ALSO FROM JOE BOOKS

Disney

GRAVITY FALLS

CINESTORY COMIC

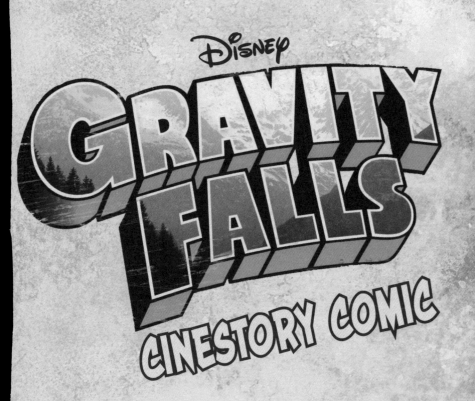

JOE BOOKS

Copyright © 2015 Disney Enterprises, Inc. All rights reserved.

Published simultaneously in the United States and Canada by Joe Books Ltd,
567 Queen St. West, Toronto, Ontario, M5V 2B6
www.joebooks.com

First Joe Books Edition: August 2015

ISBN 978-1-92651-699-8

Library and Archives Canada Cataloguing in Publication
information is available upon request

Printed and bound in Canada

3   5   7   9   10   8   6   4

For information regarding the CPSIA on this printed material, call:
(203) 595-3636 and provide reference # RICH - 613704

GRAVITY FALLS
CINESTORY COMIC

ADAPTATION, DESIGN, LETTERING, LAYOUT AND EDITING:
For Readhead Books: Greg Lockard, Heidi Roux, Salvador Navarro, Ester Salguero, Puste, Ernesto Lovera, Eduardo Alpuente, Alberto Garrido, Aaron Sparrow, and Carolynn Prior.

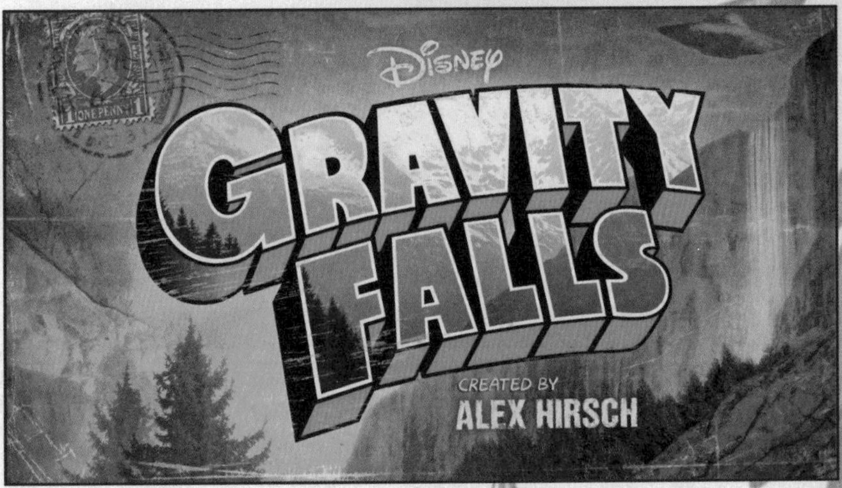
Disney
GRAVITY FALLS
CREATED BY
ALEX HIRSCH

TOURIST TRAPPED
EPISODE 1

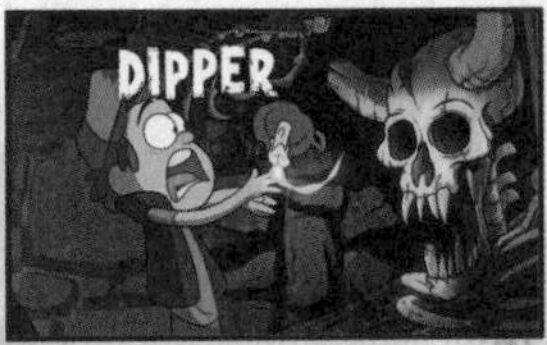
DIPPER

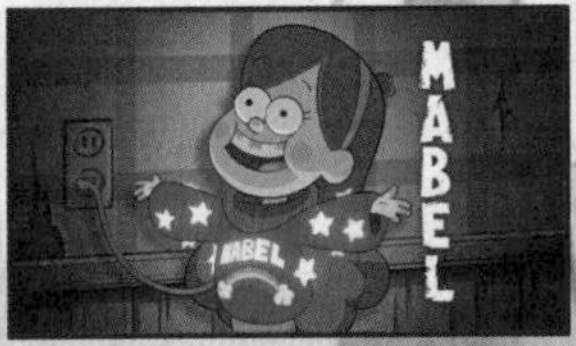
MABEL

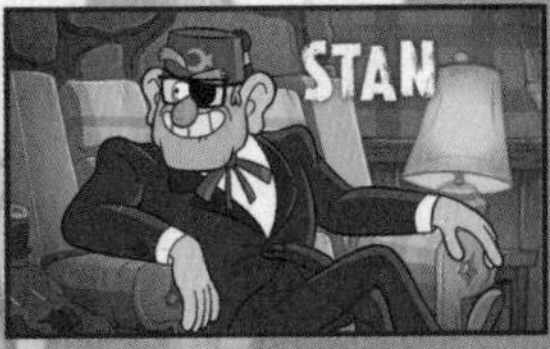
STAN

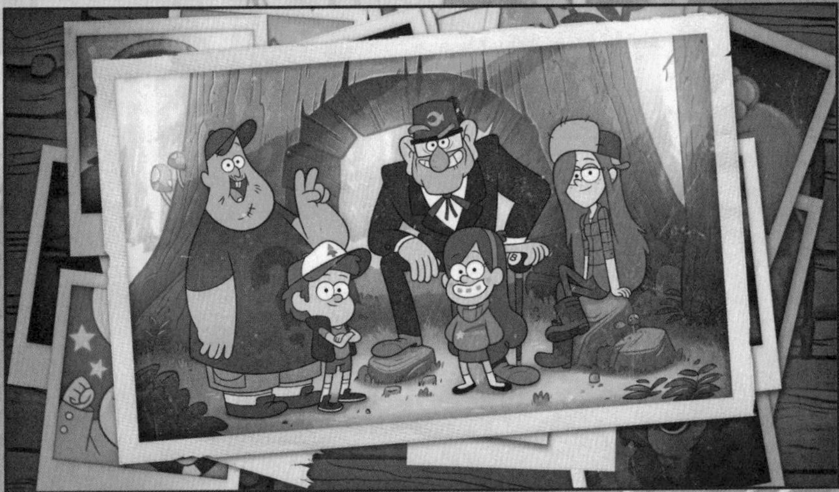

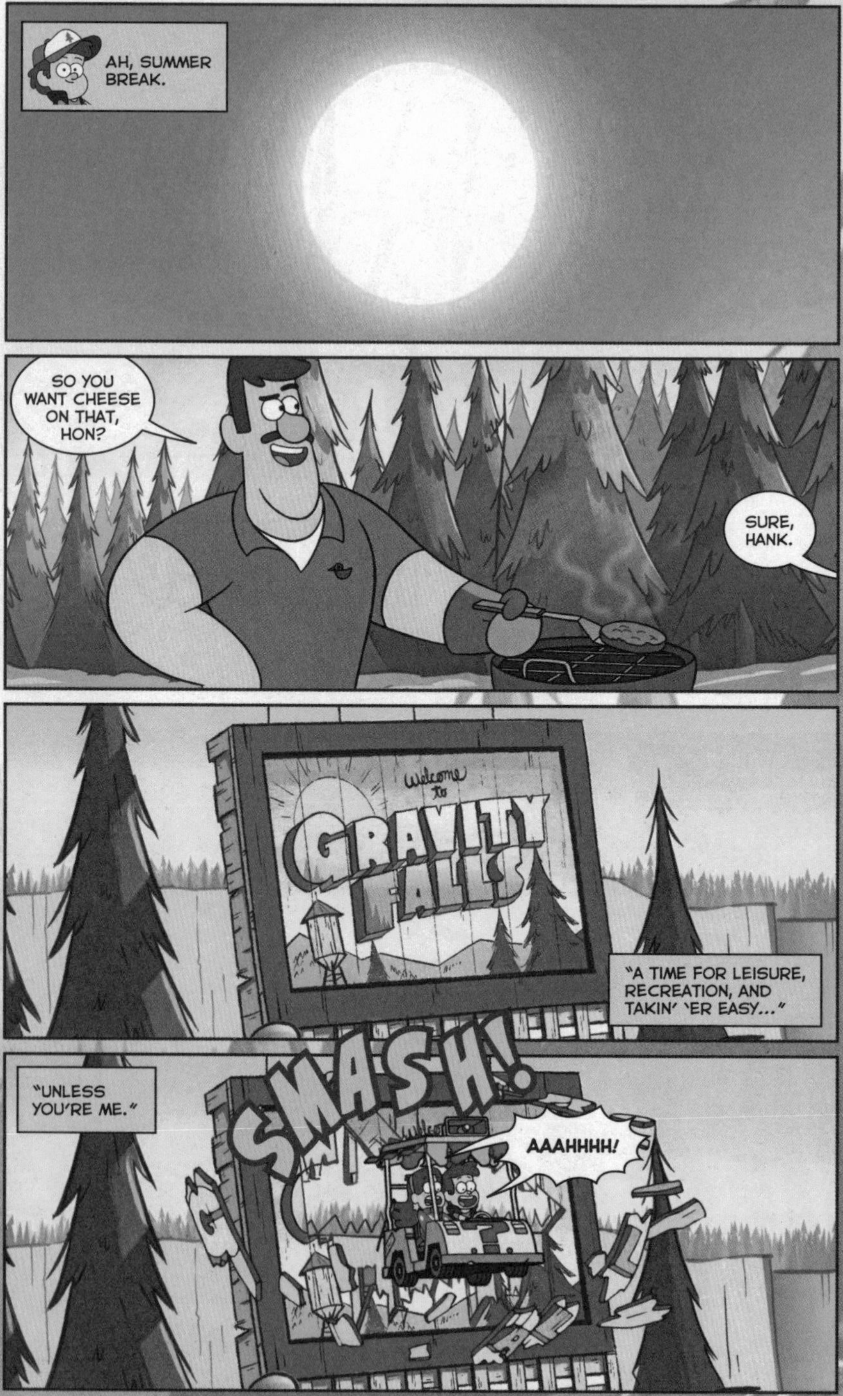
AH, SUMMER BREAK.
SO YOU WANT CHEESE ON THAT, HON?
SURE, HANK.
Welcome to
GRAVITY FALLS
"A TIME FOR LEISURE, RECREATION, AND TAKIN' 'ER EASY..."
"UNLESS YOU'RE ME."
SMASH!
AAAHHHH!

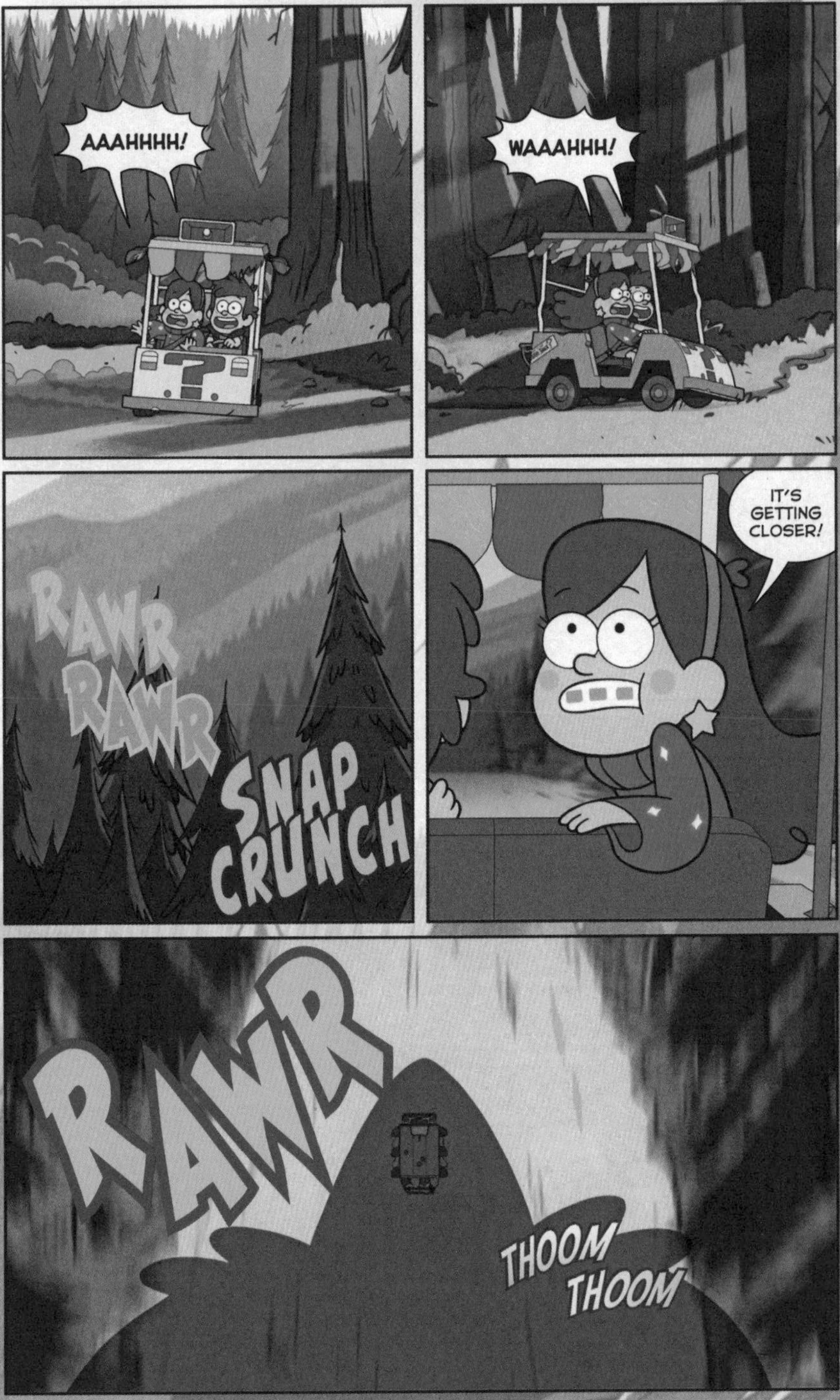
AAAHHHH!
WAAAHHH!
RAWR
RAWR
SNAP
CRUNCH
IT'S GETTING CLOSER!
RAWR
THOOM
THOOM

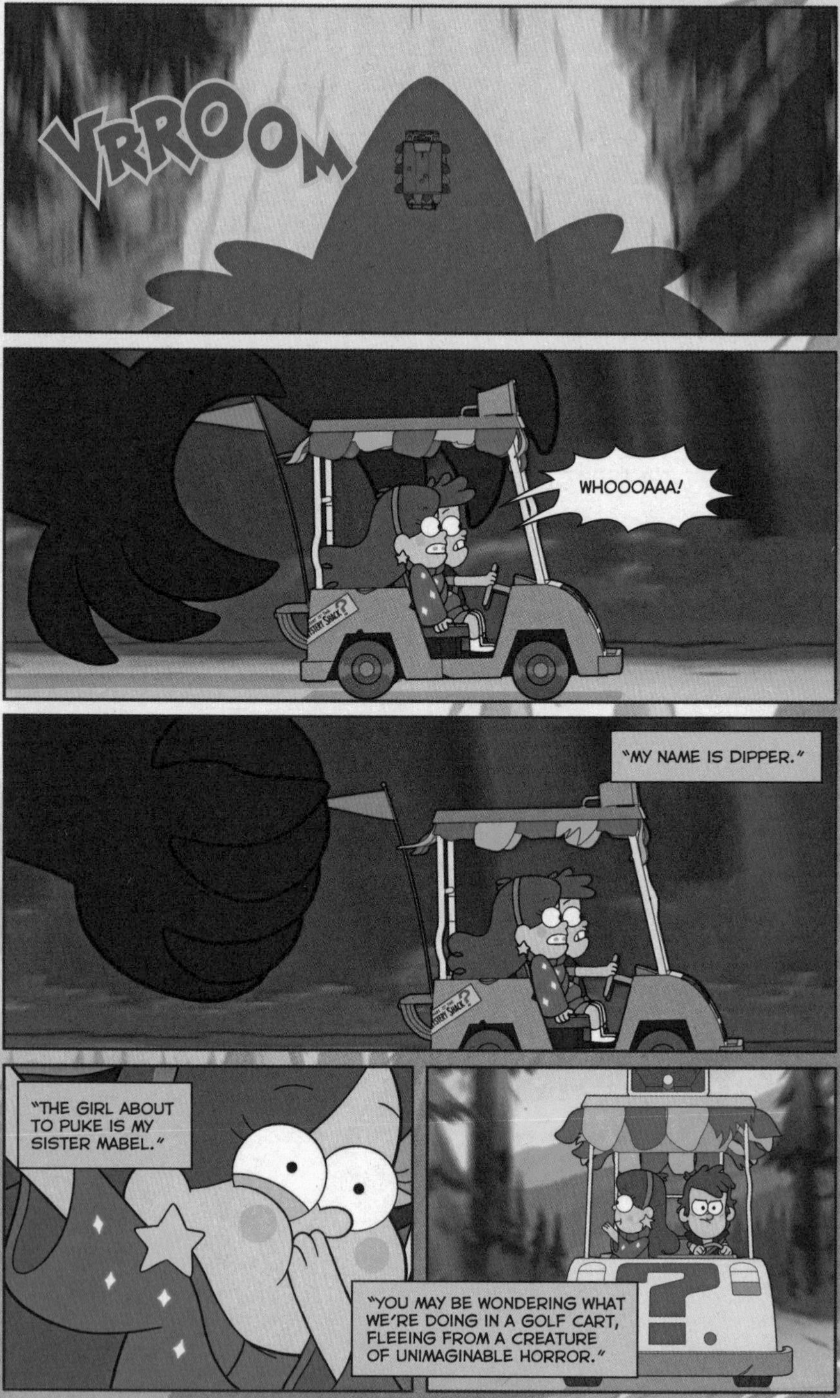

VRROOM
WHOOOAAA!
"MY NAME IS DIPPER."
"THE GIRL ABOUT TO PUKE IS MY SISTER MABEL."
"YOU MAY BE WONDERING WHAT WE'RE DOING IN A GOLF CART, FLEEING FROM A CREATURE OF UNIMAGINABLE HORROR."

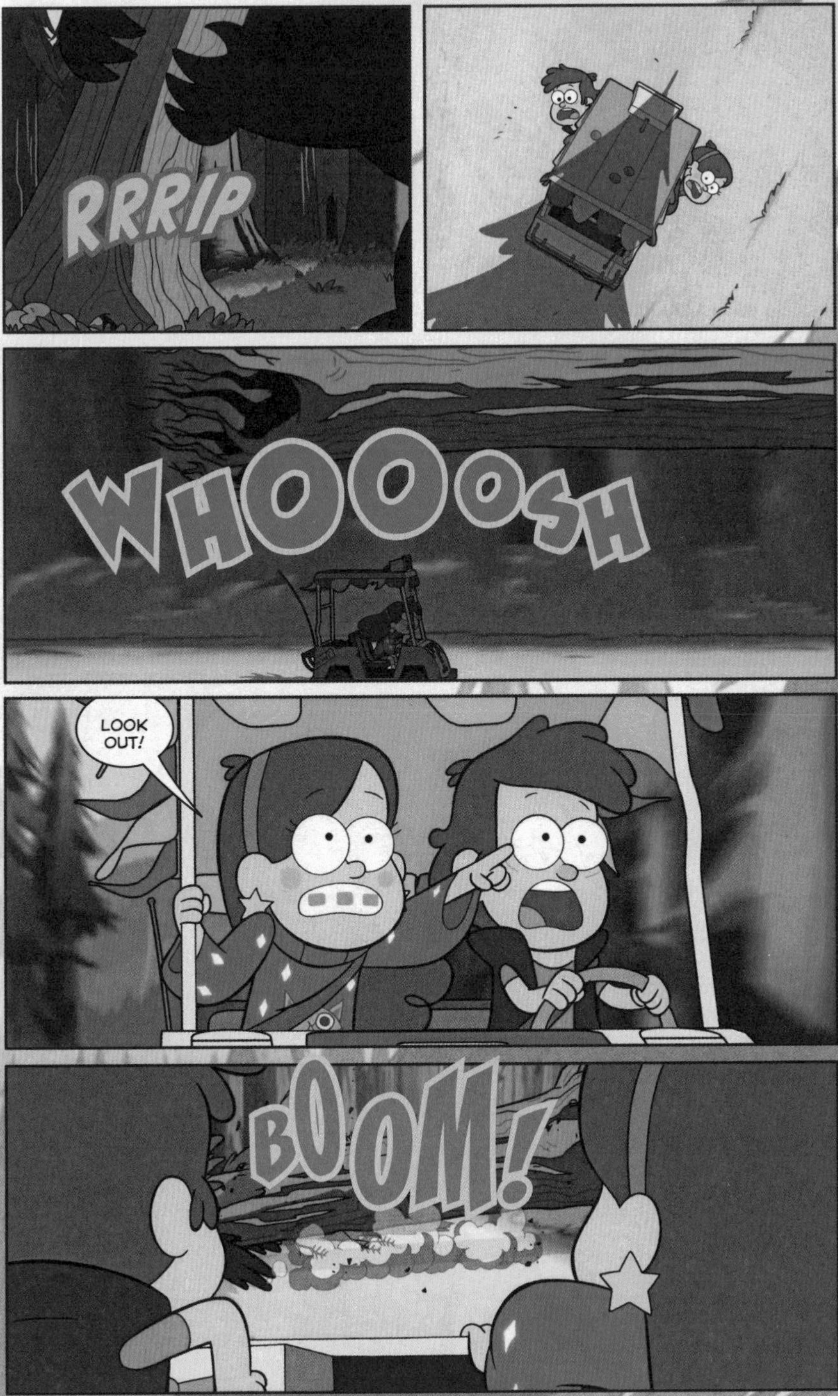
RRRIP
WHOOOSH
LOOK OUT!
BOOM!

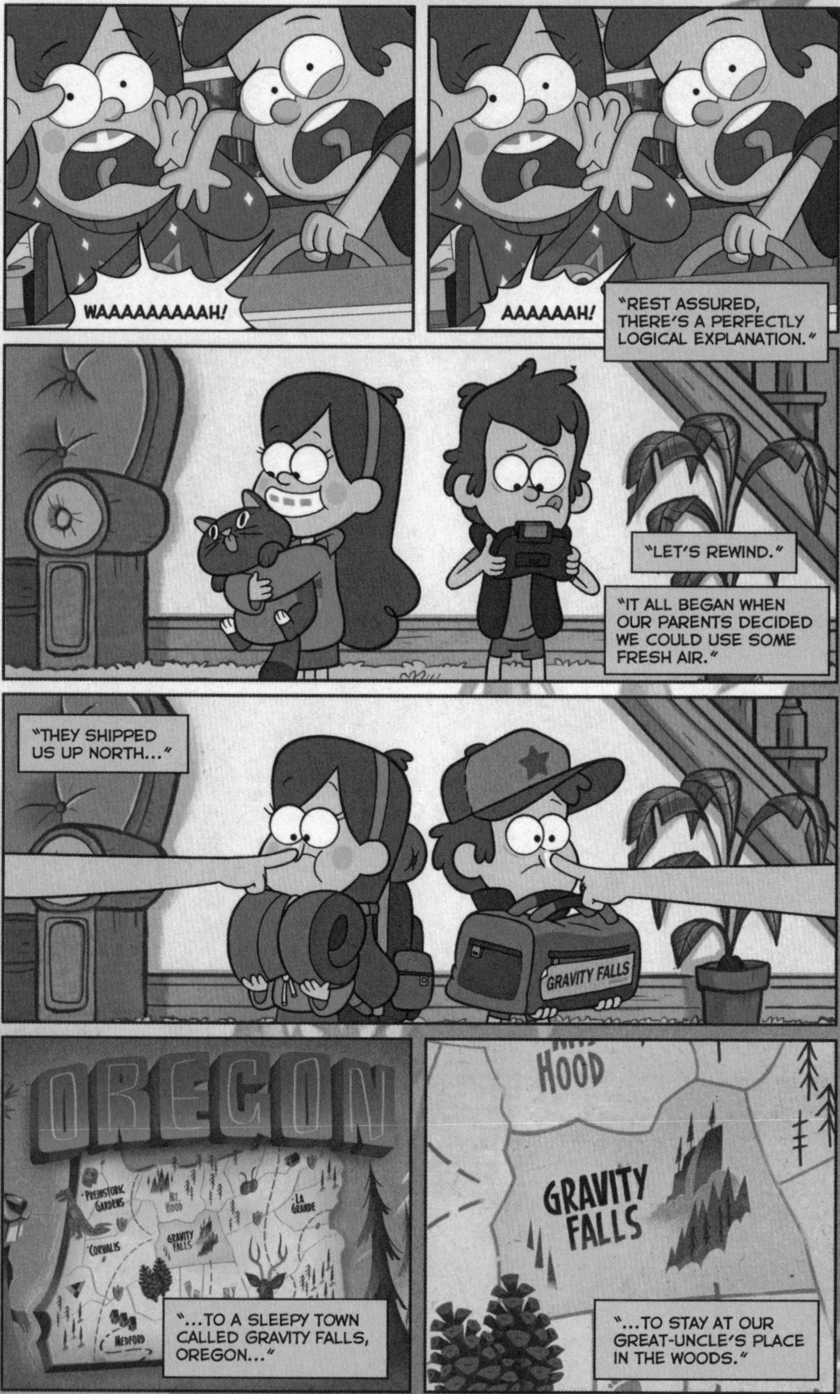
WAAAAAAAAAH!
AAAAAAH!
"REST ASSURED, THERE'S A PERFECTLY LOGICAL EXPLANATION."
"LET'S REWIND."
"IT ALL BEGAN WHEN OUR PARENTS DECIDED WE COULD USE SOME FRESH AIR."
"THEY SHIPPED US UP NORTH..."
GRAVITY FALLS
OREGON
PREHISTORIC GARDENS
MT. HOOD
LA GRANDE
GRAVITY FALLS
CORVALIS
MEDFORD
"...TO A SLEEPY TOWN CALLED GRAVITY FALLS, OREGON..."
HOOD
GRAVITY FALLS
"...TO STAY AT OUR GREAT-UNCLE'S PLACE IN THE WOODS."

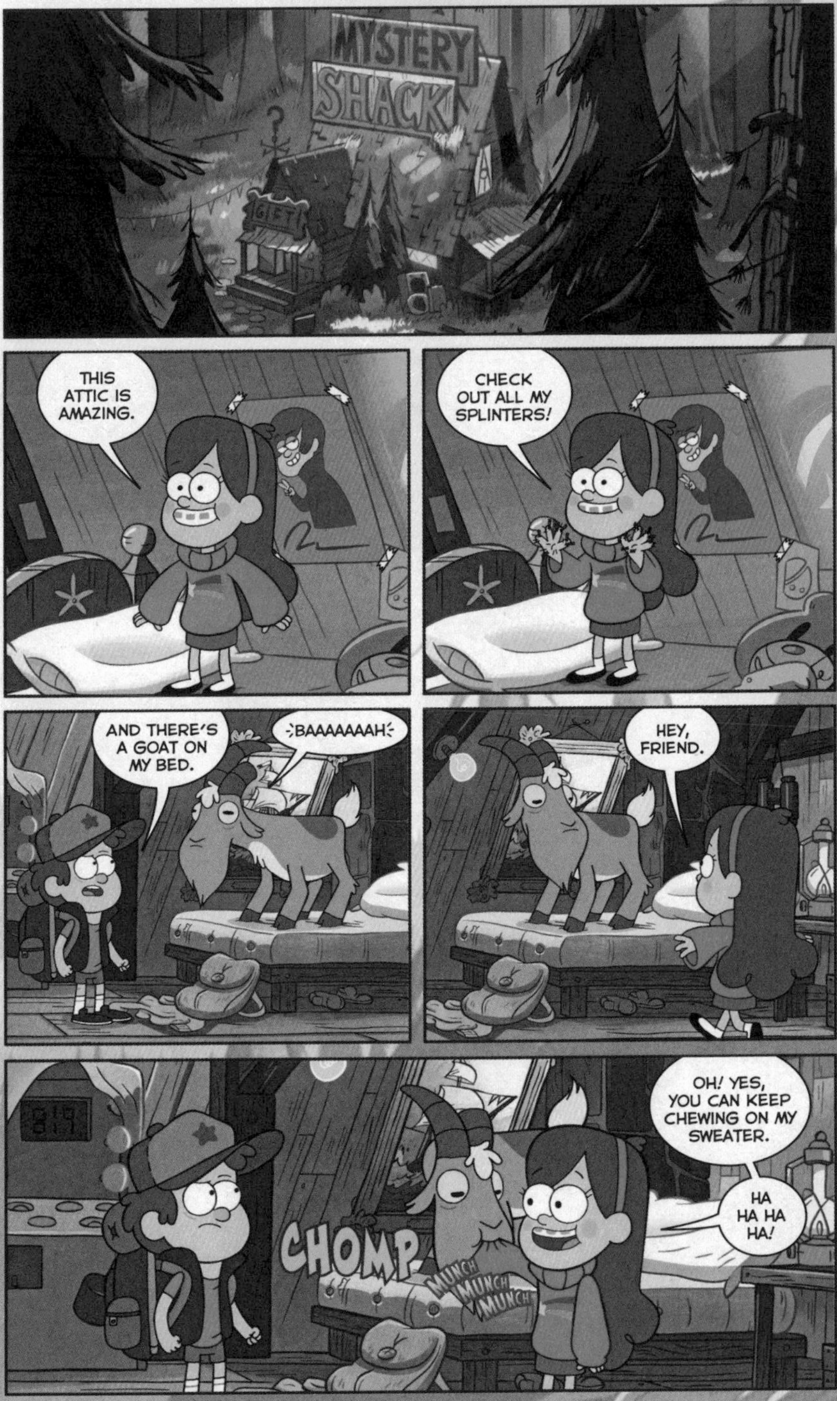
MYSTERY SHACK
GIFT
THIS ATTIC IS AMAZING.
CHECK OUT ALL MY SPLINTERS!
AND THERE'S A GOAT ON MY BED.
BAAAAAAAH
HEY, FRIEND.
CHOMP
MUNCH MUNCH MUNCH
OH! YES, YOU CAN KEEP CHEWING ON MY SWEATER.
HA HA HA HA!

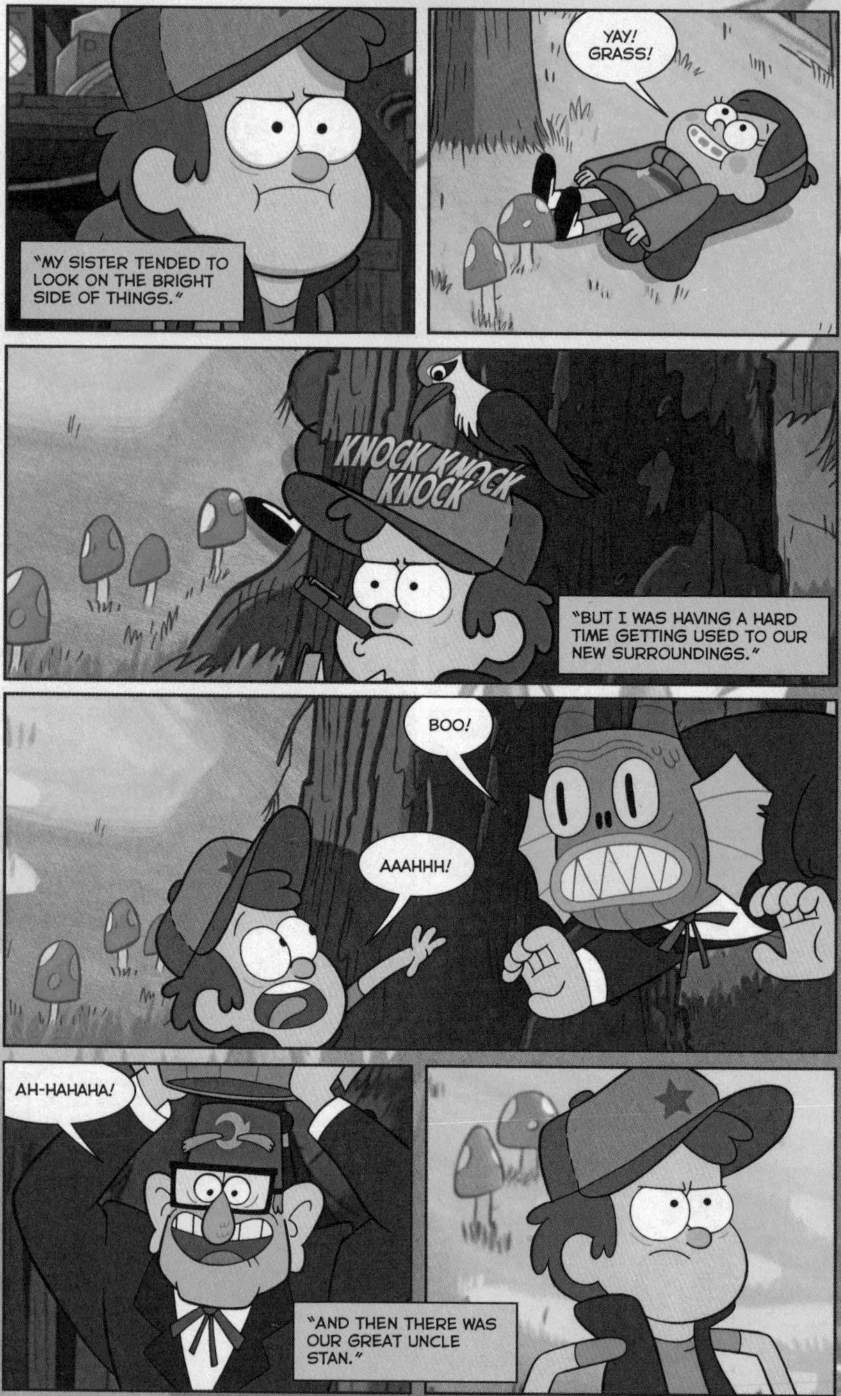
"MY SISTER TENDED TO LOOK ON THE BRIGHT SIDE OF THINGS."
YAY! GRASS!
KNOCK KNOCK KNOCK
"BUT I WAS HAVING A HARD TIME GETTING USED TO OUR NEW SURROUNDINGS."
BOO!
AAAHHH!
AH-HAHAHA!
"AND THEN THERE WAS OUR GREAT UNCLE STAN."

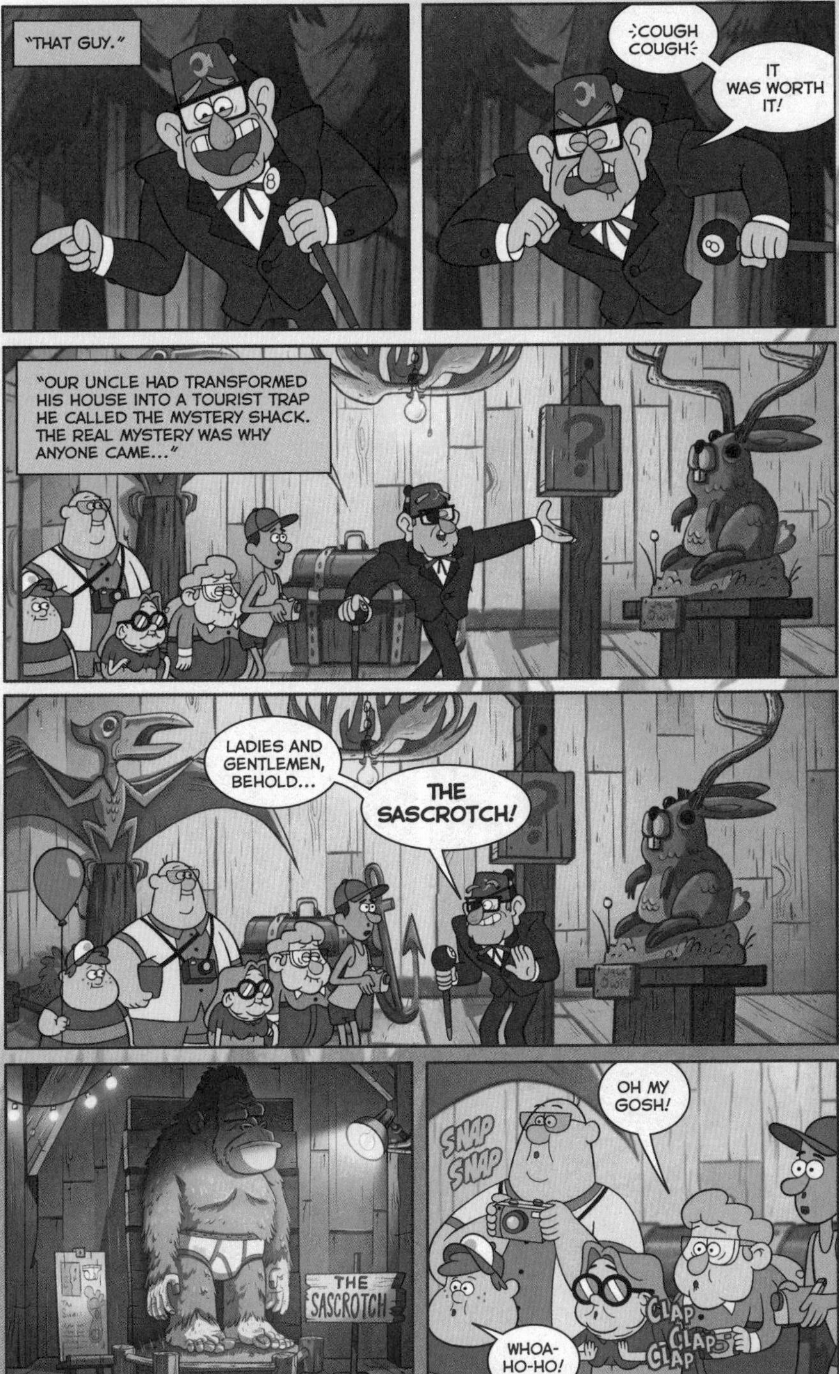
"THAT GUY."
-COUGH COUGH-
IT WAS WORTH IT!
"OUR UNCLE HAD TRANSFORMED HIS HOUSE INTO A TOURIST TRAP HE CALLED THE MYSTERY SHACK. THE REAL MYSTERY WAS WHY ANYONE CAME..."
LADIES AND GENTLEMEN, BEHOLD...
THE SASCROTCH!
THE SASCROTCH
OH MY GOSH!
SNAP SNAP
WHOA-HO-HO!
CLAP CLAP CLAP

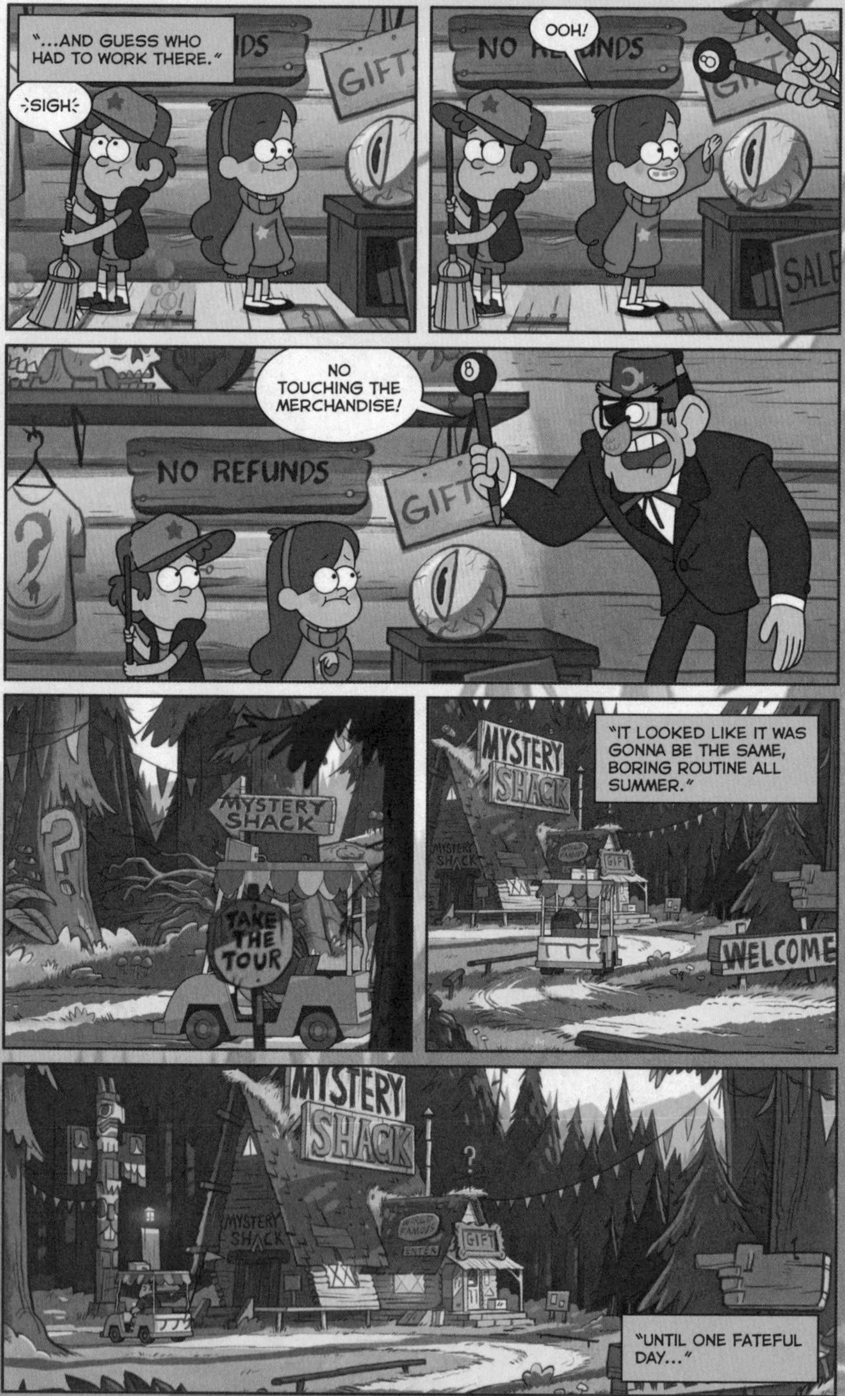
"...AND GUESS WHO HAD TO WORK THERE."
SIGH
OOH!
NO TOUCHING THE MERCHANDISE!
NO REFUNDS
GIFT
MYSTERY SHACK
TAKE THE TOUR
"IT LOOKED LIKE IT WAS GONNA BE THE SAME, BORING ROUTINE ALL SUMMER."
MYSTERY SHACK
WELCOME
MYSTERY SHACK
"UNTIL ONE FATEFUL DAY..."

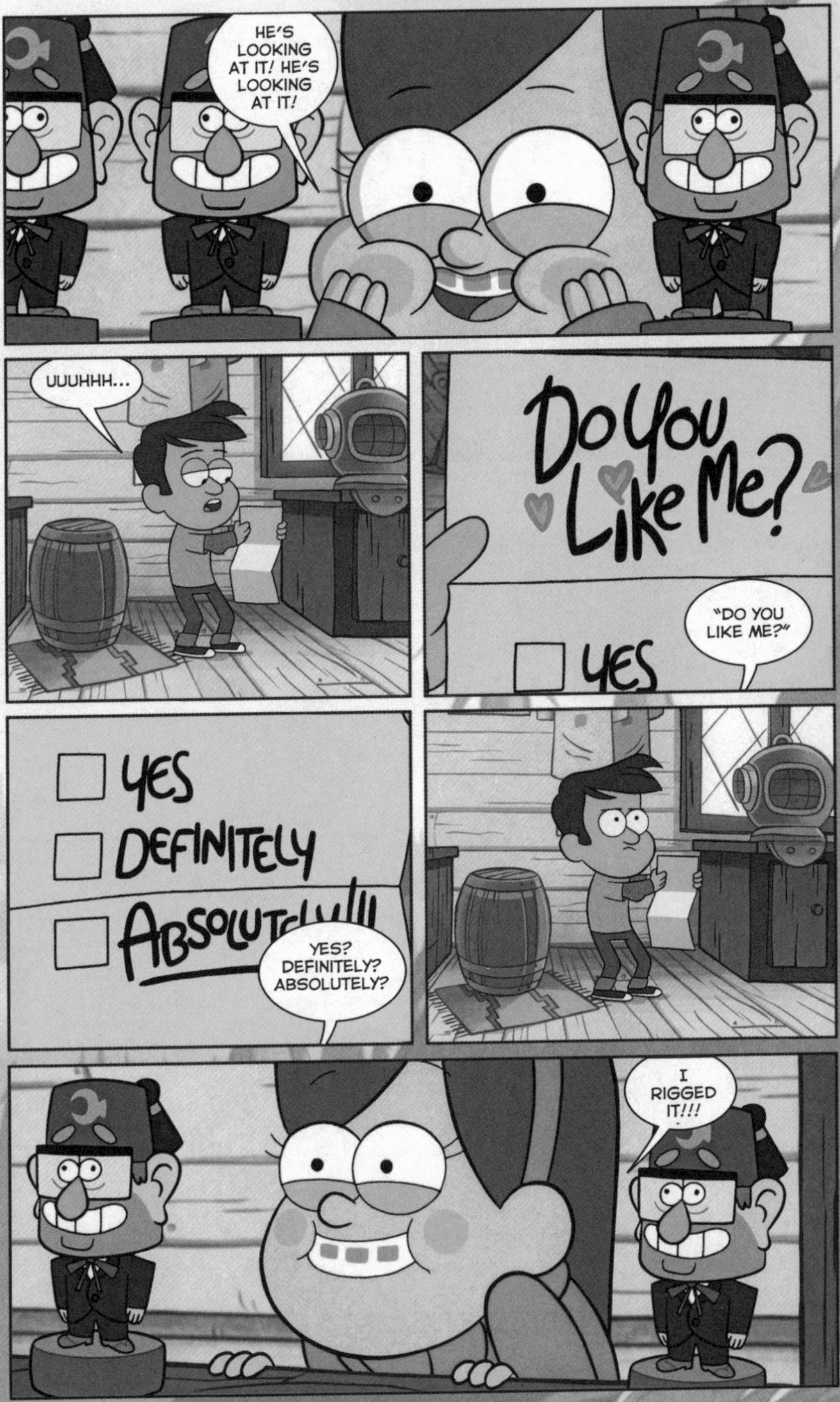

HE'S LOOKING AT IT! HE'S LOOKING AT IT!
UUUHHH...
Do You Like Me?
YES
"DO YOU LIKE ME?"
YES
DEFINITELY
YES? DEFINITELY? ABSOLUTELY?
I RIGGED IT!!!

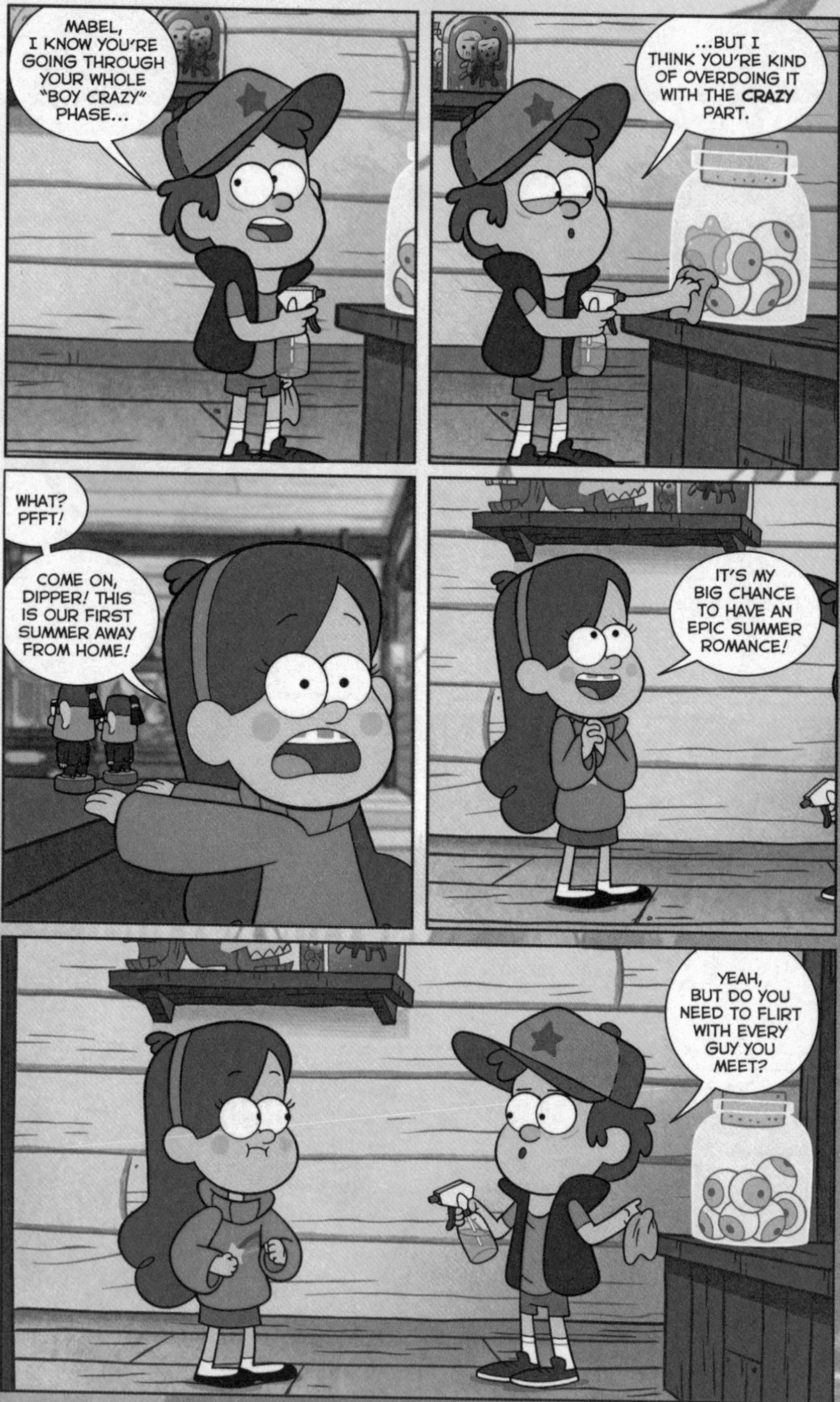
MABEL, I KNOW YOU'RE GOING THROUGH YOUR WHOLE "BOY CRAZY" PHASE...
...BUT I THINK YOU'RE KIND OF OVERDOING IT WITH THE **CRAZY** PART.
WHAT? PFFT!
COME ON, DIPPER! THIS IS OUR FIRST SUMMER AWAY FROM HOME!
IT'S MY BIG CHANCE TO HAVE AN EPIC SUMMER ROMANCE!
YEAH, BUT DO YOU NEED TO FLIRT WITH EVERY GUY YOU MEET?

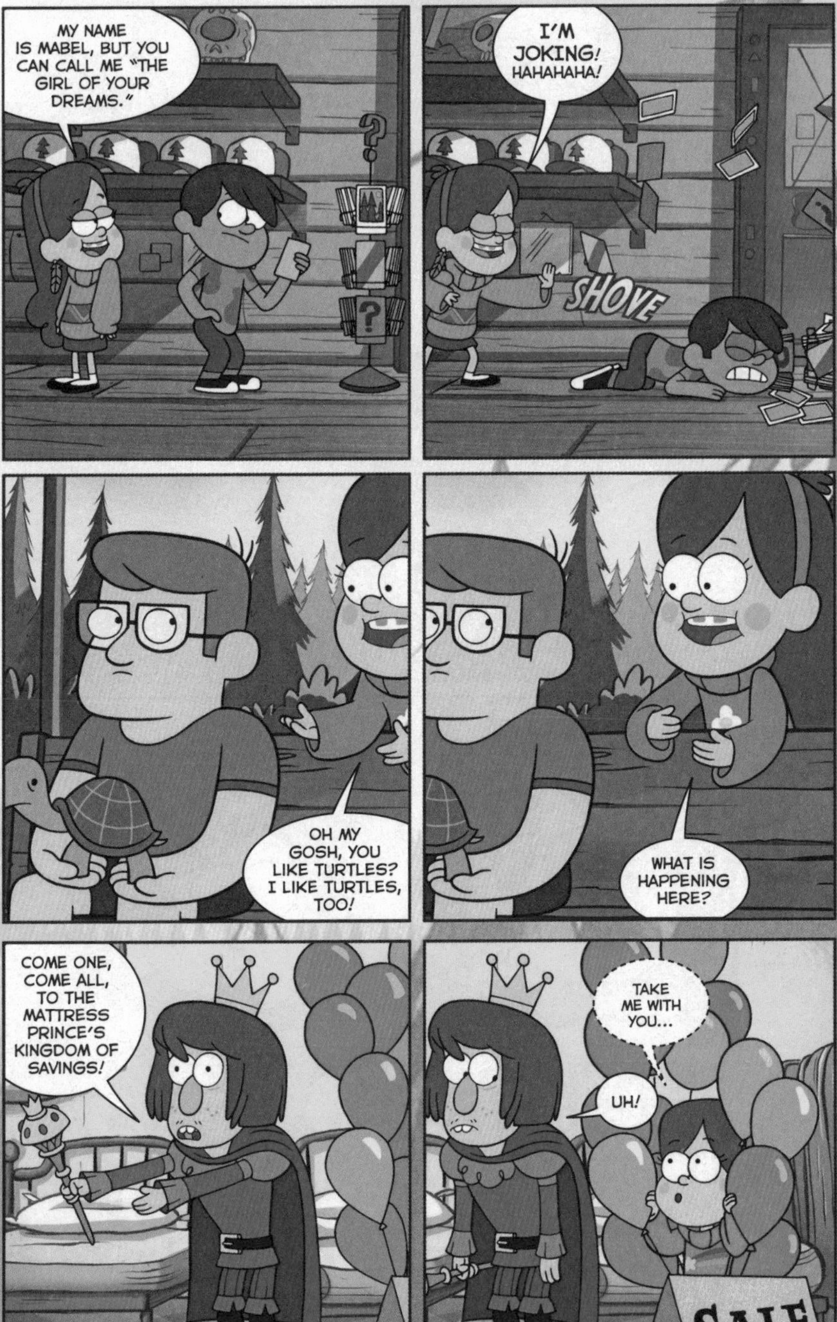
MY NAME IS MABEL, BUT YOU CAN CALL ME "THE GIRL OF YOUR DREAMS."
I'M JOKING! HAHAHAHA!
SHOVE
OH MY GOSH, YOU LIKE TURTLES? I LIKE TURTLES, TOO!
WHAT IS HAPPENING HERE?
COME ONE, COME ALL, TO THE MATTRESS PRINCE'S KINGDOM OF SAVINGS!
TAKE ME WITH YOU...
UH!
SALE

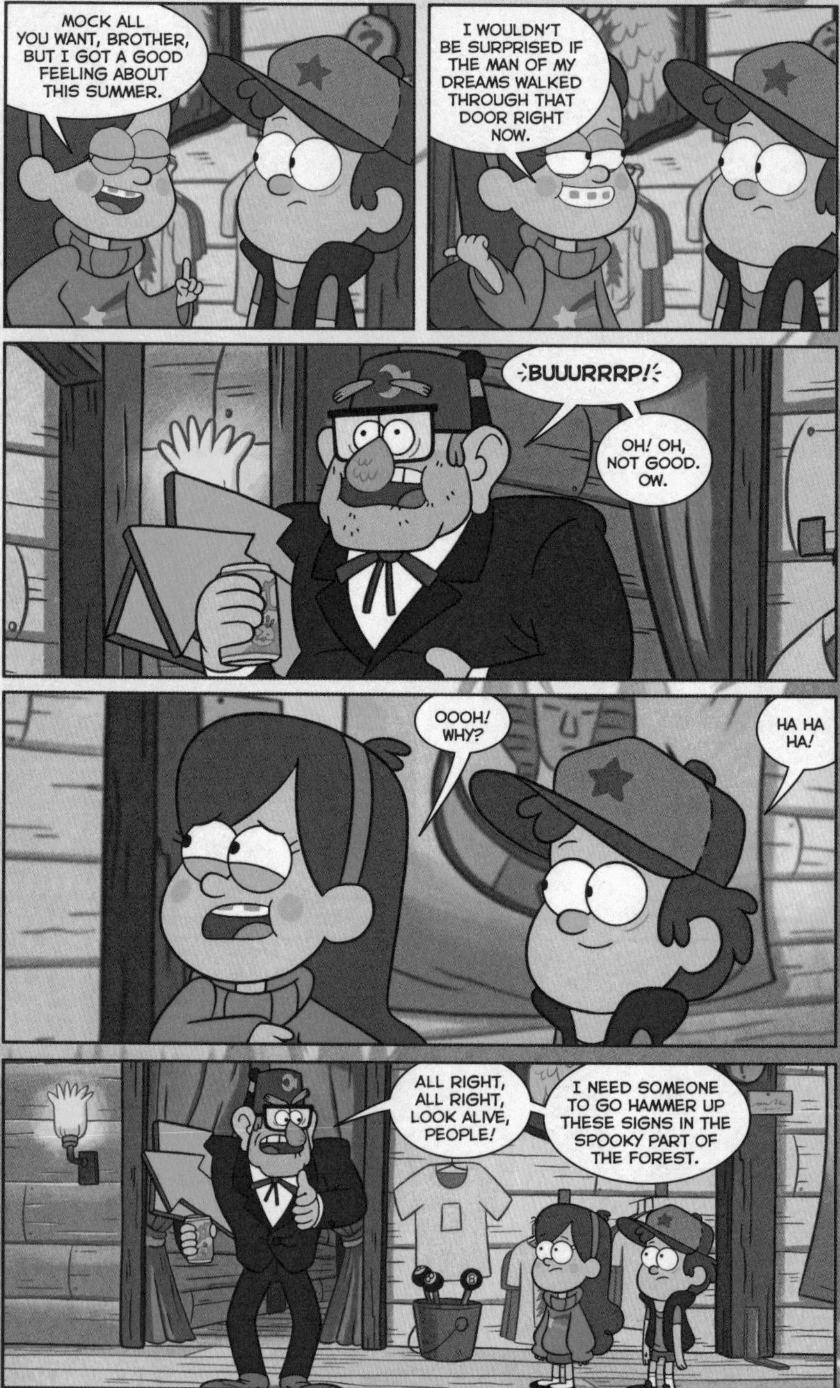
MOCK ALL YOU WANT, BROTHER, BUT I GOT A GOOD FEELING ABOUT THIS SUMMER.
I WOULDN'T BE SURPRISED IF THE MAN OF MY DREAMS WALKED THROUGH THAT DOOR RIGHT NOW.
BUUURRRP!
OH! OH, NOT GOOD. OW.
OOOH! WHY?
HA HA HA!
ALL RIGHT, ALL RIGHT, LOOK ALIVE, PEOPLE!
I NEED SOMEONE TO GO HAMMER UP THESE SIGNS IN THE SPOOKY PART OF THE FOREST.

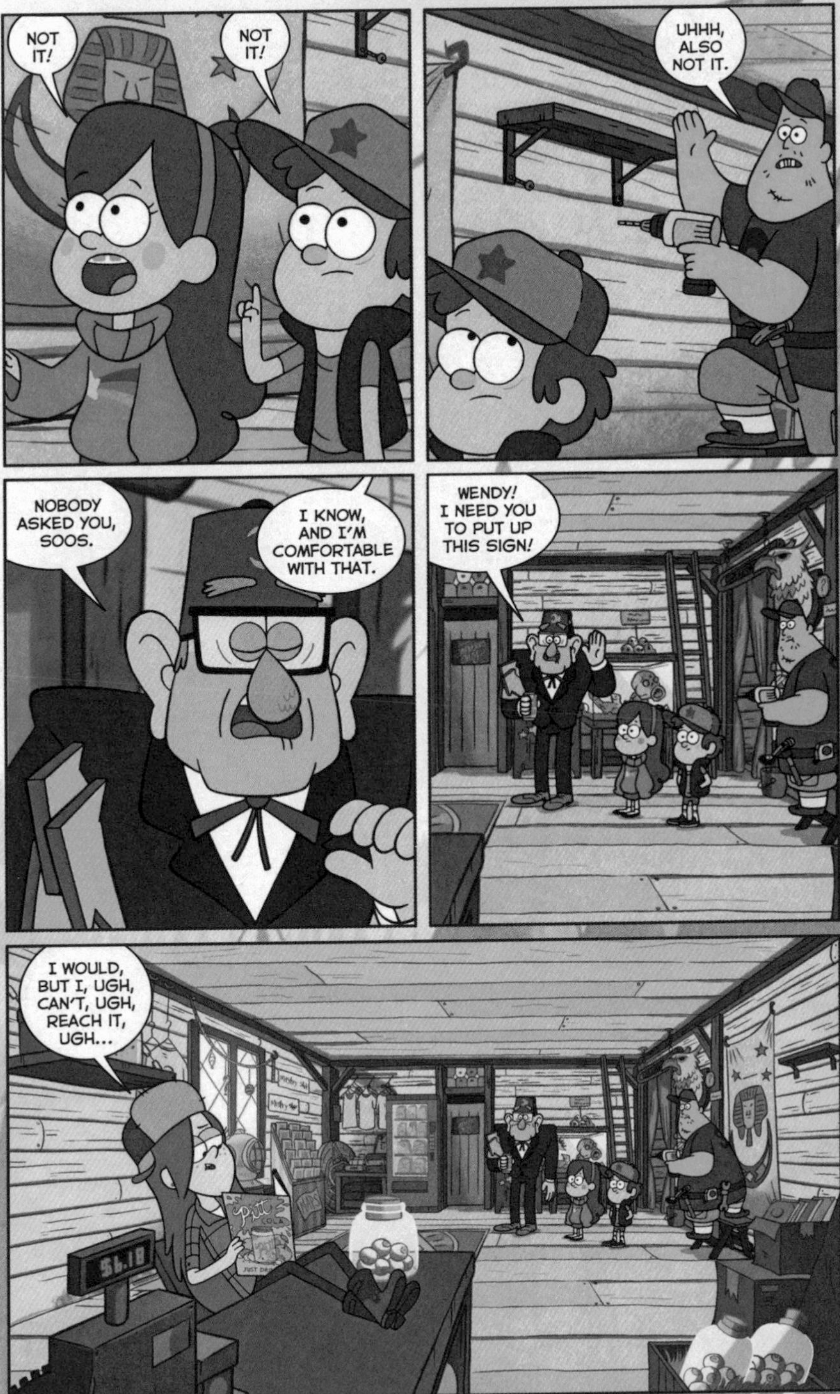
NOT IT!
NOT IT!
UHHH, ALSO NOT IT.
NOBODY ASKED YOU, SOOS.
I KNOW, AND I'M COMFORTABLE WITH THAT.
WENDY! I NEED YOU TO PUT UP THIS SIGN!
I WOULD, BUT I, UGH, CAN'T, UGH, REACH IT, UGH...
$6.18

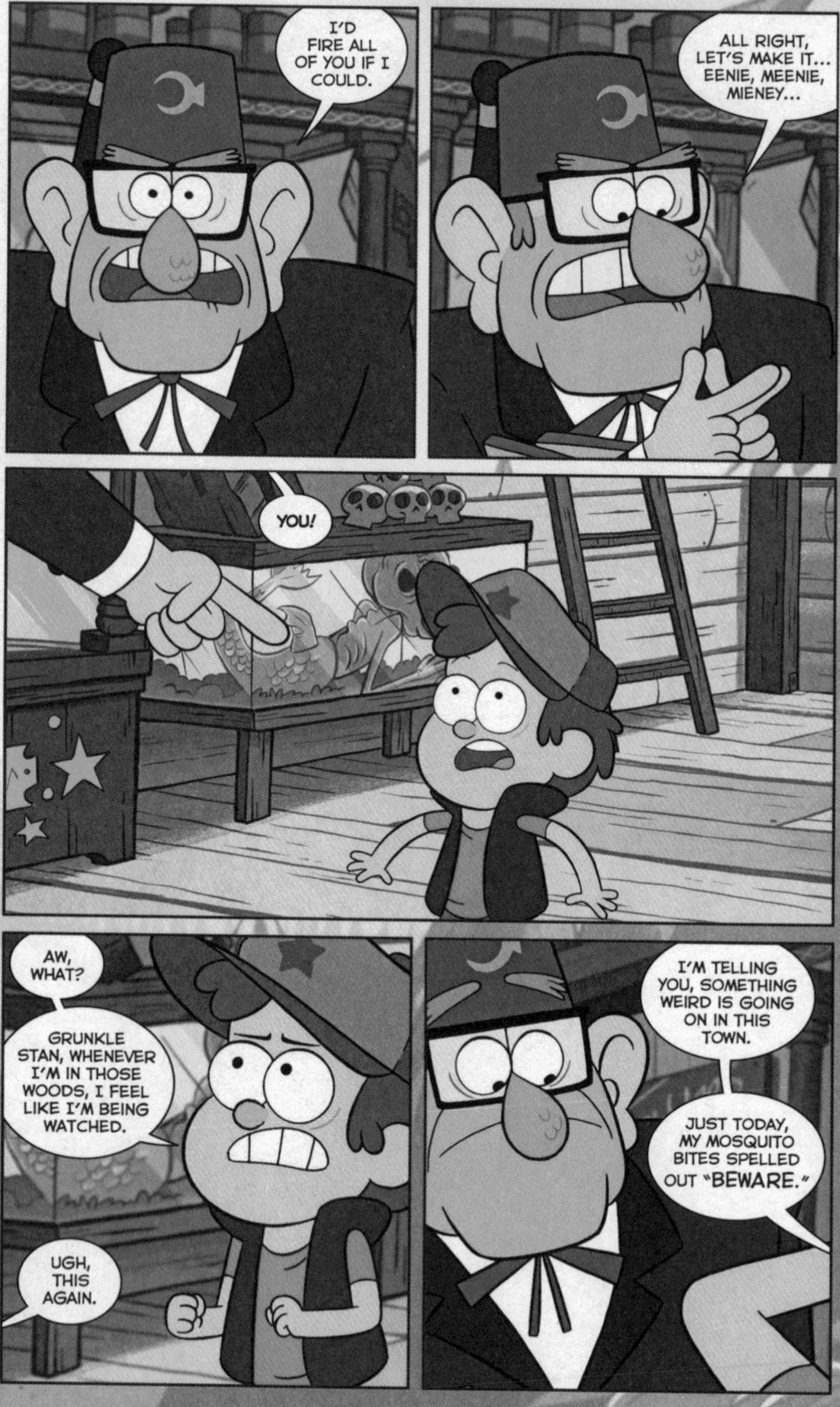
I'D FIRE ALL OF YOU IF I COULD.
ALL RIGHT, LET'S MAKE IT... EENIE, MEENIE, MIENEY...
YOU!
AW, WHAT?
GRUNKLE STAN, WHENEVER I'M IN THOSE WOODS, I FEEL LIKE I'M BEING WATCHED.
UGH, THIS AGAIN.
I'M TELLING YOU, SOMETHING WEIRD IS GOING ON IN THIS TOWN.
JUST TODAY, MY MOSQUITO BITES SPELLED OUT "BEWARE."

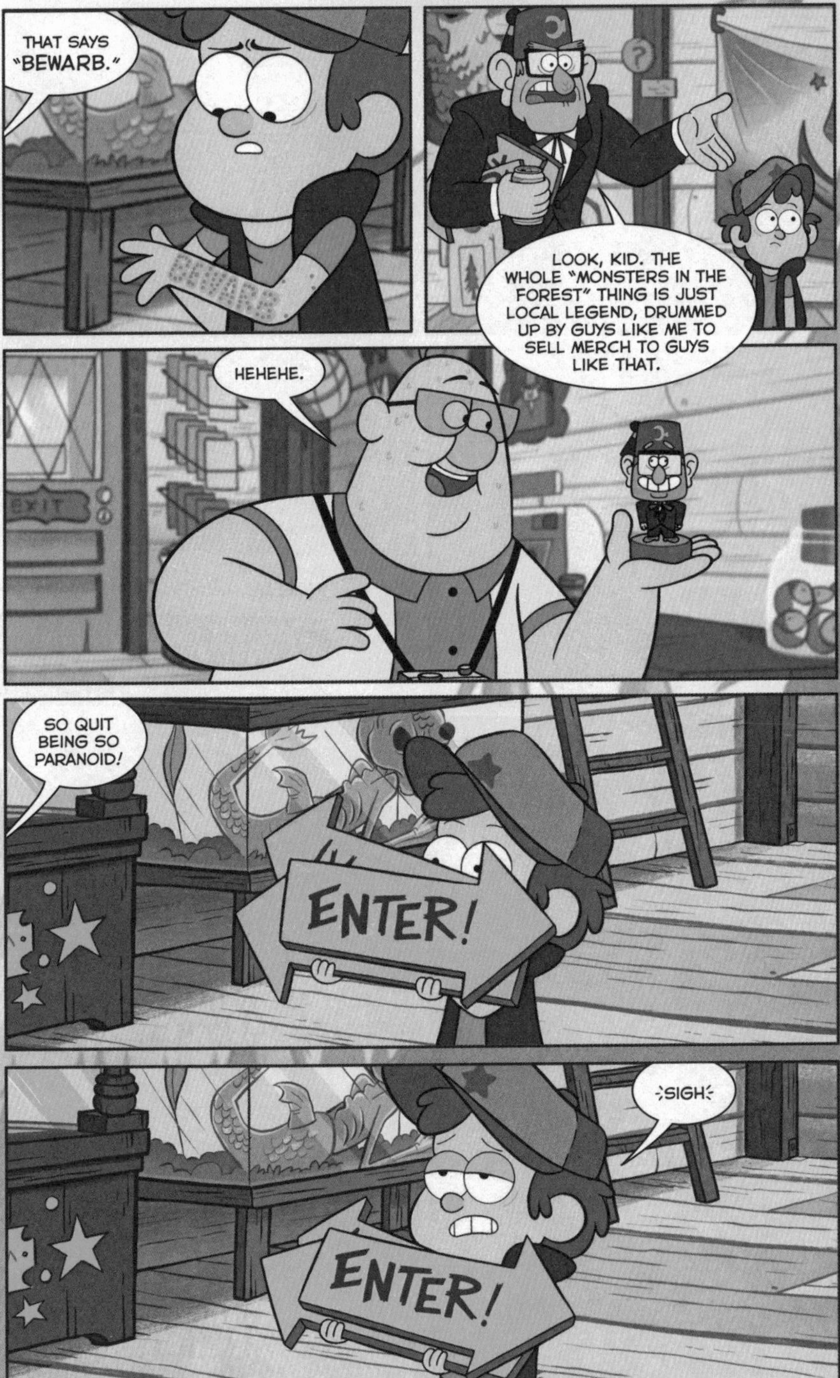
THAT SAYS "BEWARB."
BEWARB
LOOK, KID. THE WHOLE "MONSTERS IN THE FOREST" THING IS JUST LOCAL LEGEND, DRUMMED UP BY GUYS LIKE ME TO SELL MERCH TO GUYS LIKE THAT.
HEHEHE.
EXIT
SO QUIT BEING SO PARANOID!
ENTER!
SIGH
ENTER!

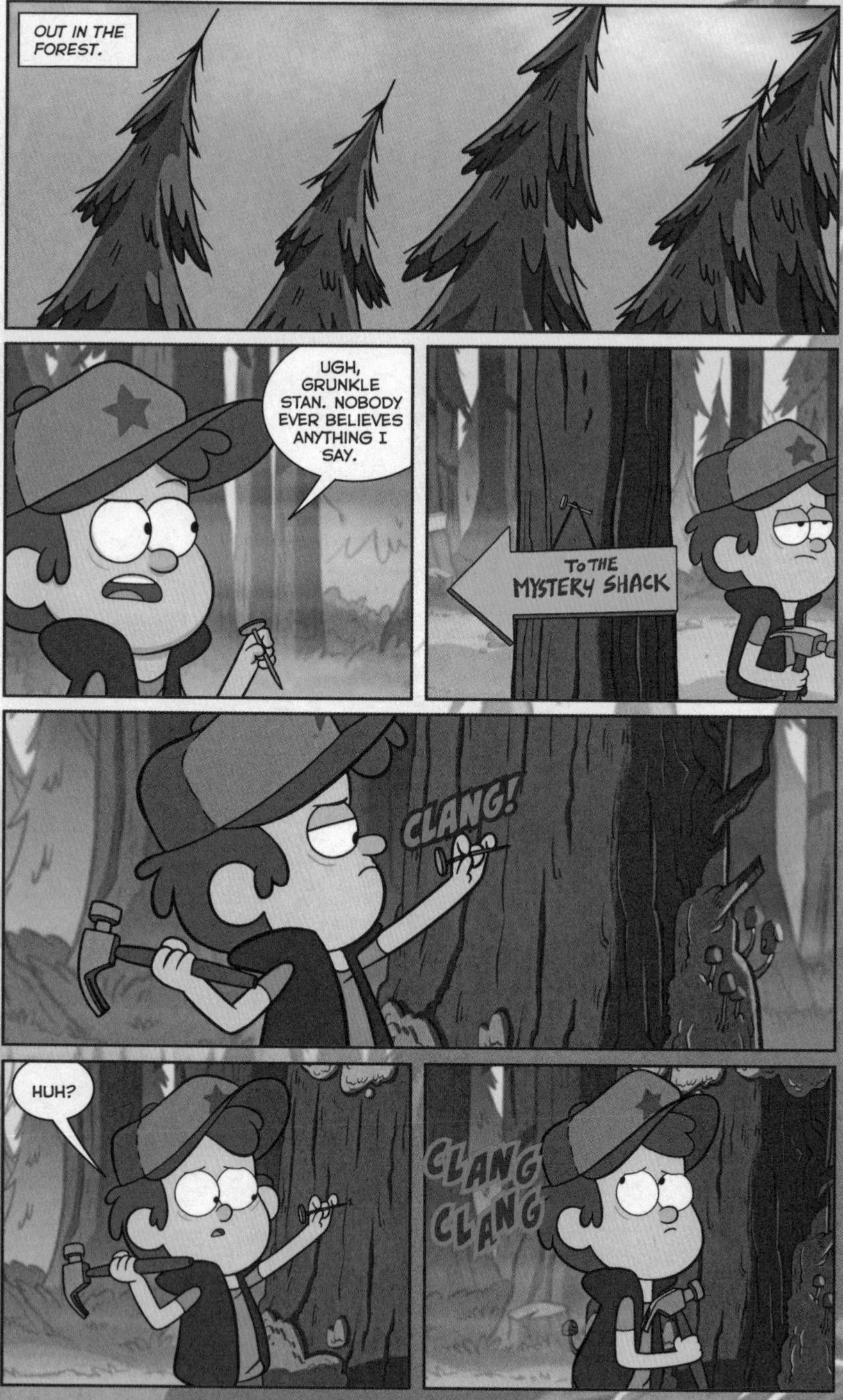
OUT IN THE FOREST.
UGH, GRUNKLE STAN. NOBODY EVER BELIEVES ANYTHING I SAY.
TO THE MYSTERY SHACK
CLANG!
HUH?
CLANG CLANG

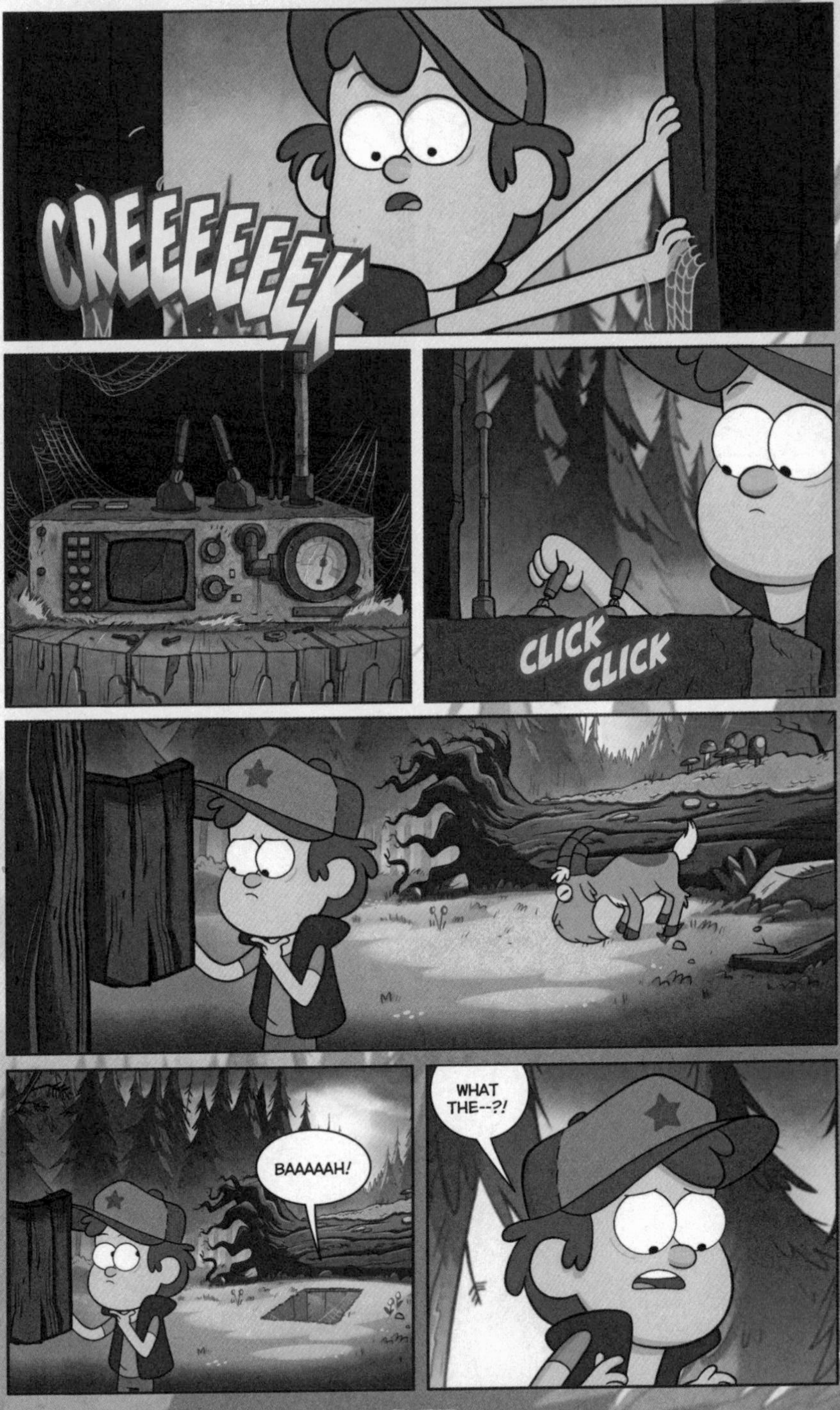
CREEEEEEK
CLICK
CLICK
BAAAAAH!
WHAT THE--?!

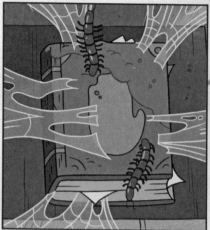

PFFF

Property of

Vol.3

"IT'S HARD TO BELIEVE IT'S BEEN SIX YEARS SINCE I BEGAN STUDYING THE STRANGE AND WONDROUS SECRETS OF GRAVITY FALLS, OREGON."

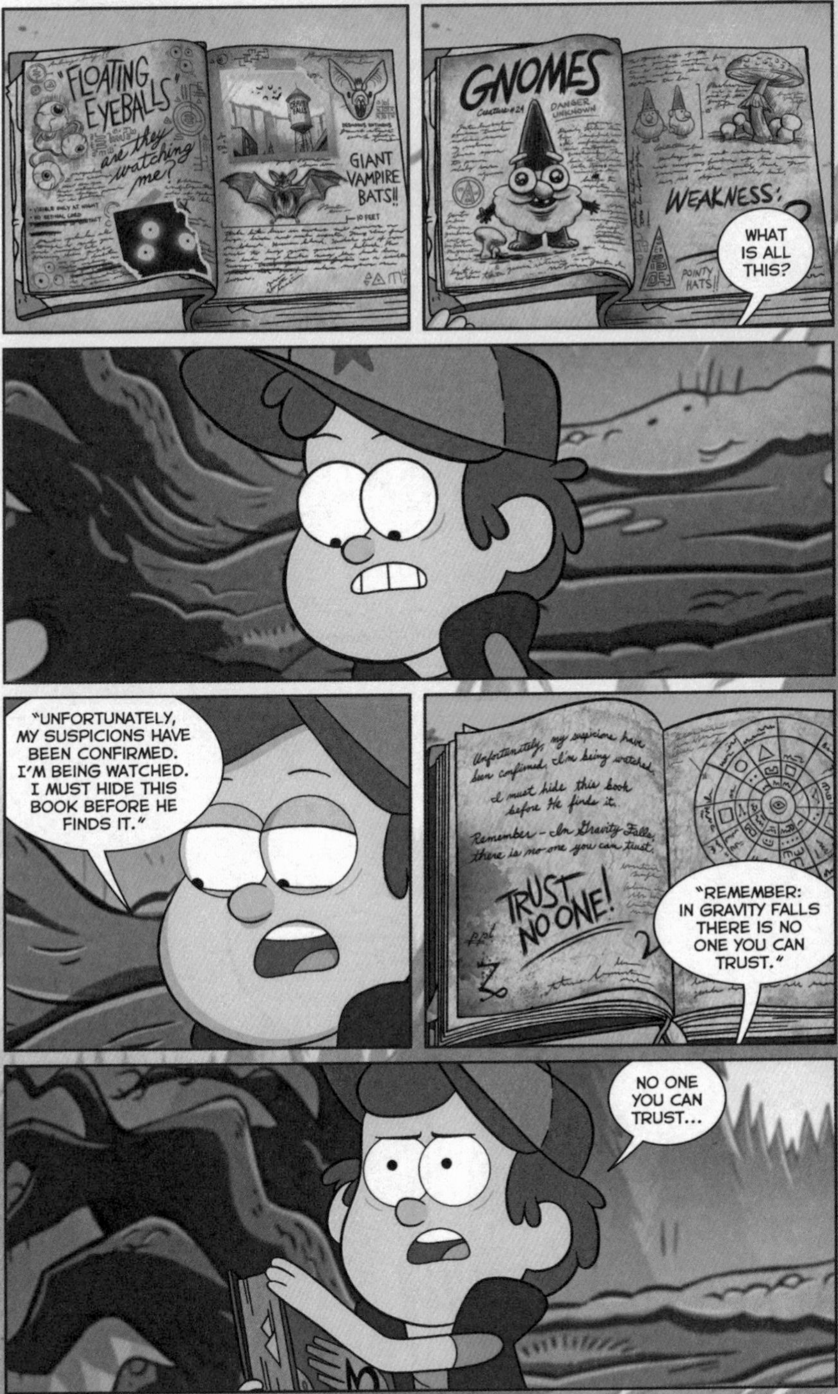
"FLOATING EYEBALLS"
are they watching me?
GIANT VAMPIRE BATS!!
GNOMES
DANGER UNKNOWN
WEAKNESS:
POINTY HATS!!
WHAT IS ALL THIS?
"UNFORTUNATELY, MY SUSPICIONS HAVE BEEN CONFIRMED. I'M BEING WATCHED. I MUST HIDE THIS BOOK BEFORE HE FINDS IT."
Unfortunately, my suspicions have been confirmed, I'm being watched.
I must hide this book before He finds it.
Remember - In Gravity Falls, there is no one you can trust.
TRUST NO ONE!
"REMEMBER: IN GRAVITY FALLS THERE IS NO ONE YOU CAN TRUST."
NO ONE YOU CAN TRUST...

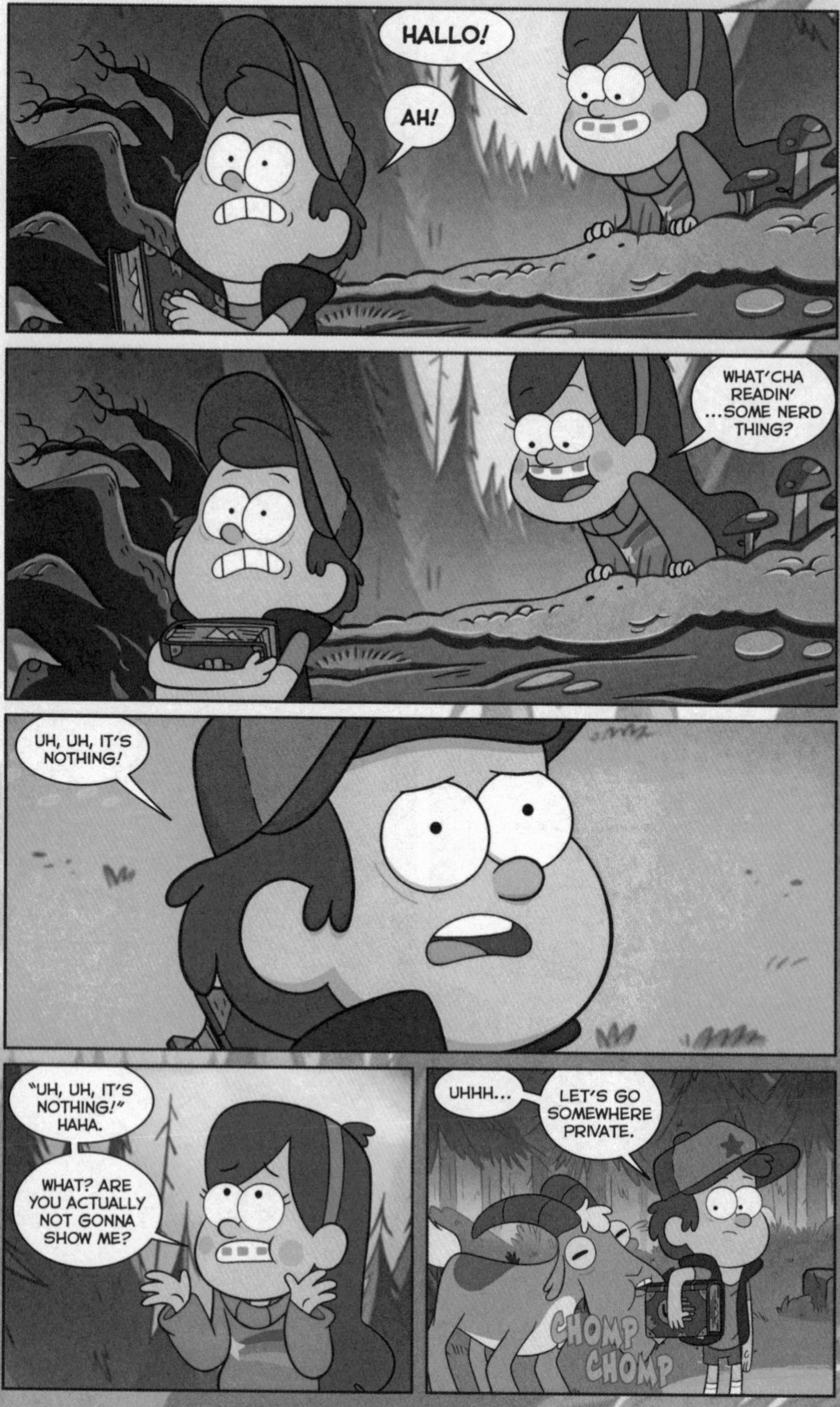
HALLO!
AH!
WHAT'CHA READIN' ...SOME NERD THING?
UH, UH, IT'S NOTHING!
"UH, UH, IT'S NOTHING!" HAHA.
WHAT? ARE YOU ACTUALLY NOT GONNA SHOW ME?
UHHH...
LET'S GO SOMEWHERE PRIVATE.
CHOMP CHOMP

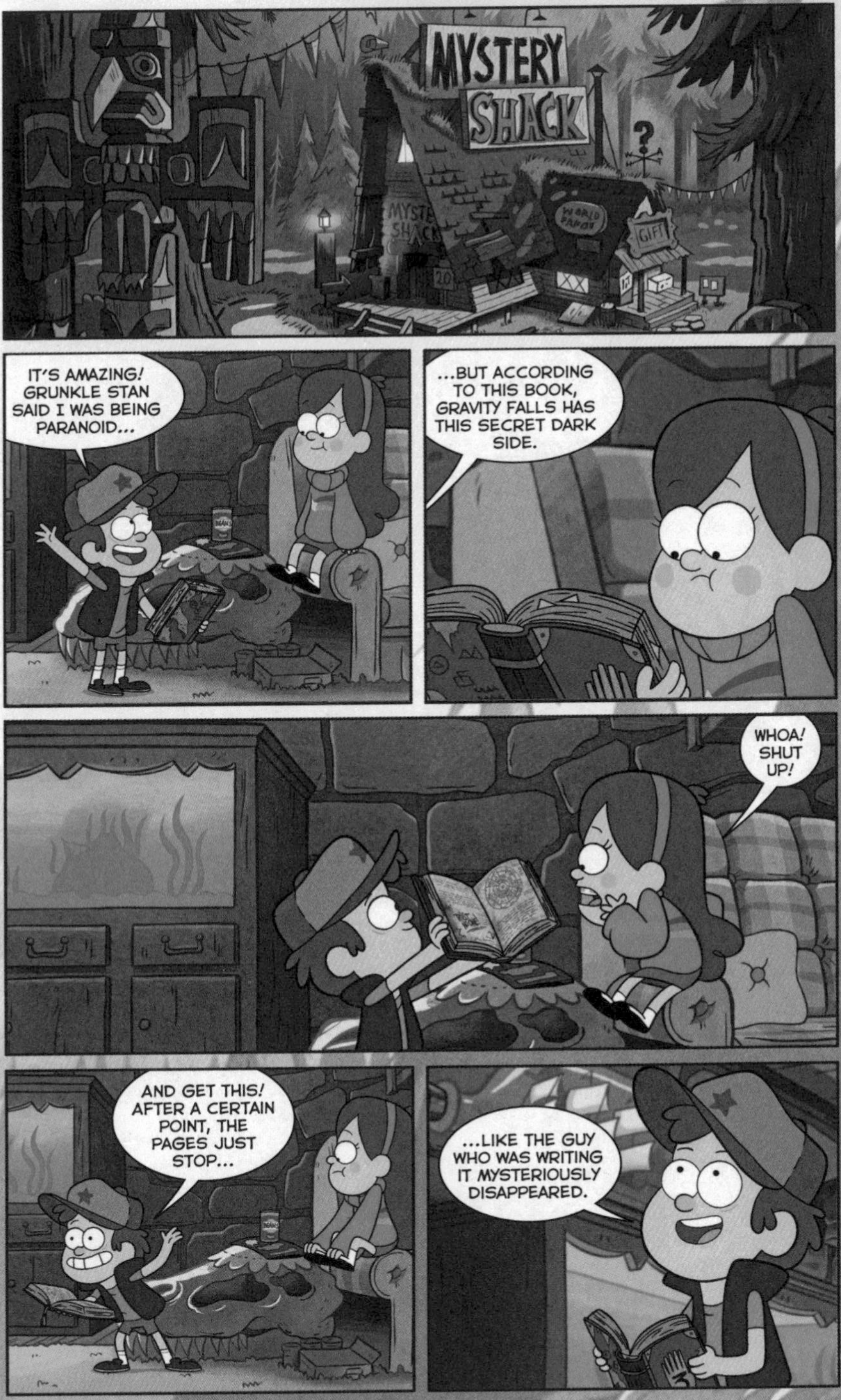
MYSTERY
SHACK
MYSTERY
SHACK
GIFT
IT'S AMAZING! GRUNKLE STAN SAID I WAS BEING PARANOID...
...BUT ACCORDING TO THIS BOOK, GRAVITY FALLS HAS THIS SECRET DARK SIDE.
WHOA! SHUT UP!
AND GET THIS! AFTER A CERTAIN POINT, THE PAGES JUST STOP...
...LIKE THE GUY WHO WAS WRITING IT MYSTERIOUSLY DISAPPEARED.

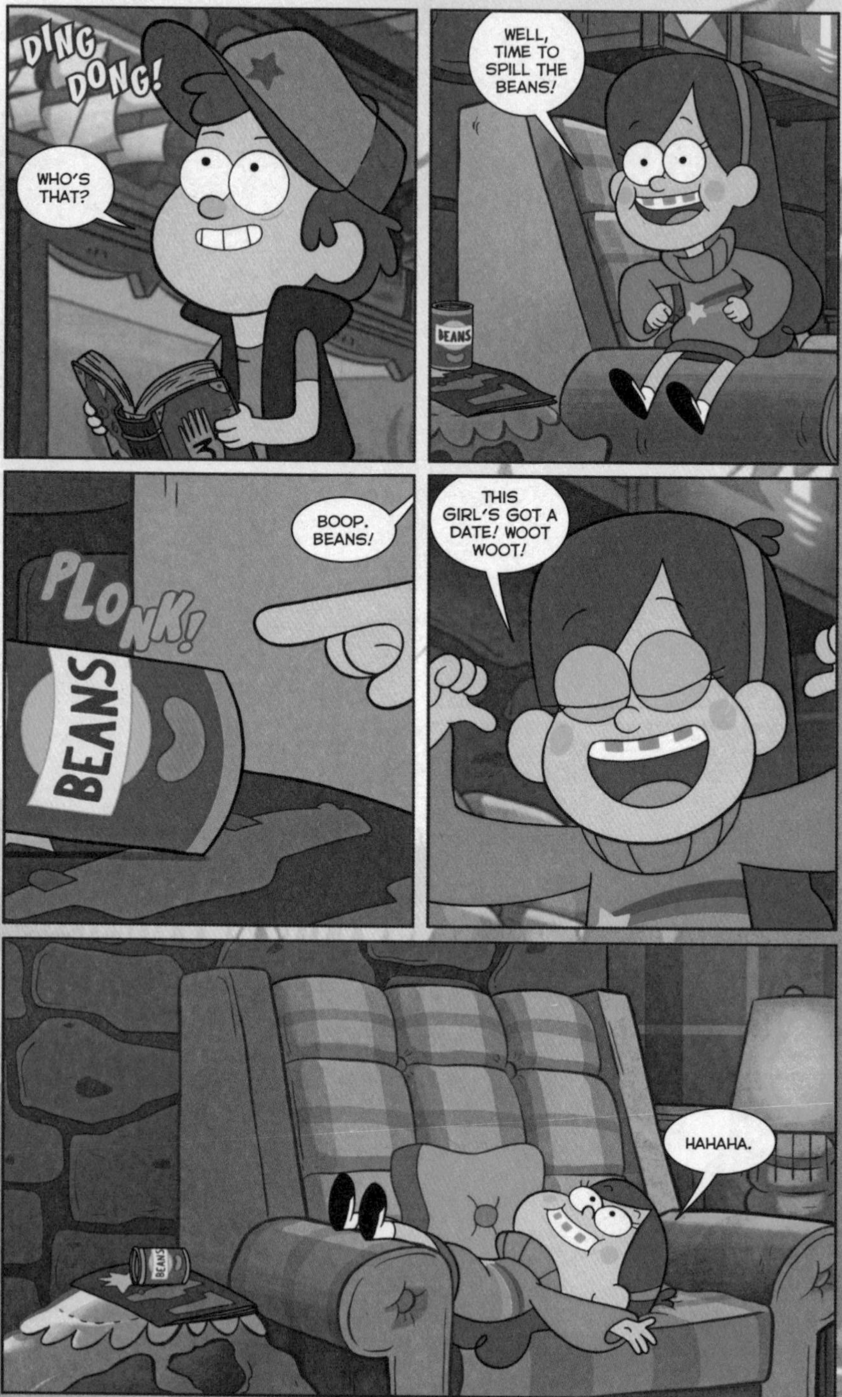
DING DONG!
WHO'S THAT?
WELL, TIME TO SPILL THE BEANS!
BEANS
BOOP. BEANS!
PLONK!
BEANS
THIS GIRL'S GOT A DATE! WOOT WOOT!
HAHAHA.
BEANS

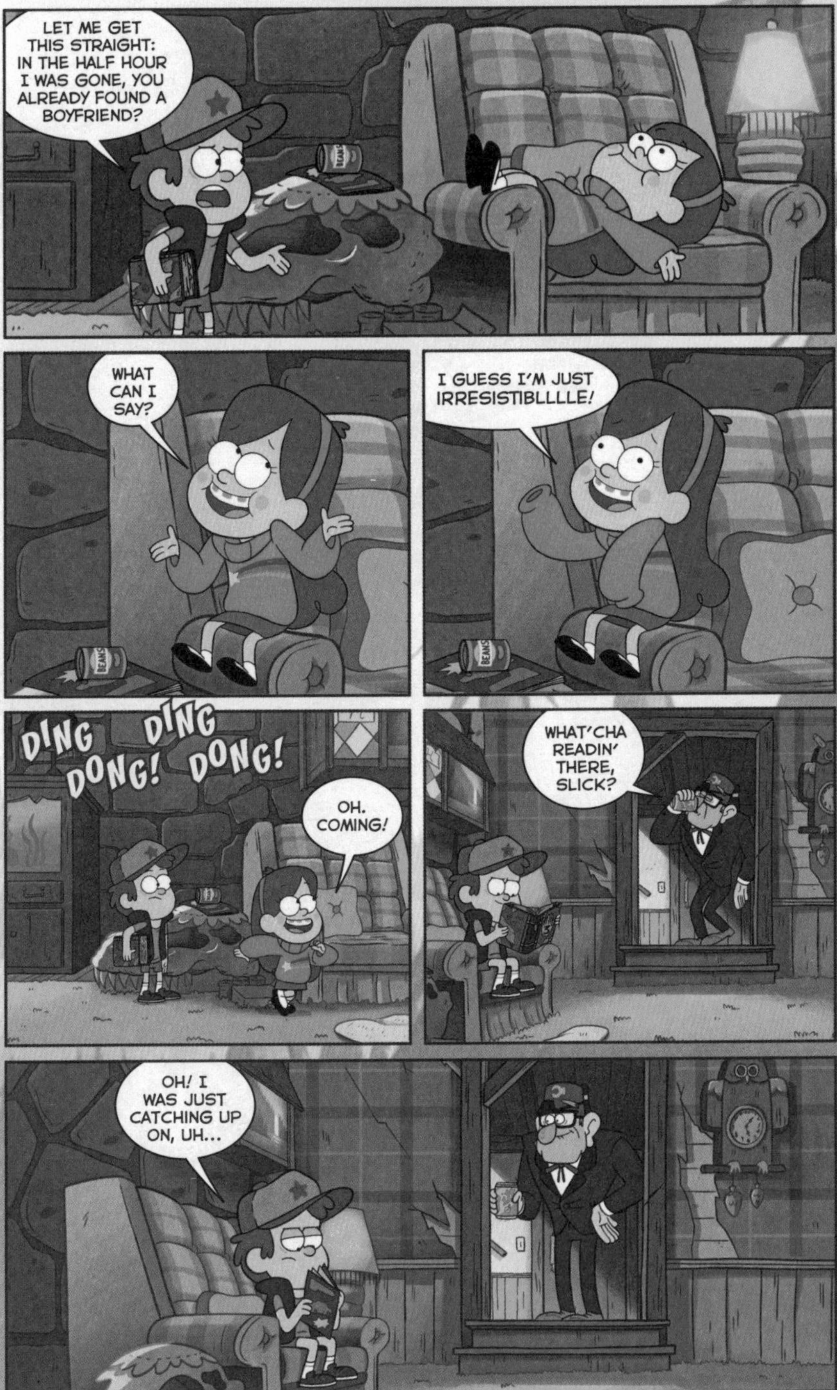
LET ME GET THIS STRAIGHT: IN THE HALF HOUR I WAS GONE, YOU ALREADY FOUND A BOYFRIEND?
WHAT CAN I SAY?
I GUESS I'M JUST IRRESISTIBLLLLE!
BEANS
DING DONG! DING DONG!
OH. COMING!
WHAT'CHA READIN' THERE, SLICK?
OH! I WAS JUST CATCHING UP ON, UH...

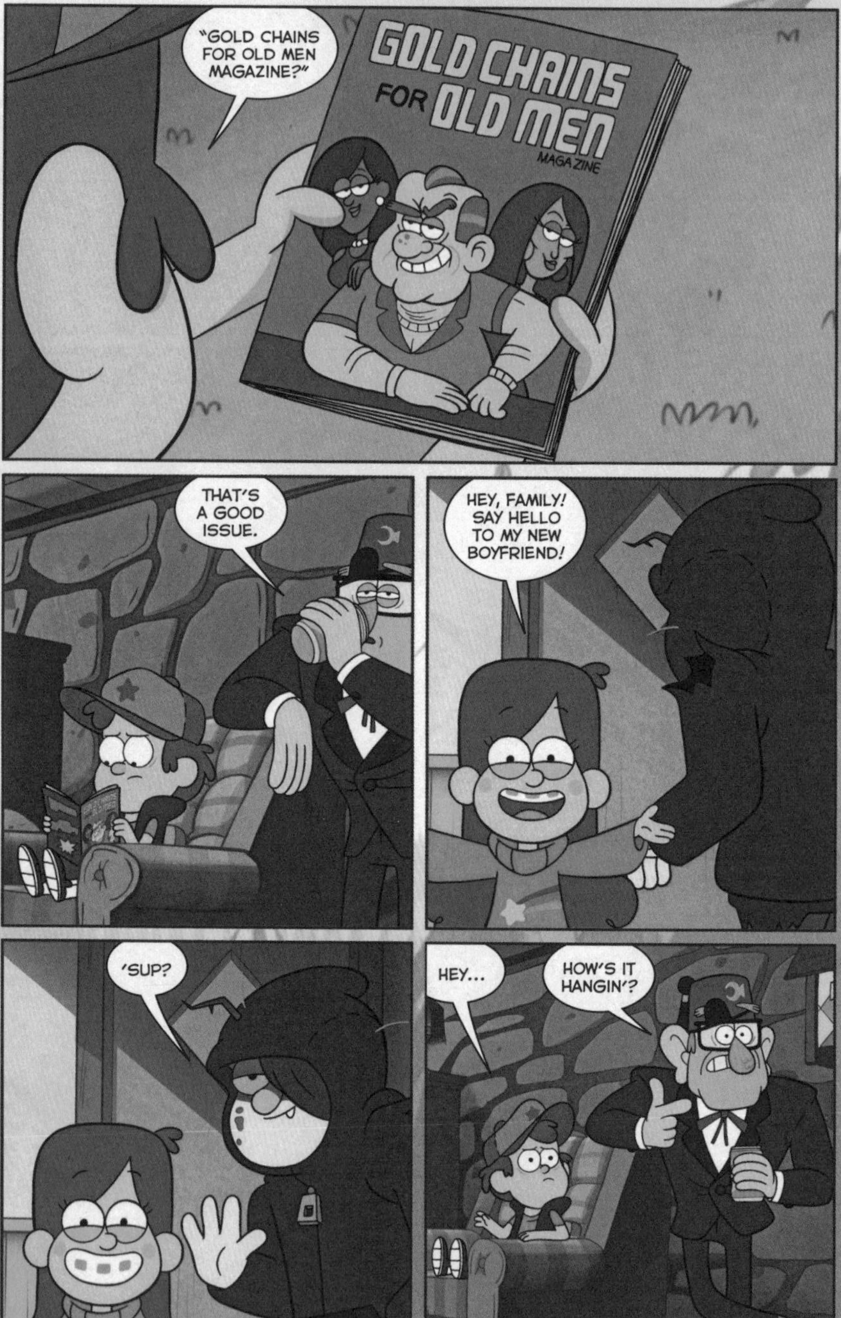
"GOLD CHAINS FOR OLD MEN MAGAZINE?"
GOLD CHAINS FOR OLD MEN MAGAZINE
THAT'S A GOOD ISSUE.
HEY, FAMILY! SAY HELLO TO MY NEW BOYFRIEND!
'SUP?
HEY...
HOW'S IT HANGIN'?

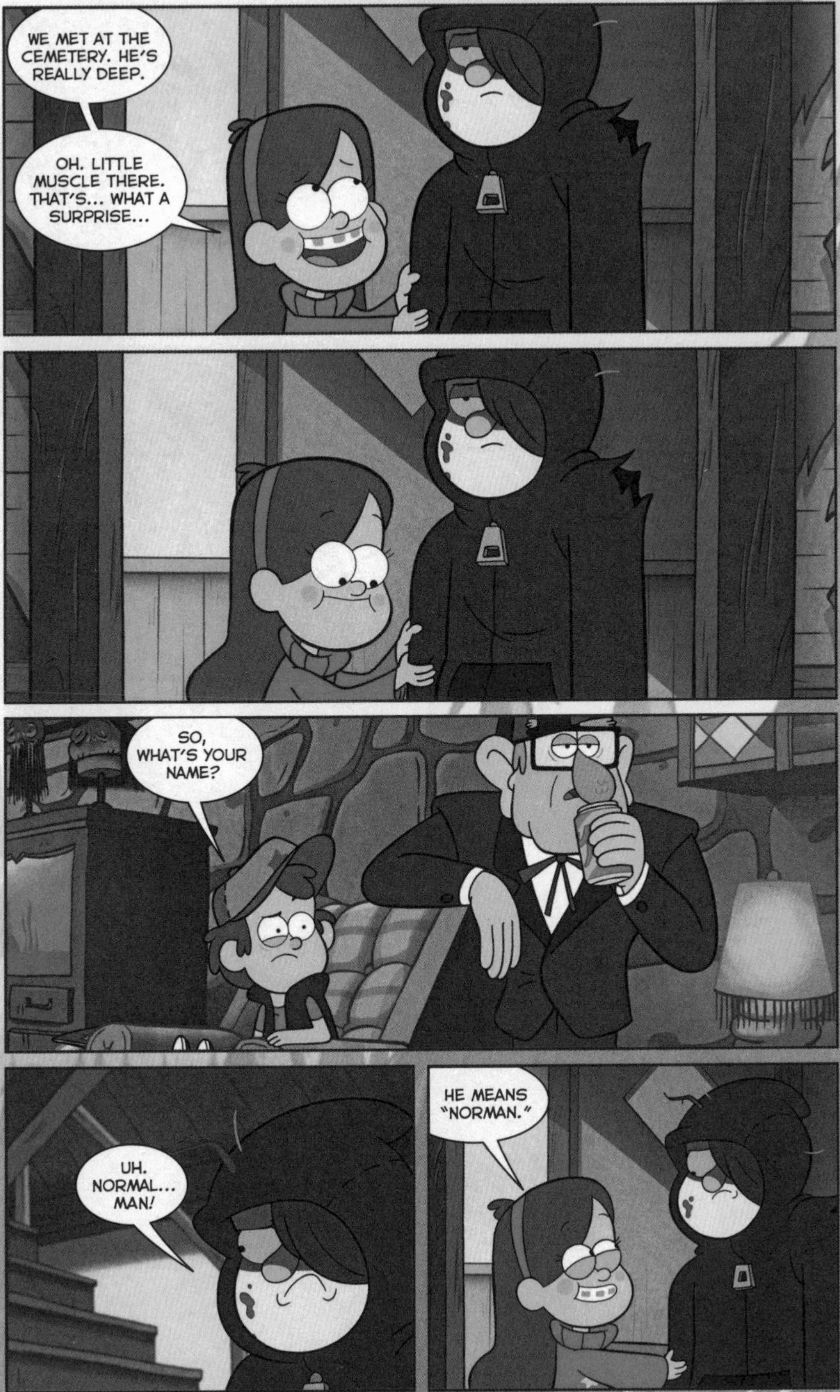
WE MET AT THE CEMETERY. HE'S REALLY DEEP.
OH. LITTLE MUSCLE THERE. THAT'S... WHAT A SURPRISE...
SO, WHAT'S YOUR NAME?
UH. NORMAL... MAN!
HE MEANS "NORMAN."

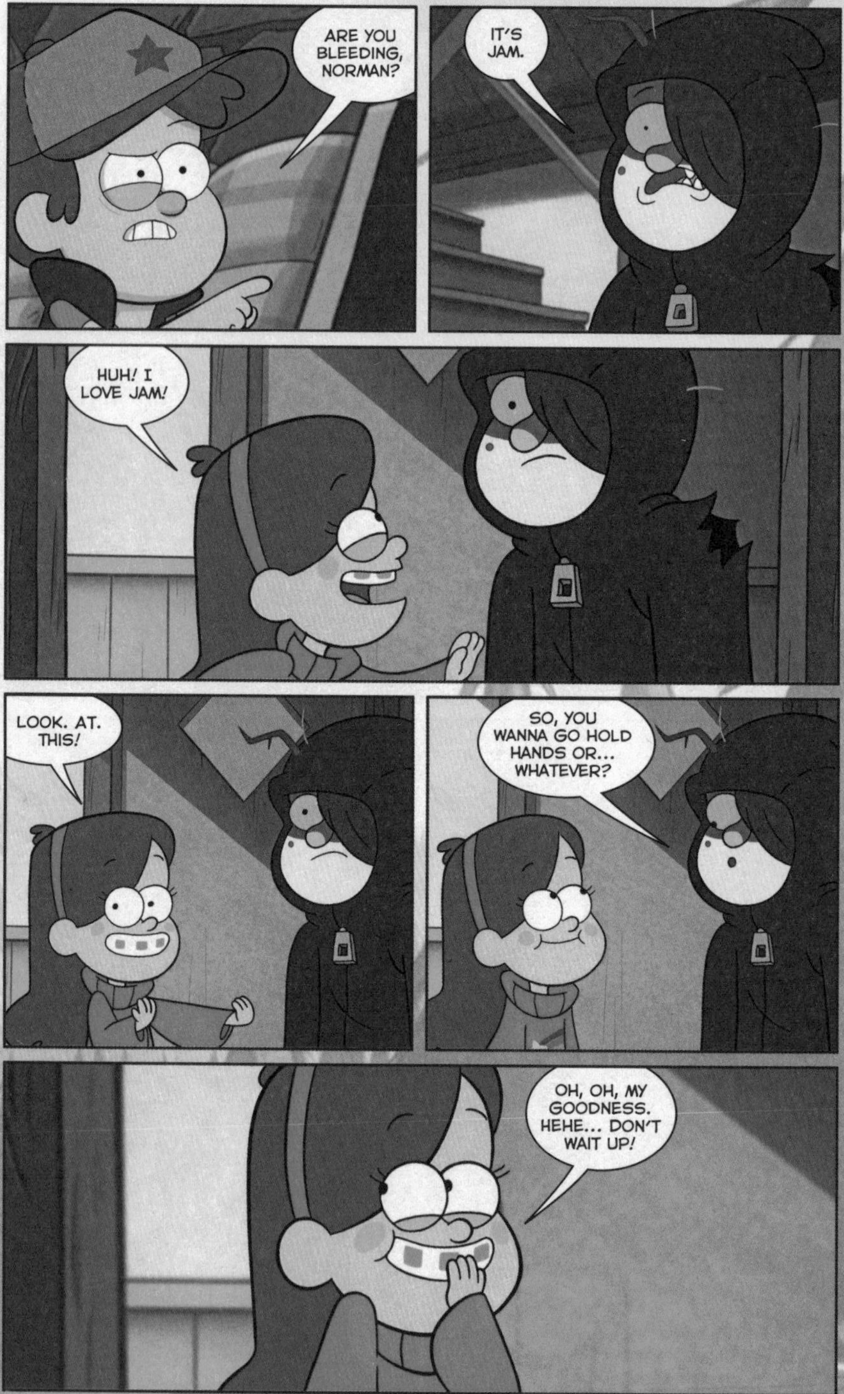
ARE YOU BLEEDING, NORMAN?
IT'S JAM.
HUH! I LOVE JAM!
LOOK. AT. THIS!
SO, YOU WANNA GO HOLD HANDS OR... WHATEVER?
OH, OH, MY GOODNESS. HEHE... DON'T WAIT UP!

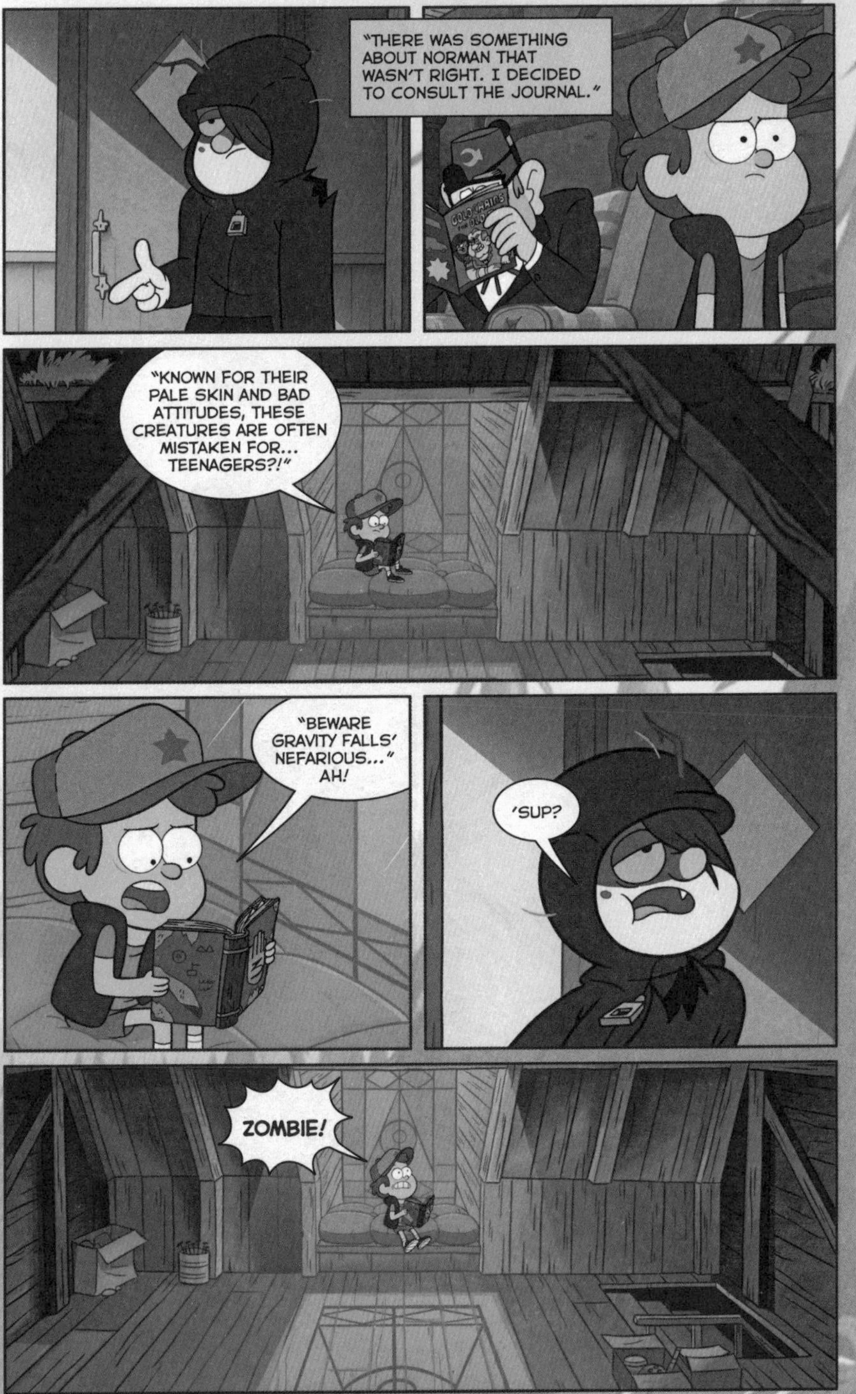
"THERE WAS SOMETHING ABOUT NORMAN THAT WASN'T RIGHT. I DECIDED TO CONSULT THE JOURNAL."
"KNOWN FOR THEIR PALE SKIN AND BAD ATTITUDES, THESE CREATURES ARE OFTEN MISTAKEN FOR... TEENAGERS?!"
"BEWARE GRAVITY FALLS' NEFARIOUS..." AH!
'SUP?
ZOMBIE!

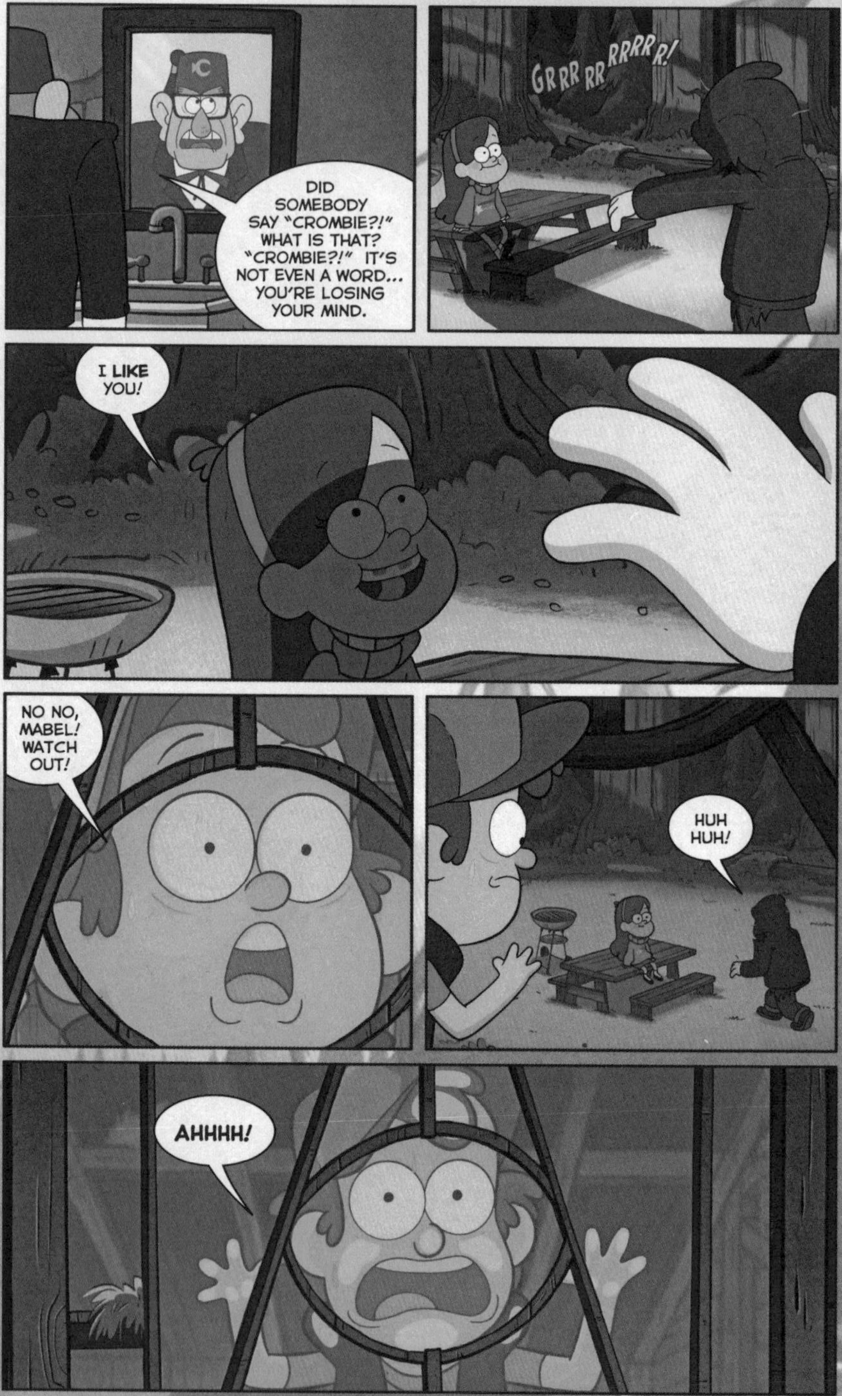
DID SOMEBODY SAY "CROMBIE?!" WHAT IS THAT? "CROMBIE?!" IT'S NOT EVEN A WORD... YOU'RE LOSING YOUR MIND.
GRRRRRRRRRR!
I LIKE YOU!
NO NO, MABEL! WATCH OUT!
HUH HUH!
AHHHH!

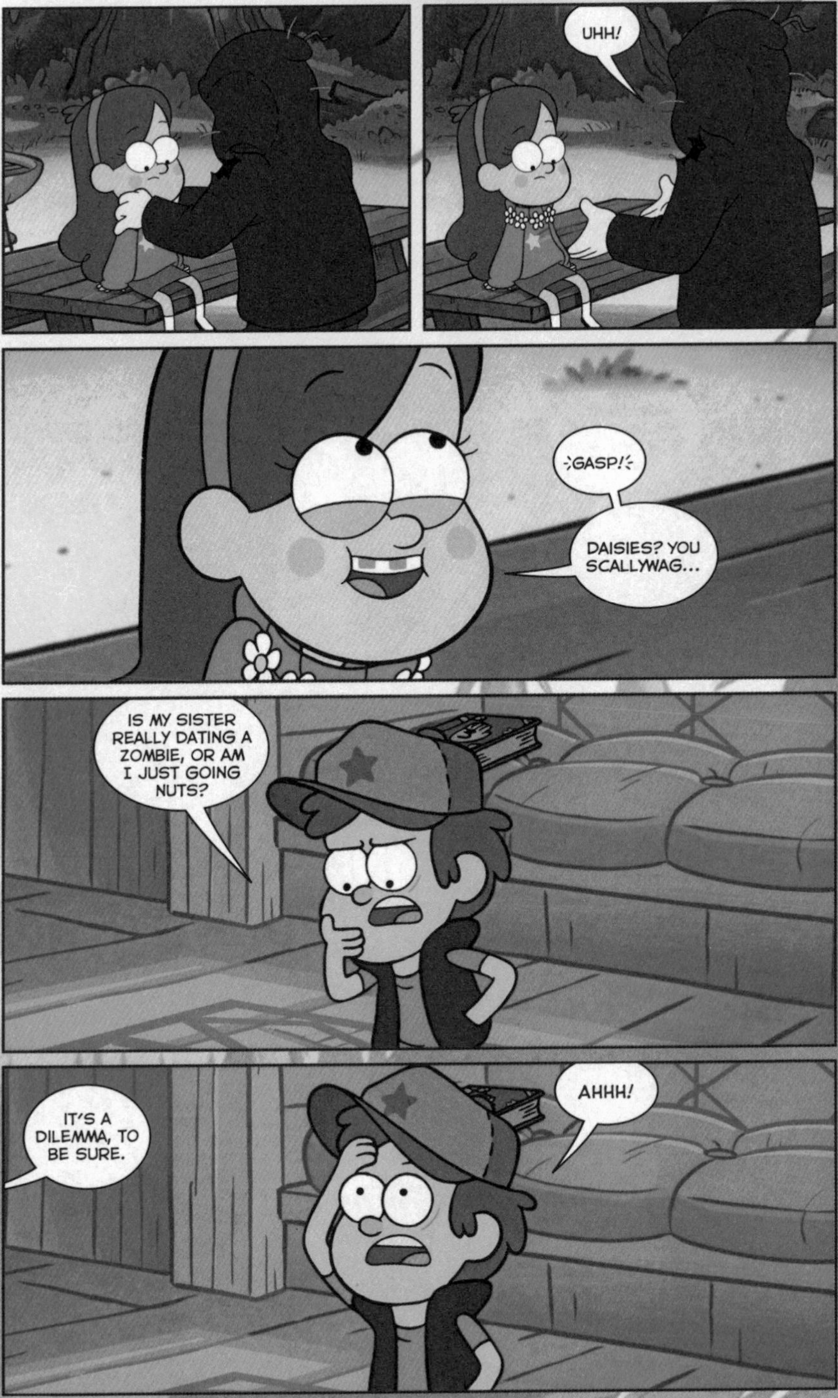
UHH!
⁑GASP!⁑
DAISIES? YOU SCALLYWAG...
IS MY SISTER REALLY DATING A ZOMBIE, OR AM I JUST GOING NUTS?
IT'S A DILEMMA, TO BE SURE.
AHHH!

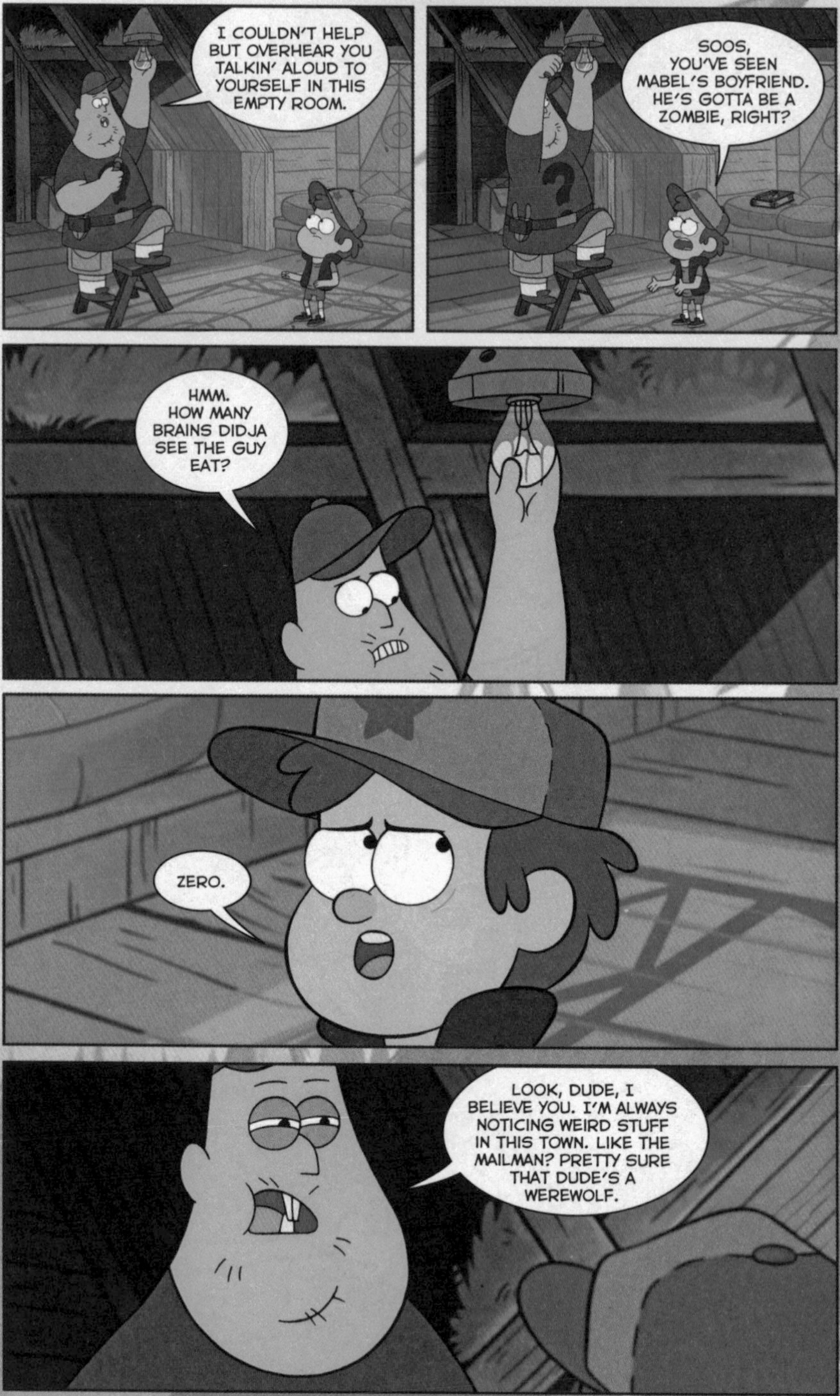
I COULDN'T HELP BUT OVERHEAR YOU TALKIN' ALOUD TO YOURSELF IN THIS EMPTY ROOM.
SOOS, YOU'VE SEEN MABEL'S BOYFRIEND. HE'S GOTTA BE A ZOMBIE, RIGHT?
HMM. HOW MANY BRAINS DIDJA SEE THE GUY EAT?
ZERO.
LOOK, DUDE, I BELIEVE YOU. I'M ALWAYS NOTICING WEIRD STUFF IN THIS TOWN. LIKE THE MAILMAN? PRETTY SURE THAT DUDE'S A WEREWOLF.

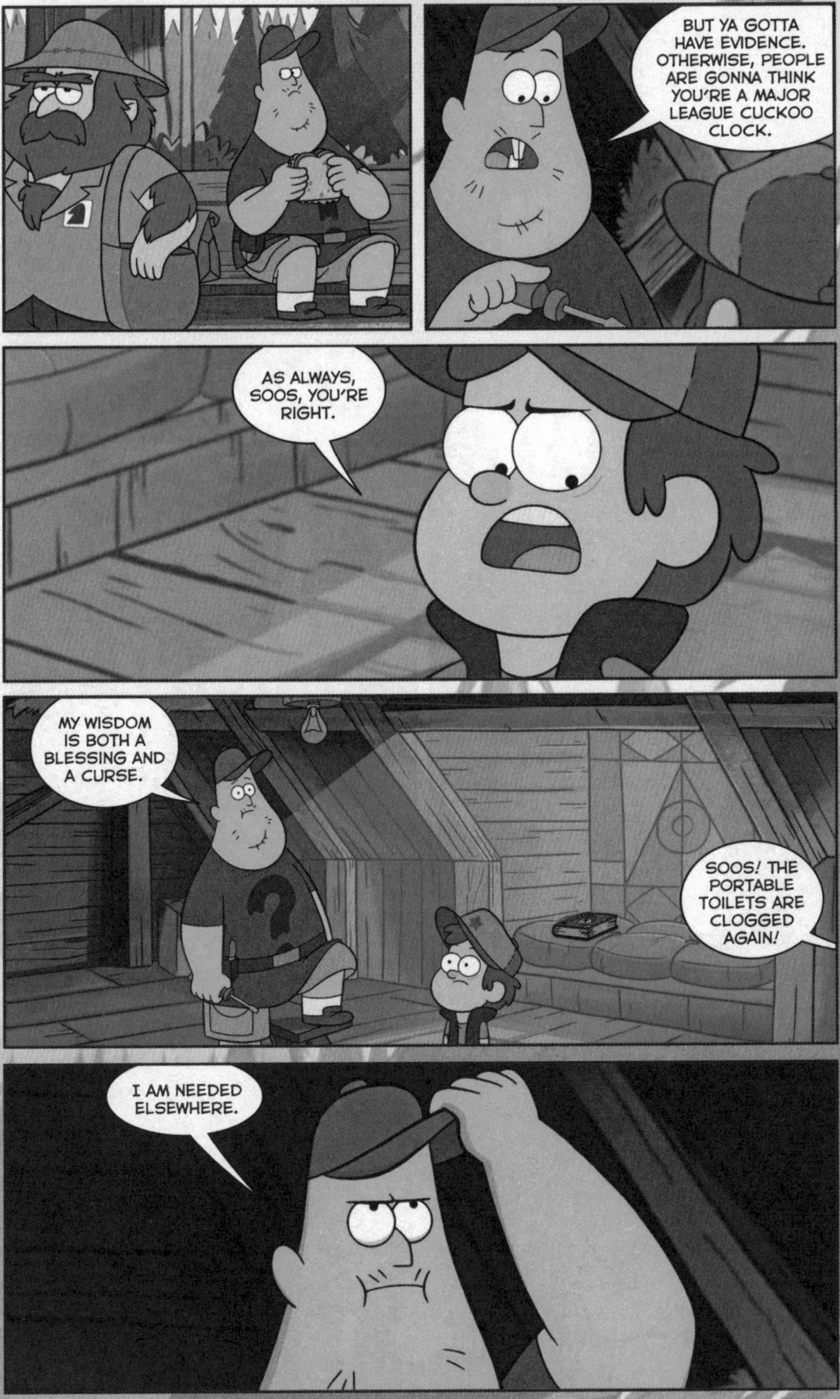
BUT YA GOTTA HAVE EVIDENCE. OTHERWISE, PEOPLE ARE GONNA THINK YOU'RE A MAJOR LEAGUE CUCKOO CLOCK.
AS ALWAYS, SOOS, YOU'RE RIGHT.
MY WISDOM IS BOTH A BLESSING AND A CURSE.
SOOS! THE PORTABLE TOILETS ARE CLOGGED AGAIN!
I AM NEEDED ELSEWHERE.

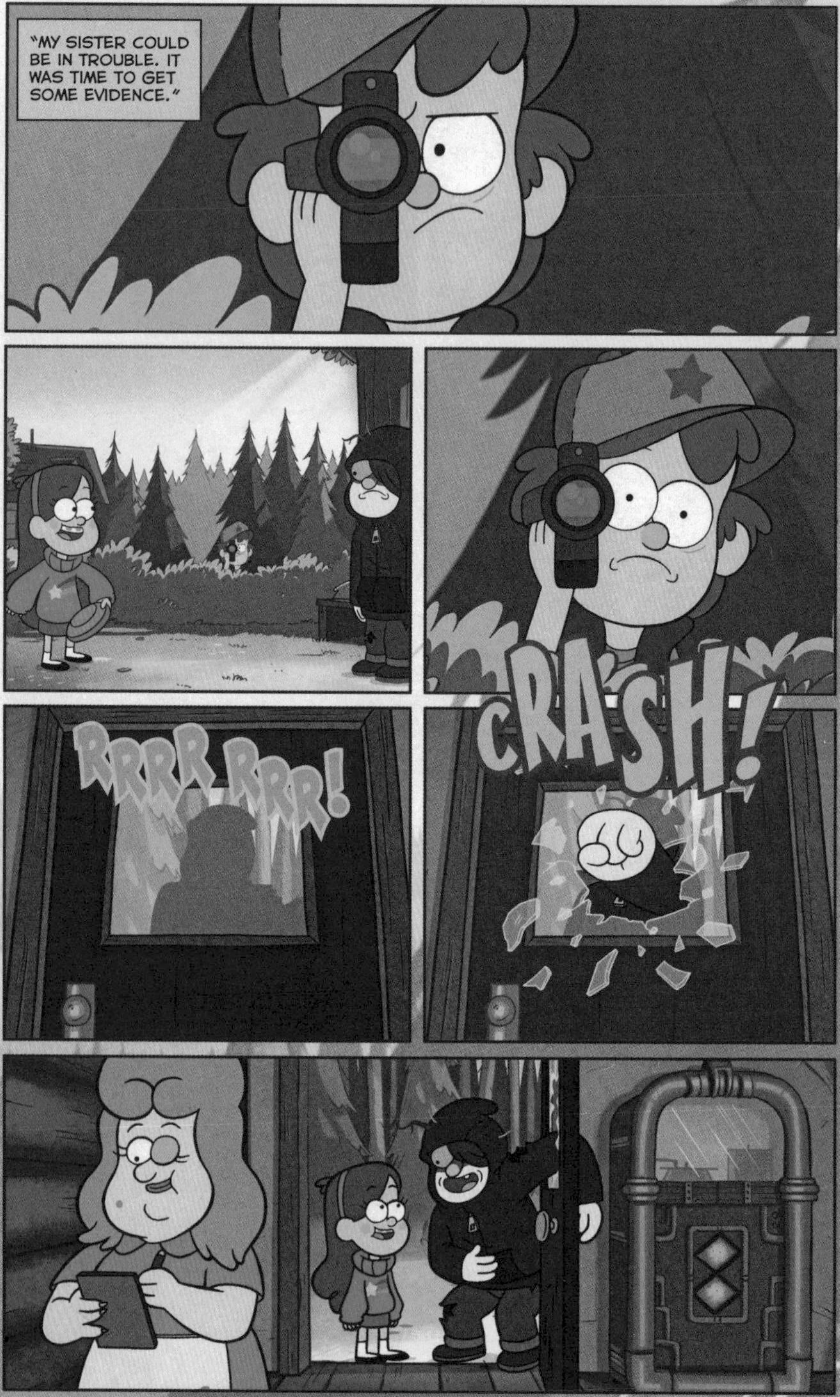
"MY SISTER COULD BE IN TROUBLE. IT WAS TIME TO GET SOME EVIDENCE."
RRRR RRRR!
CRASH!

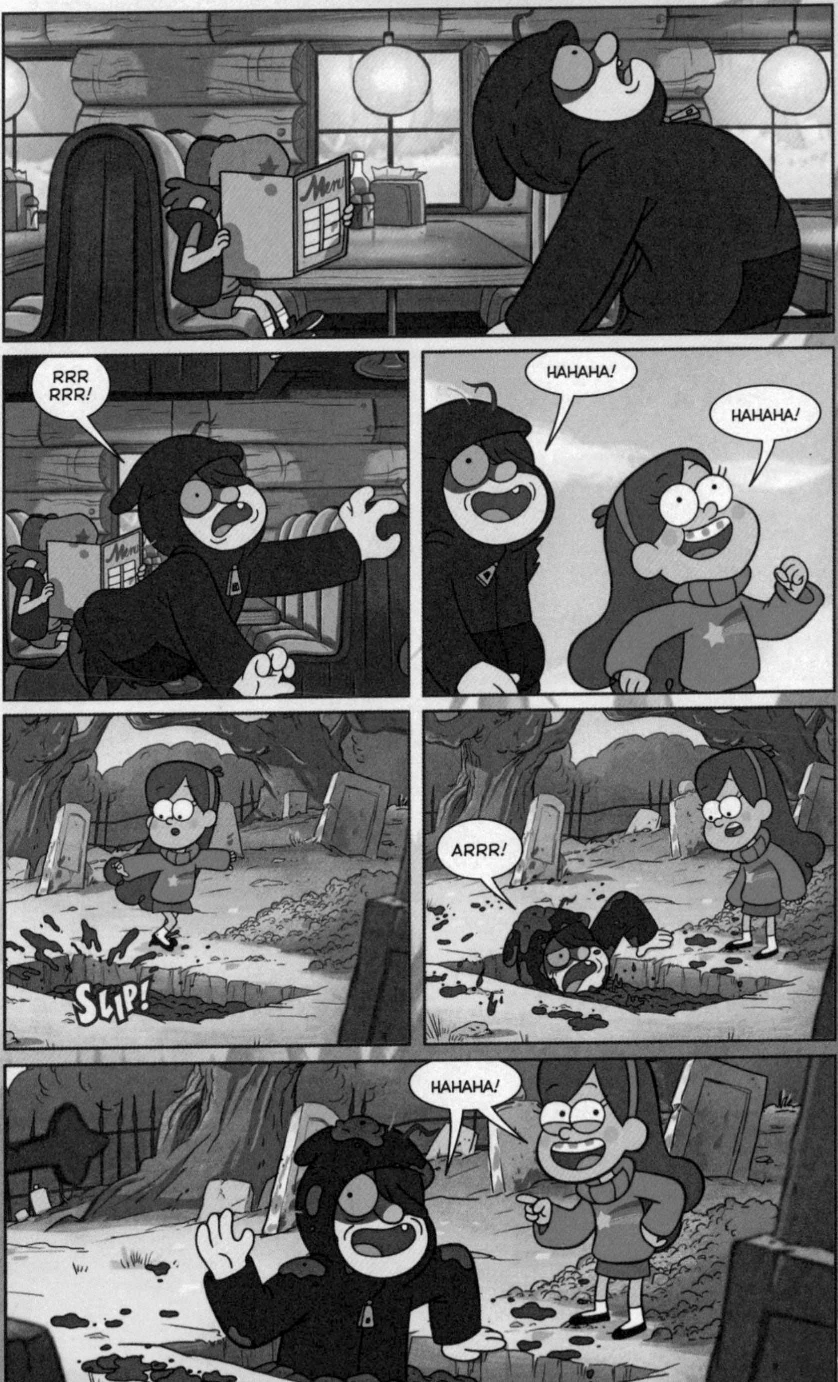
RRR
RRR!
HAHAHA!
HAHAHA!
SLIP!
ARRR!
HAHAHA!

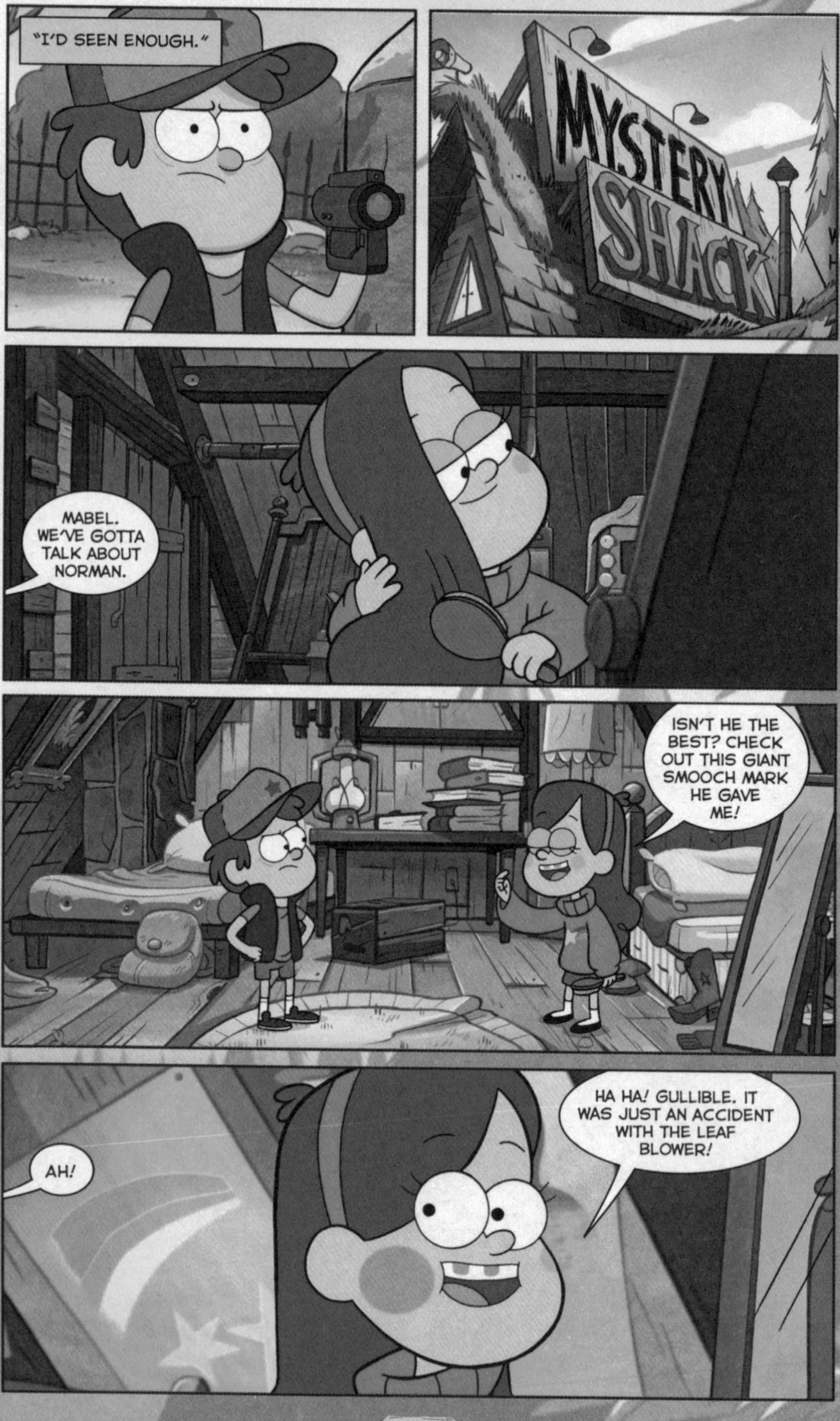
"I'D SEEN ENOUGH."
MYSTERY SHACK
MABEL. WE'VE GOTTA TALK ABOUT NORMAN.
ISN'T HE THE BEST? CHECK OUT THIS GIANT SMOOCH MARK HE GAVE ME!
AH!
HA HA! GULLIBLE. IT WAS JUST AN ACCIDENT WITH THE LEAF BLOWER!

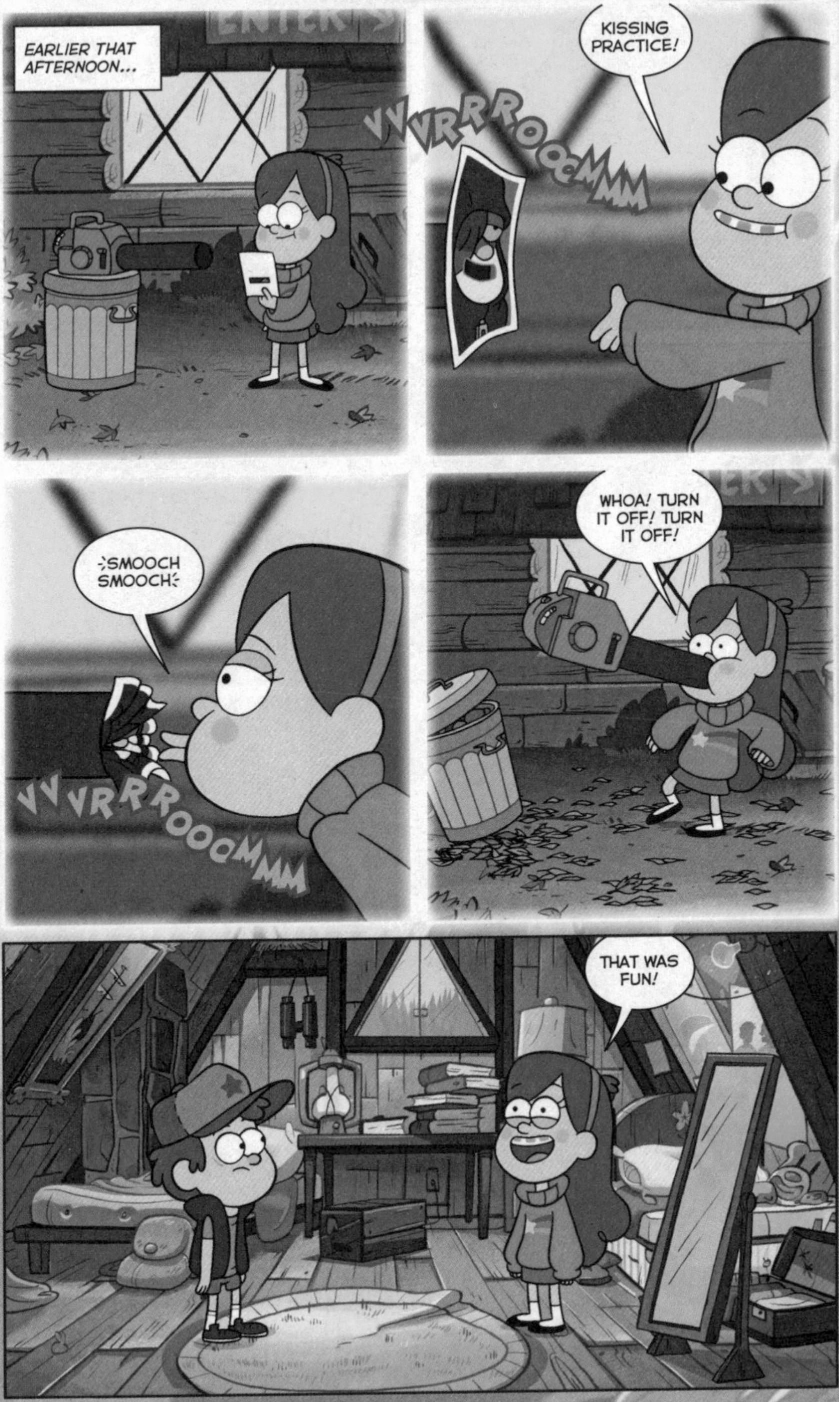
EARLIER THAT AFTERNOON...
KISSING PRACTICE!
VVVRRROOOMMM
SMOOCH SMOOCH
VVVRRROOOMMM
WHOA! TURN IT OFF! TURN IT OFF!
THAT WAS FUN!

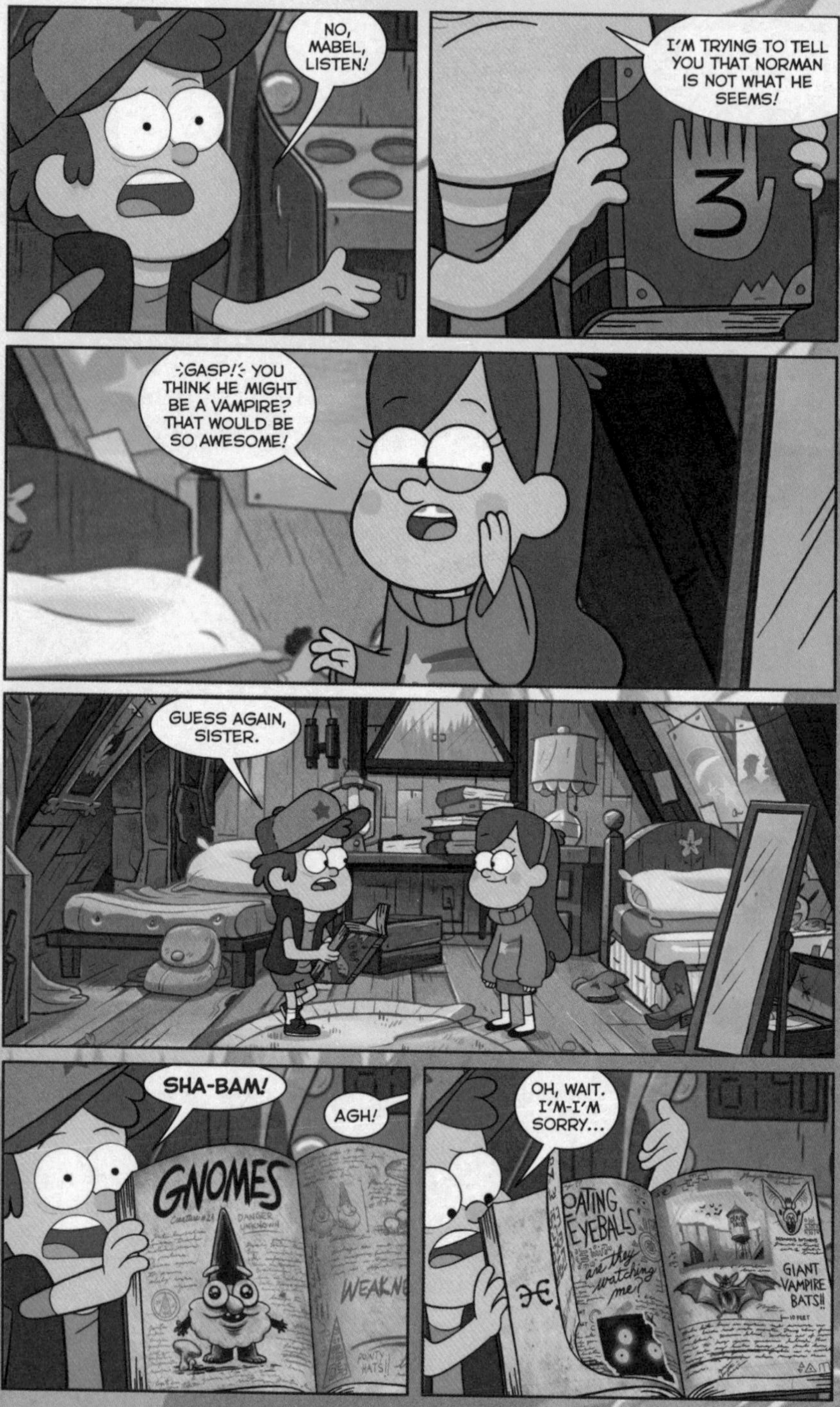
NO, MABEL, LISTEN!
I'M TRYING TO TELL YOU THAT NORMAN IS NOT WHAT HE SEEMS!
3
GASP! YOU THINK HE MIGHT BE A VAMPIRE? THAT WOULD BE SO AWESOME!
GUESS AGAIN, SISTER.
SHA-BAM!
AGH!
GNOMES
DANGER UNKNOWN
POINTY HATS!!
OH, WAIT. I'M-I'M SORRY...
EYEBALLS
are they watching me?
GIANT VAMPIRE BATS!!

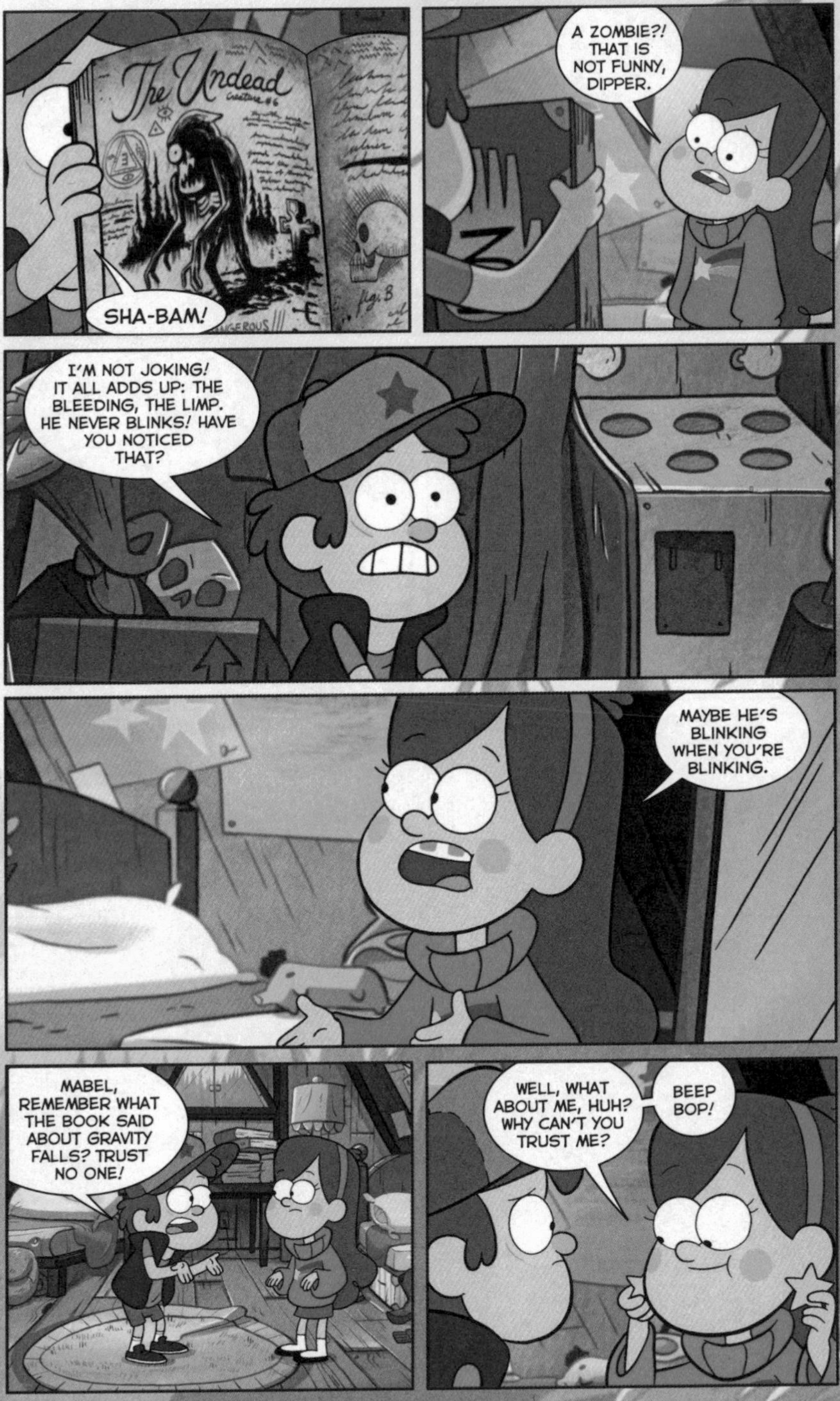
The Undead
SHA-BAM!
A ZOMBIE?! THAT IS NOT FUNNY, DIPPER.
I'M NOT JOKING! IT ALL ADDS UP: THE BLEEDING, THE LIMP. HE NEVER BLINKS! HAVE YOU NOTICED THAT?
MAYBE HE'S BLINKING WHEN YOU'RE BLINKING.
MABEL, REMEMBER WHAT THE BOOK SAID ABOUT GRAVITY FALLS? TRUST NO ONE!
WELL, WHAT ABOUT ME, HUH? WHY CAN'T YOU TRUST ME?
BEEP BOP!

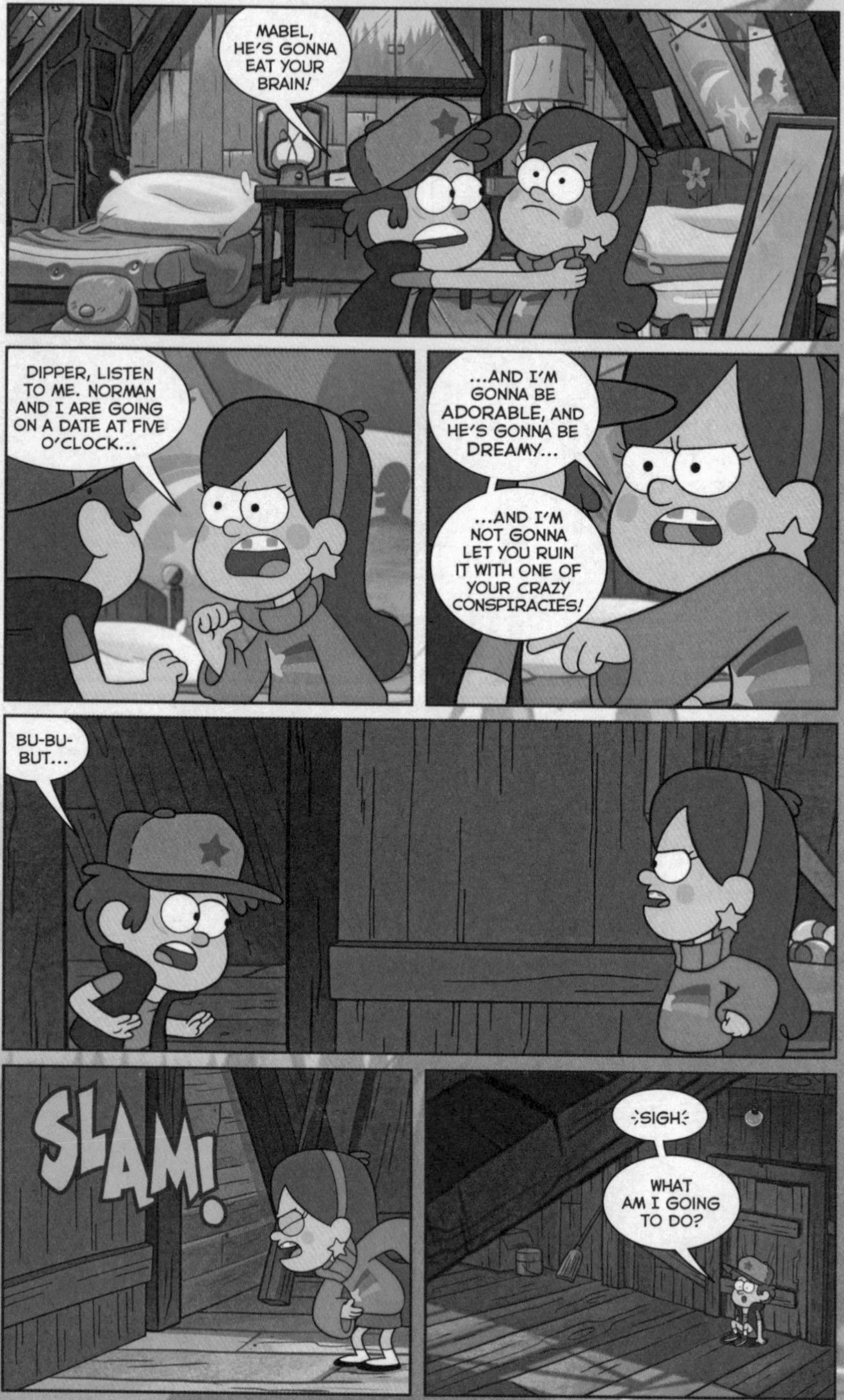
MABEL, HE'S GONNA EAT YOUR BRAIN!
DIPPER, LISTEN TO ME. NORMAN AND I ARE GOING ON A DATE AT FIVE O'CLOCK...
...AND I'M GONNA BE ADORABLE, AND HE'S GONNA BE DREAMY...
...AND I'M NOT GONNA LET YOU RUIN IT WITH ONE OF YOUR CRAZY CONSPIRACIES!
BU-BU-BUT...
SLAM!
SIGH
WHAT AM I GOING TO DO?

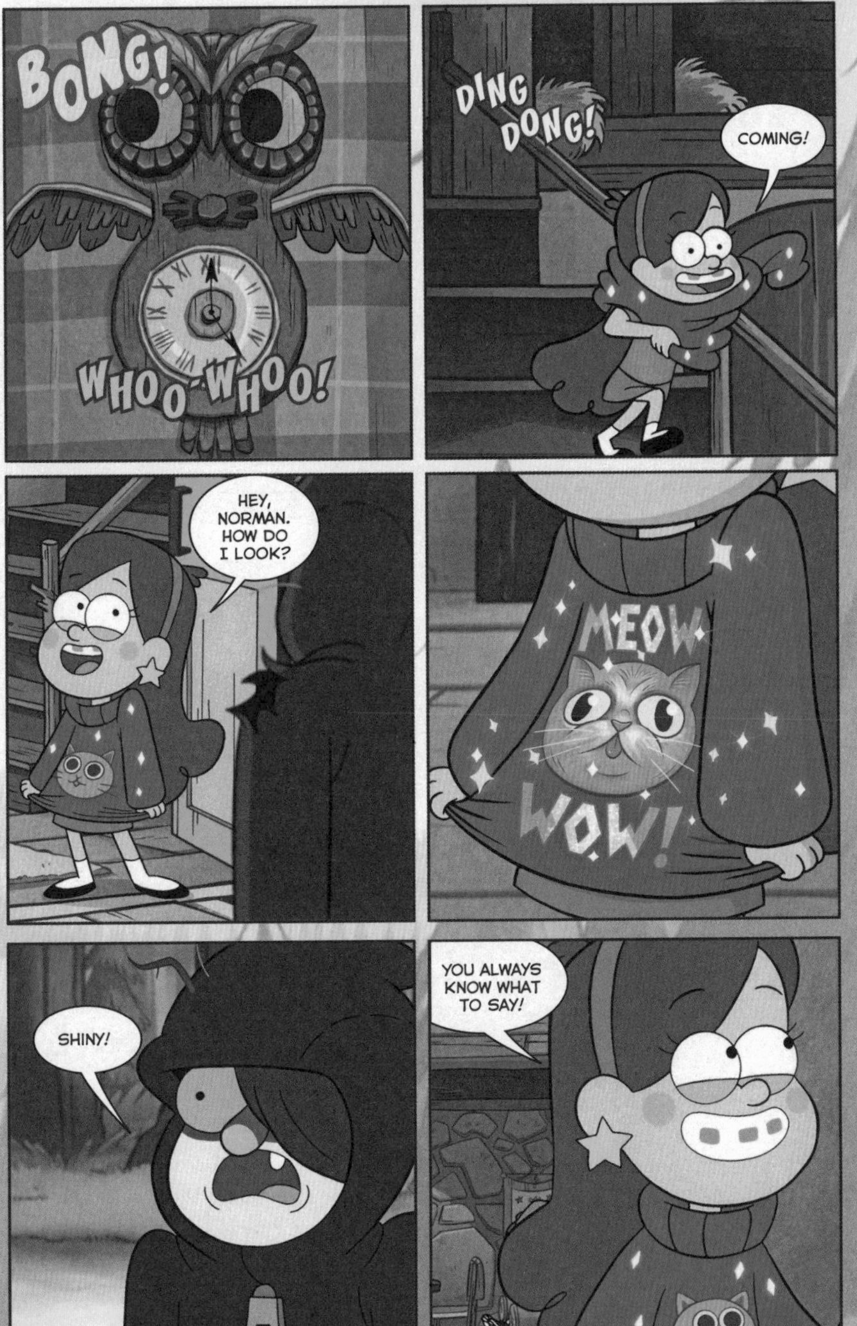
BONG!
WHOO-WHOO!
DING DONG!
COMING!
HEY, NORMAN. HOW DO I LOOK?
MEOW
WOW!
SHINY!
YOU ALWAYS KNOW WHAT TO SAY!

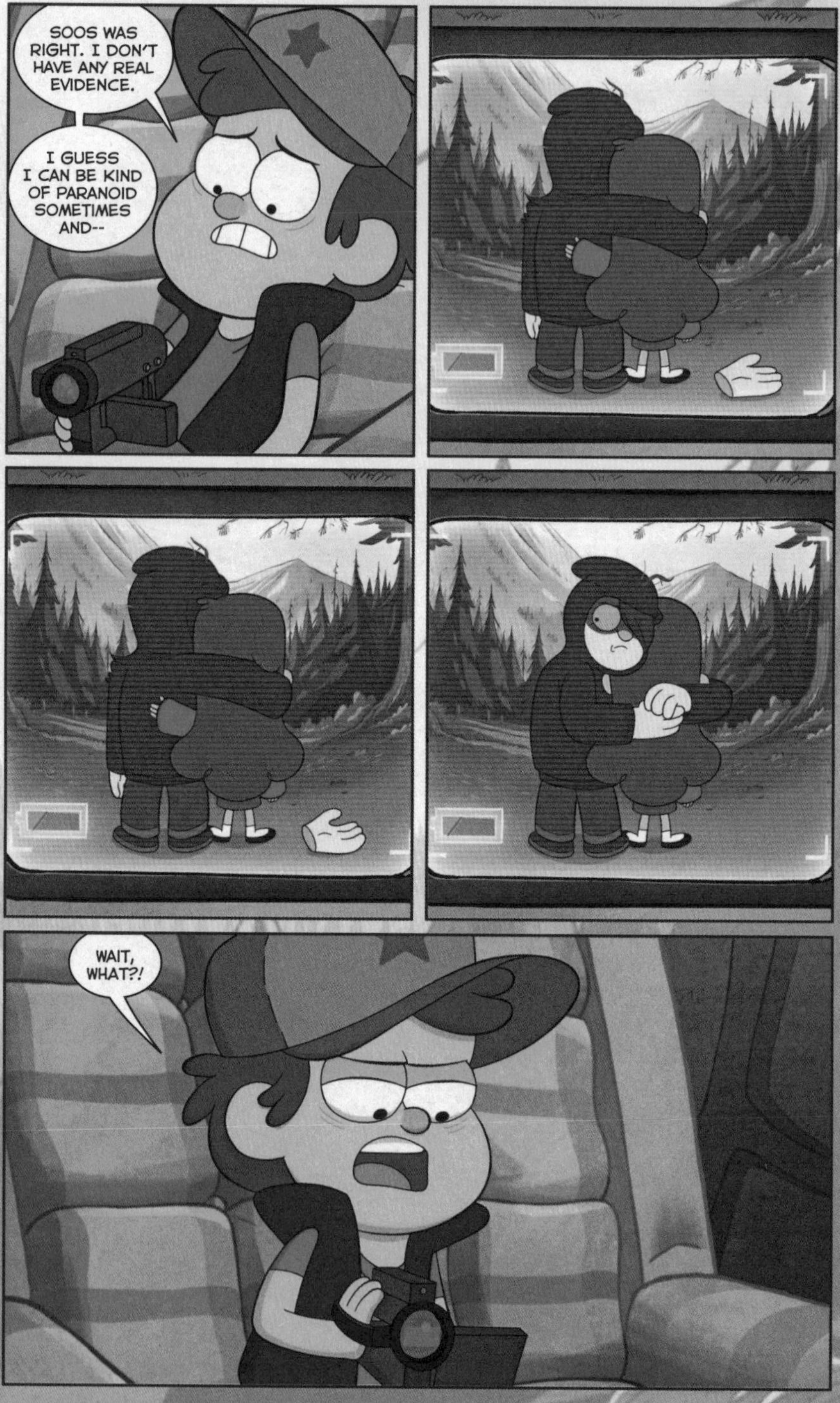
SOOS WAS RIGHT. I DON'T HAVE ANY REAL EVIDENCE.
I GUESS I CAN BE KIND OF PARANOID SOMETIMES AND--
WAIT, WHAT?!

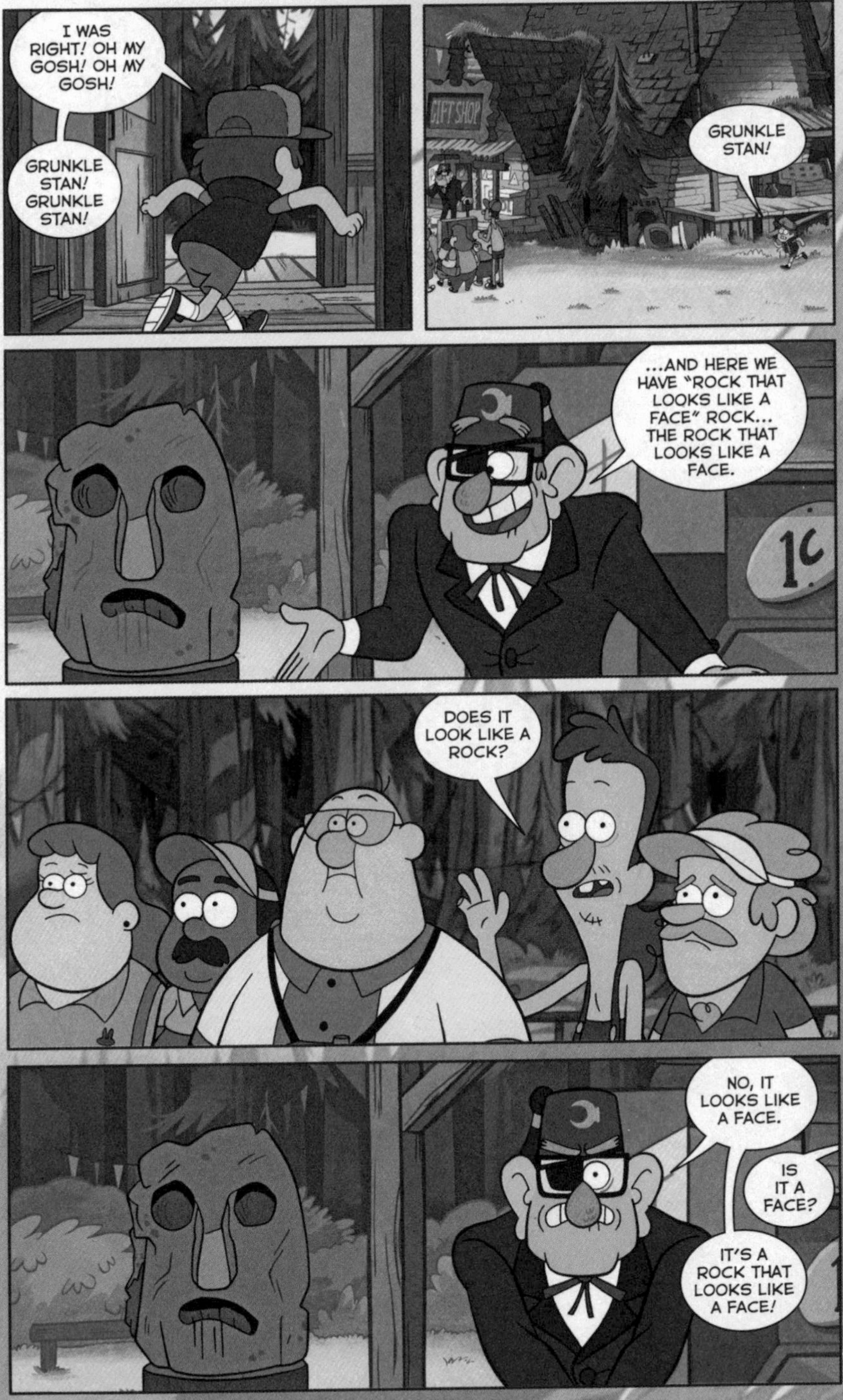
I WAS RIGHT! OH MY GOSH! OH MY GOSH!
GRUNKLE STAN! GRUNKLE STAN!
GIFT SHOP
GRUNKLE STAN!
...AND HERE WE HAVE "ROCK THAT LOOKS LIKE A FACE" ROCK... THE ROCK THAT LOOKS LIKE A FACE.
1¢
DOES IT LOOK LIKE A ROCK?
NO, IT LOOKS LIKE A FACE.
IS IT A FACE?
IT'S A ROCK THAT LOOKS LIKE A FACE!

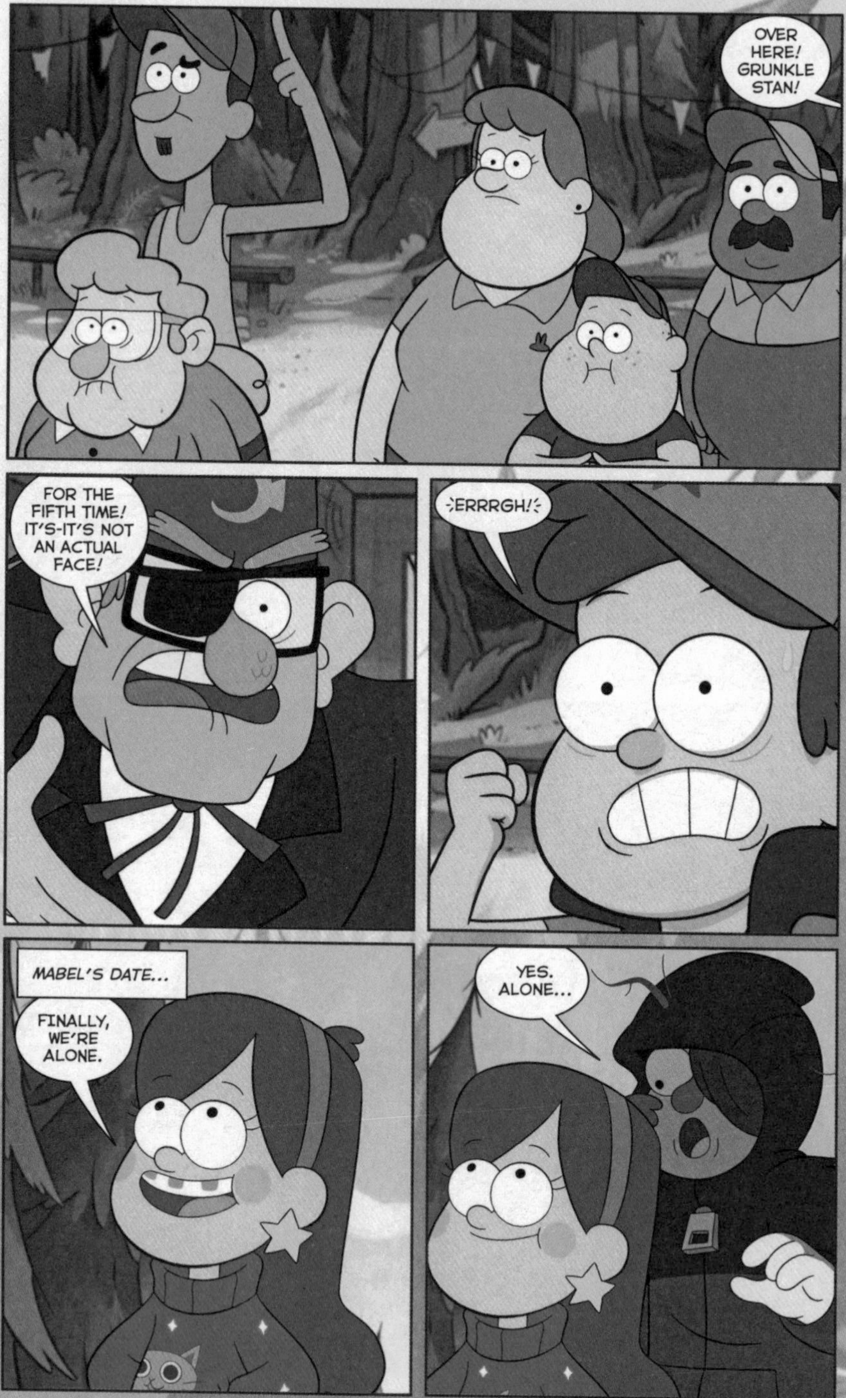
OVER HERE! GRUNKLE STAN!
FOR THE FIFTH TIME! IT'S-IT'S NOT AN ACTUAL FACE!
ERRRGH!
MABEL'S DATE...
FINALLY, WE'RE ALONE.
YES. ALONE...

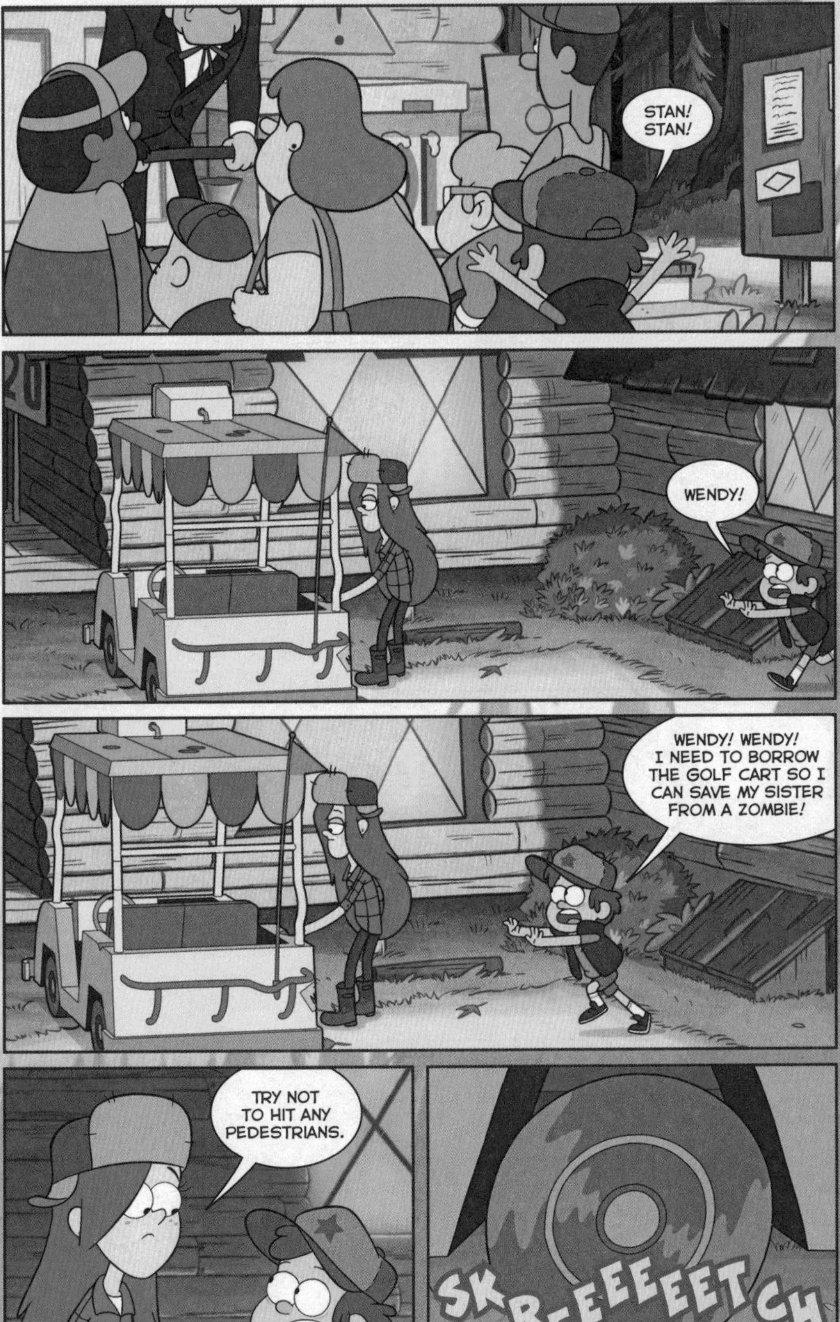
STAN! STAN!
WENDY!
WENDY! WENDY! I NEED TO BORROW THE GOLF CART SO I CAN SAVE MY SISTER FROM A ZOMBIE!
TRY NOT TO HIT ANY PEDESTRIANS.
SKREEEEEETCH

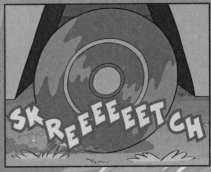

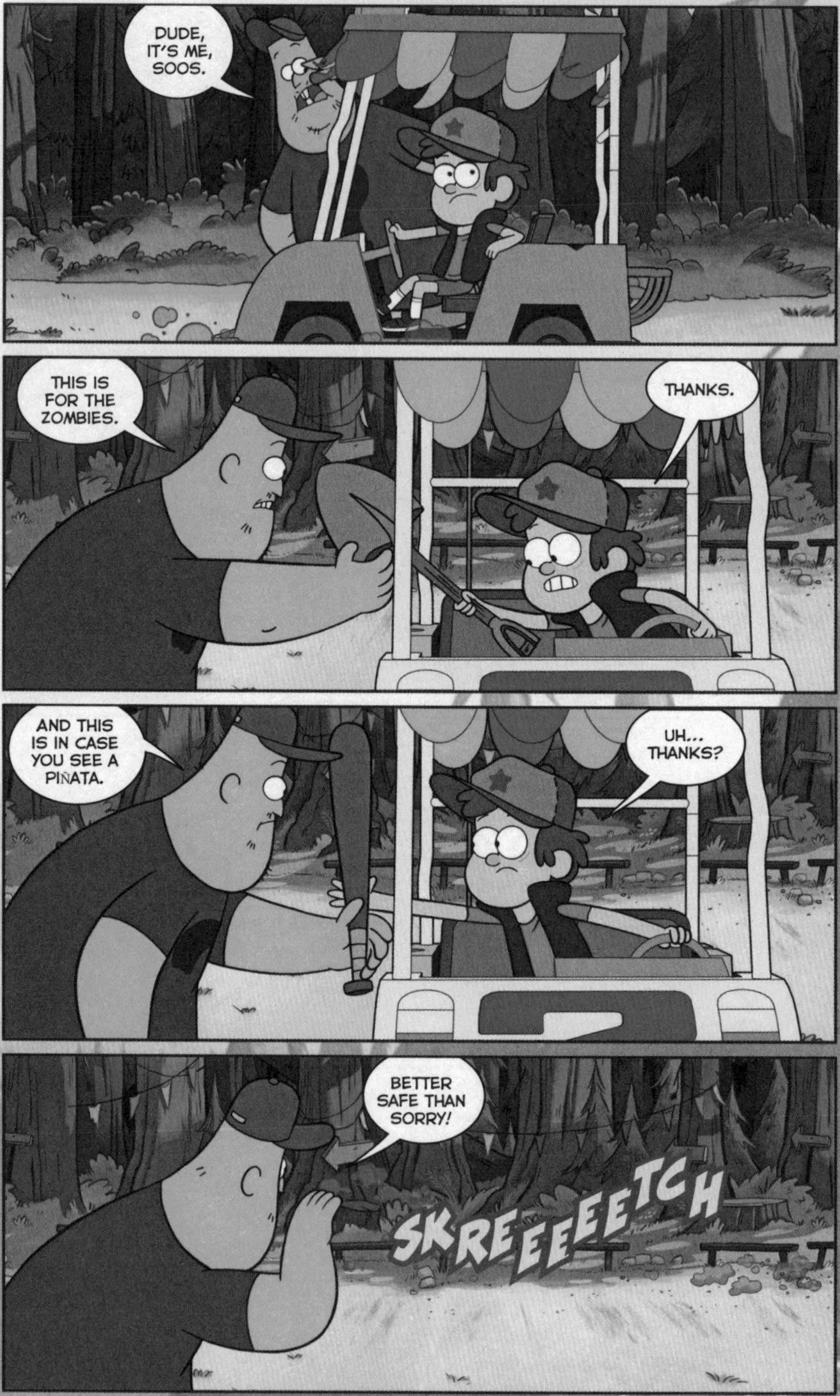
DUDE, IT'S ME, SOOS.
THIS IS FOR THE ZOMBIES.
THANKS.
AND THIS IS IN CASE YOU SEE A PIÑATA.
UH... THANKS?
BETTER SAFE THAN SORRY!
SKREEEEEETCH

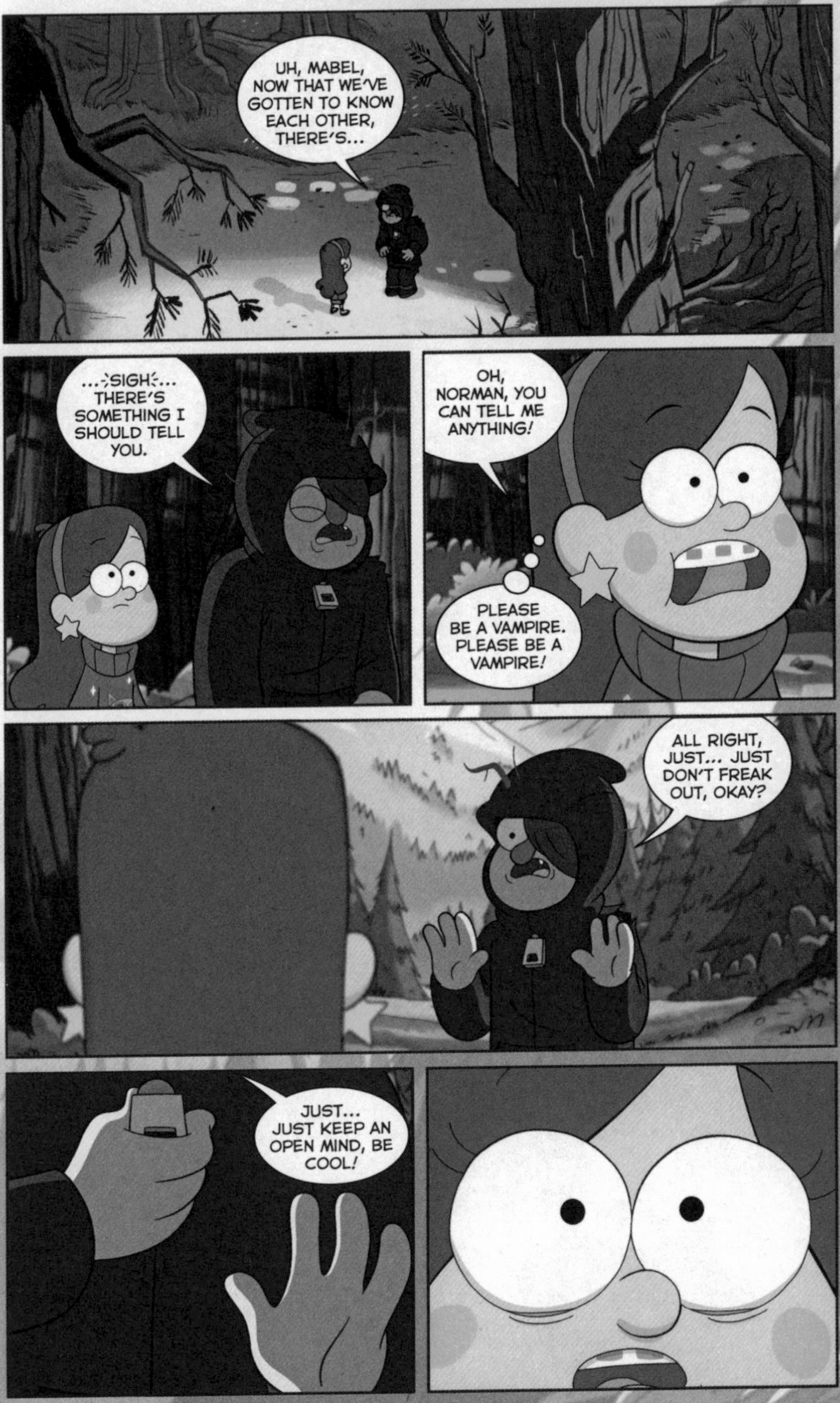
UH, MABEL, NOW THAT WE'VE GOTTEN TO KNOW EACH OTHER, THERE'S...
...SIGH... THERE'S SOMETHING I SHOULD TELL YOU.
OH, NORMAN, YOU CAN TELL ME ANYTHING!
PLEASE BE A VAMPIRE. PLEASE BE A VAMPIRE!
ALL RIGHT, JUST... JUST DON'T FREAK OUT, OKAY?
JUST... JUST KEEP AN OPEN MIND, BE COOL!

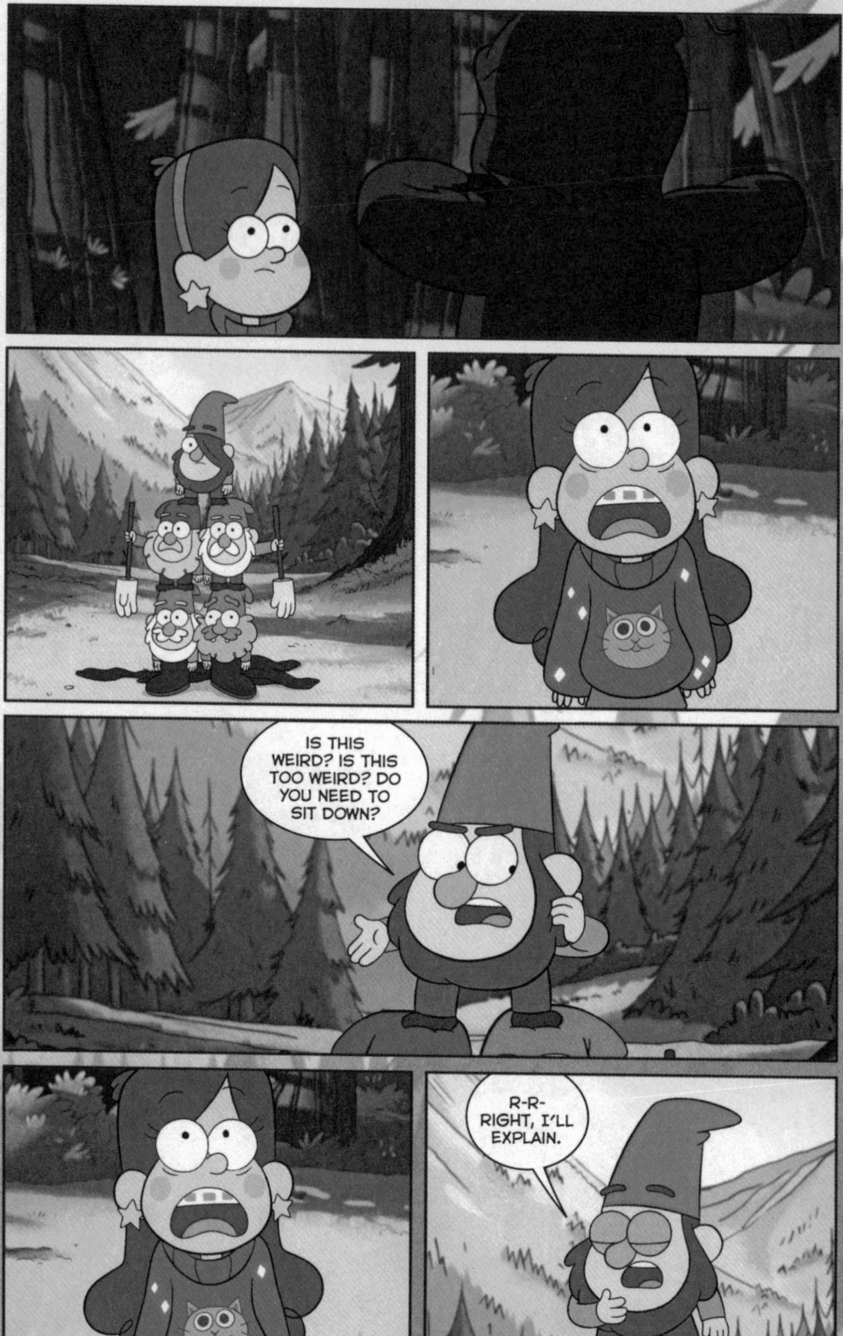
IS THIS WEIRD? IS THIS TOO WEIRD? DO YOU NEED TO SIT DOWN?
R-R-RIGHT, I'LL EXPLAIN.

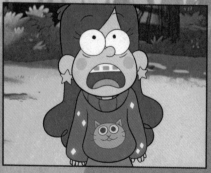

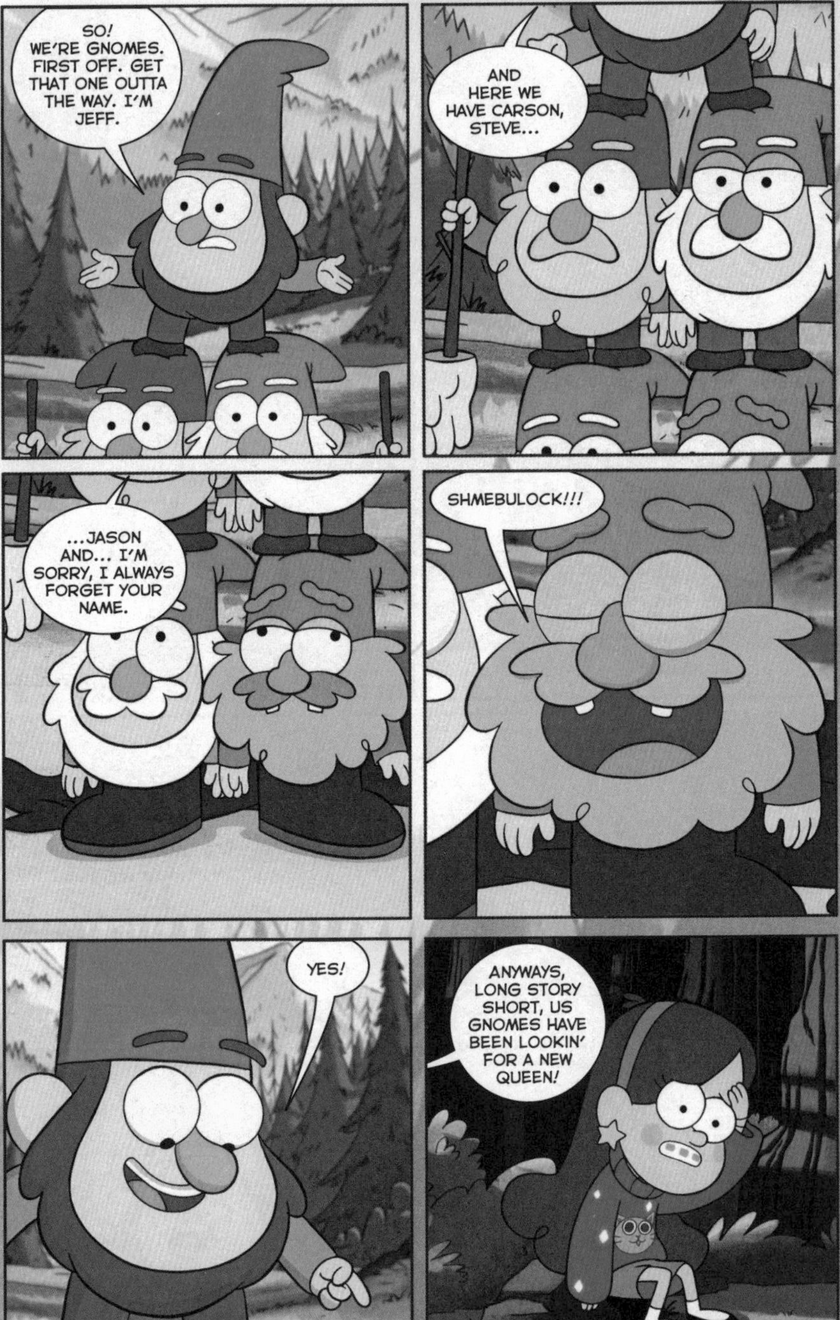
SO! WE'RE GNOMES. FIRST OFF. GET THAT ONE OUTTA THE WAY. I'M JEFF.
AND HERE WE HAVE CARSON, STEVE...
...JASON AND... I'M SORRY, I ALWAYS FORGET YOUR NAME.
SHMEBULOCK!!!
YES!
ANYWAYS, LONG STORY SHORT, US GNOMES HAVE BEEN LOOKIN' FOR A NEW QUEEN!

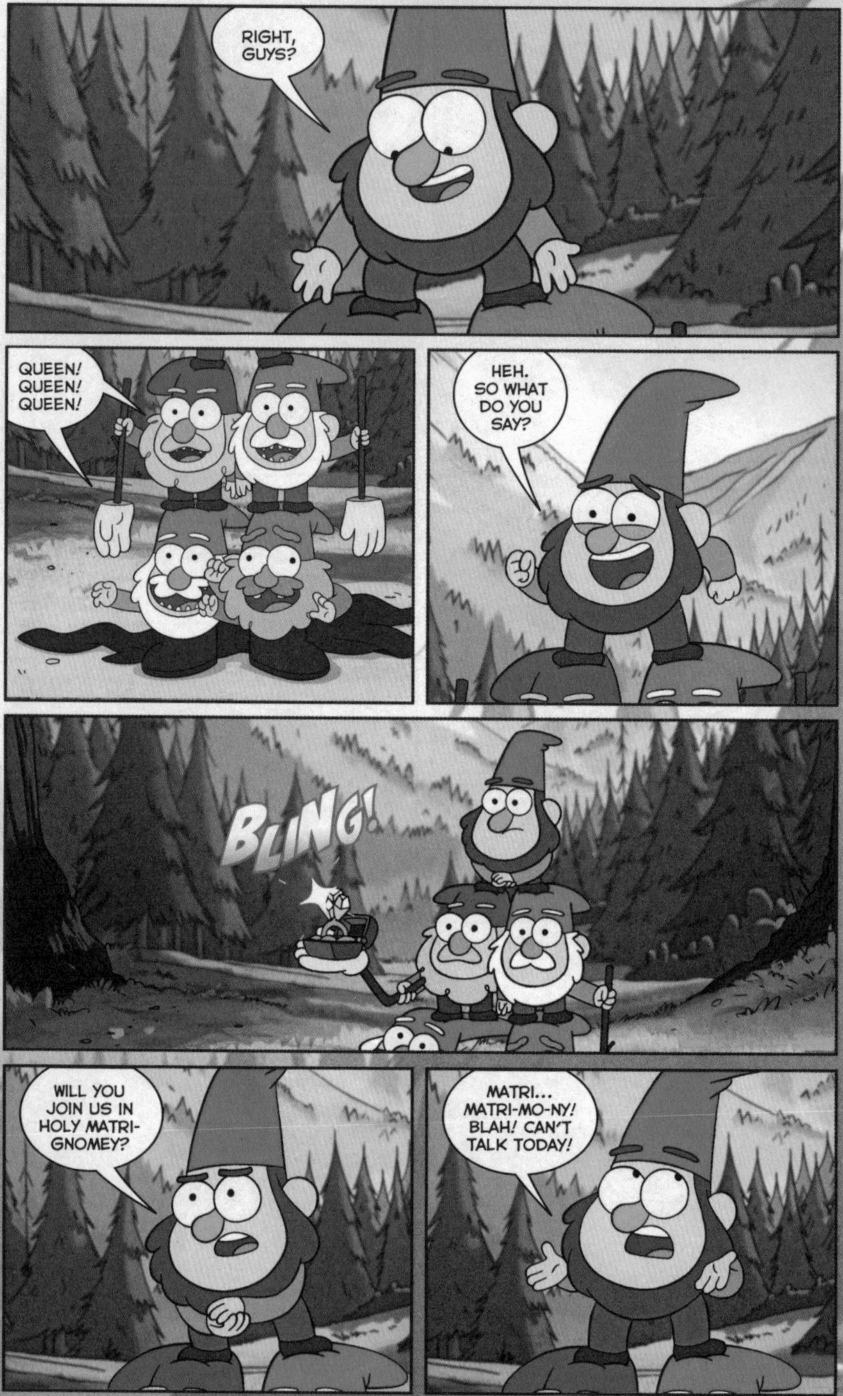
RIGHT, GUYS?
QUEEN! QUEEN! QUEEN!
HEH. SO WHAT DO YOU SAY?
BLING!
WILL YOU JOIN US IN HOLY MATRI-GNOMEY?
MATRI... MATRI-MO-NY! BLAH! CAN'T TALK TODAY!

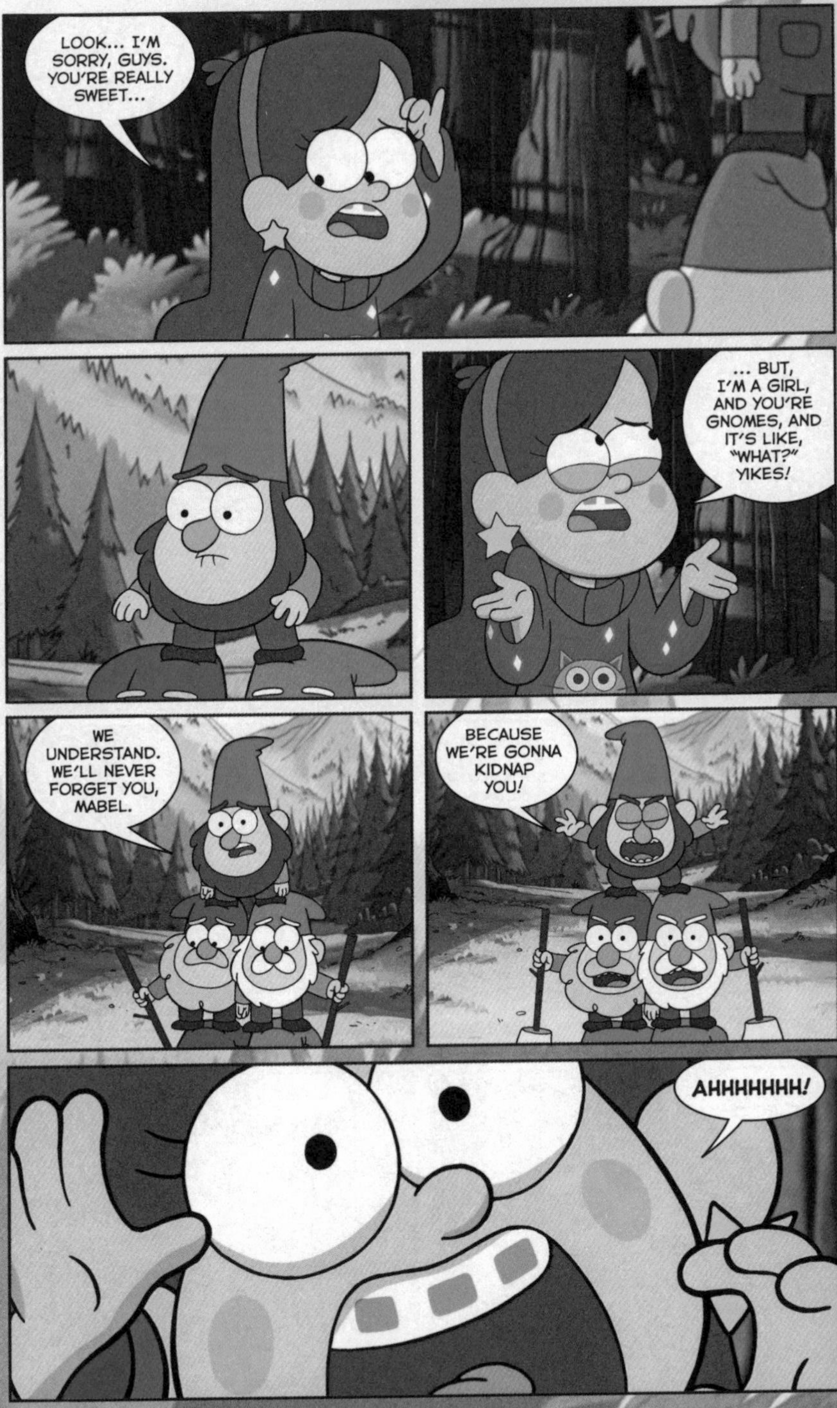
LOOK... I'M SORRY, GUYS. YOU'RE REALLY SWEET...
... BUT, I'M A GIRL, AND YOU'RE GNOMES, AND IT'S LIKE, "WHAT?" YIKES!
WE UNDERSTAND. WE'LL NEVER FORGET YOU, MABEL.
BECAUSE WE'RE GONNA KIDNAP YOU!
AHHHHHHH!

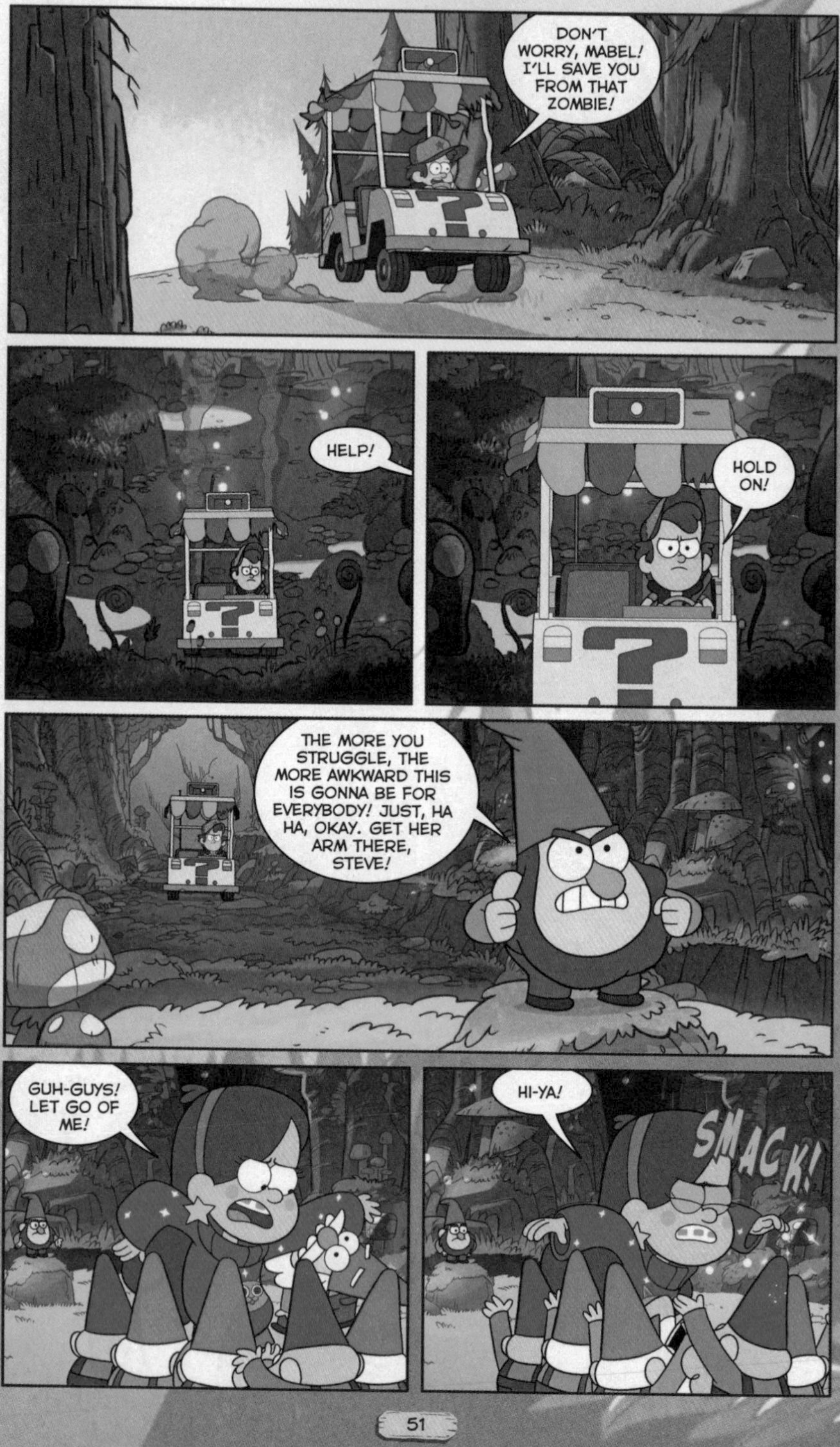
DON'T WORRY, MABEL! I'LL SAVE YOU FROM THAT ZOMBIE!
HELP!
HOLD ON!
THE MORE YOU STRUGGLE, THE MORE AWKWARD THIS IS GONNA BE FOR EVERYBODY! JUST, HA HA, OKAY. GET HER ARM THERE, STEVE!
GUH-GUYS! LET GO OF ME!
HI-YA!
SMACK!

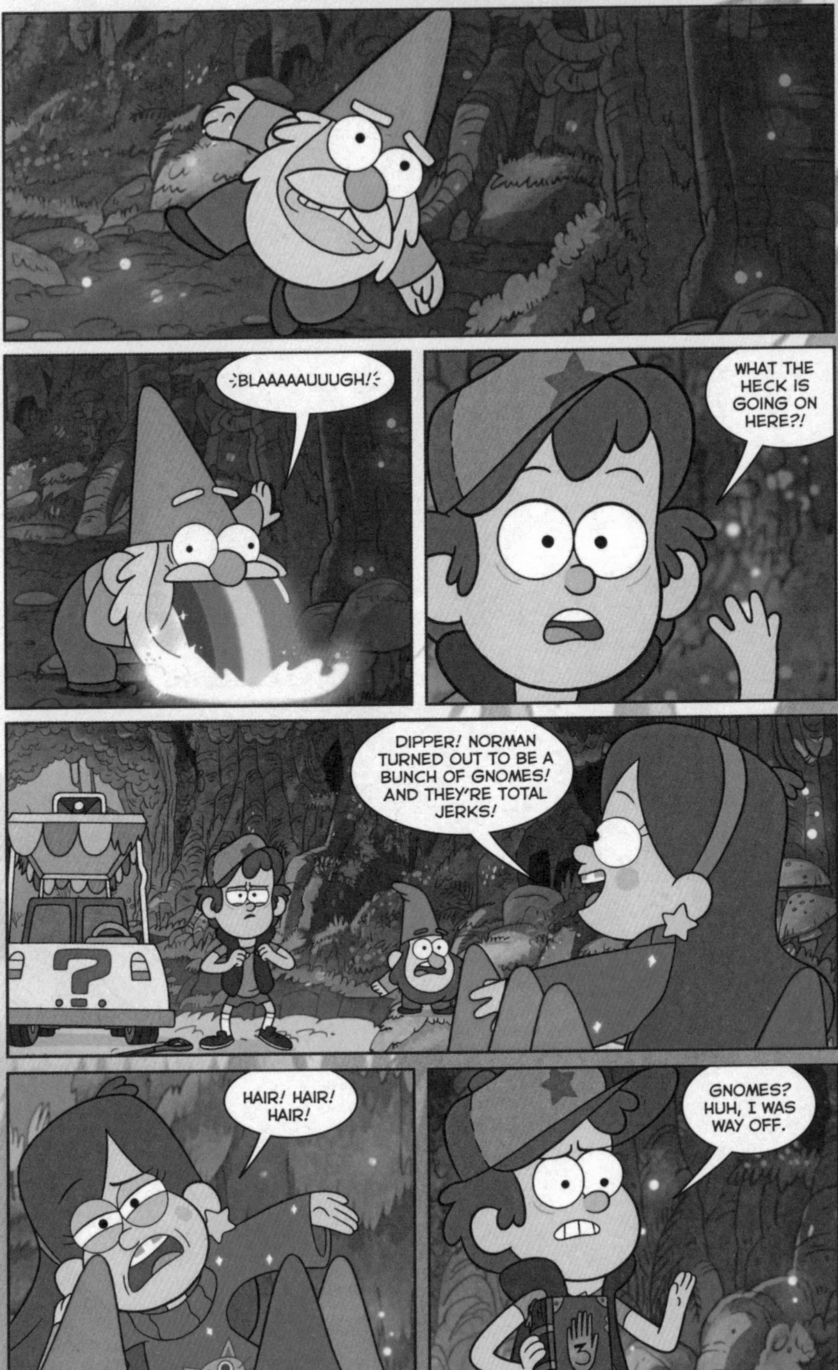
-;BLAAAAAUUUGH!;-
WHAT THE HECK IS GOING ON HERE?!
DIPPER! NORMAN TURNED OUT TO BE A BUNCH OF GNOMES! AND THEY'RE TOTAL JERKS!
HAIR! HAIR! HAIR!
GNOMES? HUH, I WAS WAY OFF.

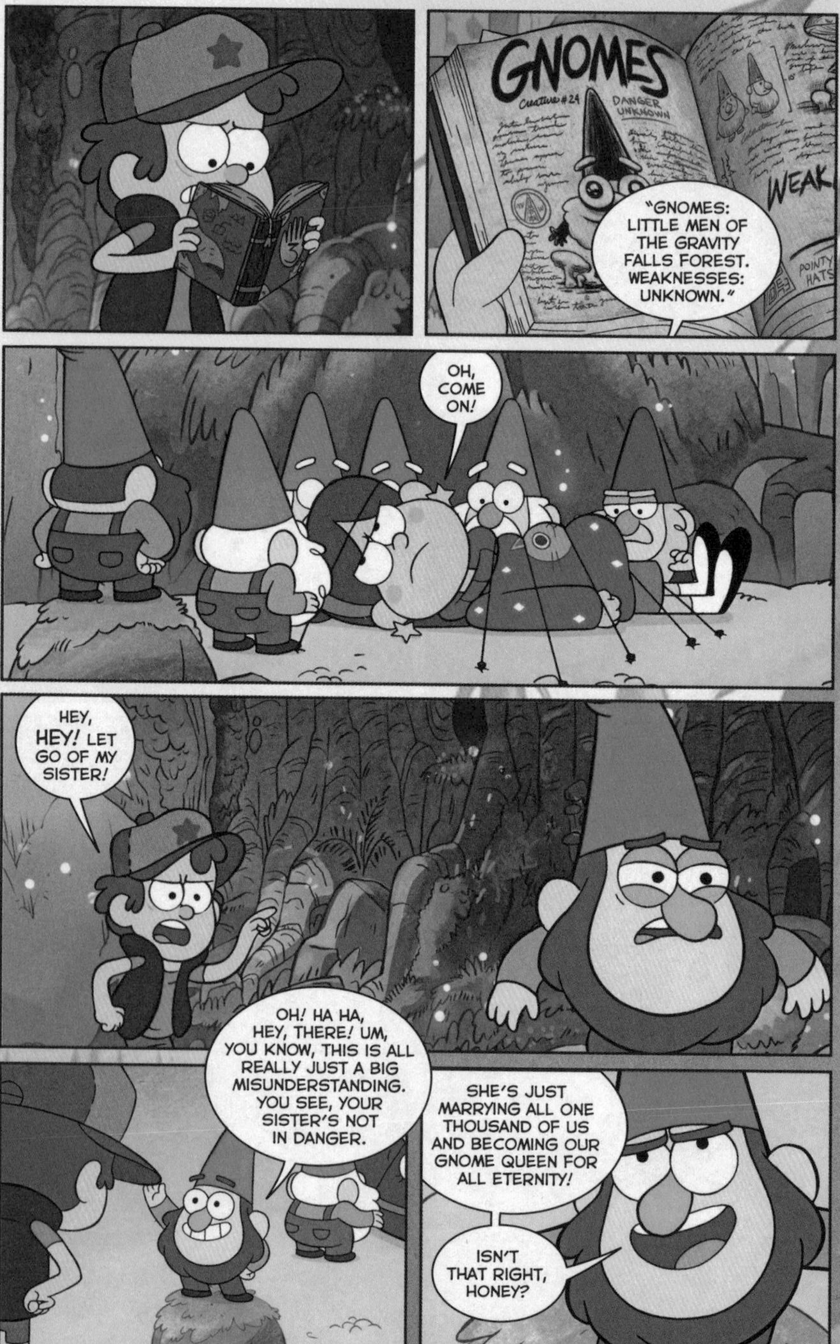
GNOMES
Creature #24
DANGER UNKNOWN
WEAK
POINTY HATS
"GNOMES: LITTLE MEN OF THE GRAVITY FALLS FOREST. WEAKNESSES: UNKNOWN."
OH, COME ON!
HEY, HEY! LET GO OF MY SISTER!
OH! HA HA, HEY, THERE! UM, YOU KNOW, THIS IS ALL REALLY JUST A BIG MISUNDERSTANDING. YOU SEE, YOUR SISTER'S NOT IN DANGER.
SHE'S JUST MARRYING ALL ONE THOUSAND OF US AND BECOMING OUR GNOME QUEEN FOR ALL ETERNITY!
ISN'T THAT RIGHT, HONEY?

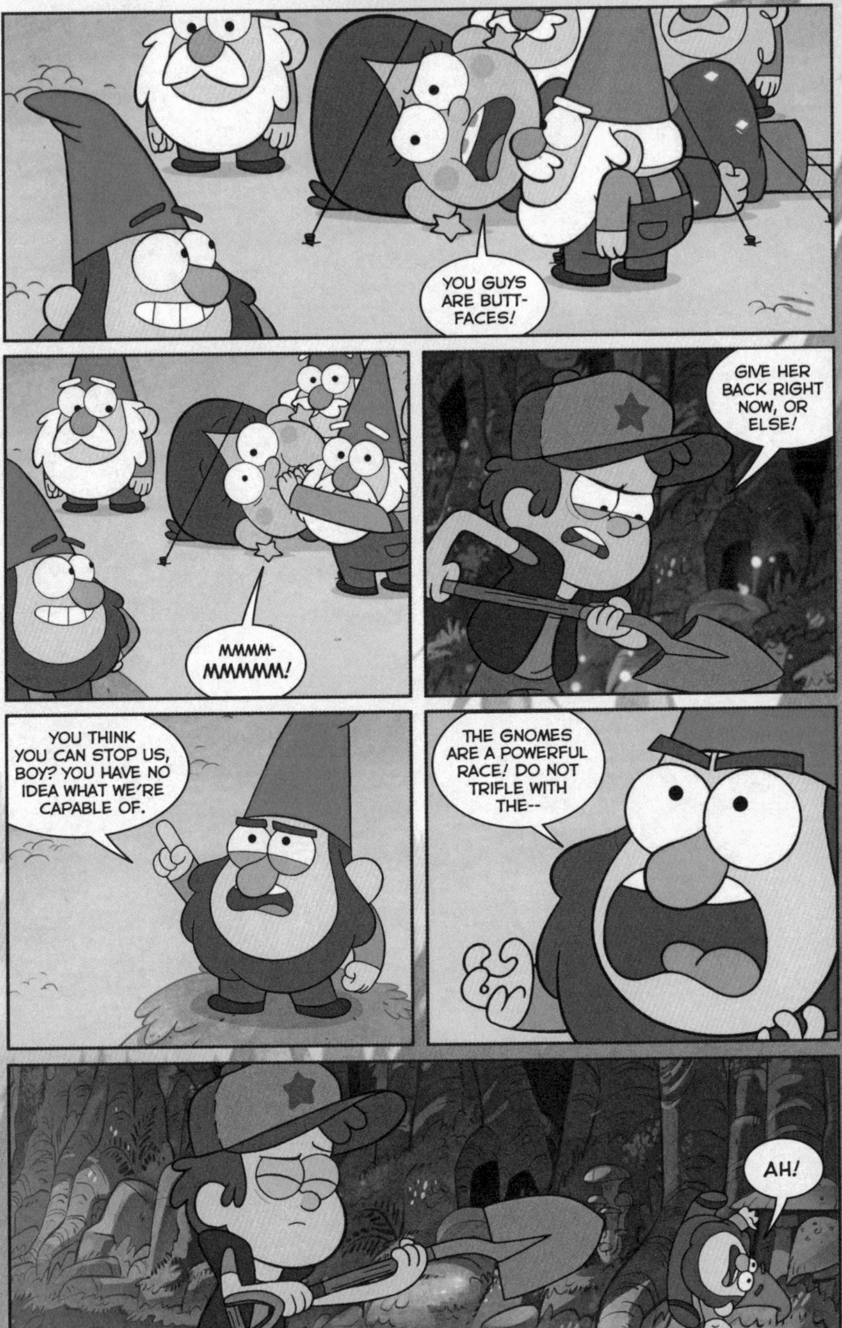
YOU GUYS ARE BUTT-FACES!
MMMM-MMMMM!
GIVE HER BACK RIGHT NOW, OR ELSE!
YOU THINK YOU CAN STOP US, BOY? YOU HAVE NO IDEA WHAT WE'RE CAPABLE OF.
THE GNOMES ARE A POWERFUL RACE! DO NOT TRIFLE WITH THE--
AH!

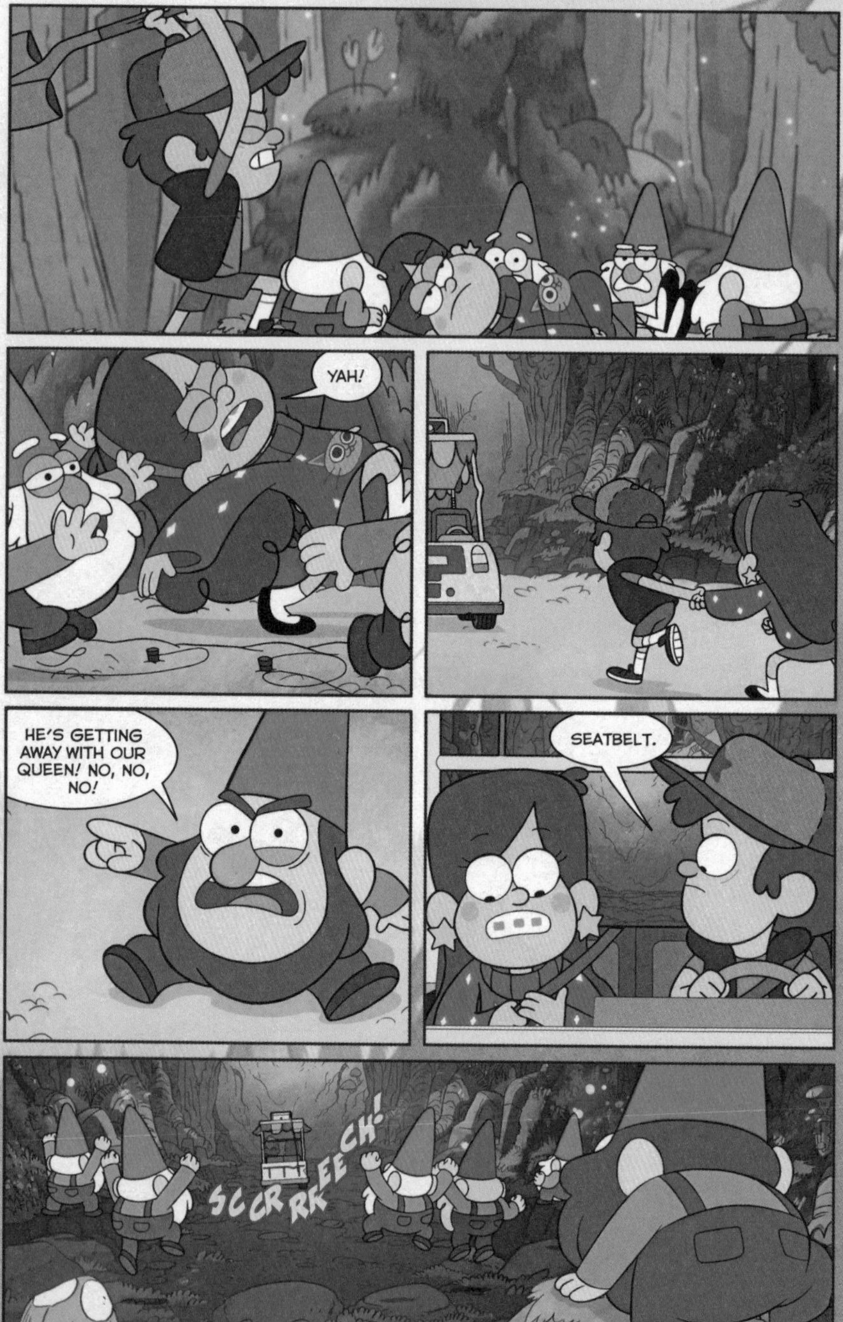

YAH!
HE'S GETTING AWAY WITH OUR QUEEN! NO, NO, NO!
SEATBELT.
SCCRRKEECH!

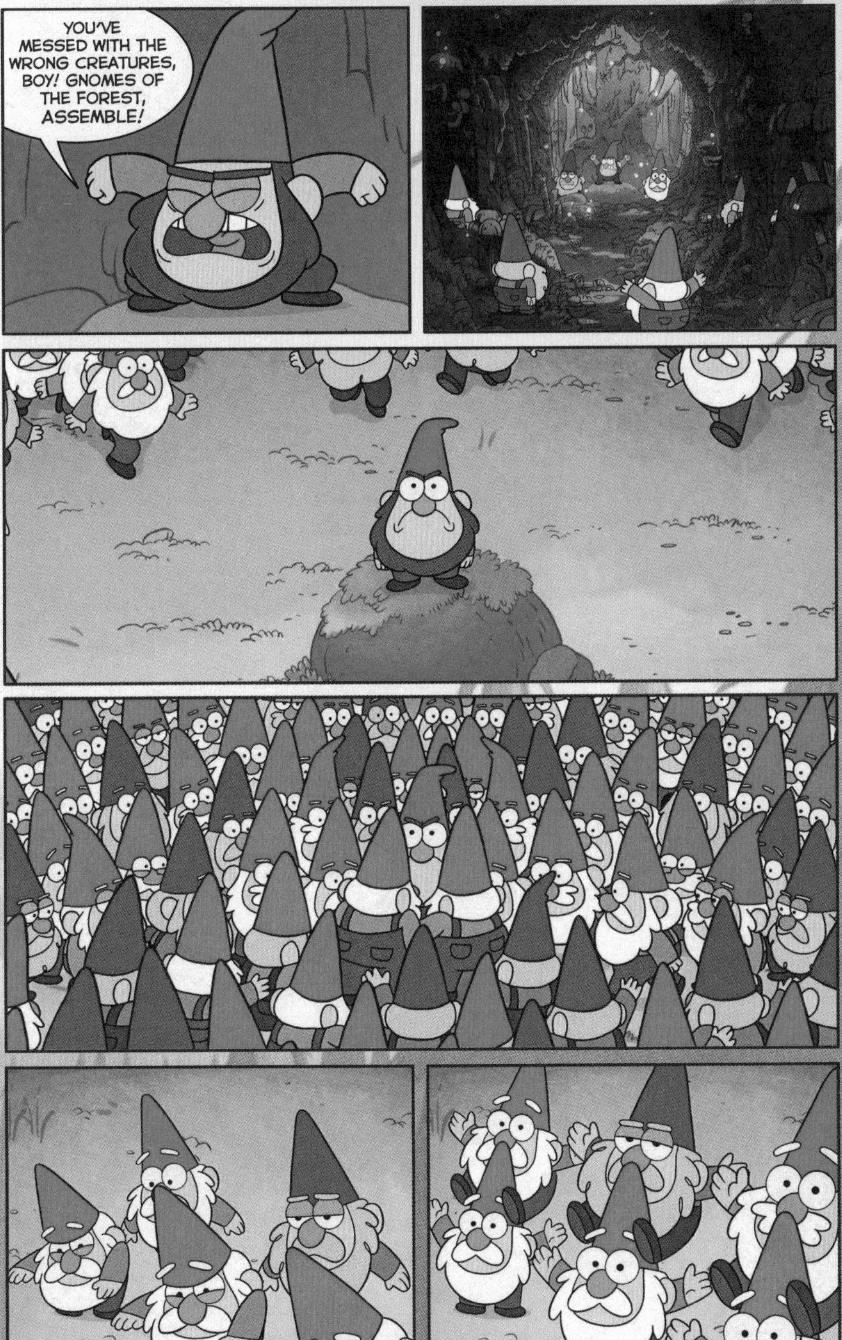
YOU'VE MESSED WITH THE WRONG CREATURES, BOY! GNOMES OF THE FOREST, ASSEMBLE!

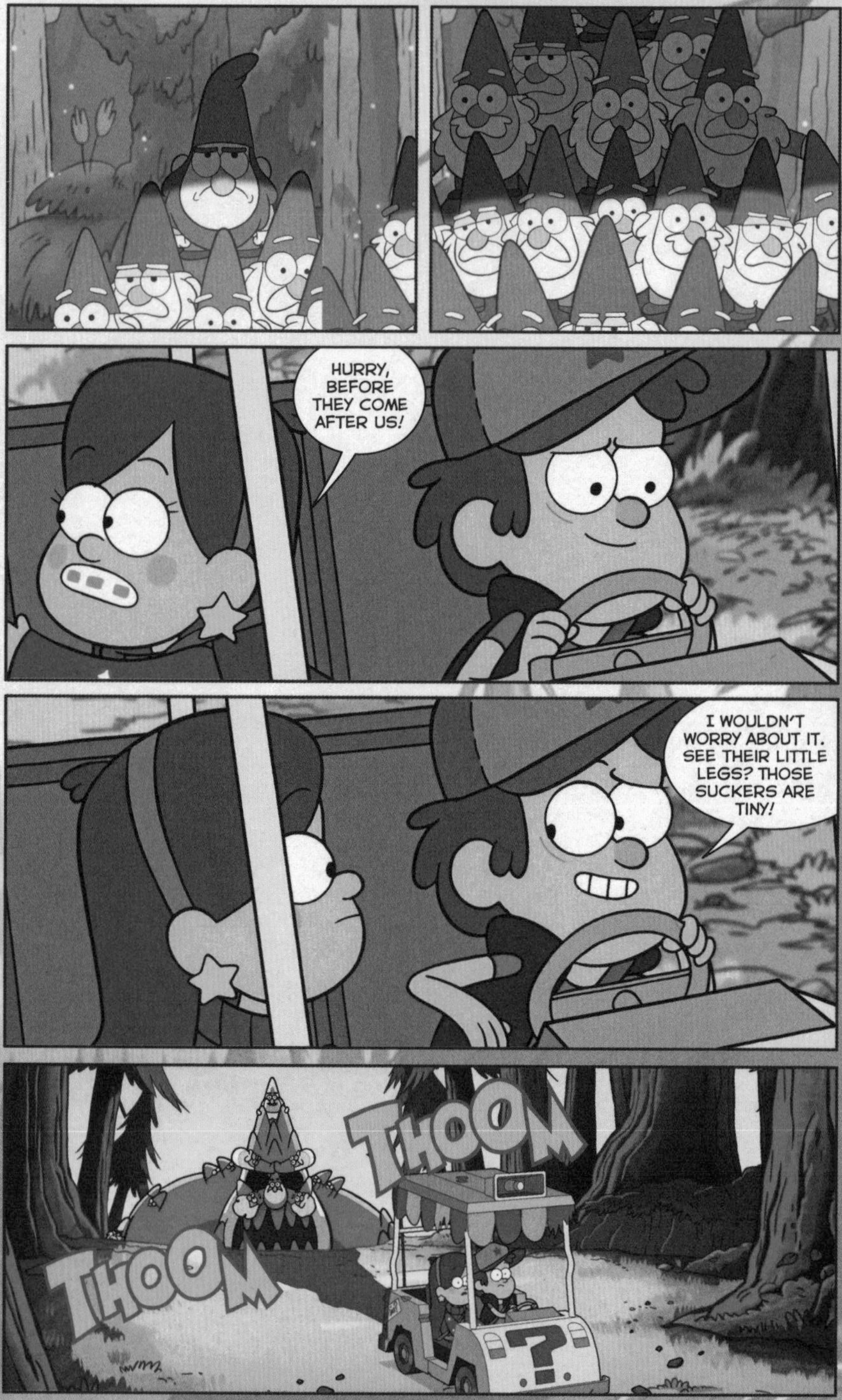
HURRY, BEFORE THEY COME AFTER US!
I WOULDN'T WORRY ABOUT IT. SEE THEIR LITTLE LEGS? THOSE SUCKERS ARE TINY!
THOOM
THOOM

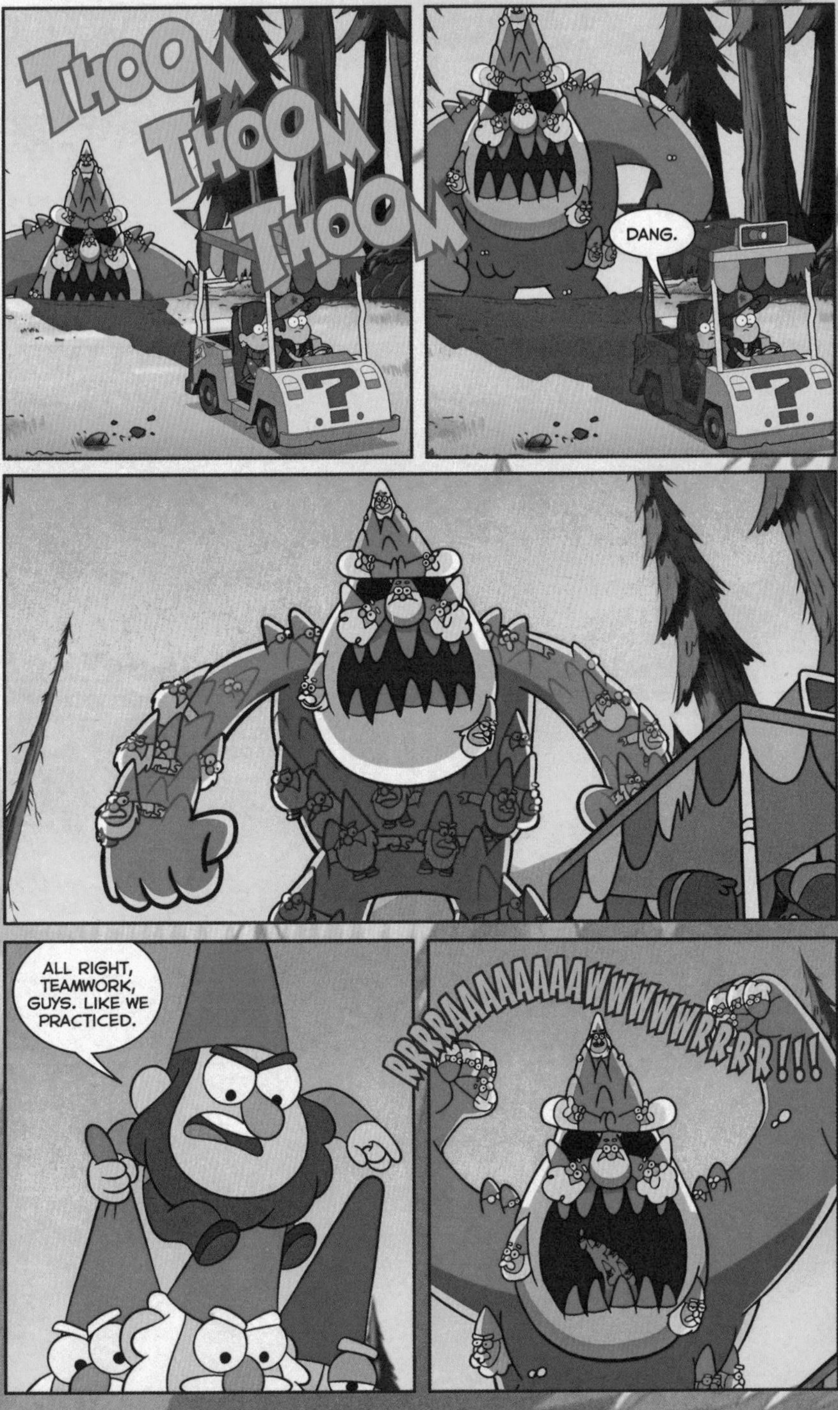
THOOM
THOOM
THOOM
DANG.
ALL RIGHT, TEAMWORK, GUYS. LIKE WE PRACTICED.
RRRRAAAAAAAAWWWWWWRRRR!!!

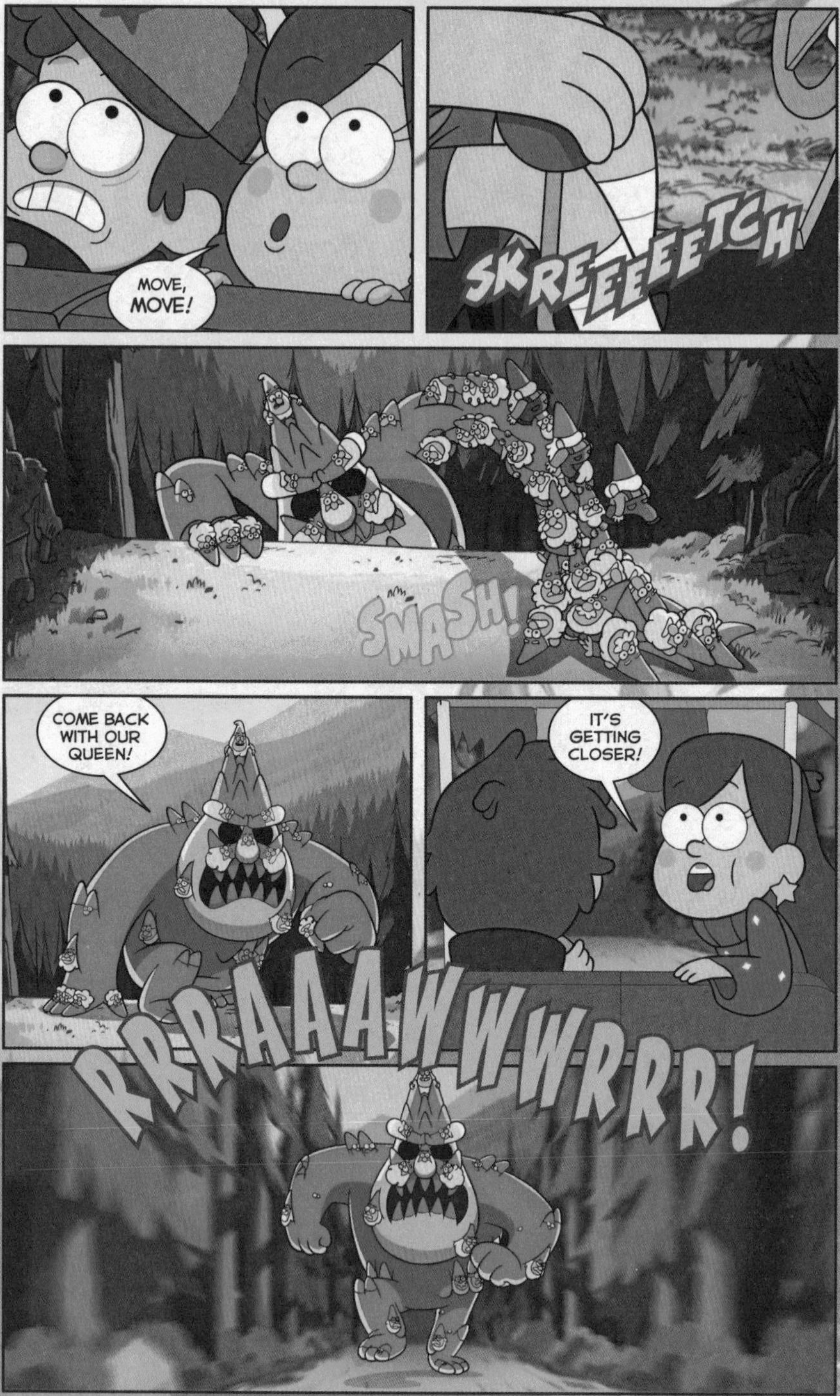
MOVE, MOVE!
SKREEEEEETCH
SMASH!
COME BACK WITH OUR QUEEN!
IT'S GETTING CLOSER!
RRRAAAWWWRRR!

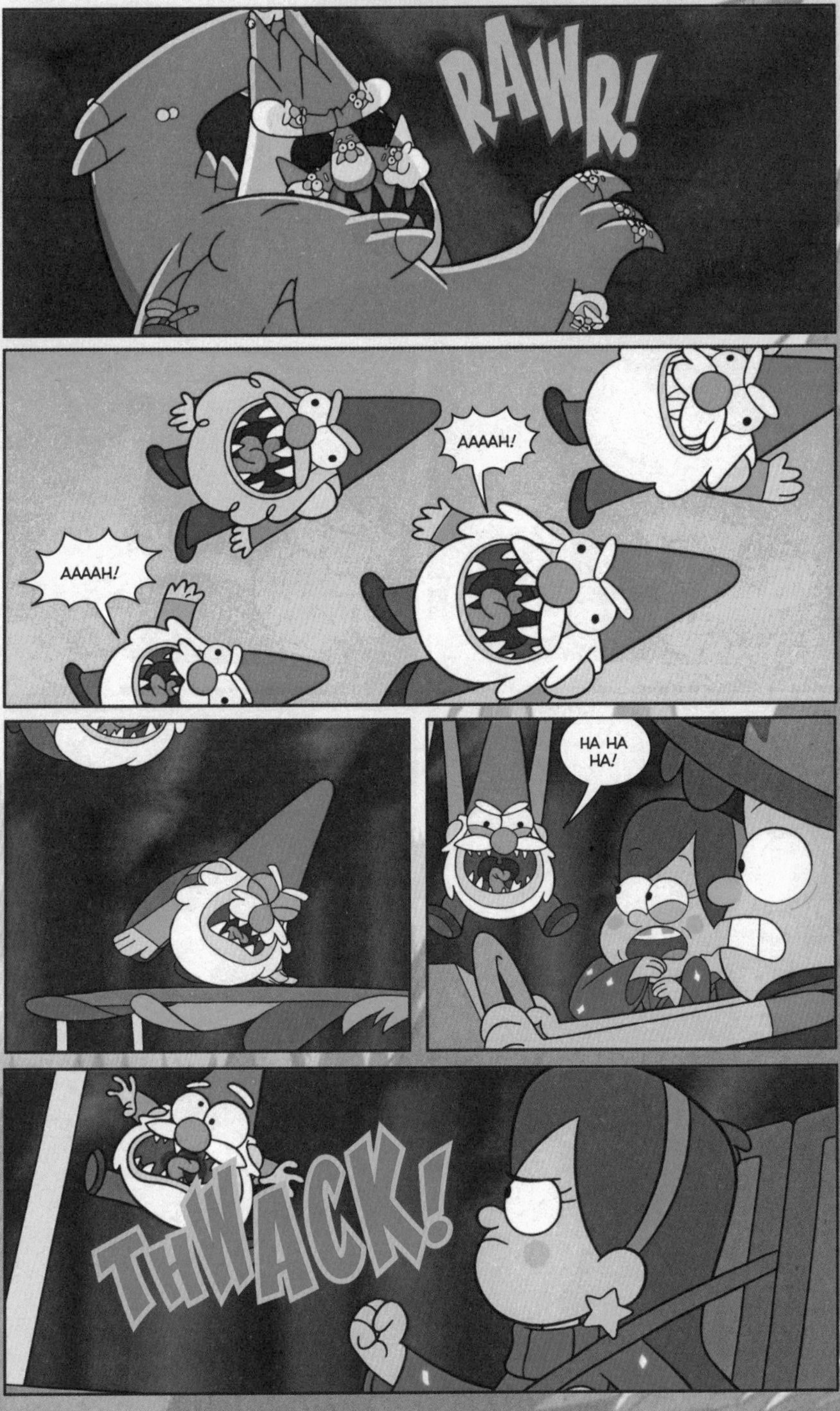
RAWR!
AAAAH!
AAAAH!
HA HA
HA!
THWACK!

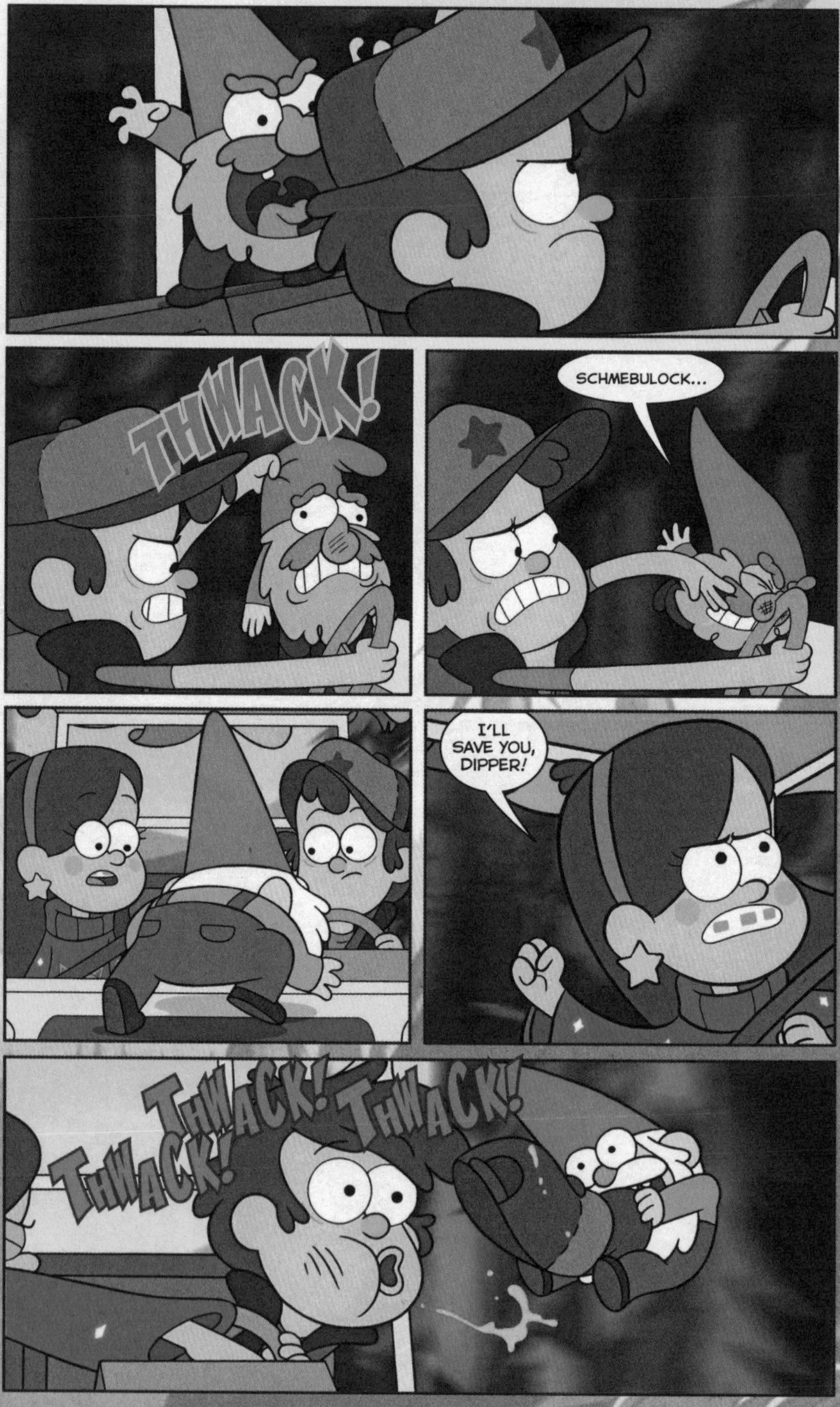
THWACK!
SCHMEBULOCK...
I'LL SAVE YOU, DIPPER!
THWACK!
THWACK!
THWACK!

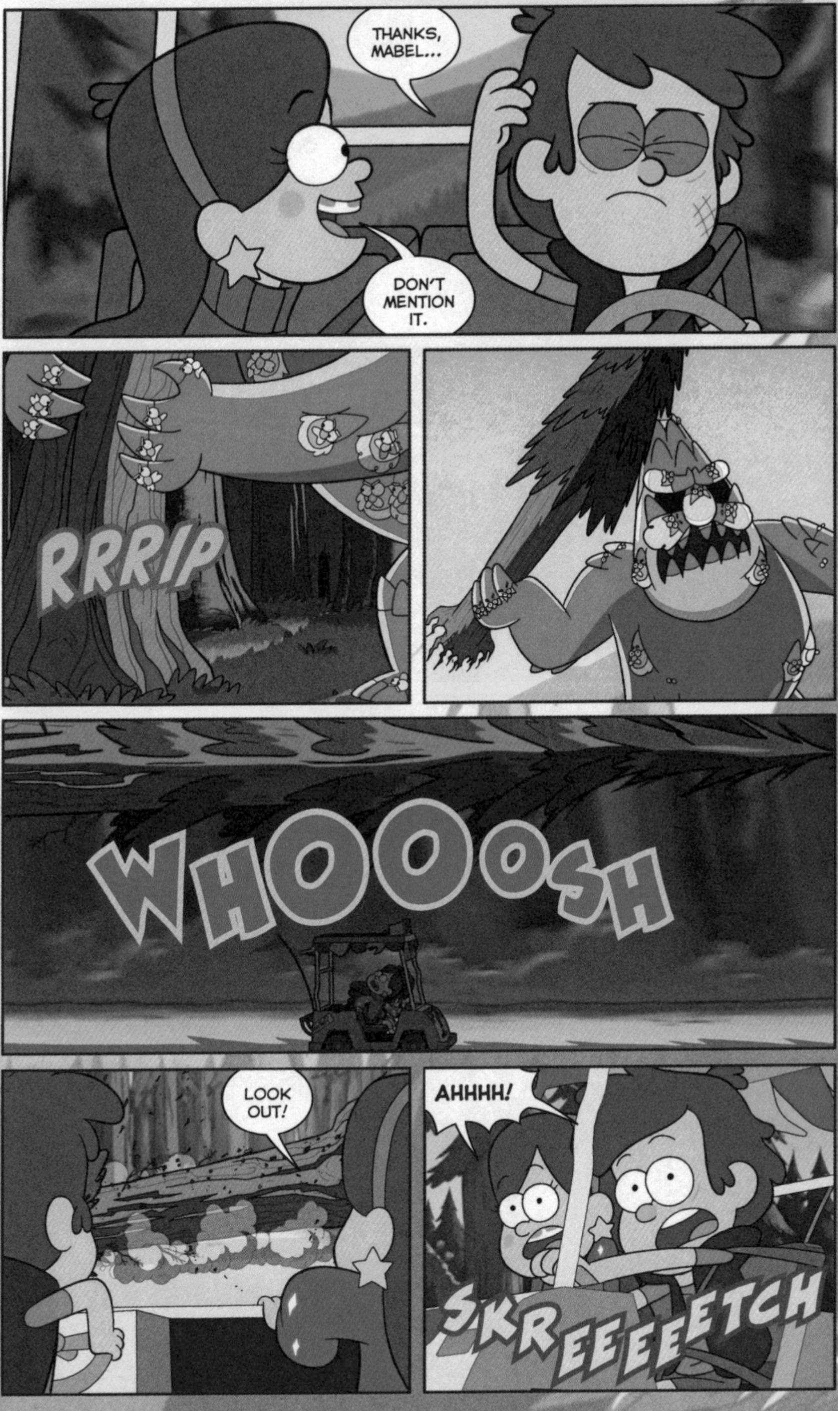
THANKS, MABEL...
DON'T MENTION IT.
RRRIP
WHOOOSH
LOOK OUT!
AHHHH!
SKREEEEEETCH

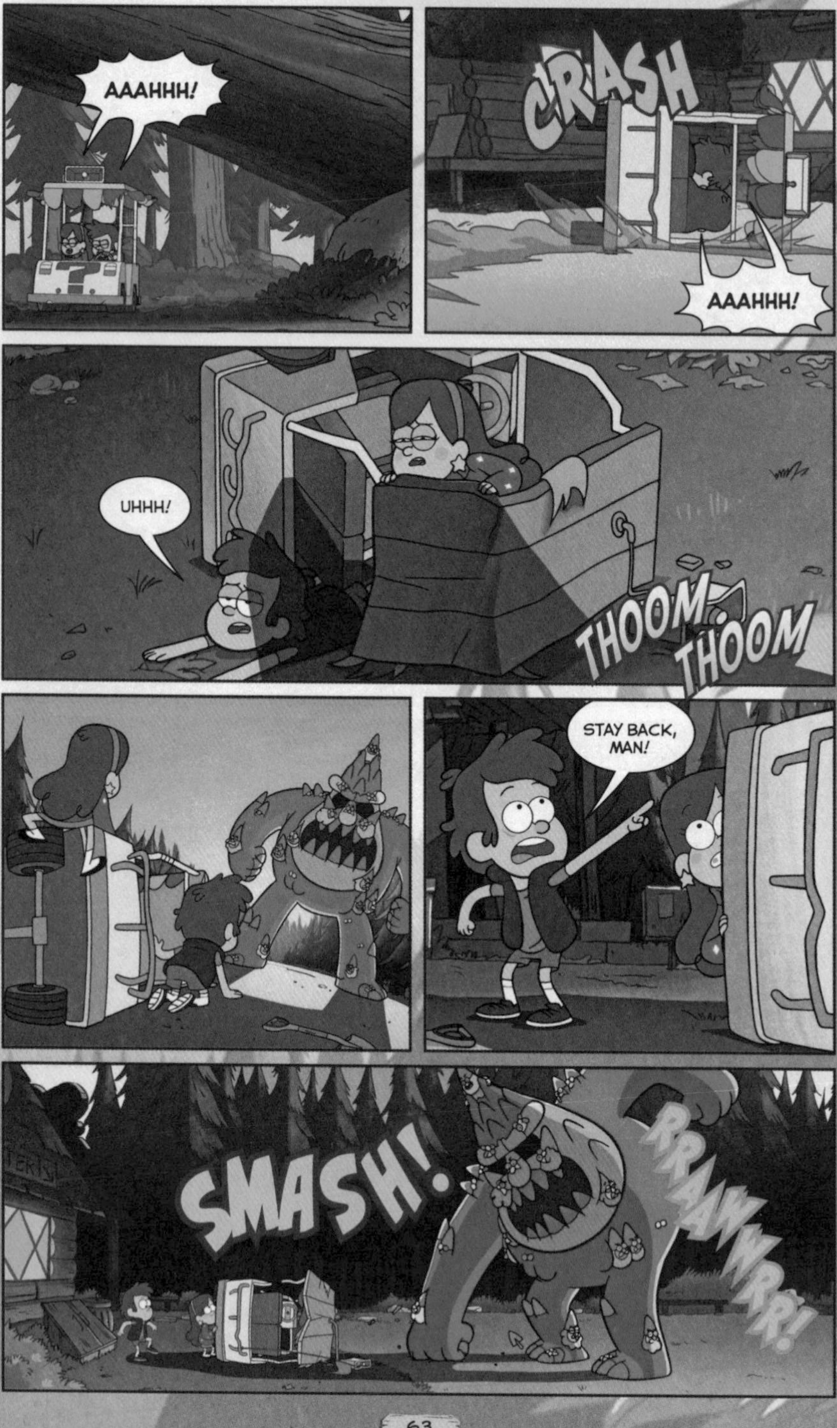
AAAHHH!
CRASH
AAAHHH!
UHHH!
THOOM THOOM
STAY BACK, MAN!
SMASH!
RRAAWWRRR!

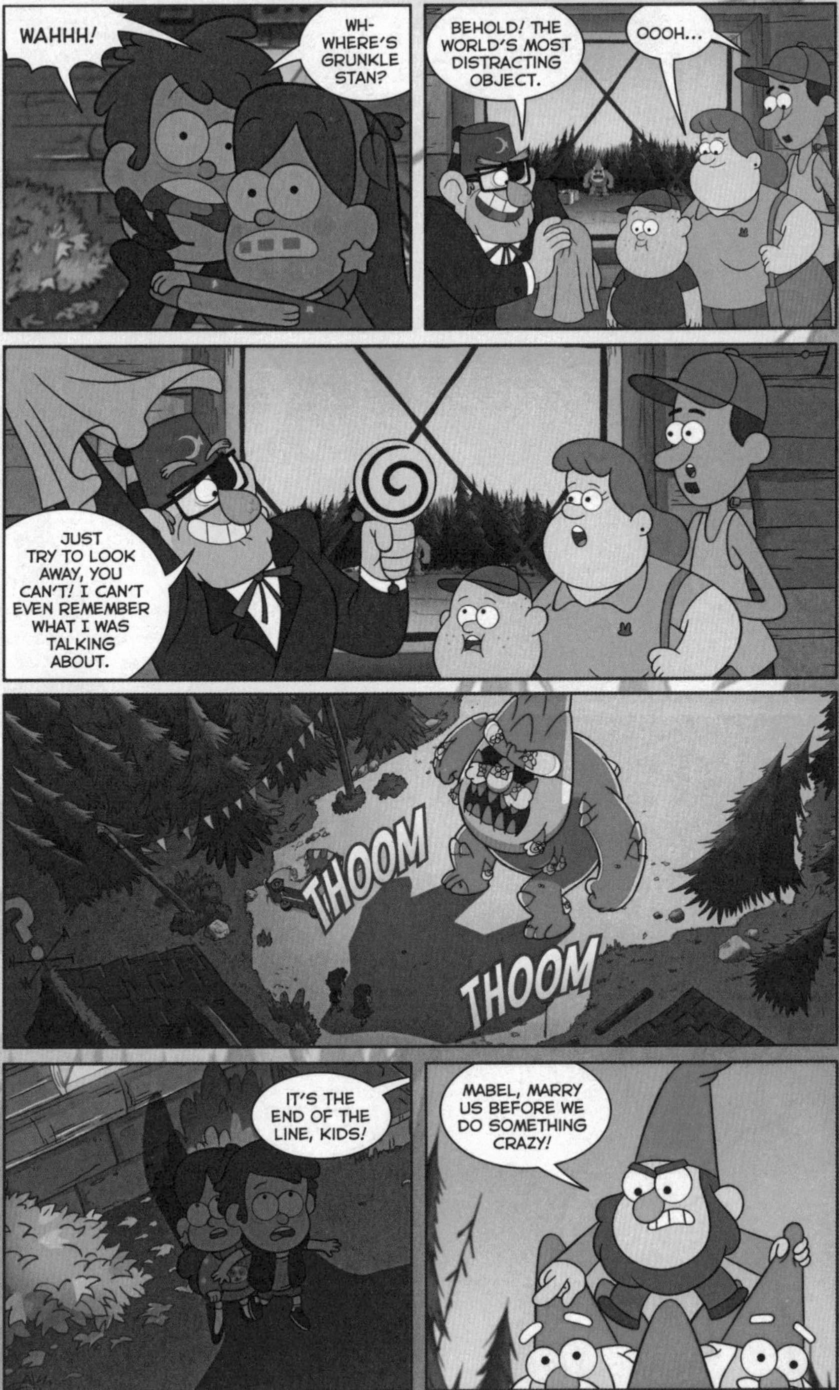
WAHHH!
WH- WHERE'S GRUNKLE STAN?
BEHOLD! THE WORLD'S MOST DISTRACTING OBJECT.
OOOH...
JUST TRY TO LOOK AWAY, YOU CAN'T! I CAN'T EVEN REMEMBER WHAT I WAS TALKING ABOUT.
THOOM
THOOM
IT'S THE END OF THE LINE, KIDS!
MABEL, MARRY US BEFORE WE DO SOMETHING CRAZY!

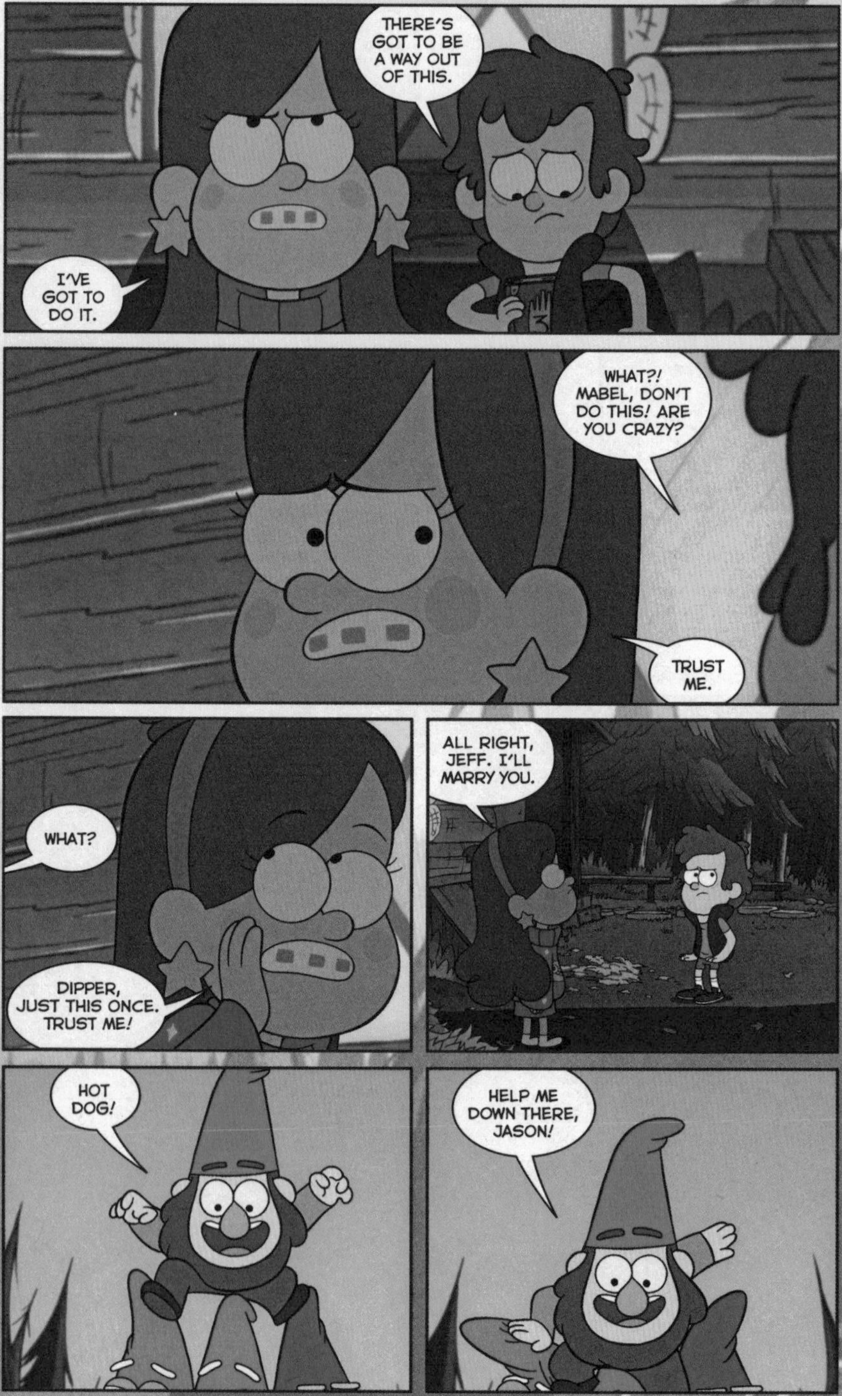
THERE'S GOT TO BE A WAY OUT OF THIS.
I'VE GOT TO DO IT.
WHAT?! MABEL, DON'T DO THIS! ARE YOU CRAZY?
TRUST ME.
WHAT?
DIPPER, JUST THIS ONCE. TRUST ME!
ALL RIGHT, JEFF. I'LL MARRY YOU.
HOT DOG!
HELP ME DOWN THERE, JASON!

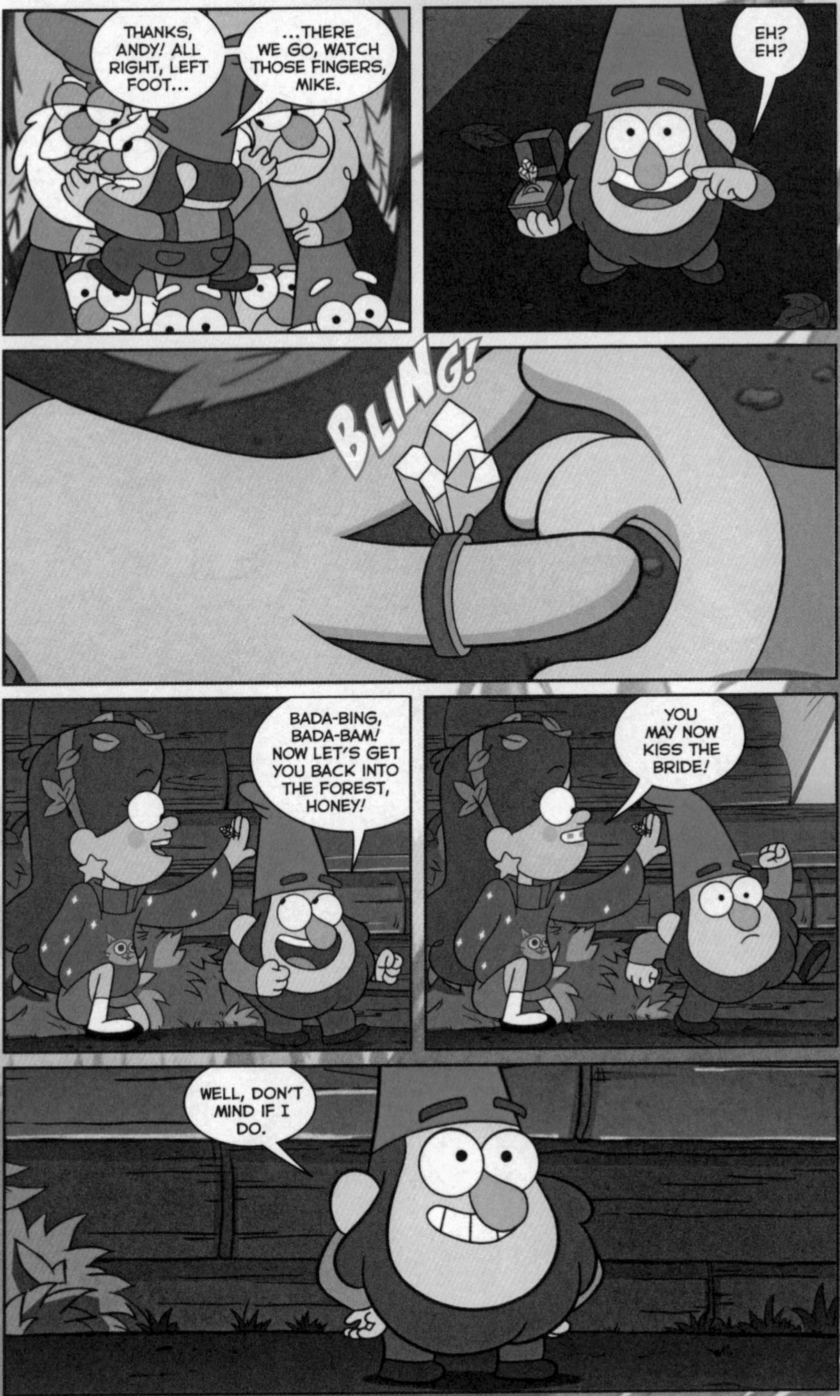
THANKS, ANDY! ALL RIGHT, LEFT FOOT...
...THERE WE GO, WATCH THOSE FINGERS, MIKE.
EH? EH?
BLING!
BADA-BING, BADA-BAM! NOW LET'S GET YOU BACK INTO THE FOREST, HONEY!
YOU MAY NOW KISS THE BRIDE!
WELL, DON'T MIND IF I DO.

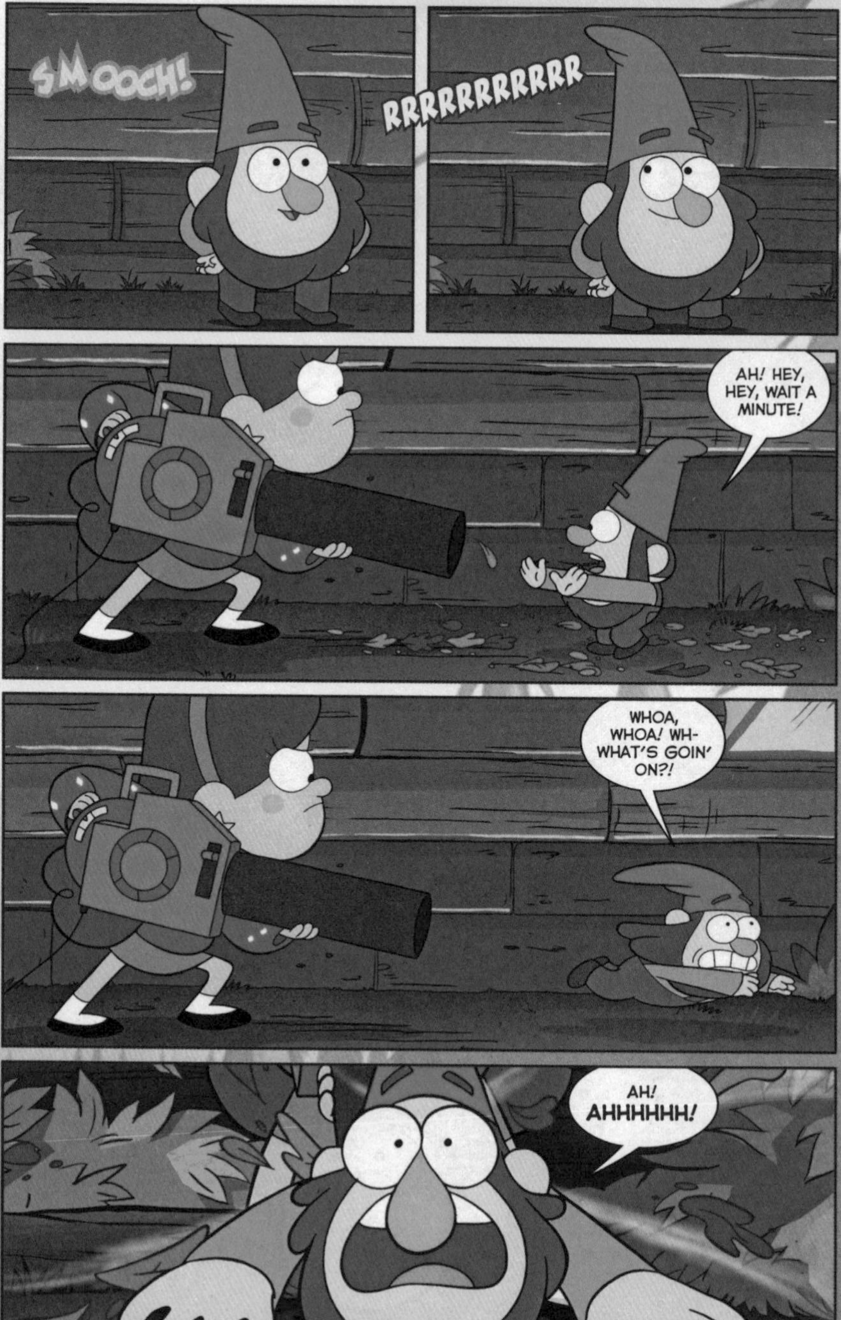
SMOOCH!
RRRRRRRRRRR
AH! HEY, HEY, WAIT A MINUTE!
WHOA, WHOA! WH-WHAT'S GOIN' ON?!
AH! AHHHHHH!

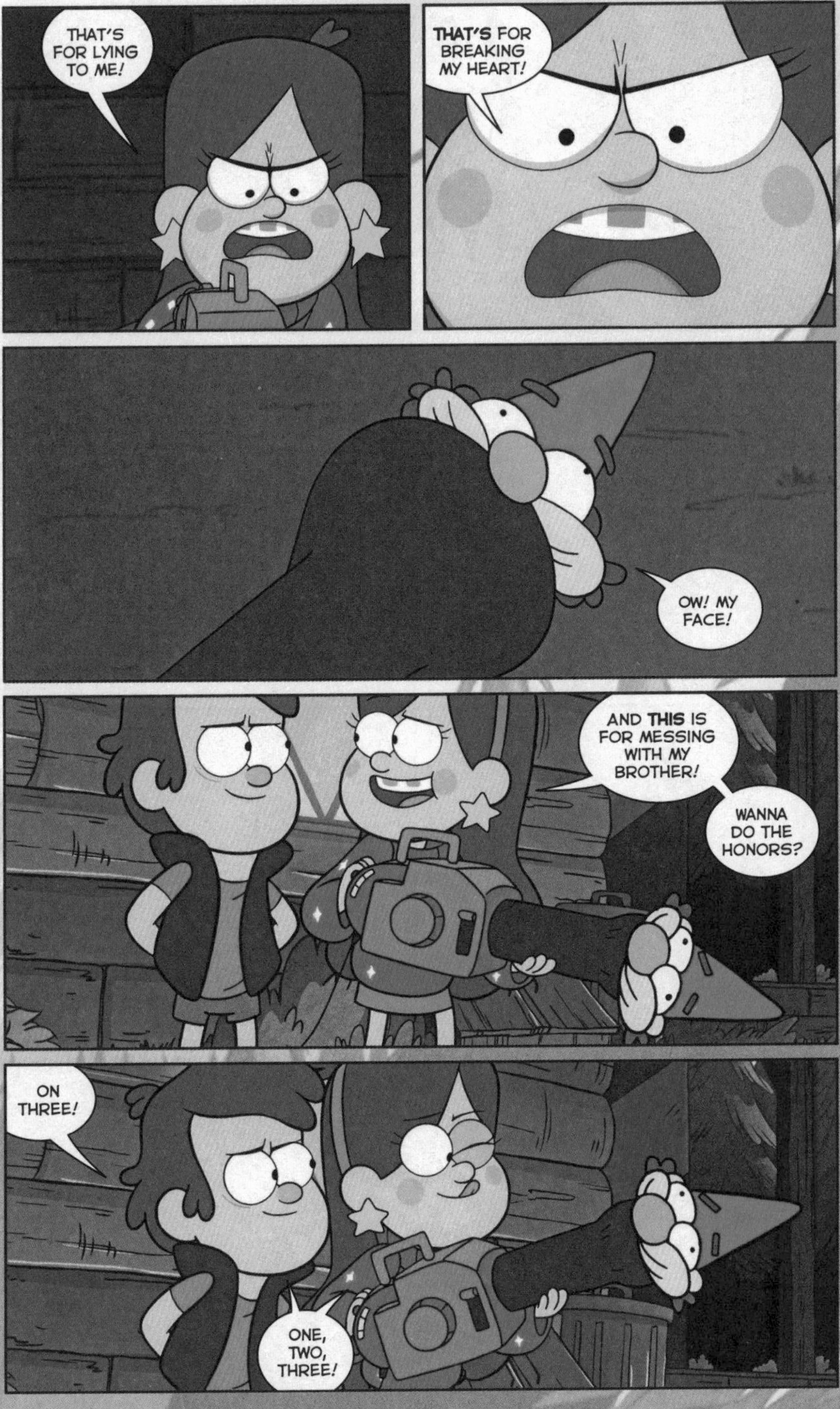
THAT'S FOR LYING TO ME!
THAT'S FOR BREAKING MY HEART!
OW! MY FACE!
AND THIS IS FOR MESSING WITH MY BROTHER!
WANNA DO THE HONORS?
ON THREE!
ONE, TWO, THREE!

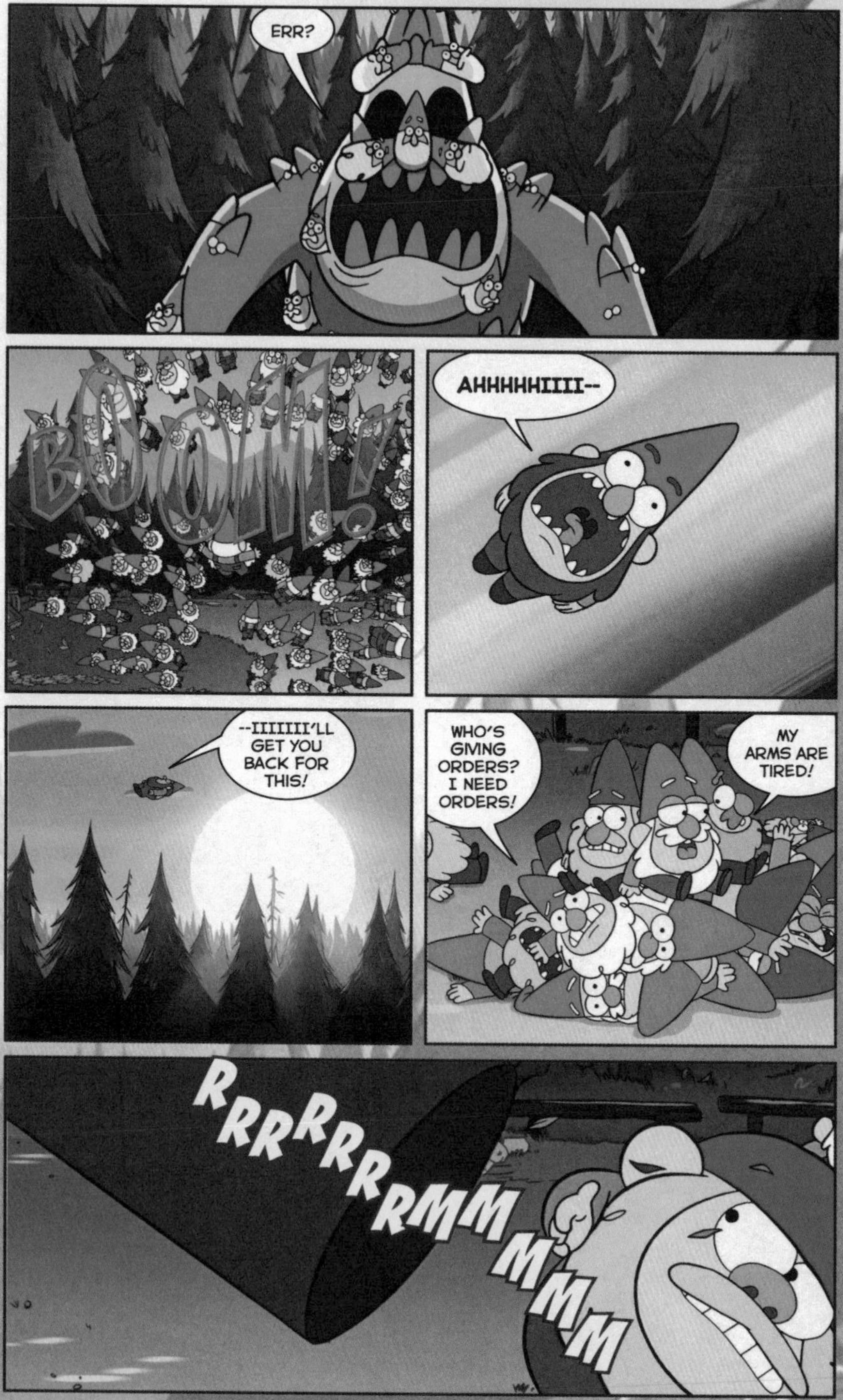
ERR?
BOOM!
AHHHHHIIII--
--IIIIIII'LL GET YOU BACK FOR THIS!
WHO'S GIVING ORDERS? I NEED ORDERS!
MY ARMS ARE TIRED!
RRRRRRRRMMMMMM

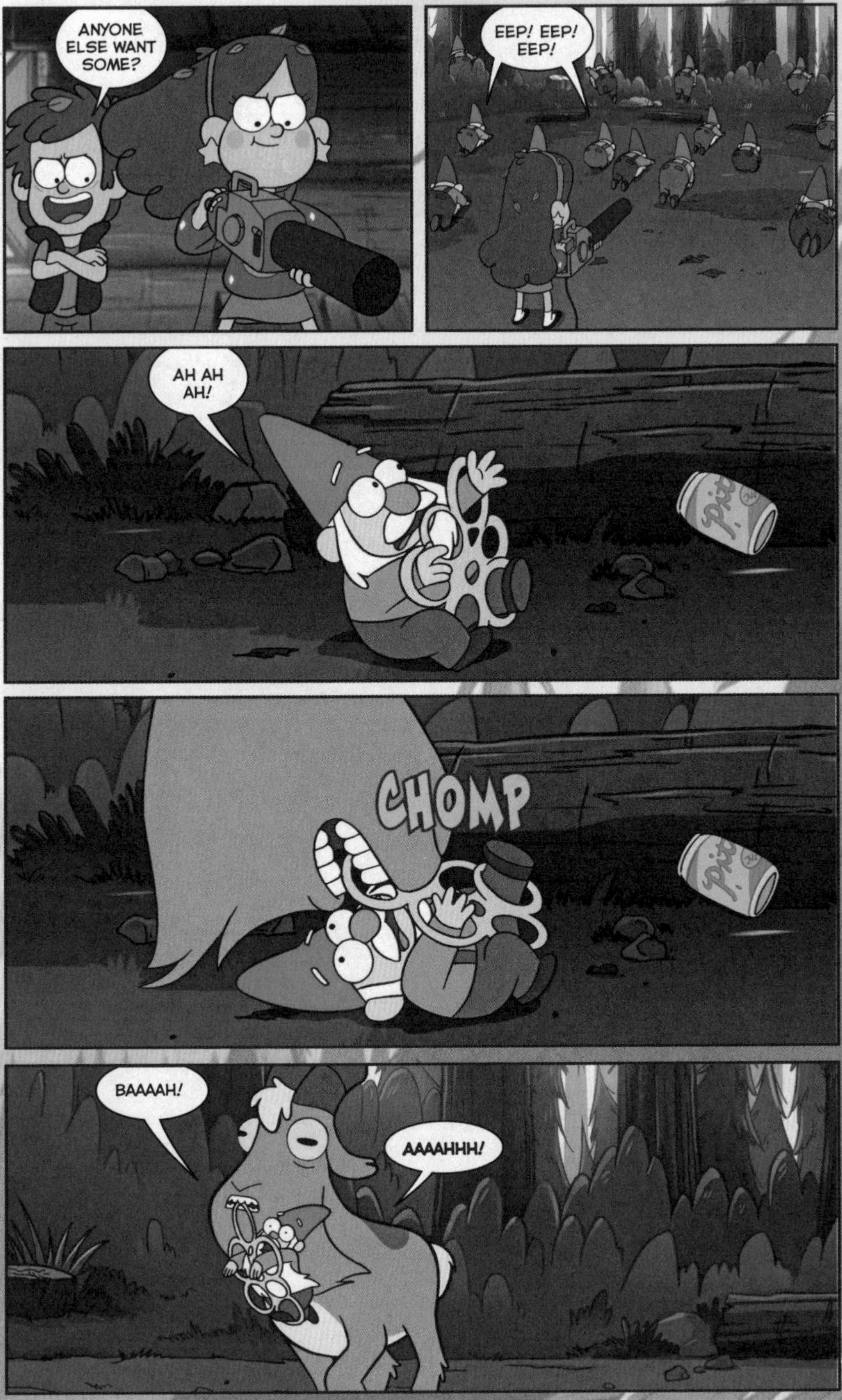
ANYONE ELSE WANT SOME?
EEP! EEP! EEP!
AH AH AH!
CHOMP
BAAAAH!
AAAAHHH!

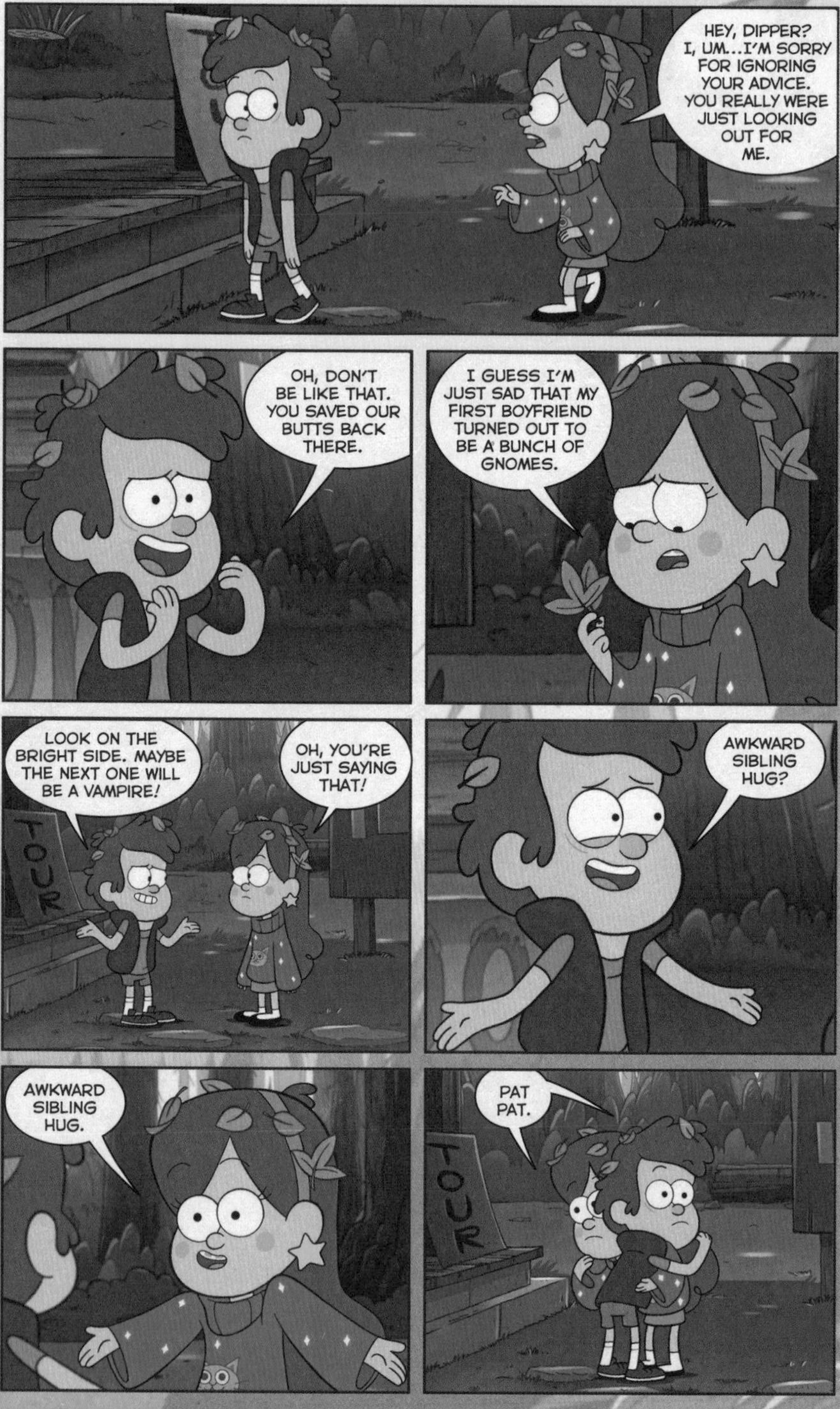
HEY, DIPPER? I, UM...I'M SORRY FOR IGNORING YOUR ADVICE. YOU REALLY WERE JUST LOOKING OUT FOR ME.
OH, DON'T BE LIKE THAT. YOU SAVED OUR BUTTS BACK THERE.
I GUESS I'M JUST SAD THAT MY FIRST BOYFRIEND TURNED OUT TO BE A BUNCH OF GNOMES.
LOOK ON THE BRIGHT SIDE. MAYBE THE NEXT ONE WILL BE A VAMPIRE!
OH, YOU'RE JUST SAYING THAT!
TOUR
AWKWARD SIBLING HUG?
AWKWARD SIBLING HUG.
PAT PAT.
TOUR

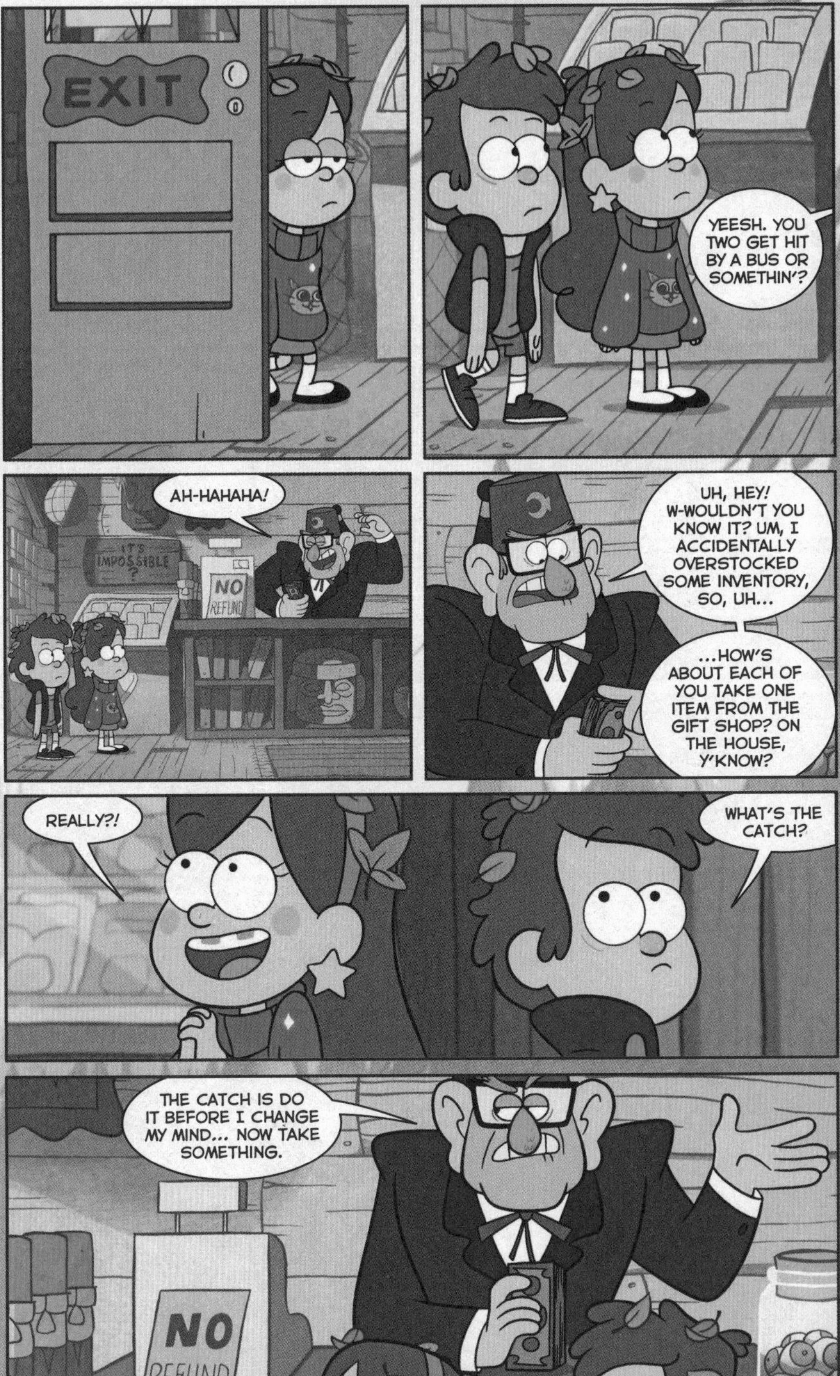
EXIT
YEESH. YOU TWO GET HIT BY A BUS OR SOMETHIN'?
AH-HAHAHA!
IT'S IMPOSSIBLE ?
NO REFUND
UH, HEY! W-WOULDN'T YOU KNOW IT? UM, I ACCIDENTALLY OVERSTOCKED SOME INVENTORY, SO, UH...
...HOW'S ABOUT EACH OF YOU TAKE ONE ITEM FROM THE GIFT SHOP? ON THE HOUSE, Y'KNOW?
REALLY?!
WHAT'S THE CATCH?
THE CATCH IS DO IT BEFORE I CHANGE MY MIND... NOW TAKE SOMETHING.
NO REFUND

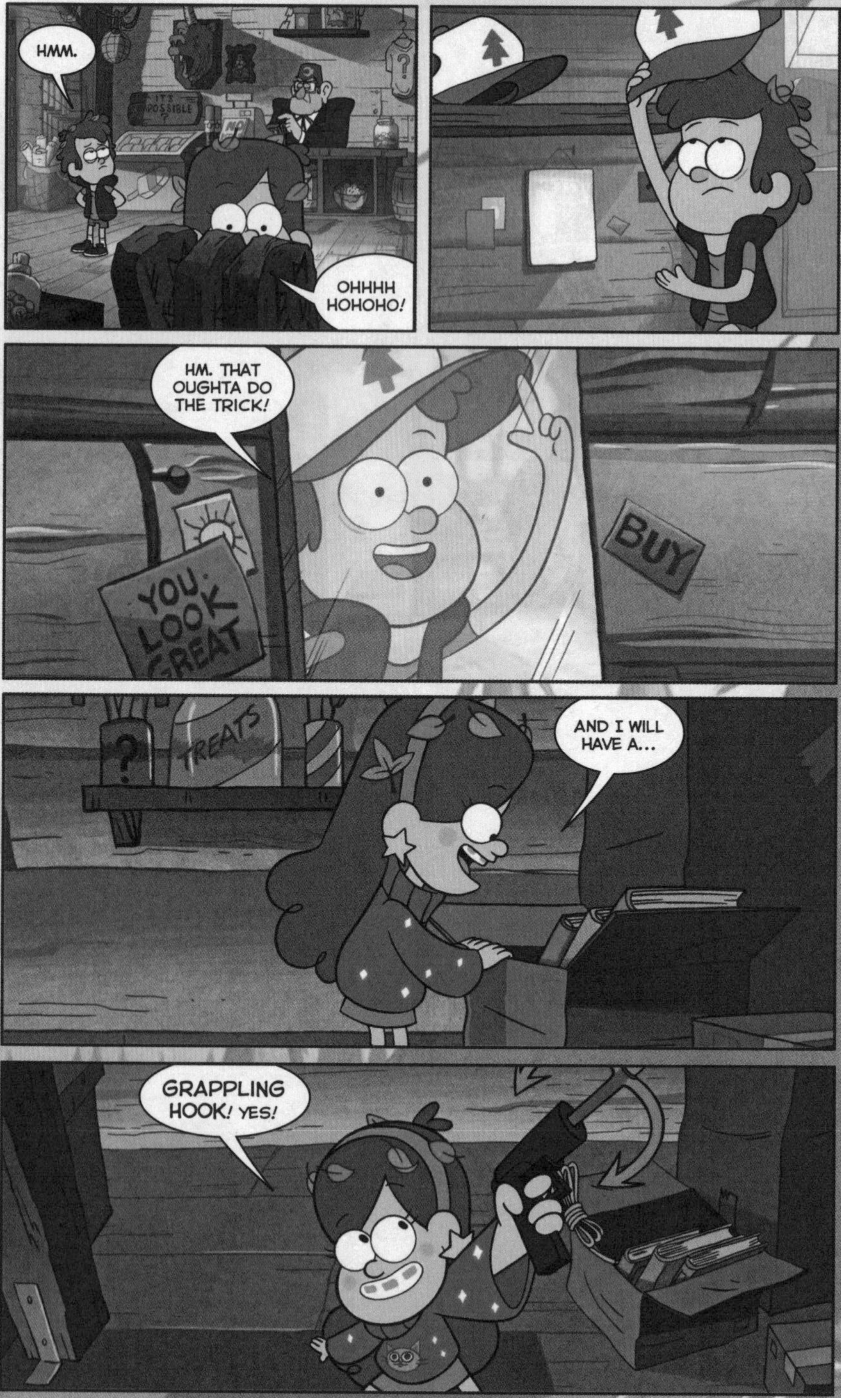
HMM.
OHHHH HOHOHO!
HM. THAT OUGHTA DO THE TRICK!
YOU LOOK GREAT
BUY
TREATS
AND I WILL HAVE A...
GRAPPLING HOOK! YES!

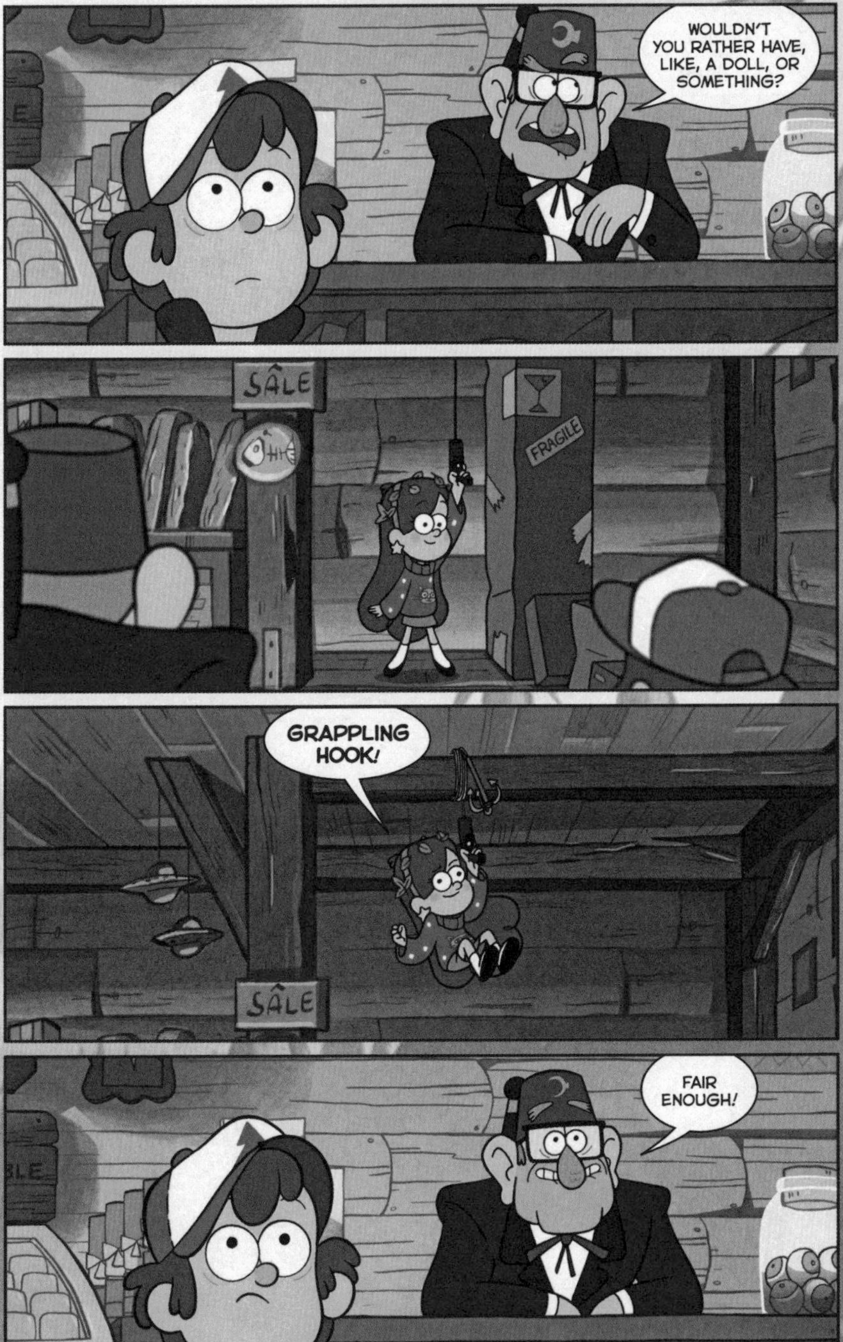
WOULDN'T YOU RATHER HAVE, LIKE, A DOLL, OR SOMETHING?
SÂLE
FRAGILE
GRAPPLING HOOK!
SÂLE
FAIR ENOUGH!

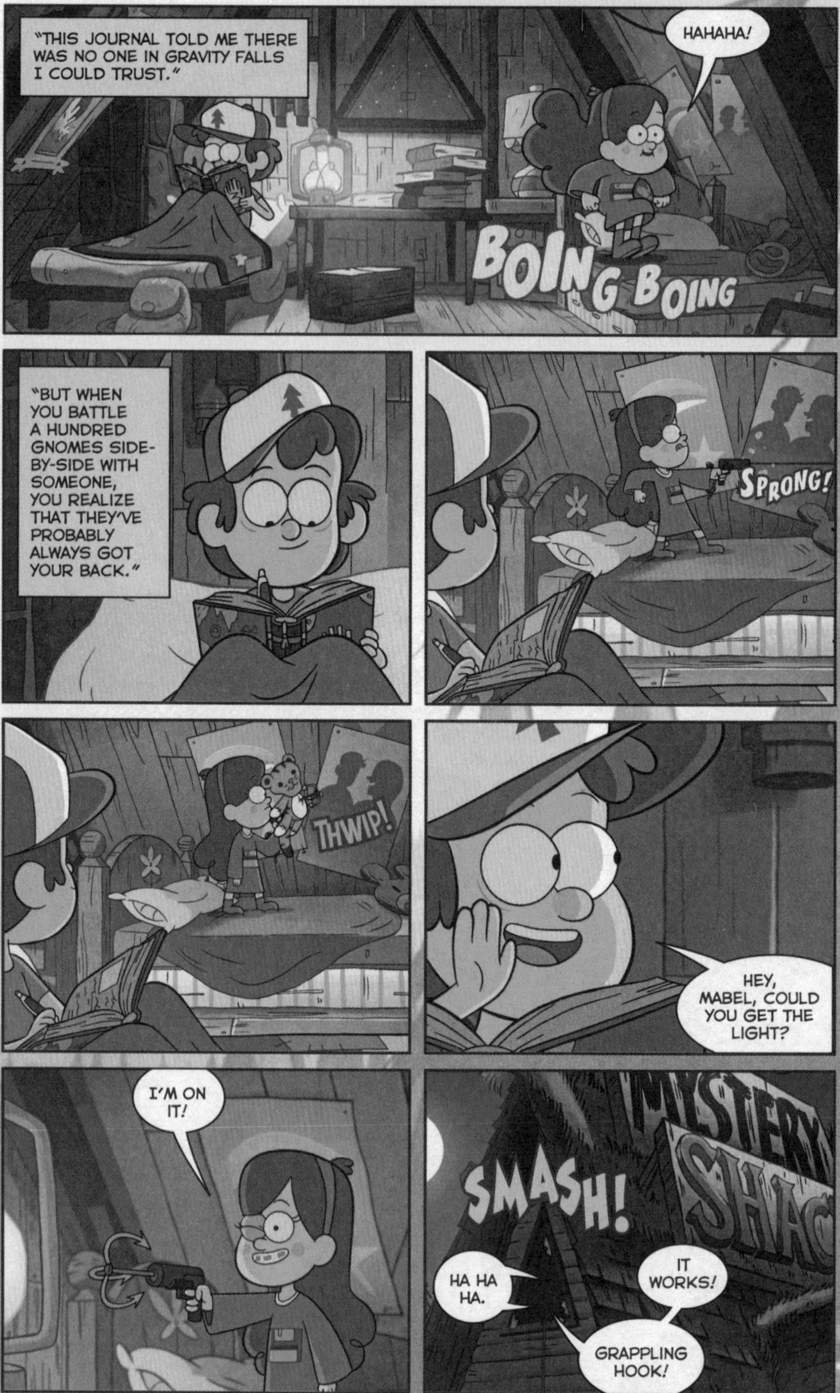
"THIS JOURNAL TOLD ME THERE WAS NO ONE IN GRAVITY FALLS I COULD TRUST."
HAHAHA!
BOING BOING
"BUT WHEN YOU BATTLE A HUNDRED GNOMES SIDE-BY-SIDE WITH SOMEONE, YOU REALIZE THAT THEY'VE PROBABLY ALWAYS GOT YOUR BACK."
SPRONG!
THWIP!
HEY, MABEL, COULD YOU GET THE LIGHT?
I'M ON IT!
MYSTERY SHAC
SMASH!
HA HA HA.
IT WORKS!
GRAPPLING HOOK!

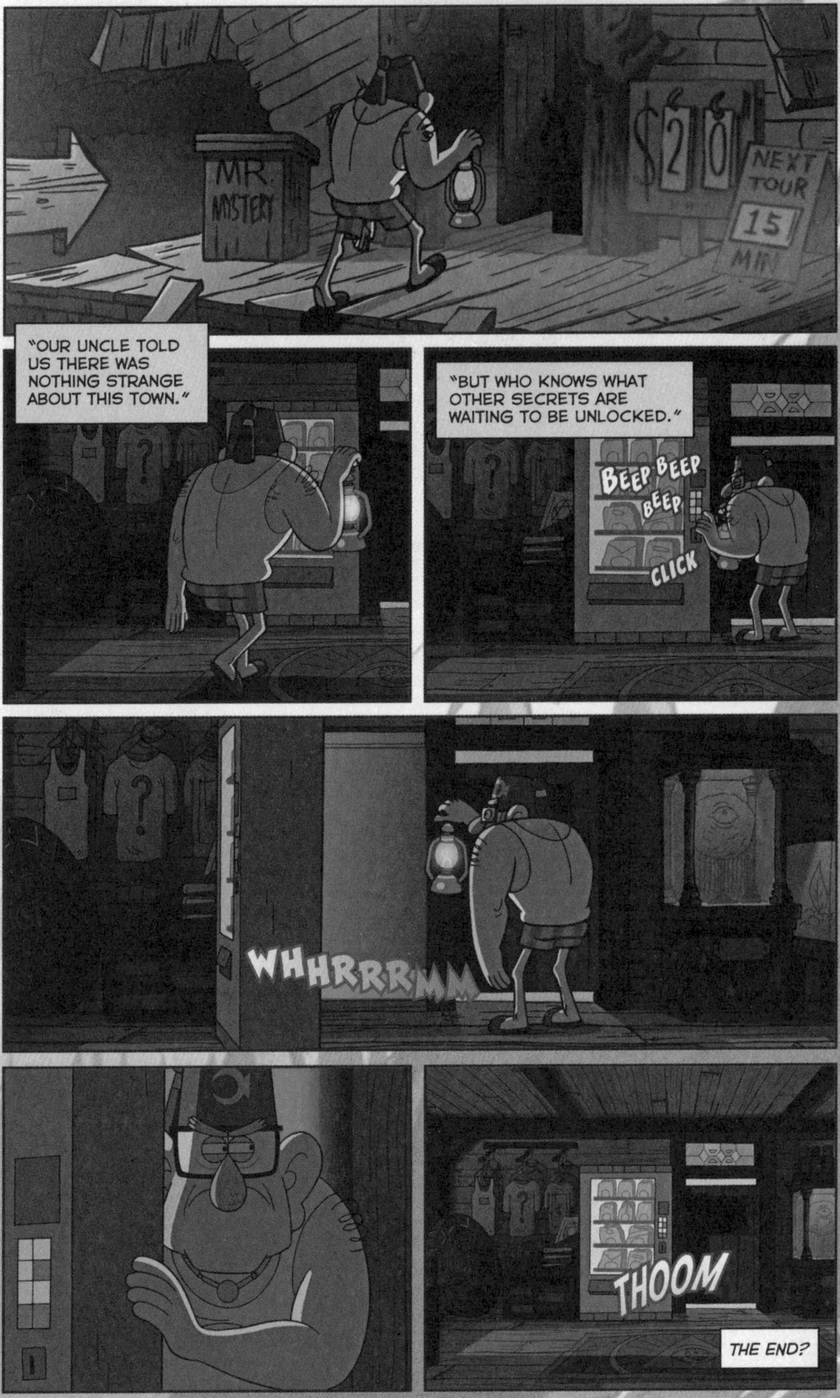
MR. MYSTERY
$20
NEXT TOUR 15 MIN
"OUR UNCLE TOLD US THERE WAS NOTHING STRANGE ABOUT THIS TOWN."
"BUT WHO KNOWS WHAT OTHER SECRETS ARE WAITING TO BE UNLOCKED."
BEEP BEEP BEEP
CLICK
WHHRRRRMM
THOOM
THE END?

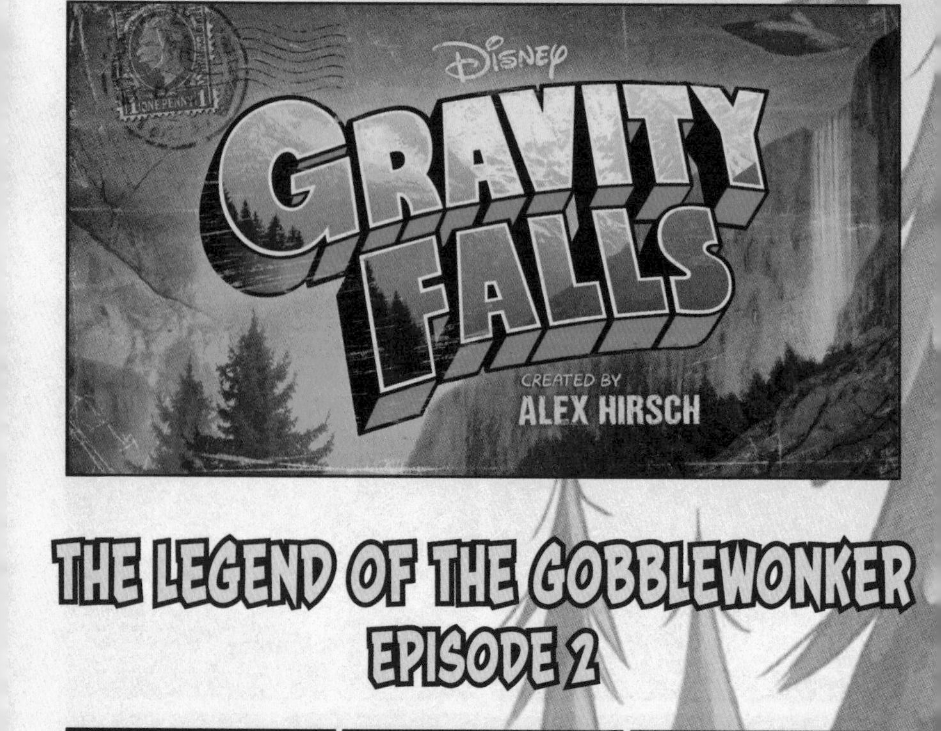
DISNEY
GRAVITY FALLS
CREATED BY
ALEX HIRSCH

THE LEGEND OF THE GOBBLEWONKER
EPISODE 2

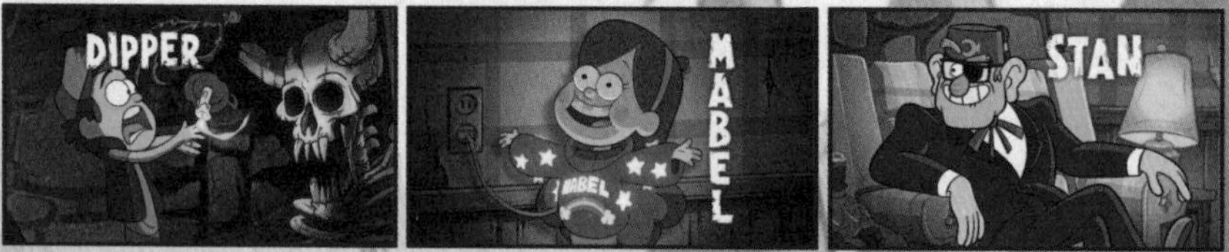
DIPPER
MABEL
STAN

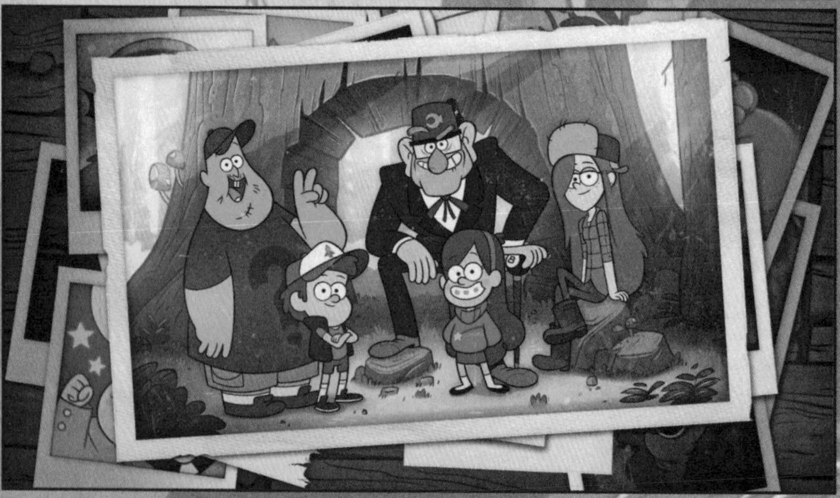

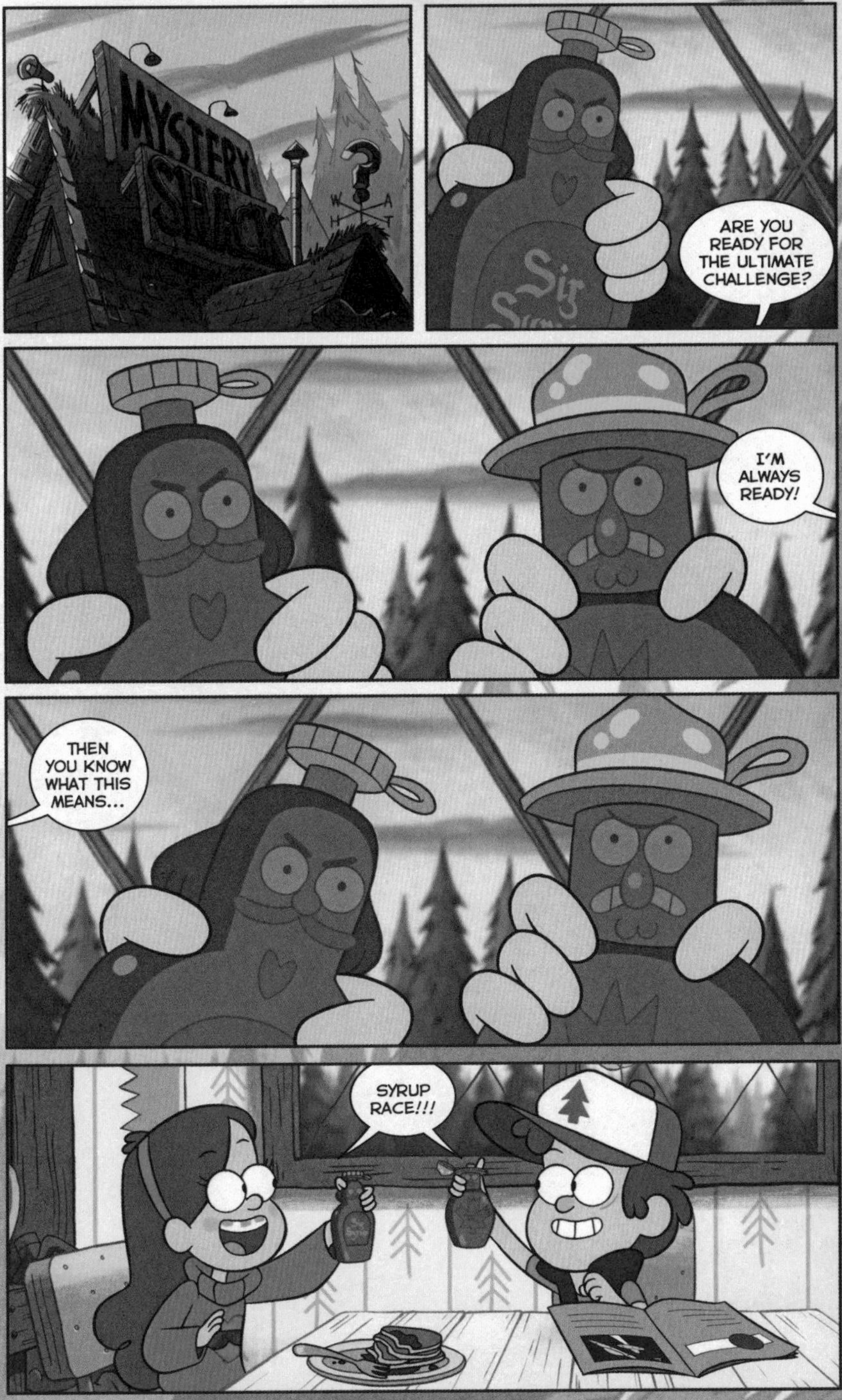
MYSTERY SHACK
ARE YOU READY FOR THE ULTIMATE CHALLENGE?
I'M ALWAYS READY!
THEN YOU KNOW WHAT THIS MEANS...
SYRUP RACE!!!

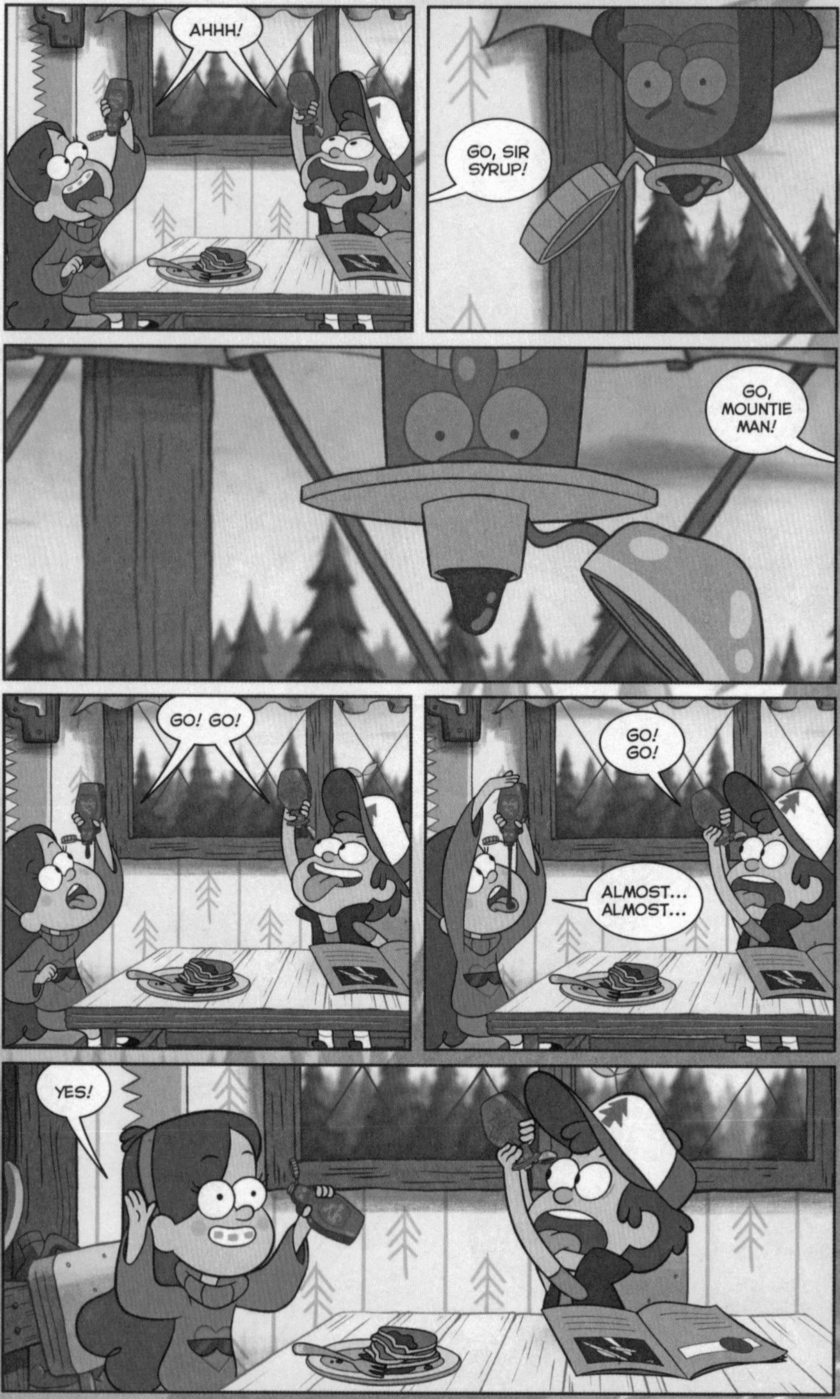
AHHH!
GO, SIR SYRUP!
GO, MOUNTIE MAN!
GO! GO!
GO! GO!
ALMOST... ALMOST...
YES!

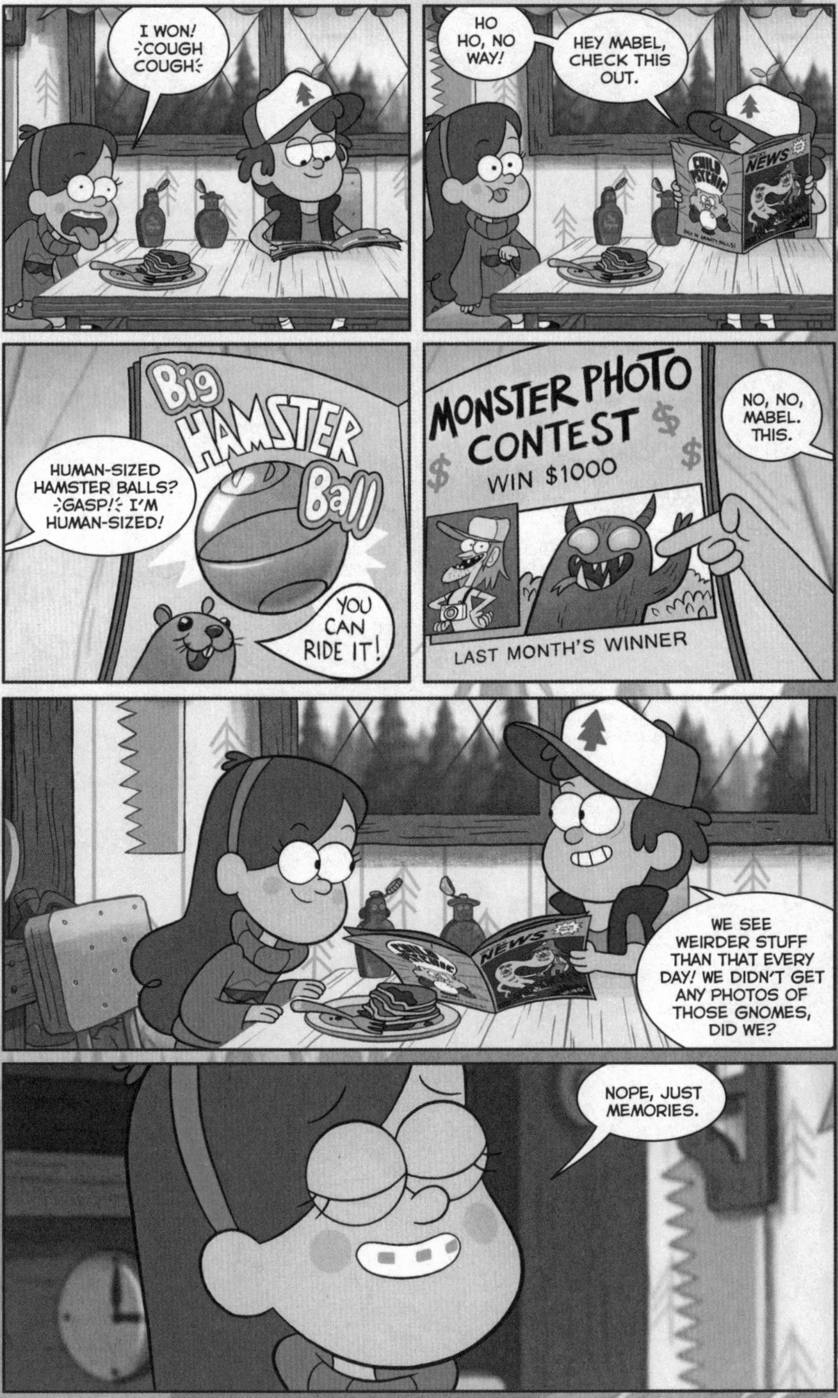
I WON! ⁒COUGH COUGH⁒
HO HO, NO WAY!
HEY MABEL, CHECK THIS OUT.
Big HAMSTER Ball
HUMAN-SIZED HAMSTER BALLS? ⁒GASP!⁒ I'M HUMAN-SIZED!
YOU CAN RIDE IT!
MONSTER PHOTO CONTEST
WIN $1000
LAST MONTH'S WINNER
NO, NO, MABEL. THIS.
WE SEE WEIRDER STUFF THAN THAT EVERY DAY! WE DIDN'T GET ANY PHOTOS OF THOSE GNOMES, DID WE?
NOPE, JUST MEMORIES.

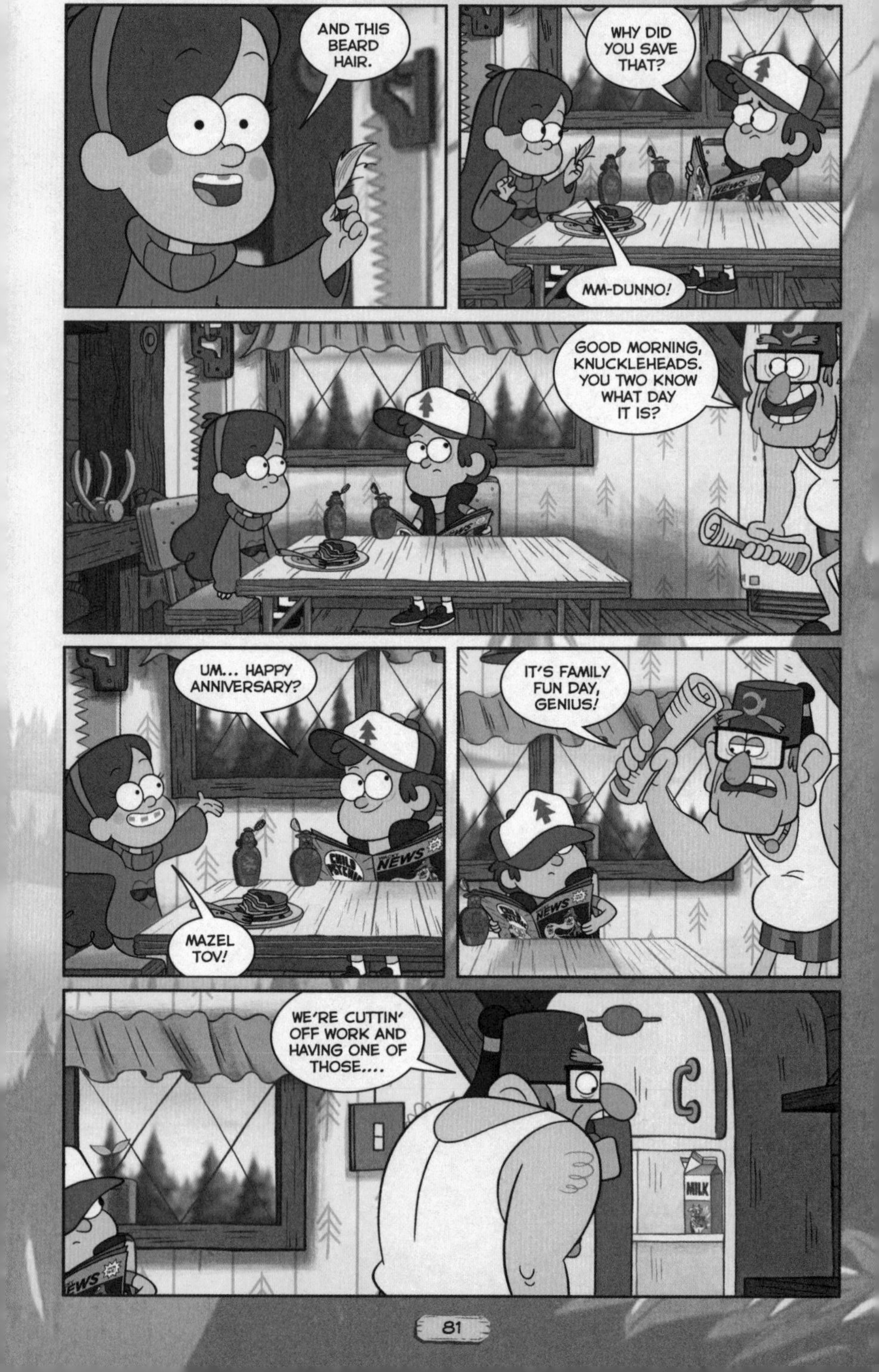
AND THIS BEARD HAIR.
WHY DID YOU SAVE THAT?
MM-DUNNO!
GOOD MORNING, KNUCKLEHEADS. YOU TWO KNOW WHAT DAY IT IS?
UM... HAPPY ANNIVERSARY?
MAZEL TOV!
IT'S FAMILY FUN DAY, GENIUS!
WE'RE CUTTIN' OFF WORK AND HAVING ONE OF THOSE....
MILK

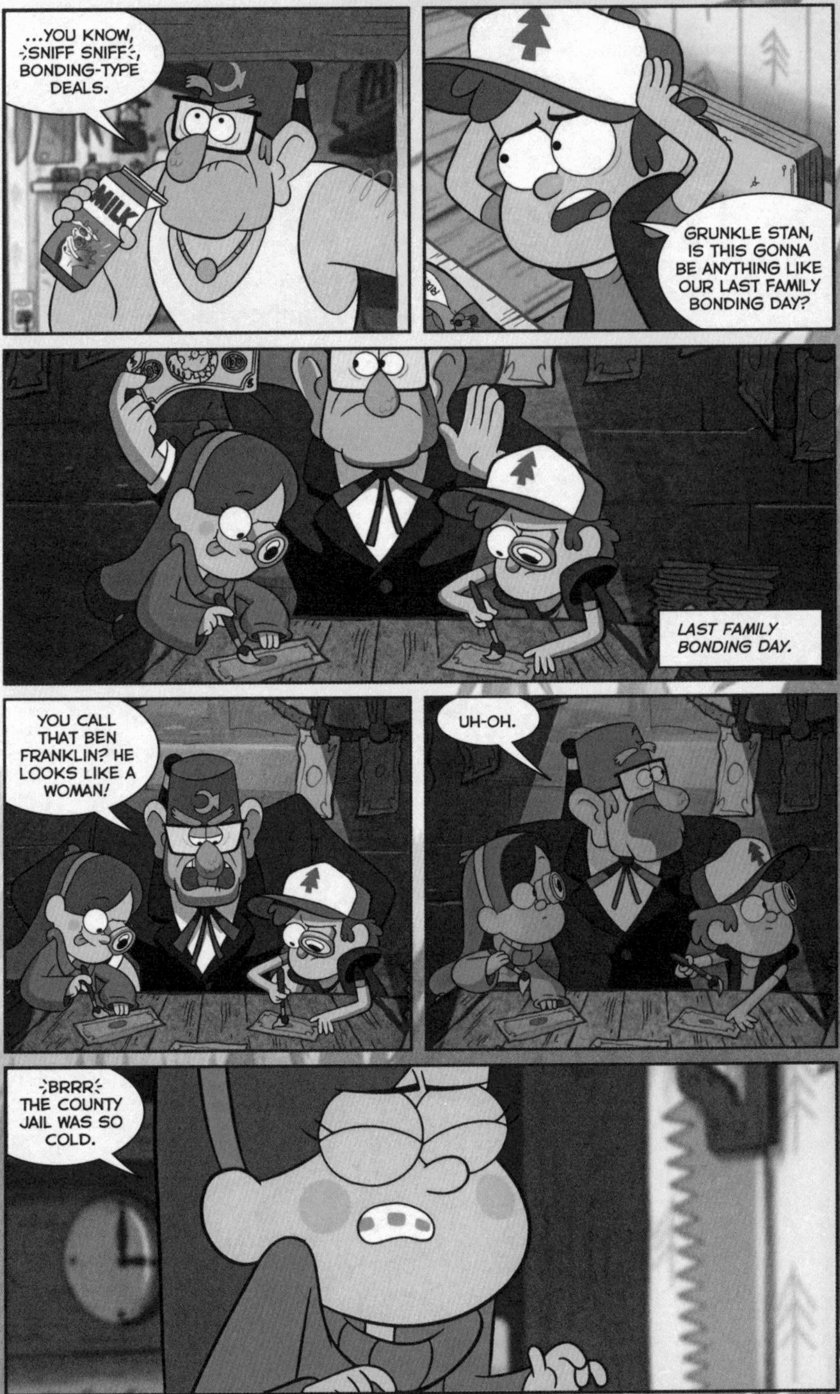
...YOU KNOW, ⁏SNIFF SNIFF⁏, BONDING-TYPE DEALS.
MILK
GRUNKLE STAN, IS THIS GONNA BE ANYTHING LIKE OUR LAST FAMILY BONDING DAY?
LAST FAMILY BONDING DAY.
YOU CALL THAT BEN FRANKLIN? HE LOOKS LIKE A WOMAN!
UH-OH.
⁏BRRR⁏ THE COUNTY JAIL WAS SO COLD.

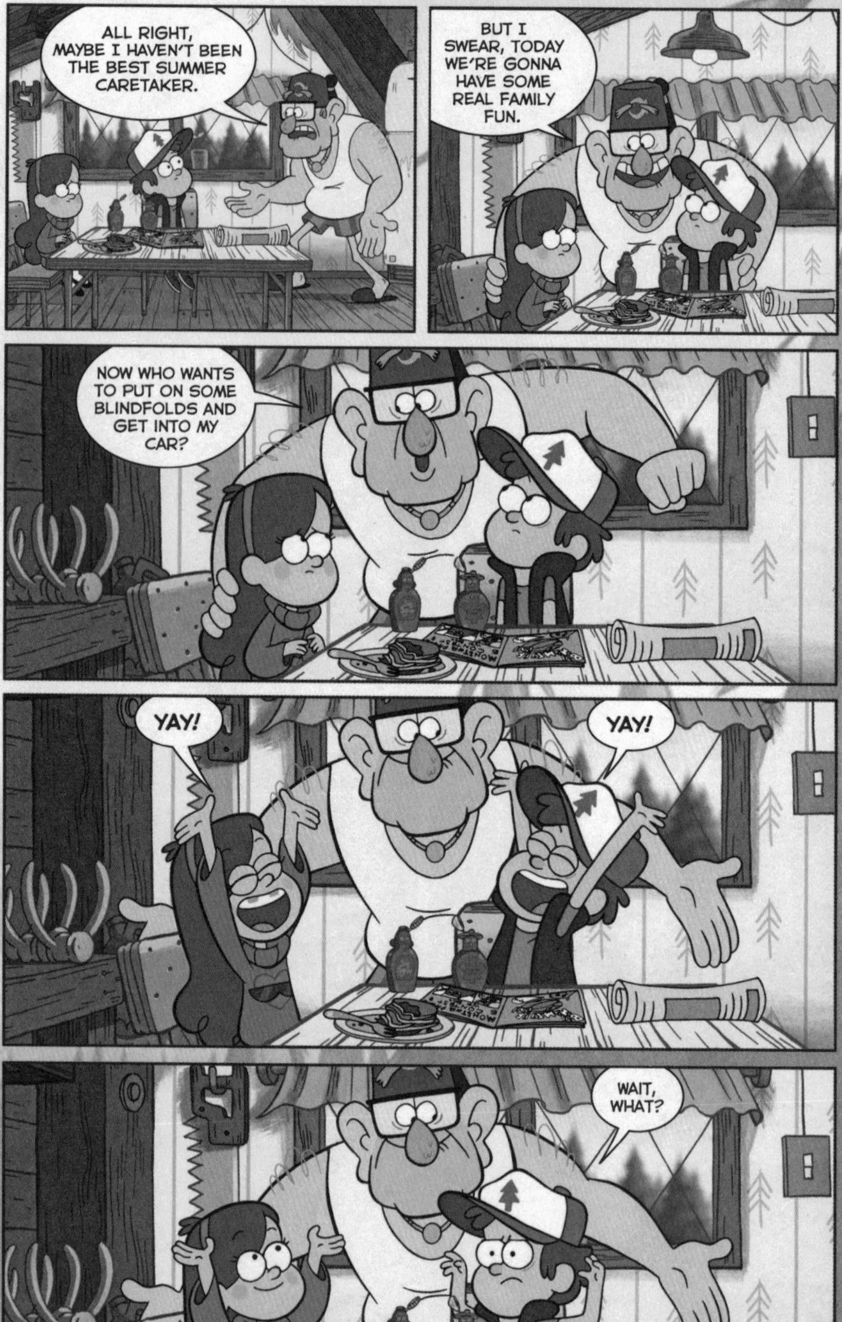
ALL RIGHT, MAYBE I HAVEN'T BEEN THE BEST SUMMER CARETAKER.
BUT I SWEAR, TODAY WE'RE GONNA HAVE SOME REAL FAMILY FUN.
NOW WHO WANTS TO PUT ON SOME BLINDFOLDS AND GET INTO MY CAR?
YAY!
YAY!
WAIT, WHAT?

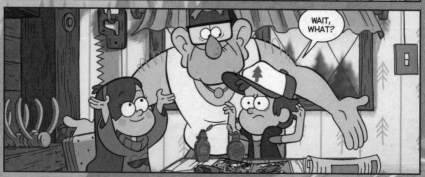

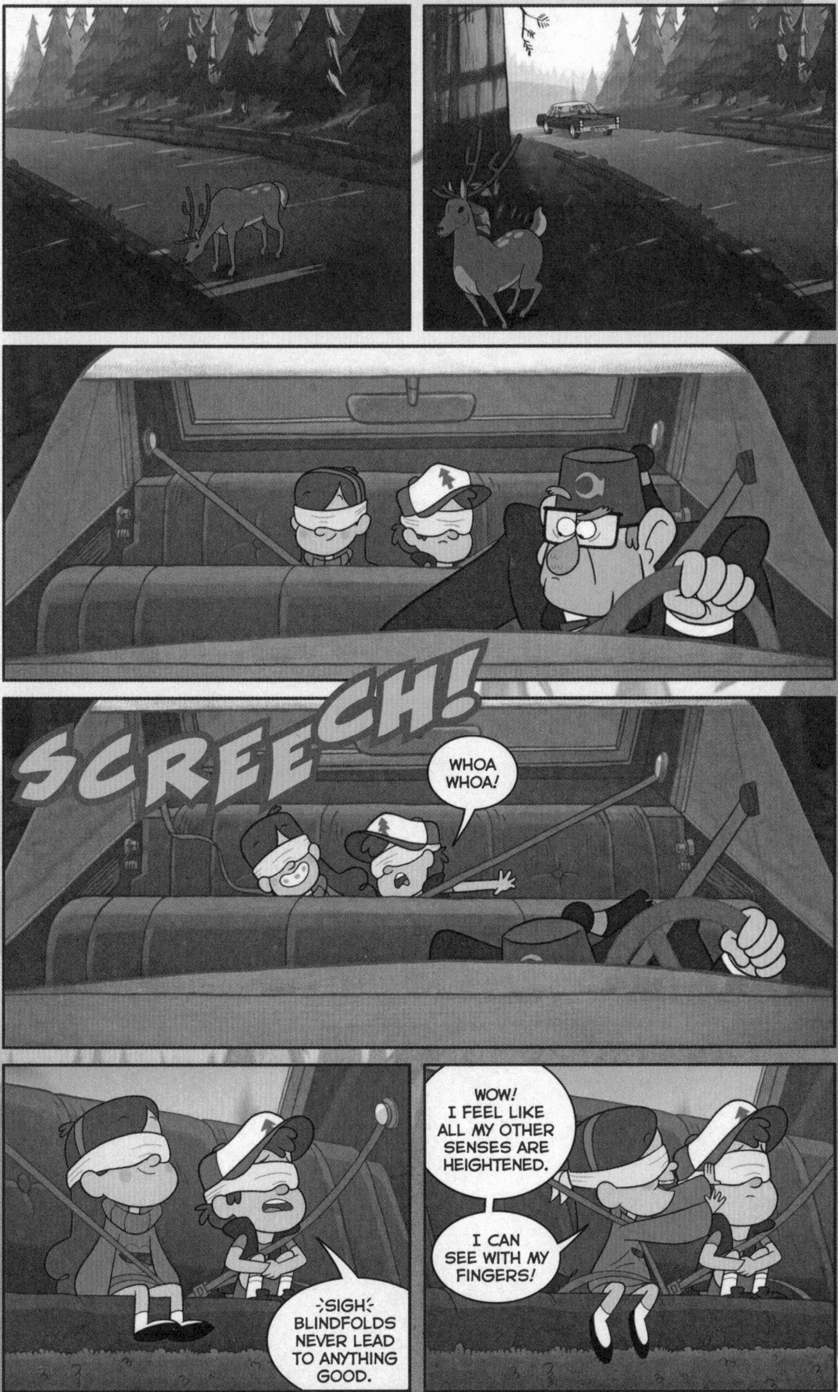
SCREECH!
WHOA WHOA!
SIGH BLINDFOLDS NEVER LEAD TO ANYTHING GOOD.
WOW! I FEEL LIKE ALL MY OTHER SENSES ARE HEIGHTENED.
I CAN SEE WITH MY FINGERS!

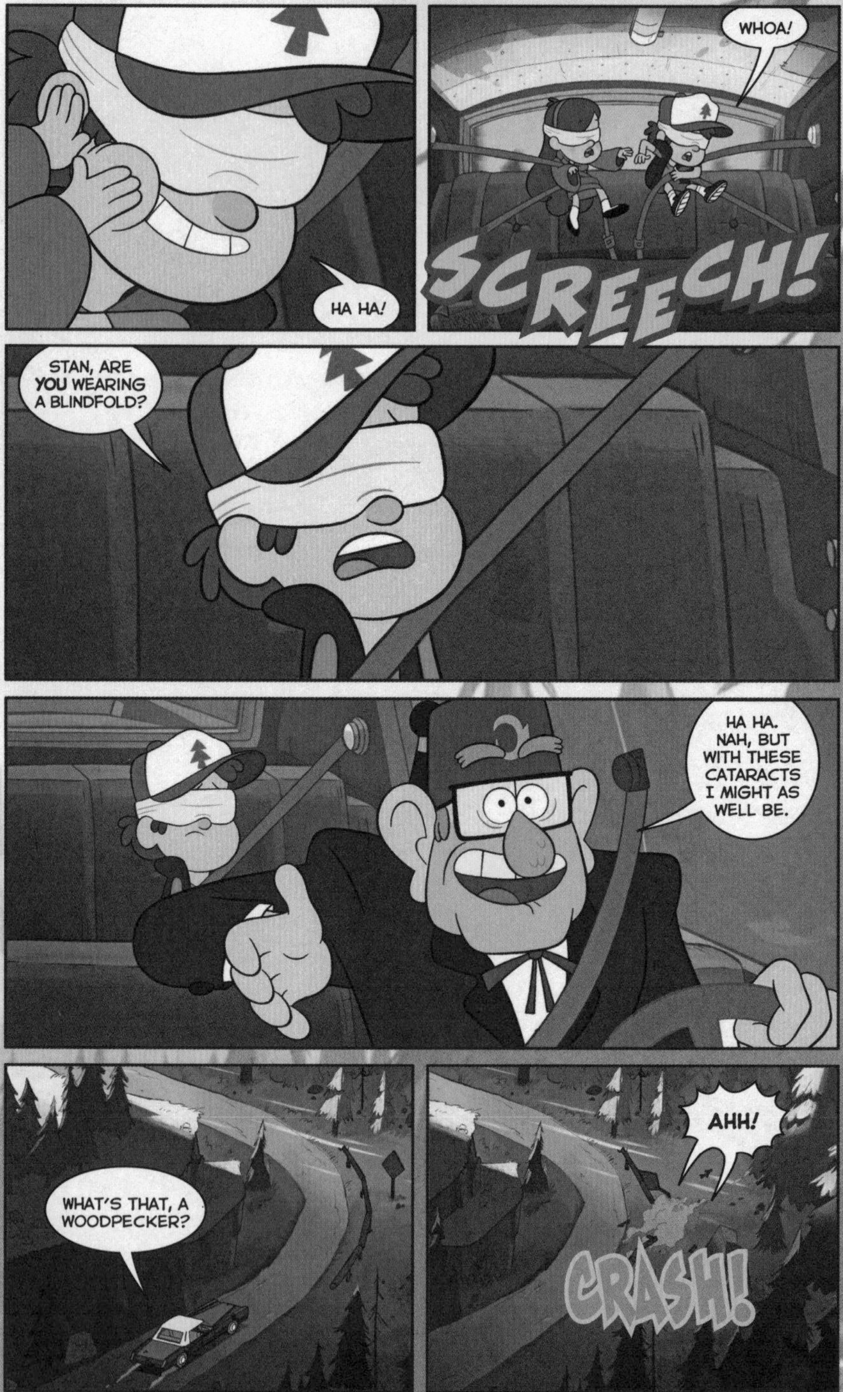
HA HA!
WHOA!
SCREECH!
STAN, ARE YOU WEARING A BLINDFOLD?
HA HA. NAH, BUT WITH THESE CATARACTS I MIGHT AS WELL BE.
WHAT'S THAT, A WOODPECKER?
AHH!
CRASH!

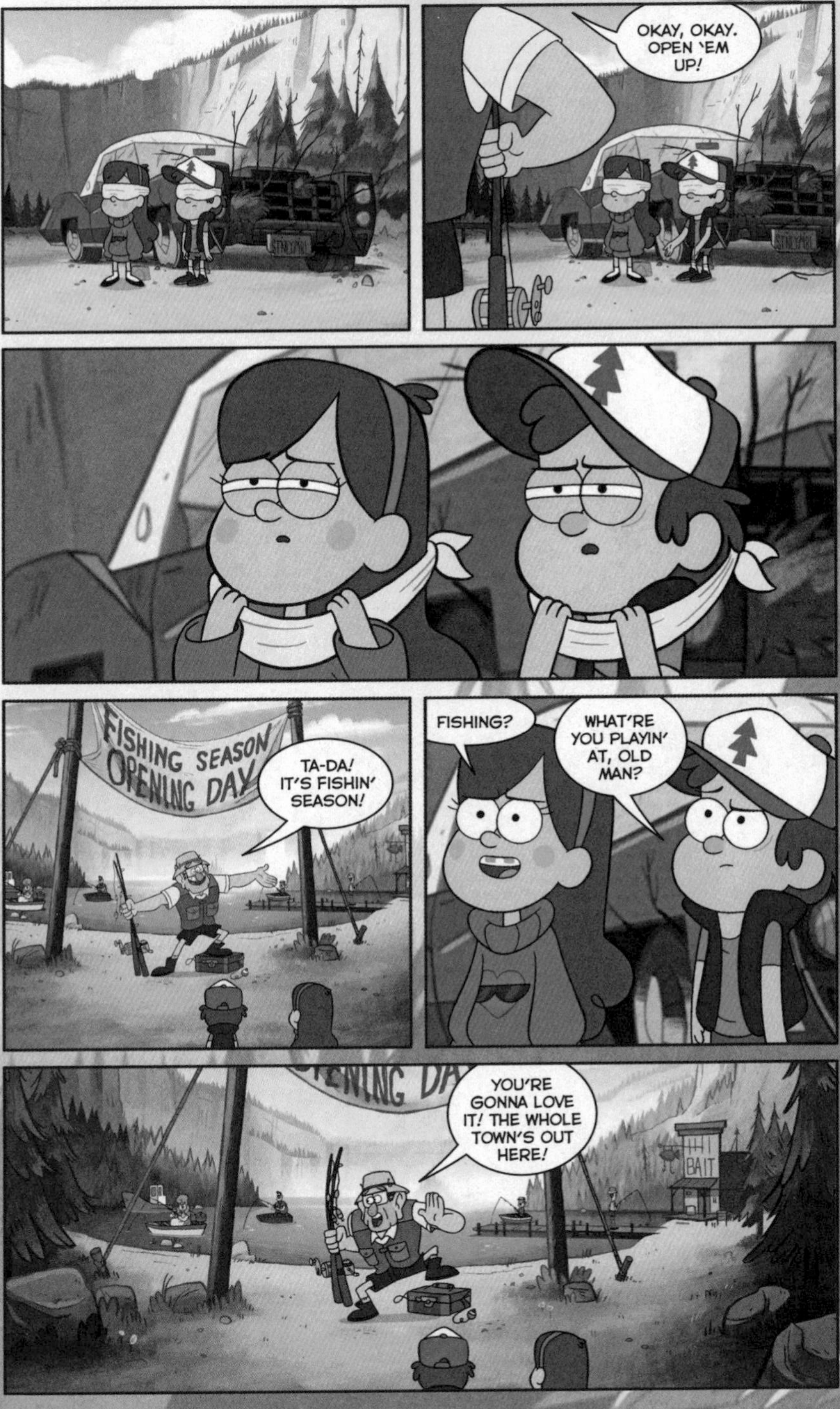
OKAY, OKAY. OPEN 'EM UP!
FISHING SEASON OPENING DAY
TA-DA! IT'S FISHIN' SEASON!
FISHING?
WHAT'RE YOU PLAYIN' AT, OLD MAN?
YOU'RE GONNA LOVE IT! THE WHOLE TOWN'S OUT HERE!
BAIT

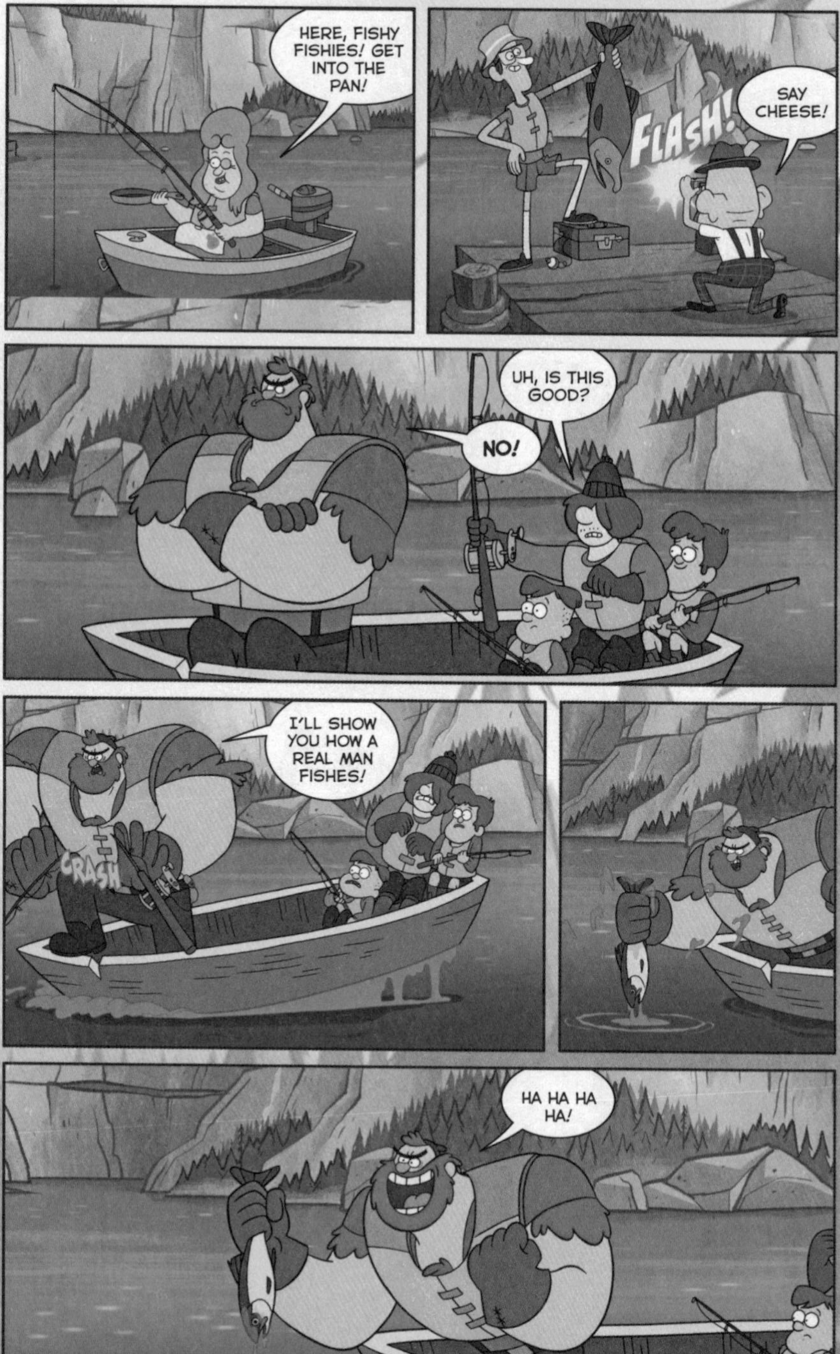
HERE, FISHY FISHIES! GET INTO THE PAN!
FLASH!
SAY CHEESE!
UH, IS THIS GOOD?
NO!
I'LL SHOW YOU HOW A REAL MAN FISHES!
CRASH
HA HA HA HA!

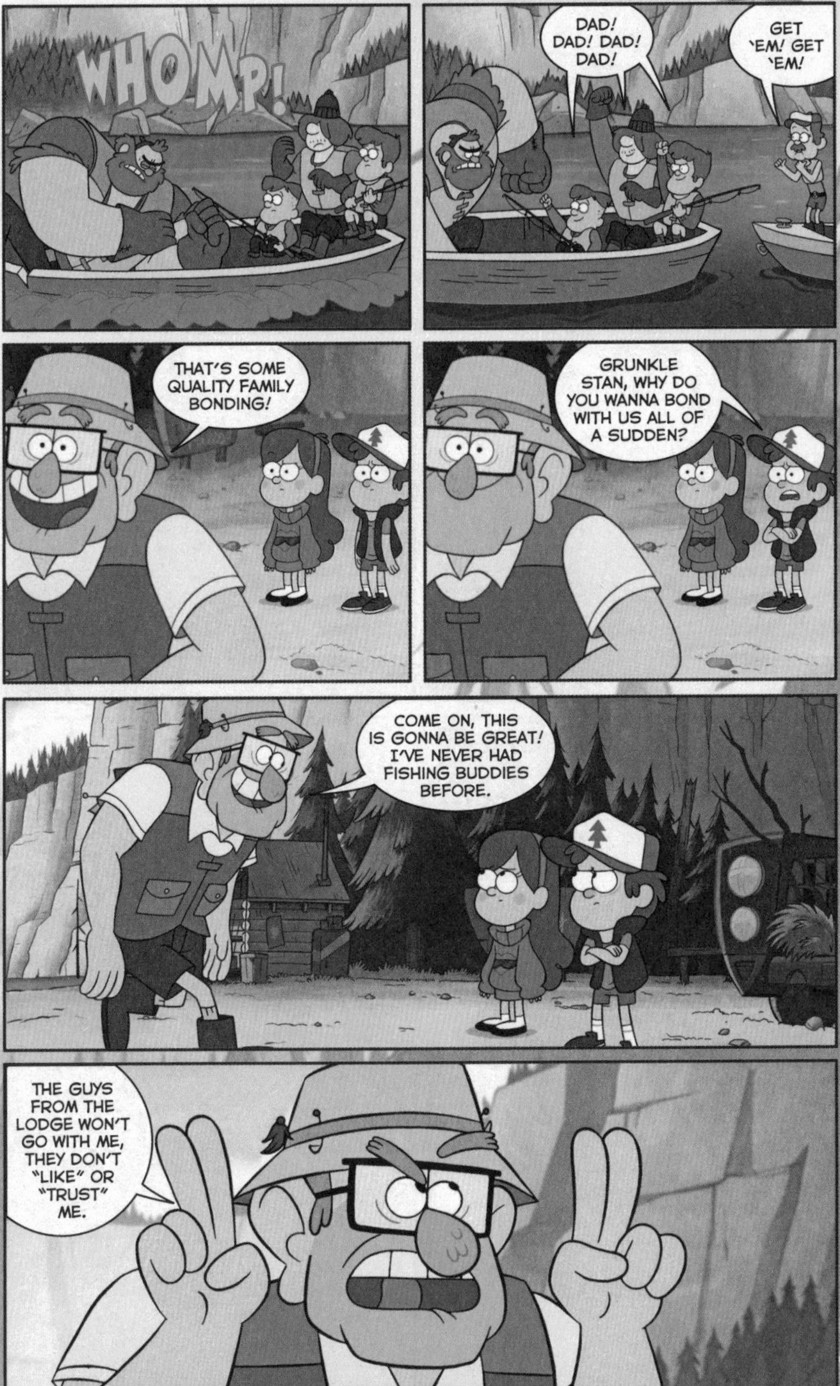

WHOMP!
DAD! DAD! DAD! DAD!
GET 'EM! GET 'EM!
THAT'S SOME QUALITY FAMILY BONDING!
GRUNKLE STAN, WHY DO YOU WANNA BOND WITH US ALL OF A SUDDEN?
COME ON, THIS IS GONNA BE GREAT! I'VE NEVER HAD FISHING BUDDIES BEFORE.
THE GUYS FROM THE LODGE WON'T GO WITH ME, THEY DON'T "LIKE" OR "TRUST" ME.

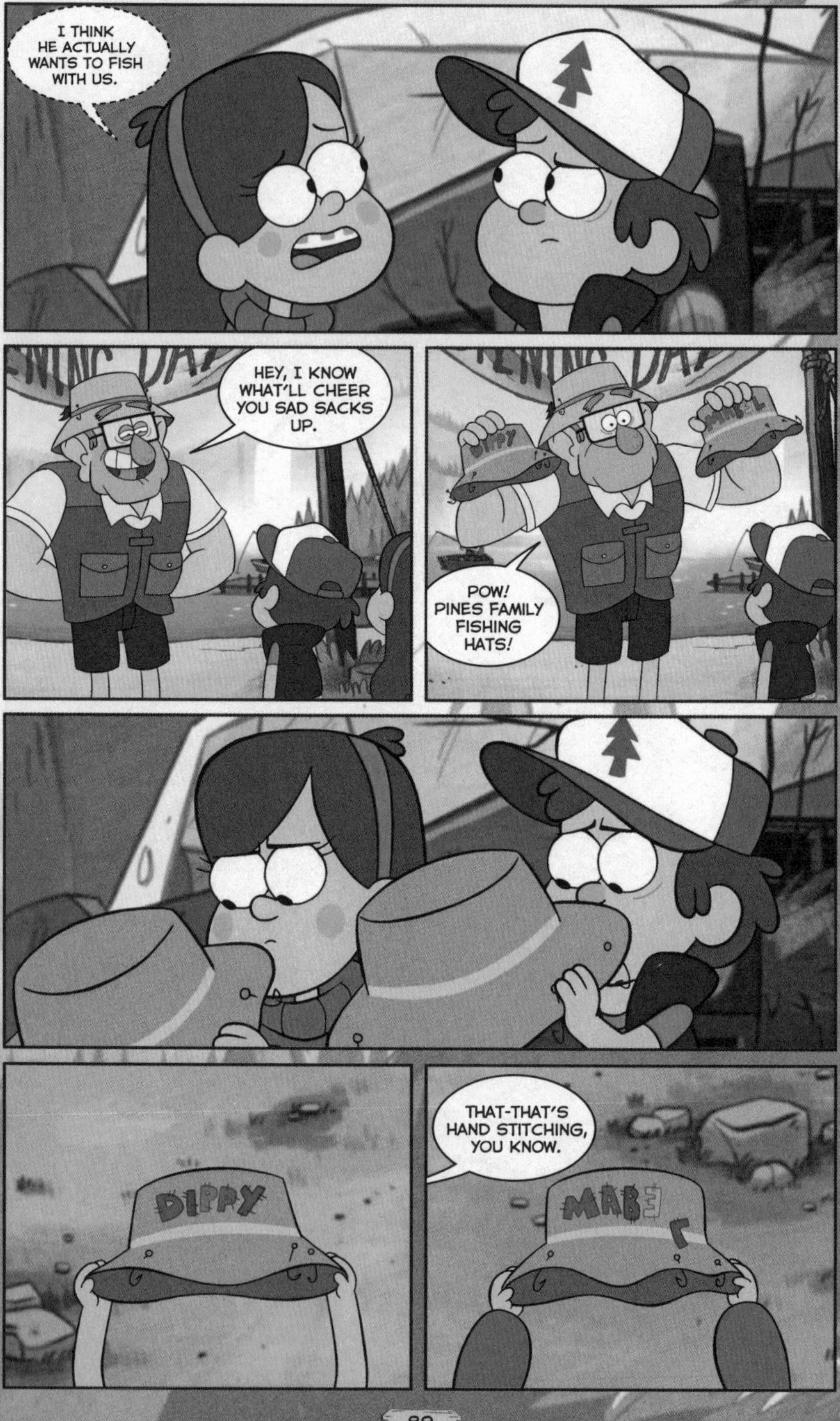
I THINK HE ACTUALLY WANTS TO FISH WITH US.
HEY, I KNOW WHAT'LL CHEER YOU SAD SACKS UP.
DIPPY
POW! PINES FAMILY FISHING HATS!
DIPPY
THAT-THAT'S HAND STITCHING, YOU KNOW.

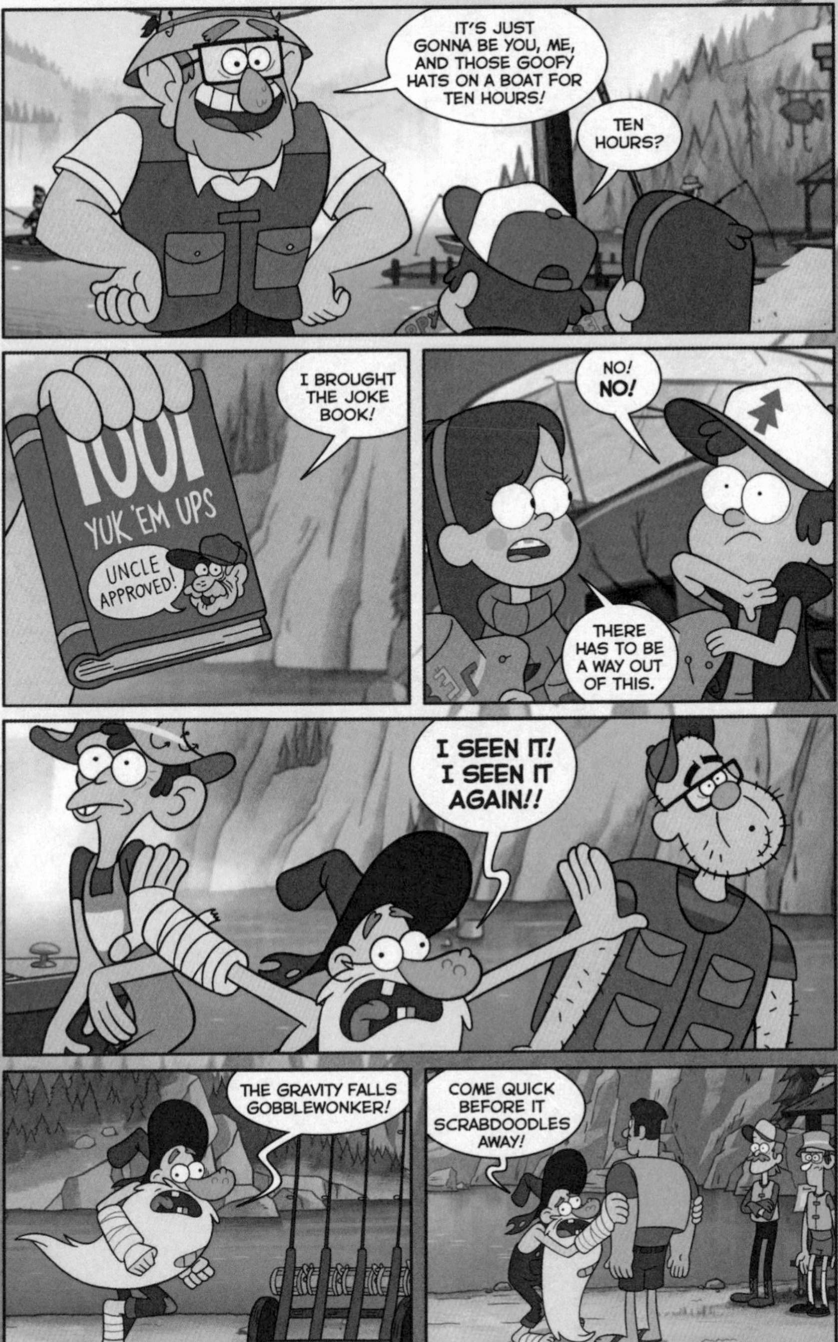
IT'S JUST GONNA BE YOU, ME, AND THOSE GOOFY HATS ON A BOAT FOR TEN HOURS!
TEN HOURS?
1001
YUK 'EM UPS
UNCLE APPROVED!
I BROUGHT THE JOKE BOOK!
NO! NO!
THERE HAS TO BE A WAY OUT OF THIS.
I SEEN IT! I SEEN IT AGAIN!!
THE GRAVITY FALLS GOBBLEWONKER!
COME QUICK BEFORE IT SCRABDOODLES AWAY!

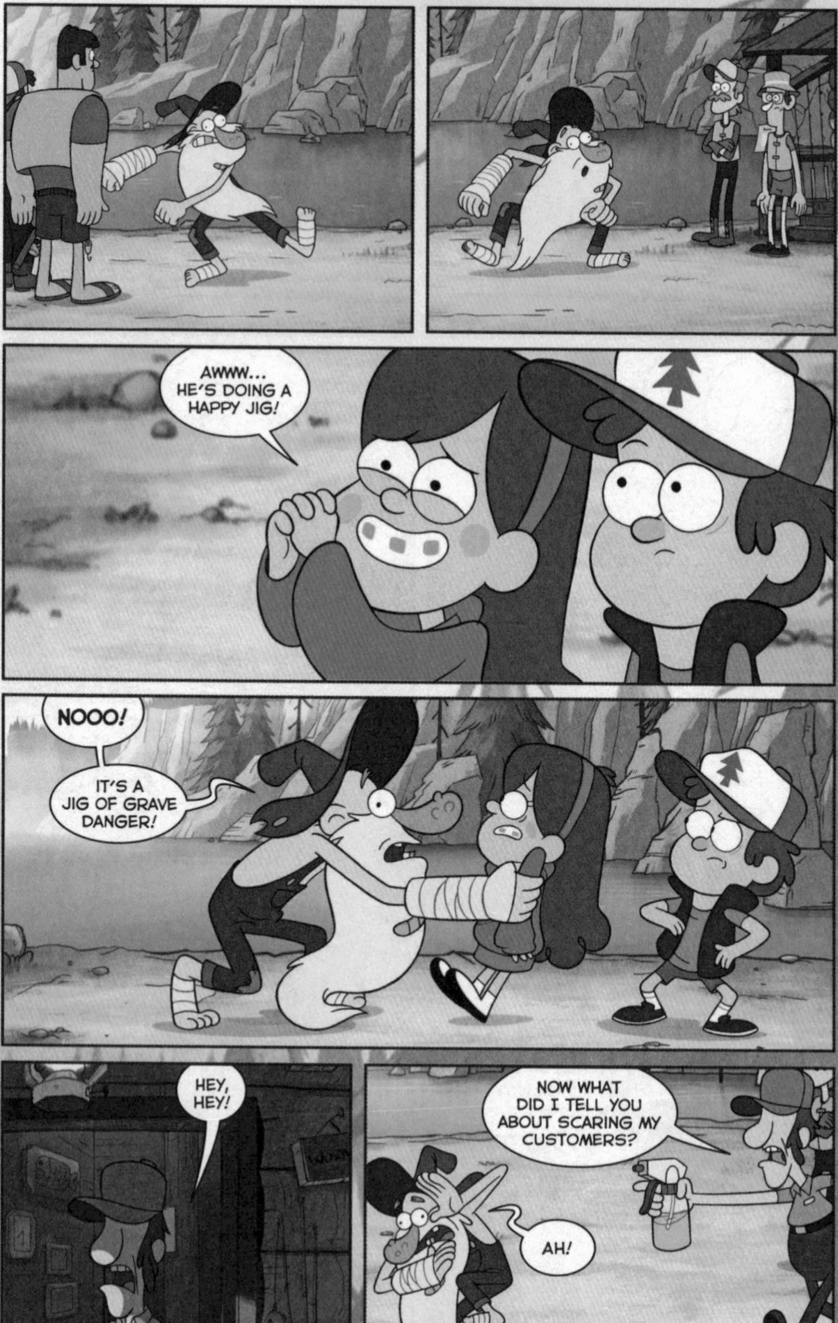
AWWW...
HE'S DOING A
HAPPY JIG!
NOOO!
IT'S A
JIG OF GRAVE
DANGER!
HEY,
HEY!
NOW WHAT
DID I TELL YOU
ABOUT SCARING MY
CUSTOMERS?
AH!

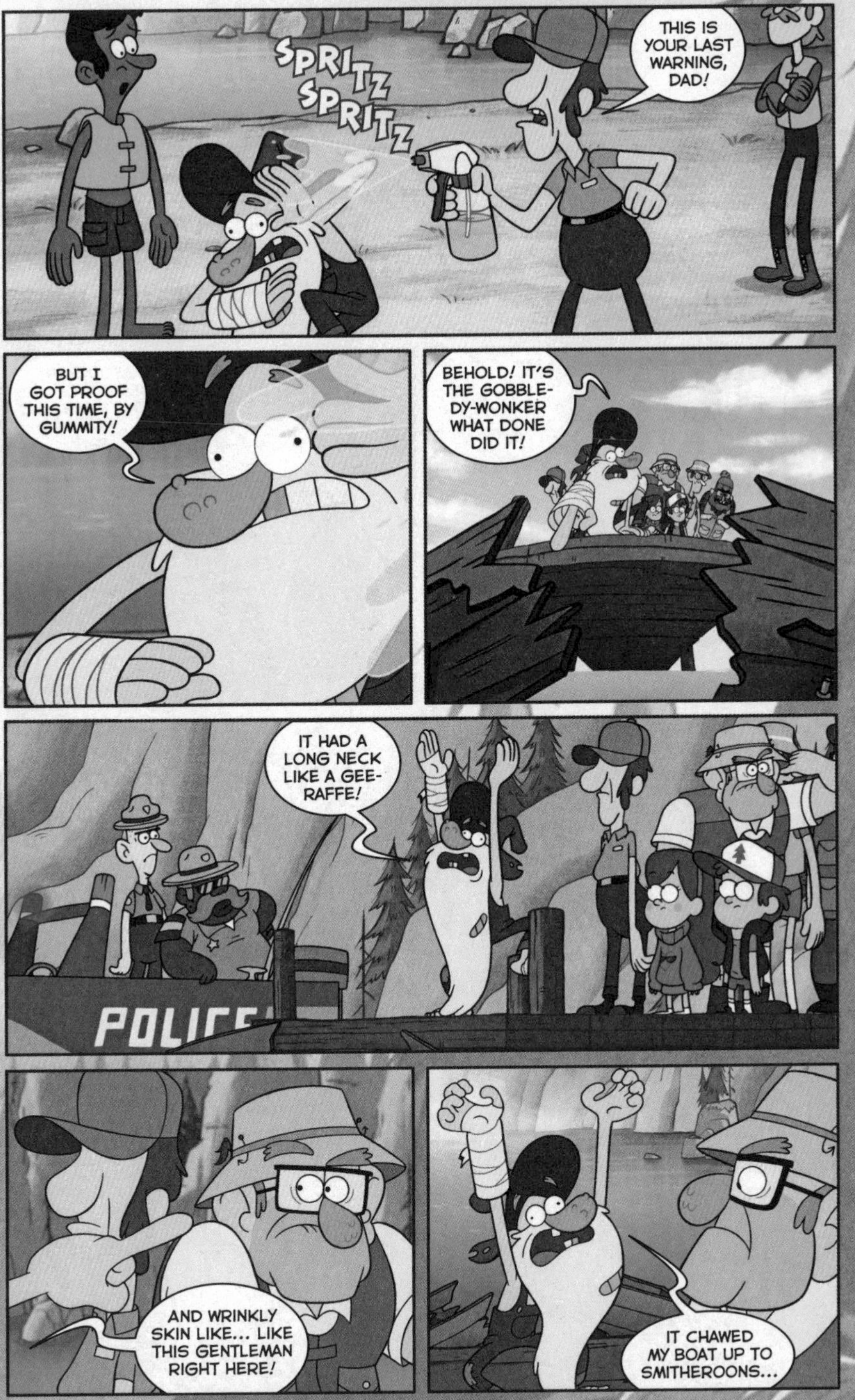
SPRITZ SPRITZ
THIS IS YOUR LAST WARNING, DAD!
BUT I GOT PROOF THIS TIME, BY GUMMITY!
BEHOLD! IT'S THE GOBBLE-DY-WONKER WHAT DONE DID IT!
IT HAD A LONG NECK LIKE A GEE-RAFFE!
POLICE
AND WRINKLY SKIN LIKE... LIKE THIS GENTLEMAN RIGHT HERE!
IT CHAWED MY BOAT UP TO SMITHEROONS...

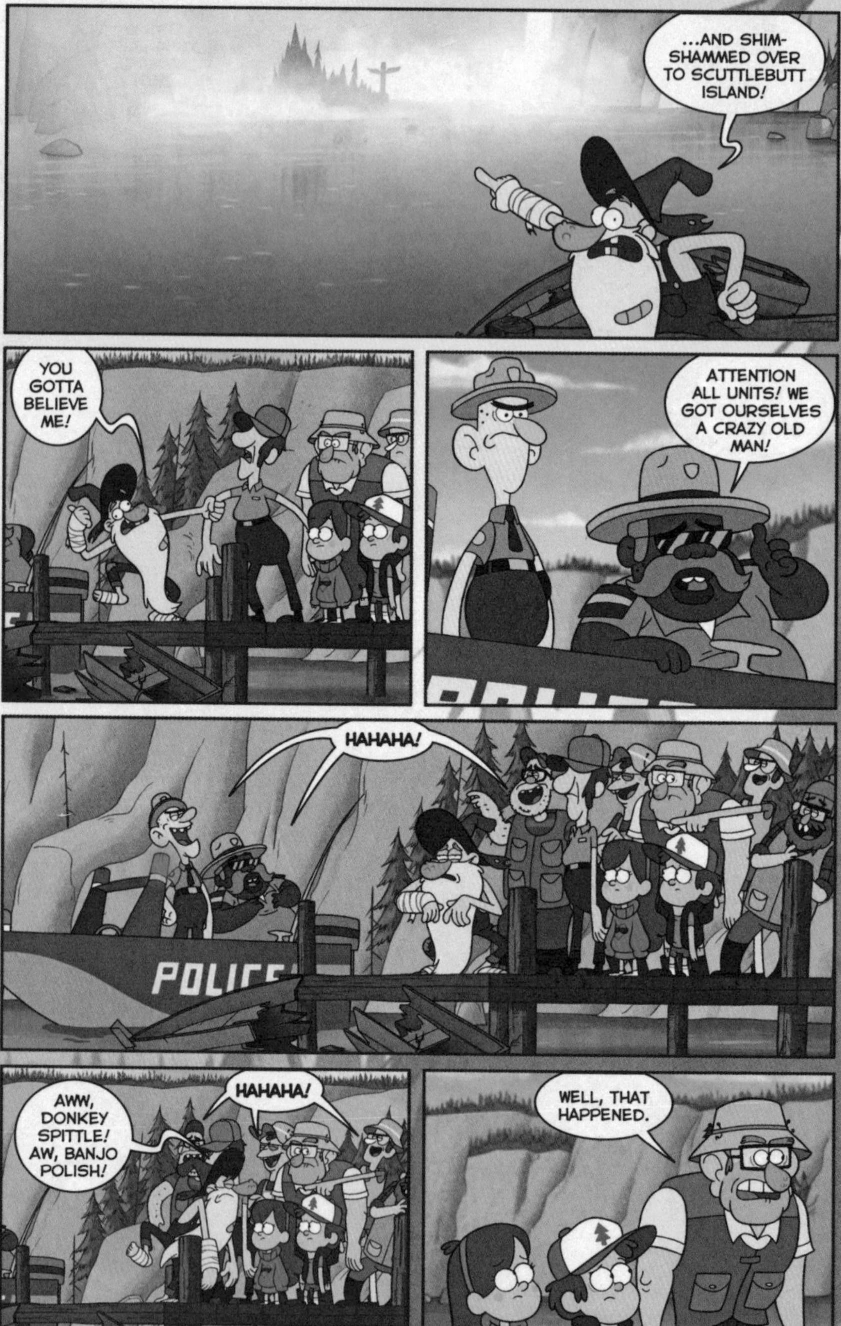
...AND SHIM-SHAMMED OVER TO SCUTTLEBUTT ISLAND!
YOU GOTTA BELIEVE ME!
ATTENTION ALL UNITS! WE GOT OURSELVES A CRAZY OLD MAN!
HAHAHA!
POLICE
AWW, DONKEY SPITTLE! AW, BANJO POLISH!
HAHAHA!
WELL, THAT HAPPENED.

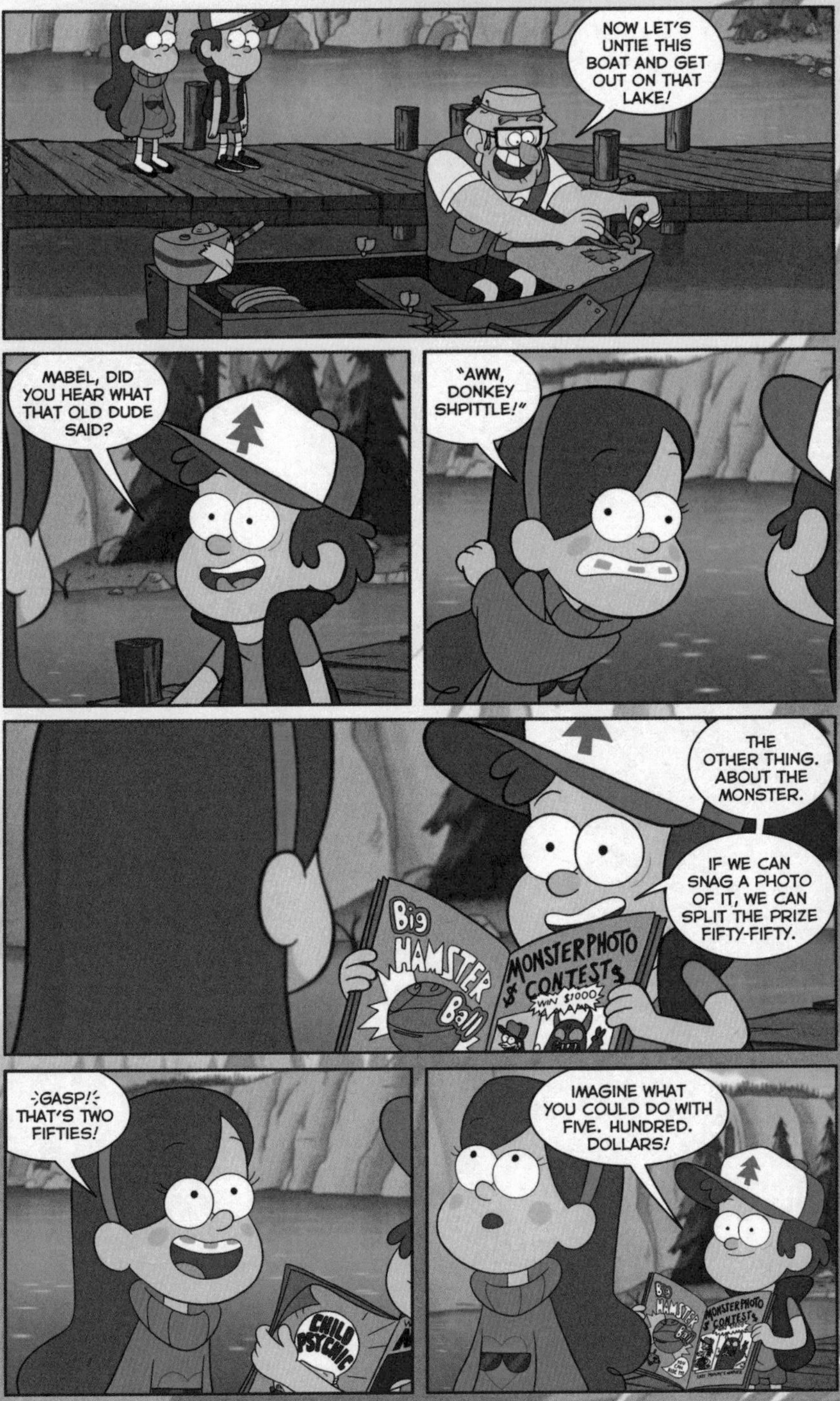
NOW LET'S UNTIE THIS BOAT AND GET OUT ON THAT LAKE!
MABEL, DID YOU HEAR WHAT THAT OLD DUDE SAID?
"AWW, DONKEY SHPITTLE!"
THE OTHER THING. ABOUT THE MONSTER.
IF WE CAN SNAG A PHOTO OF IT, WE CAN SPLIT THE PRIZE FIFTY-FIFTY.
Big HAMSTER Ball
MONSTER PHOTO CONTEST
WIN $1000
GASP! THAT'S TWO FIFTIES!
CHILD PSYCHIC
IMAGINE WHAT YOU COULD DO WITH FIVE. HUNDRED. DOLLARS!

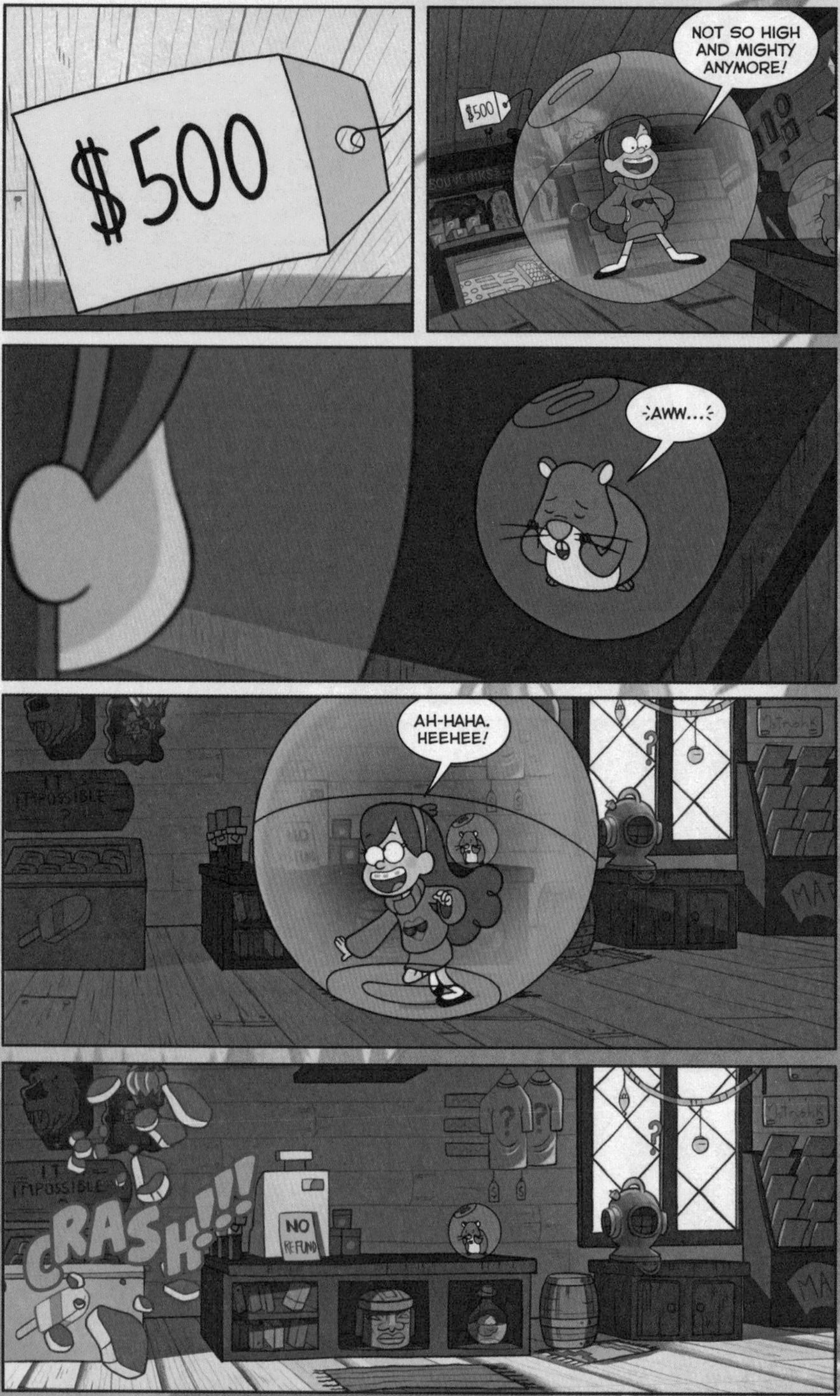
$500
$500
NOT SO HIGH AND MIGHTY ANYMORE!
AWW...
AH-HAHA. HEEHEE!
CRASH!!!
NO REFUND

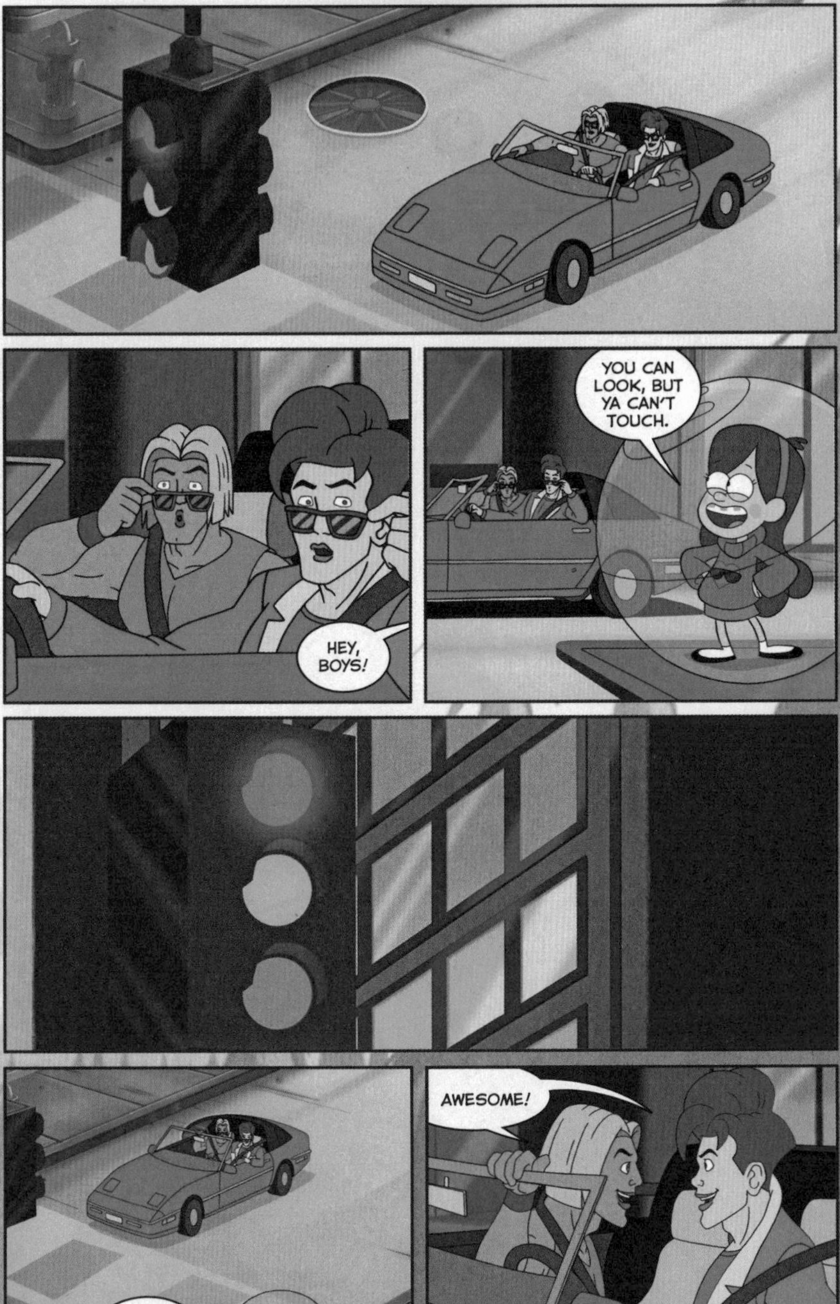
HEY, BOYS!
YOU CAN LOOK, BUT YA CAN'T TOUCH.
SQUEAK, SQUEAK, SQUEAK, SQUEAK!
AWESOME!

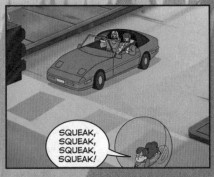

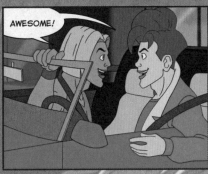

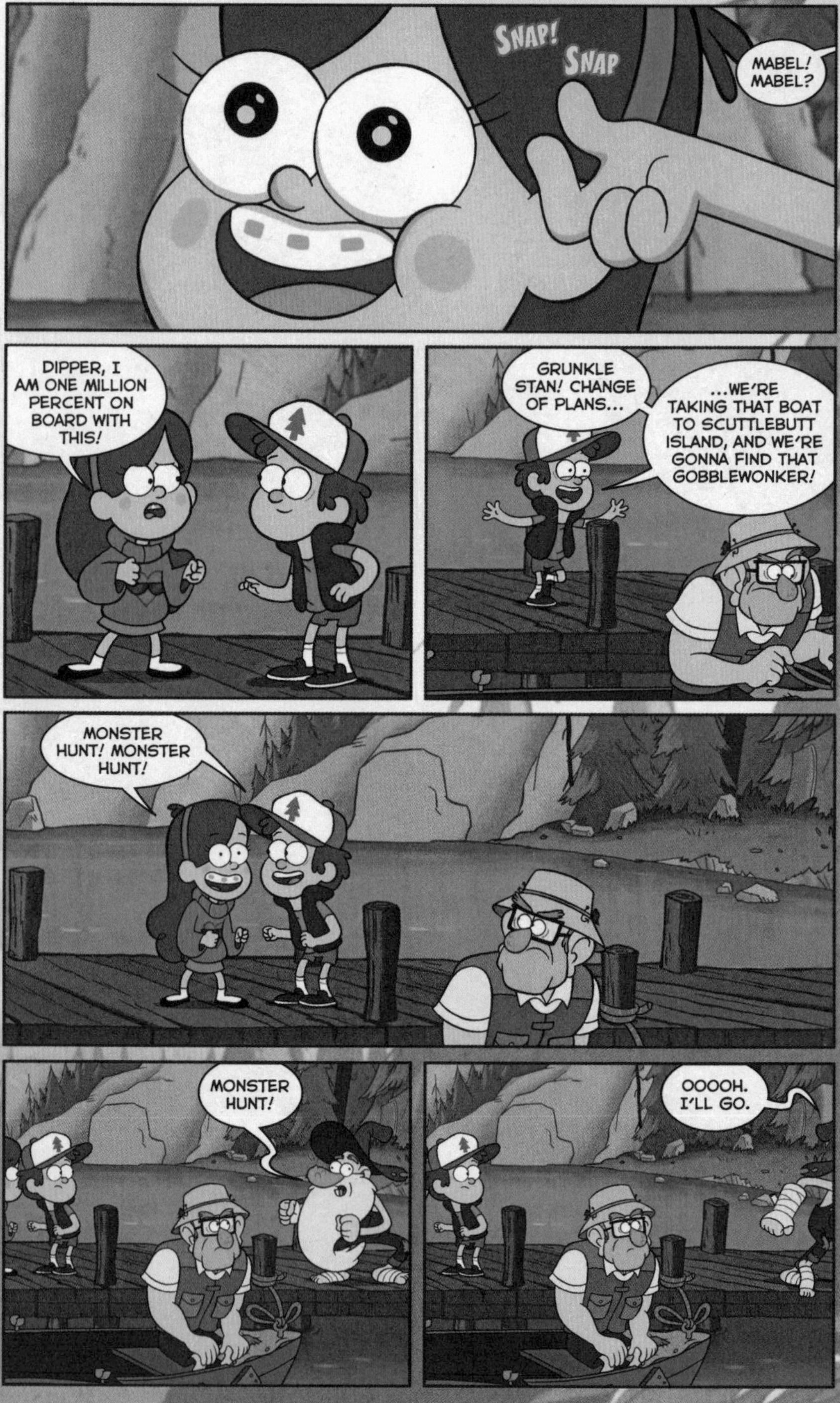
SNAP! SNAP
MABEL! MABEL?
DIPPER, I AM ONE MILLION PERCENT ON BOARD WITH THIS!
GRUNKLE STAN! CHANGE OF PLANS...
...WE'RE TAKING THAT BOAT TO SCUTTLEBUTT ISLAND, AND WE'RE GONNA FIND THAT GOBBLEWONKER!
MONSTER HUNT! MONSTER HUNT!
MONSTER HUNT!
OOOOH. I'LL GO.

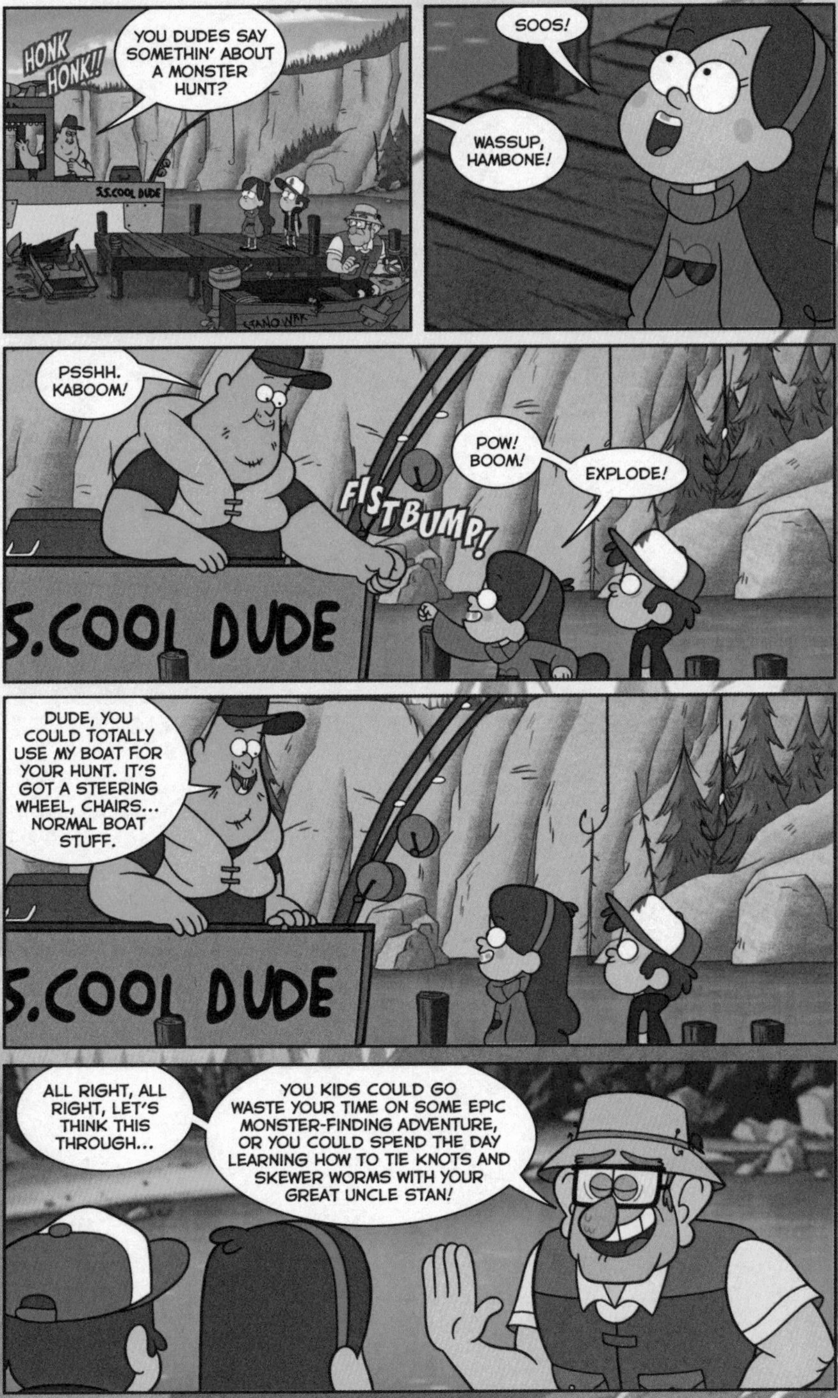
HONK HONK!!
YOU DUDES SAY SOMETHIN' ABOUT A MONSTER HUNT?
S.S.COOL DUDE
SOOS!
WASSUP, HAMBONE!
PSSHH. KABOOM!
POW! BOOM!
EXPLODE!
FISTBUMP!
S.COOL DUDE
DUDE, YOU COULD TOTALLY USE MY BOAT FOR YOUR HUNT. IT'S GOT A STEERING WHEEL, CHAIRS... NORMAL BOAT STUFF.
S.COOL DUDE
ALL RIGHT, ALL RIGHT, LET'S THINK THIS THROUGH...
YOU KIDS COULD GO WASTE YOUR TIME ON SOME EPIC MONSTER-FINDING ADVENTURE, OR YOU COULD SPEND THE DAY LEARNING HOW TO TIE KNOTS AND SKEWER WORMS WITH YOUR GREAT UNCLE STAN!

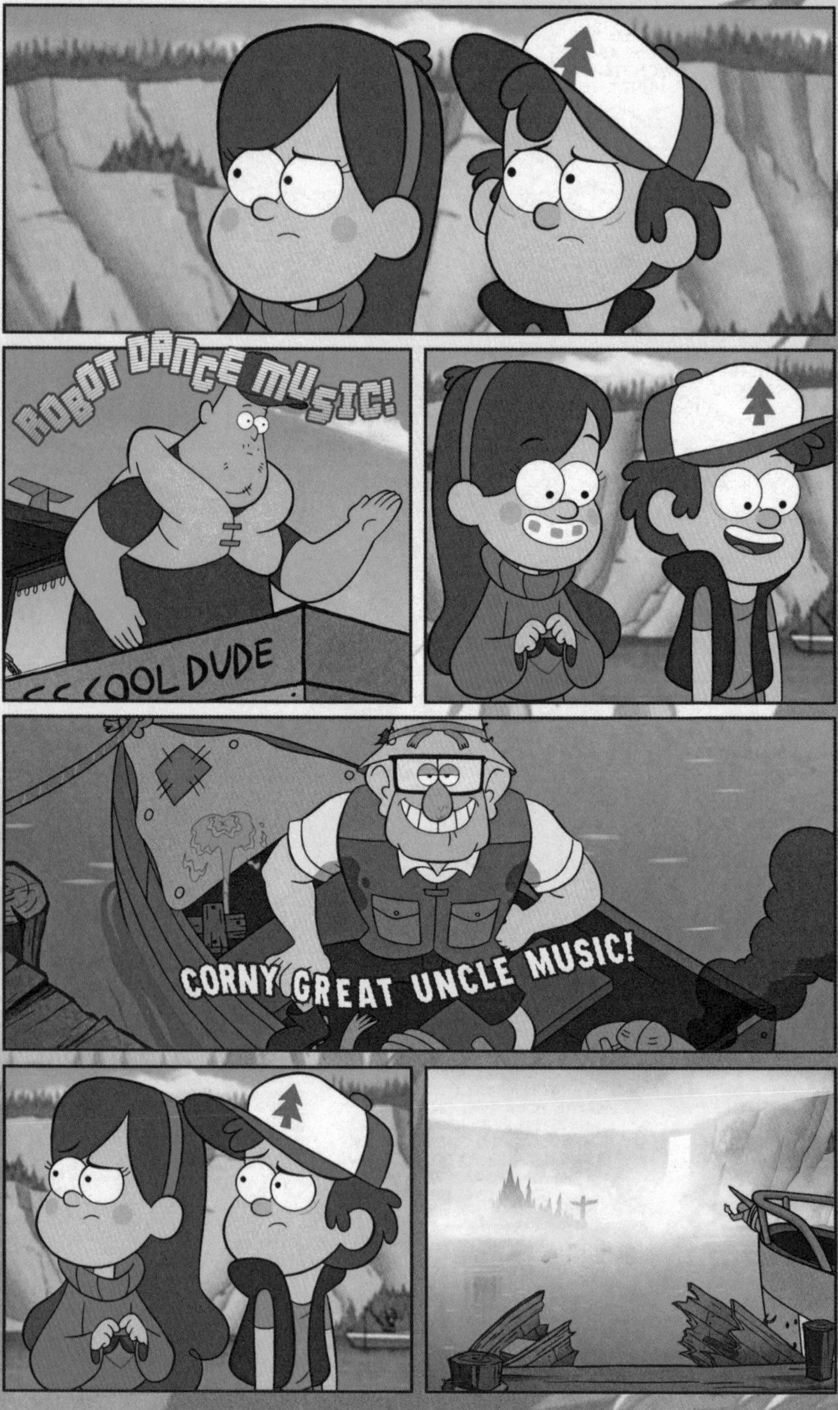
ROBOT DANCE MUSIC!
COOL DUDE
CORNY GREAT UNCLE MUSIC!

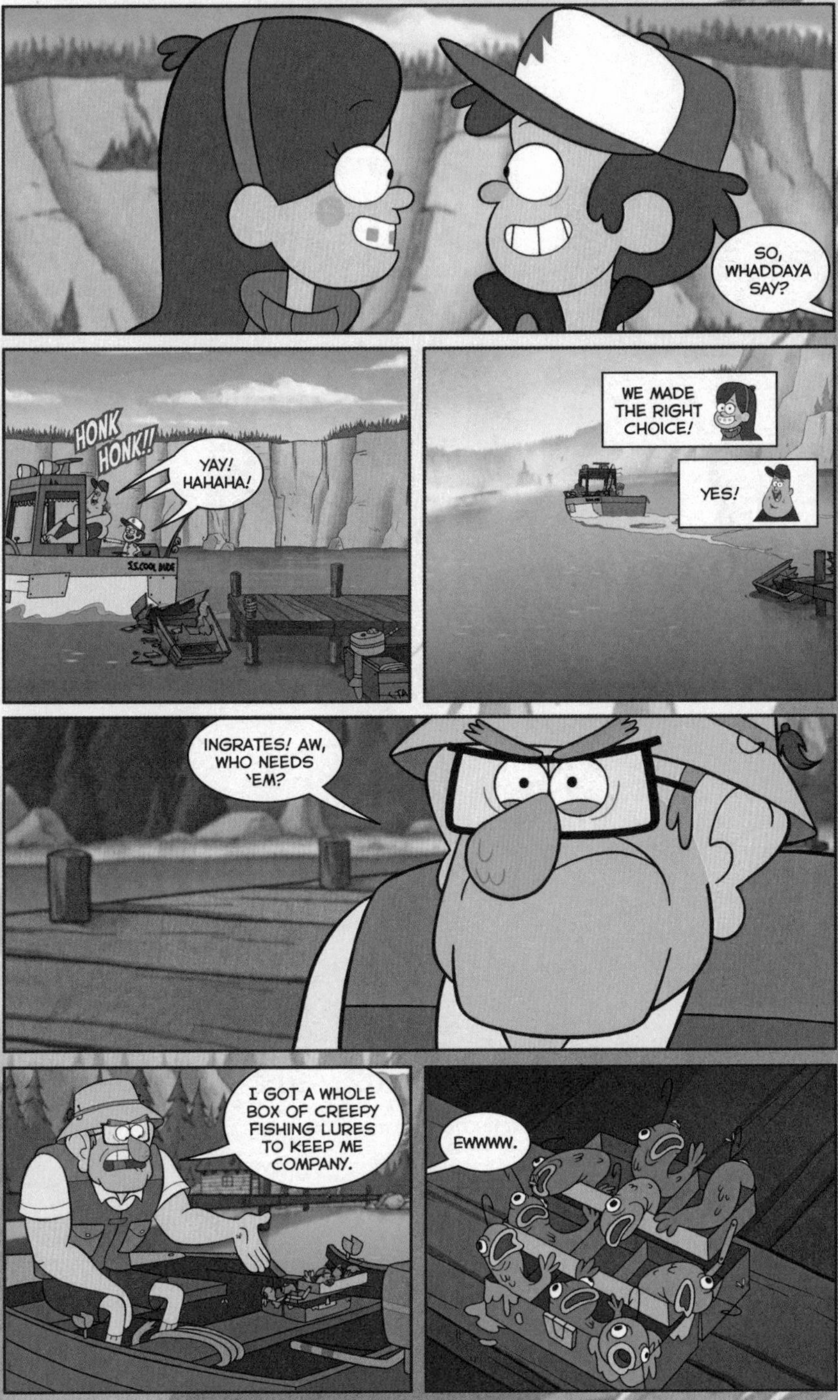
SO, WHADDAYA SAY?
HONK HONK!!
YAY! HAHAHA!
S.S. COOL BIRD
WE MADE THE RIGHT CHOICE!
YES!
INGRATES! AW, WHO NEEDS 'EM?
I GOT A WHOLE BOX OF CREEPY FISHING LURES TO KEEP ME COMPANY.
EWWWW.

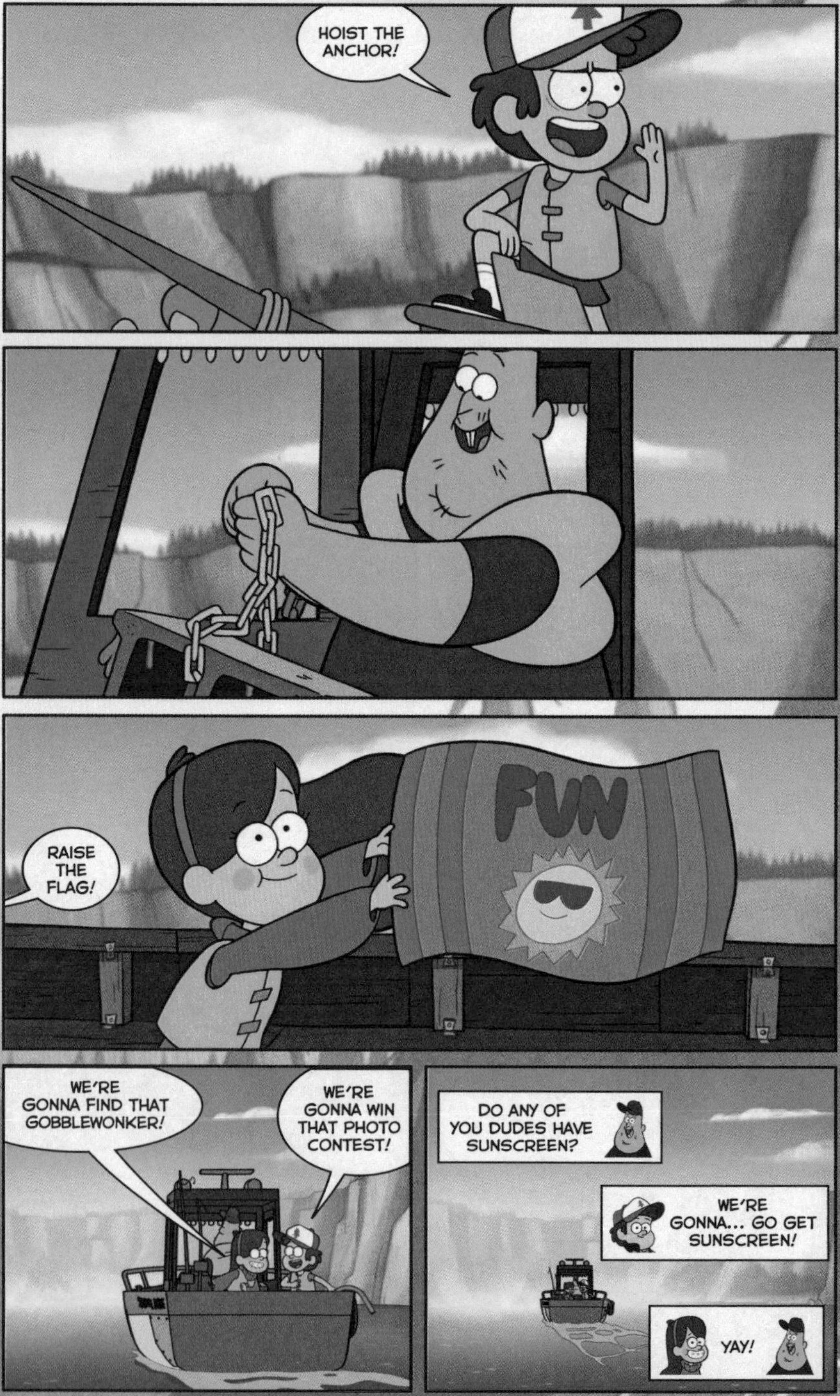
HOIST THE ANCHOR!
RAISE THE FLAG!
FUN
WE'RE GONNA FIND THAT GOBBLEWONKER!
WE'RE GONNA WIN THAT PHOTO CONTEST!
DO ANY OF YOU DUDES HAVE SUNSCREEN?
WE'RE GONNA... GO GET SUNSCREEN!
YAY!

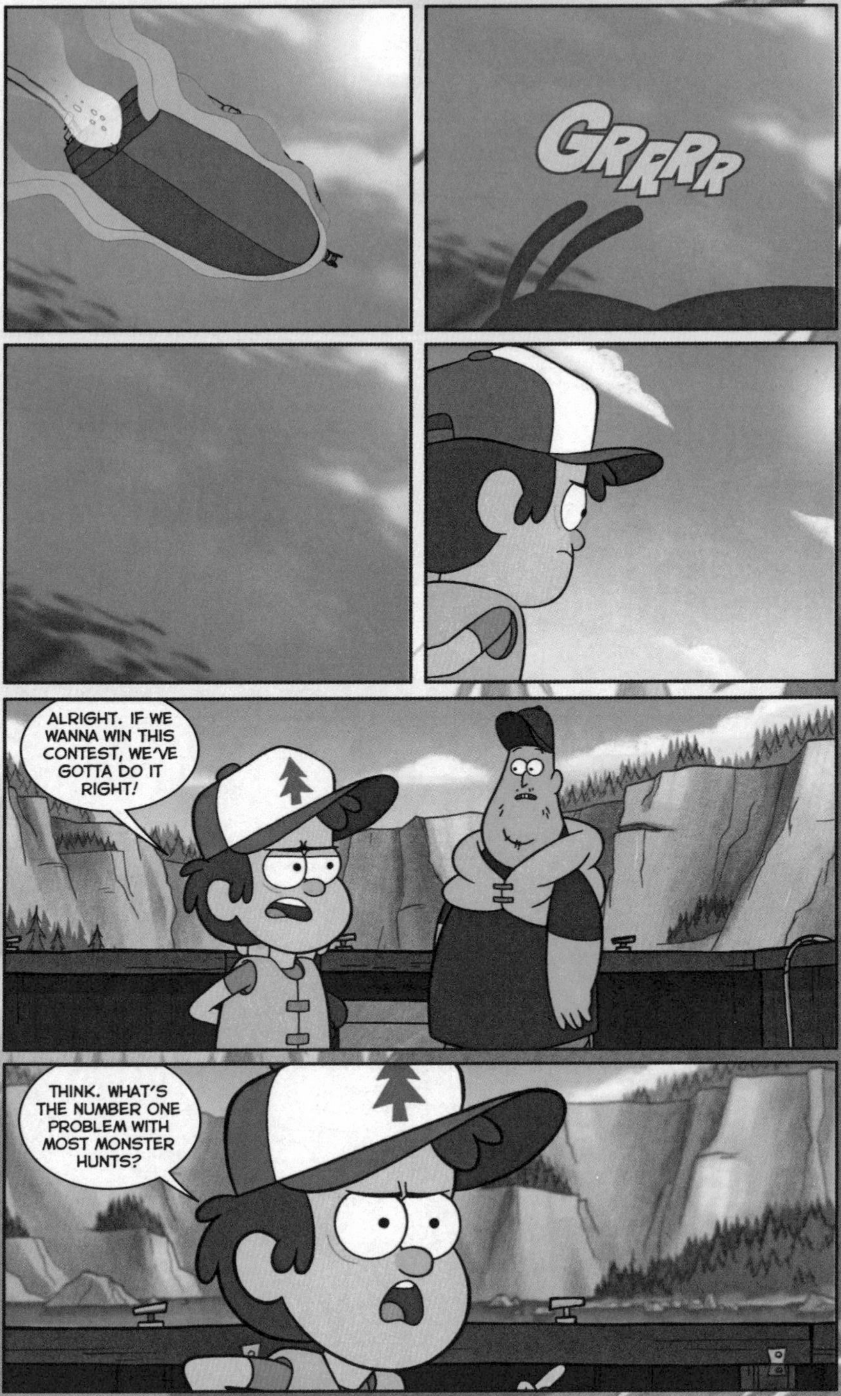
GRRRR
ALRIGHT. IF WE WANNA WIN THIS CONTEST, WE'VE GOTTA DO IT RIGHT!
THINK. WHAT'S THE NUMBER ONE PROBLEM WITH MOST MONSTER HUNTS?

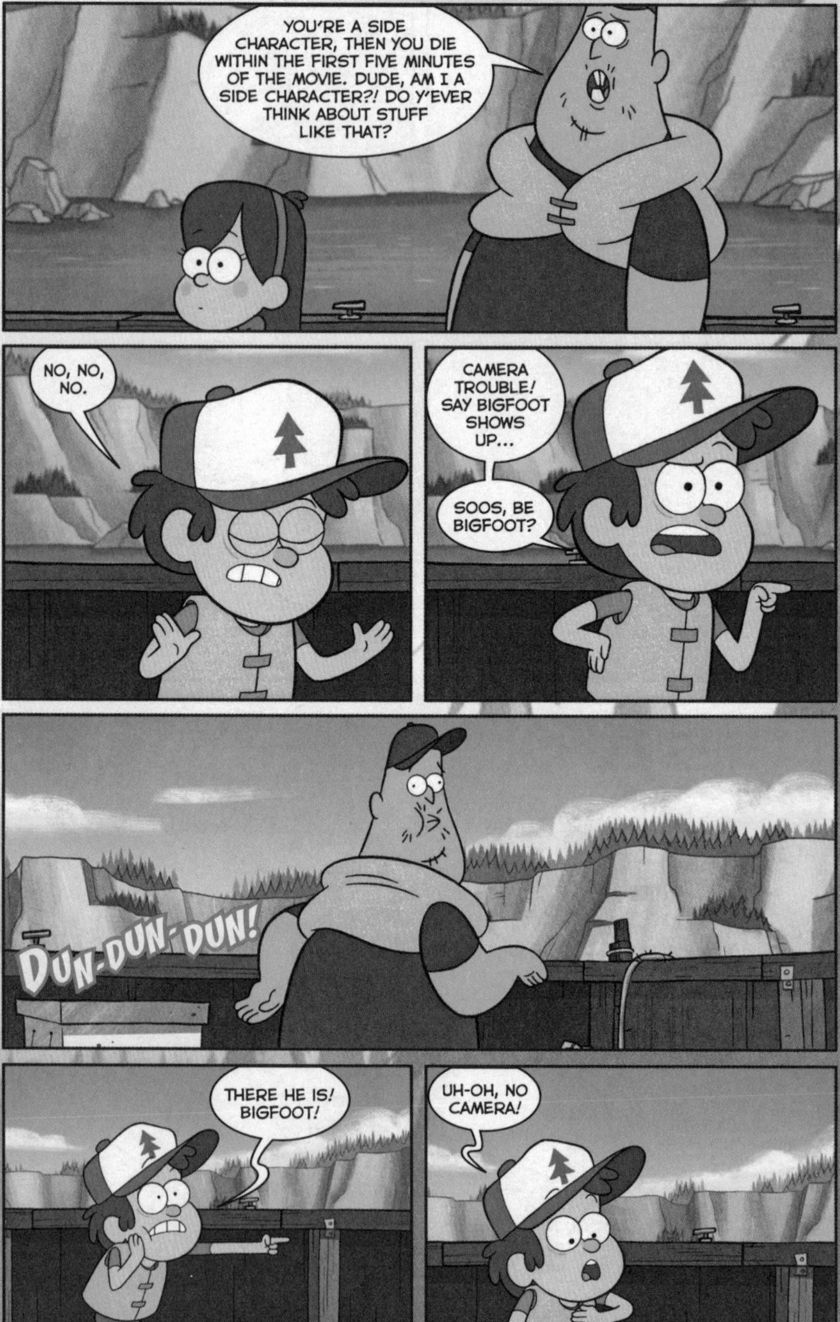
YOU'RE A SIDE CHARACTER, THEN YOU DIE WITHIN THE FIRST FIVE MINUTES OF THE MOVIE. DUDE, AM I A SIDE CHARACTER?! DO Y'EVER THINK ABOUT STUFF LIKE THAT?
NO, NO, NO.
CAMERA TROUBLE! SAY BIGFOOT SHOWS UP...
SOOS, BE BIGFOOT?
DUN-DUN-DUN!
THERE HE IS! BIGFOOT!
UH-OH, NO CAMERA!

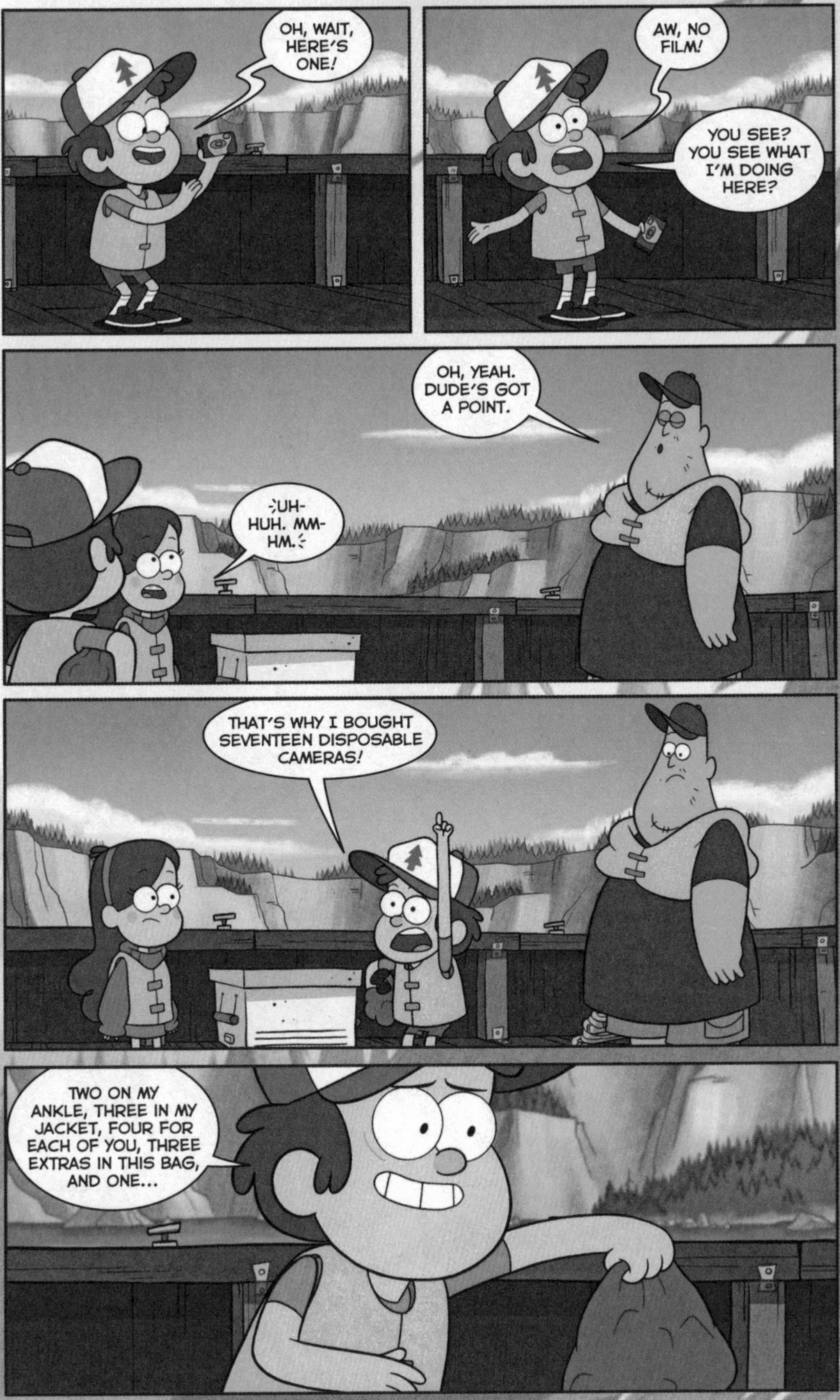
OH, WAIT, HERE'S ONE!
AW, NO FILM!
YOU SEE? YOU SEE WHAT I'M DOING HERE?
OH, YEAH. DUDE'S GOT A POINT.
UH-HUH. MM-HM.
THAT'S WHY I BOUGHT SEVENTEEN DISPOSABLE CAMERAS!
TWO ON MY ANKLE, THREE IN MY JACKET, FOUR FOR EACH OF YOU, THREE EXTRAS IN THIS BAG, AND ONE...

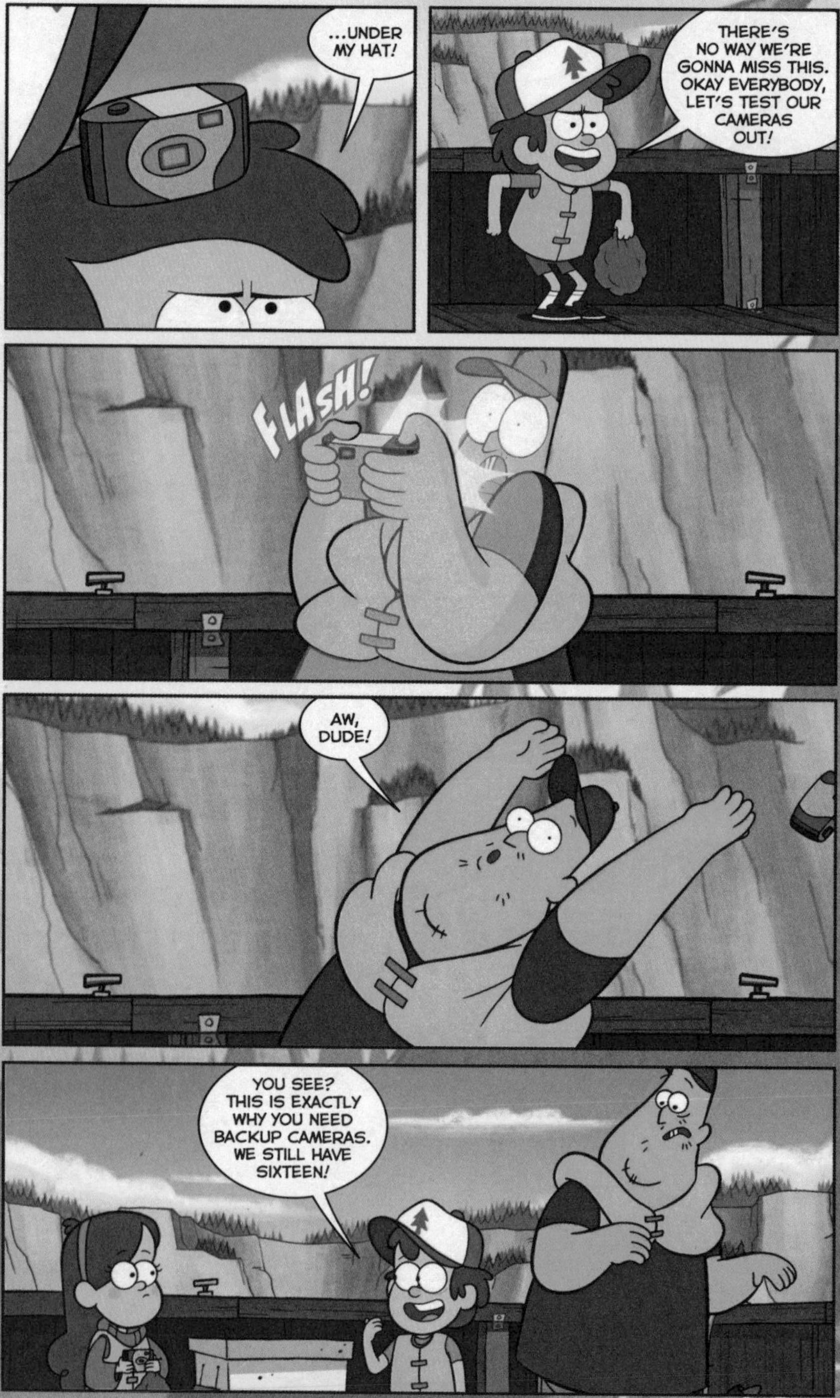
...UNDER MY HAT!
THERE'S NO WAY WE'RE GONNA MISS THIS. OKAY EVERYBODY, LET'S TEST OUR CAMERAS OUT!
FLASH!
AW, DUDE!
YOU SEE? THIS IS EXACTLY WHY YOU NEED BACKUP CAMERAS. WE STILL HAVE SIXTEEN!

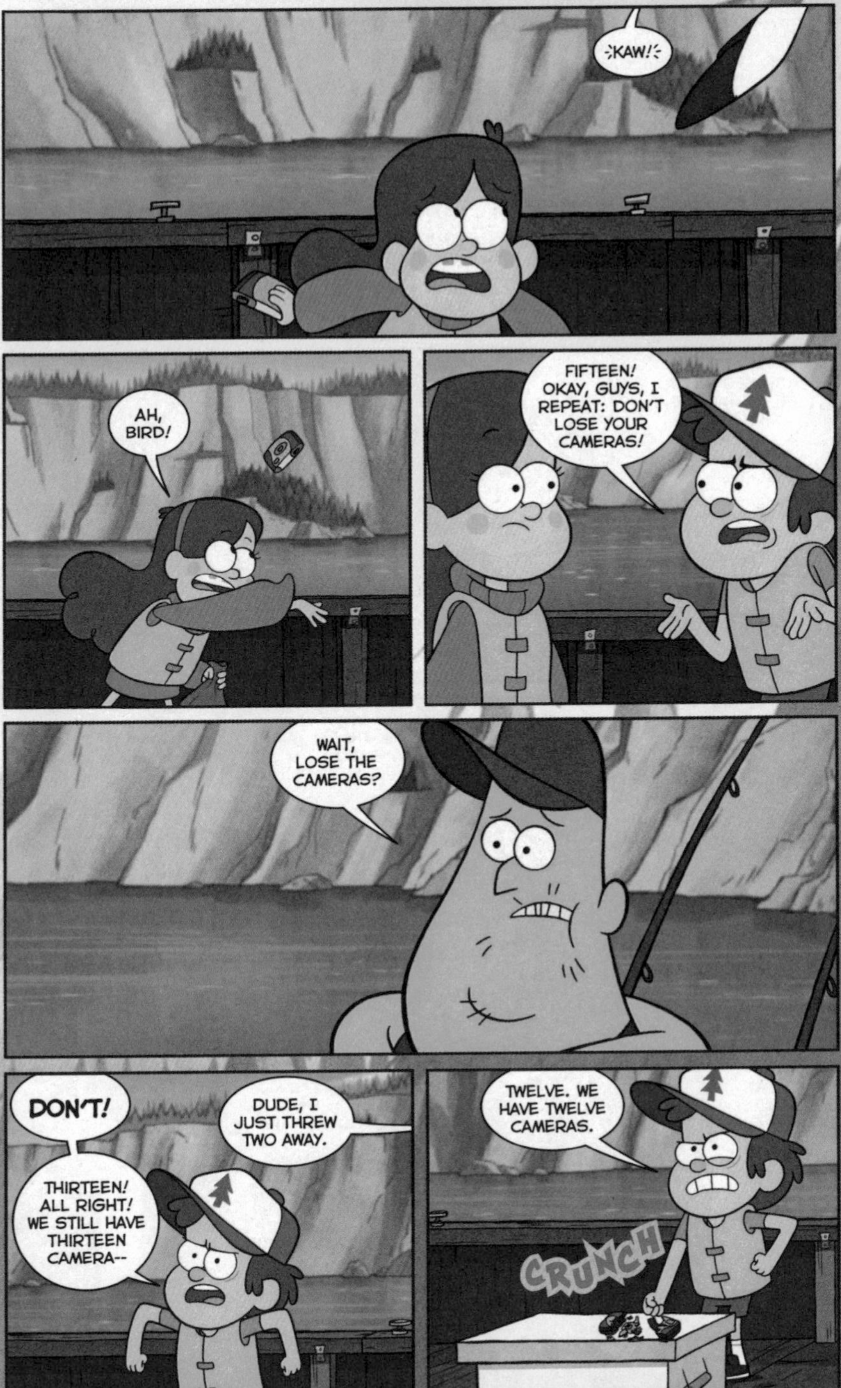
KAW!
AH, BIRD!
FIFTEEN! OKAY, GUYS, I REPEAT: DON'T LOSE YOUR CAMERAS!
WAIT, LOSE THE CAMERAS?
DON'T!
DUDE, I JUST THREW TWO AWAY.
THIRTEEN! ALL RIGHT! WE STILL HAVE THIRTEEN CAMERA--
TWELVE. WE HAVE TWELVE CAMERAS.
CRUNCH

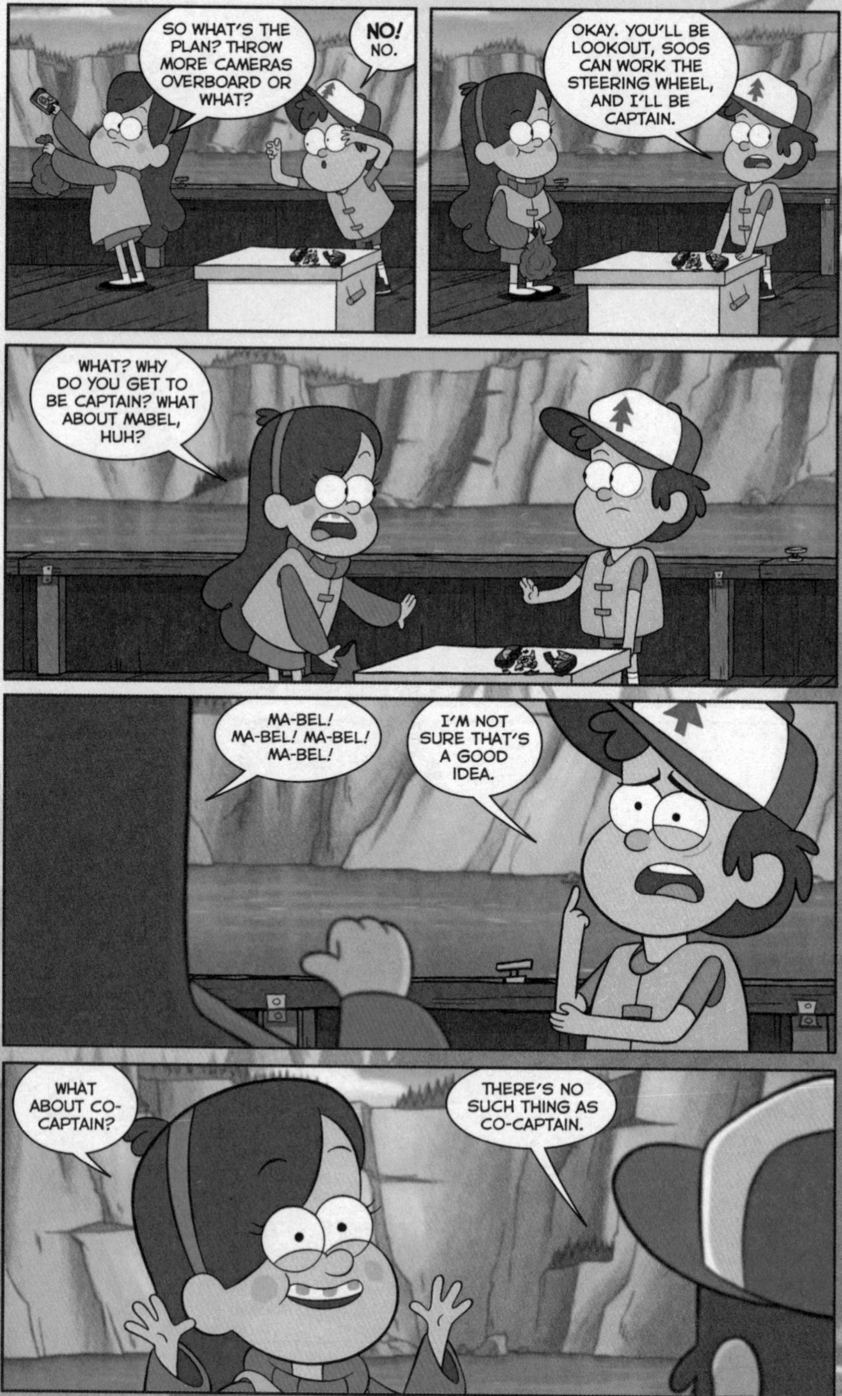
SO WHAT'S THE PLAN? THROW MORE CAMERAS OVERBOARD OR WHAT?
NO! NO.
OKAY. YOU'LL BE LOOKOUT, SOOS CAN WORK THE STEERING WHEEL, AND I'LL BE CAPTAIN.
WHAT? WHY DO YOU GET TO BE CAPTAIN? WHAT ABOUT MABEL, HUH?
MA-BEL! MA-BEL! MA-BEL! MA-BEL!
I'M NOT SURE THAT'S A GOOD IDEA.
WHAT ABOUT CO-CAPTAIN?
THERE'S NO SUCH THING AS CO-CAPTAIN.

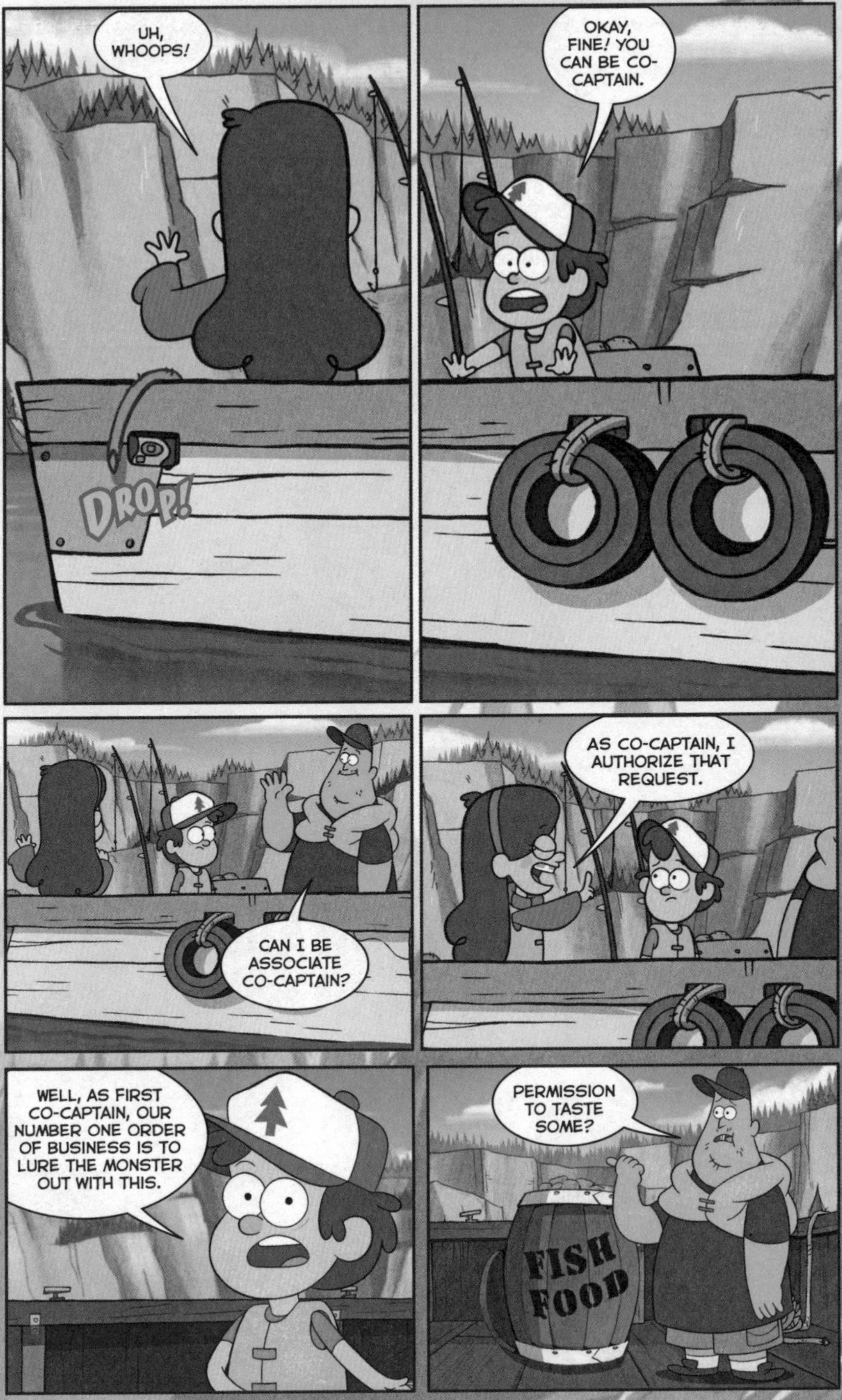
UH, WHOOPS!
DROP!
OKAY, FINE! YOU CAN BE CO-CAPTAIN.
CAN I BE ASSOCIATE CO-CAPTAIN?
AS CO-CAPTAIN, I AUTHORIZE THAT REQUEST.
WELL, AS FIRST CO-CAPTAIN, OUR NUMBER ONE ORDER OF BUSINESS IS TO LURE THE MONSTER OUT WITH THIS.
PERMISSION TO TASTE SOME?
FISH FOOD

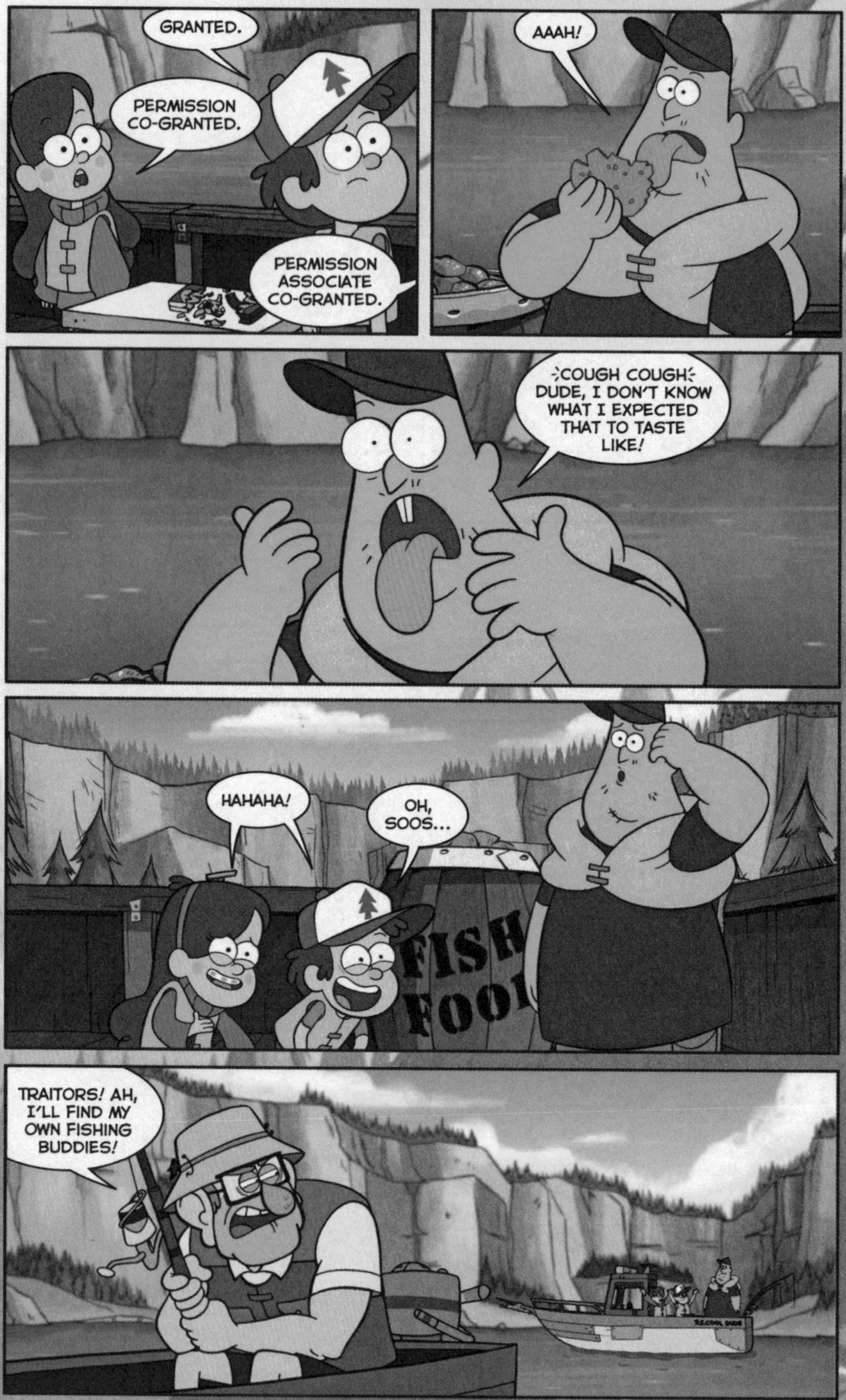
GRANTED.
PERMISSION CO-GRANTED.
PERMISSION ASSOCIATE CO-GRANTED.
AAAH!
COUGH COUGH DUDE, I DON'T KNOW WHAT I EXPECTED THAT TO TASTE LIKE!
HAHAHA!
OH, SOOS...
FISH FOO
TRAITORS! AH, I'LL FIND MY OWN FISHING BUDDIES!

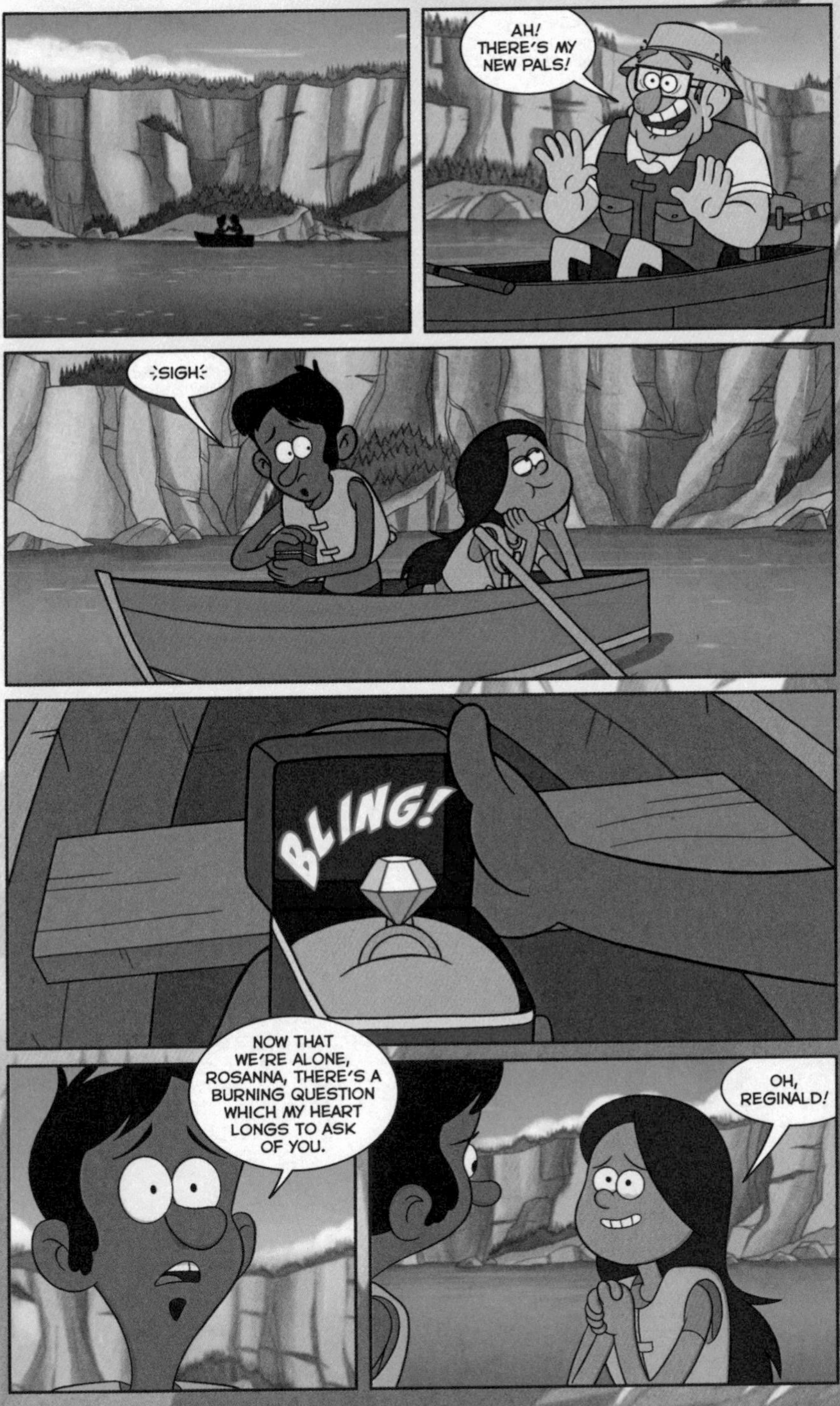
AH! THERE'S MY NEW PALS!
SIGH
BLING!
NOW THAT WE'RE ALONE, ROSANNA, THERE'S A BURNING QUESTION WHICH MY HEART LONGS TO ASK OF YOU.
OH, REGINALD!

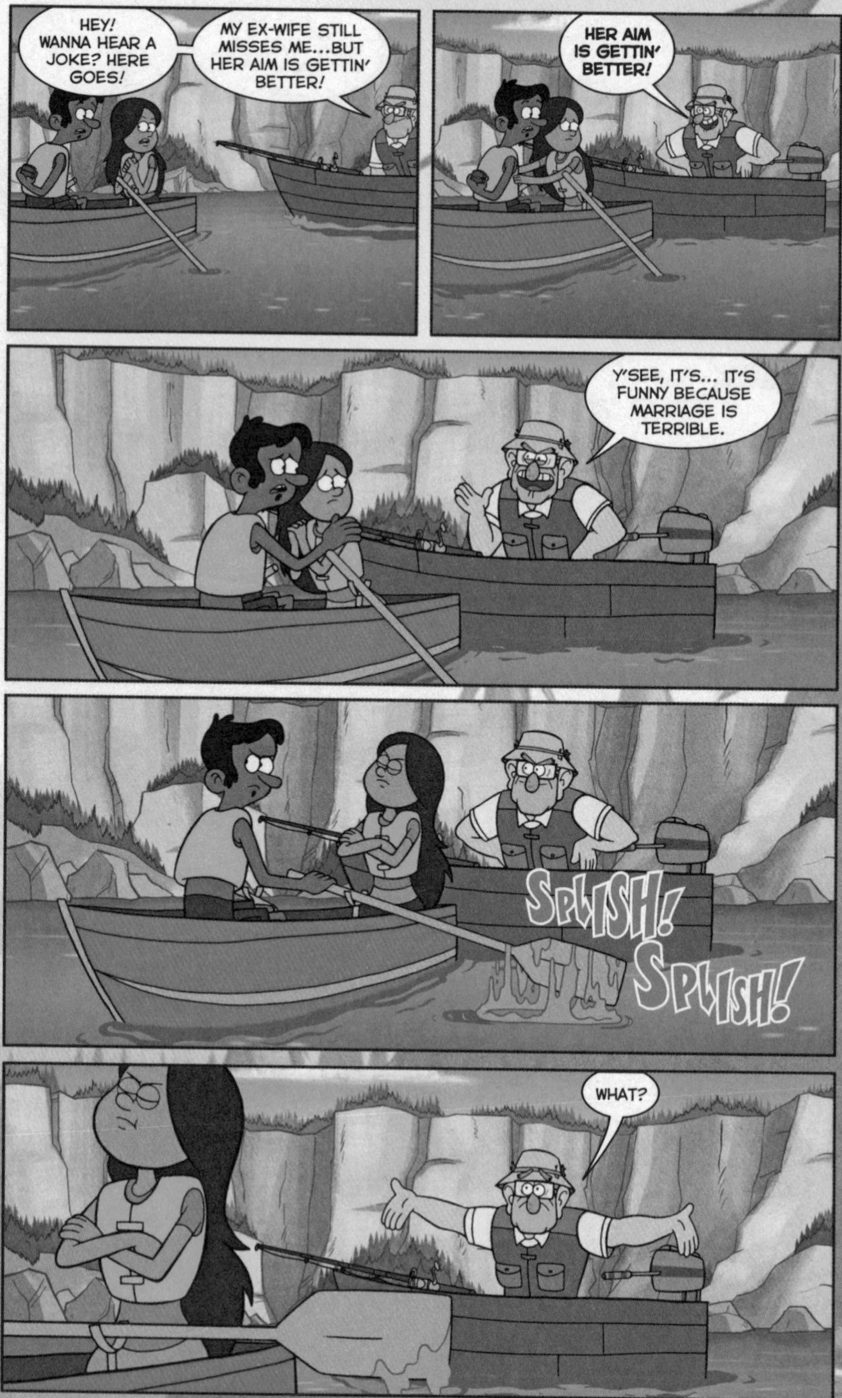
HEY! WANNA HEAR A JOKE? HERE GOES!
MY EX-WIFE STILL MISSES ME...BUT HER AIM IS GETTIN' BETTER!
HER AIM IS GETTIN' BETTER!
Y'SEE, IT'S... IT'S FUNNY BECAUSE MARRIAGE IS TERRIBLE.
SPLISH! SPLISH!
WHAT?

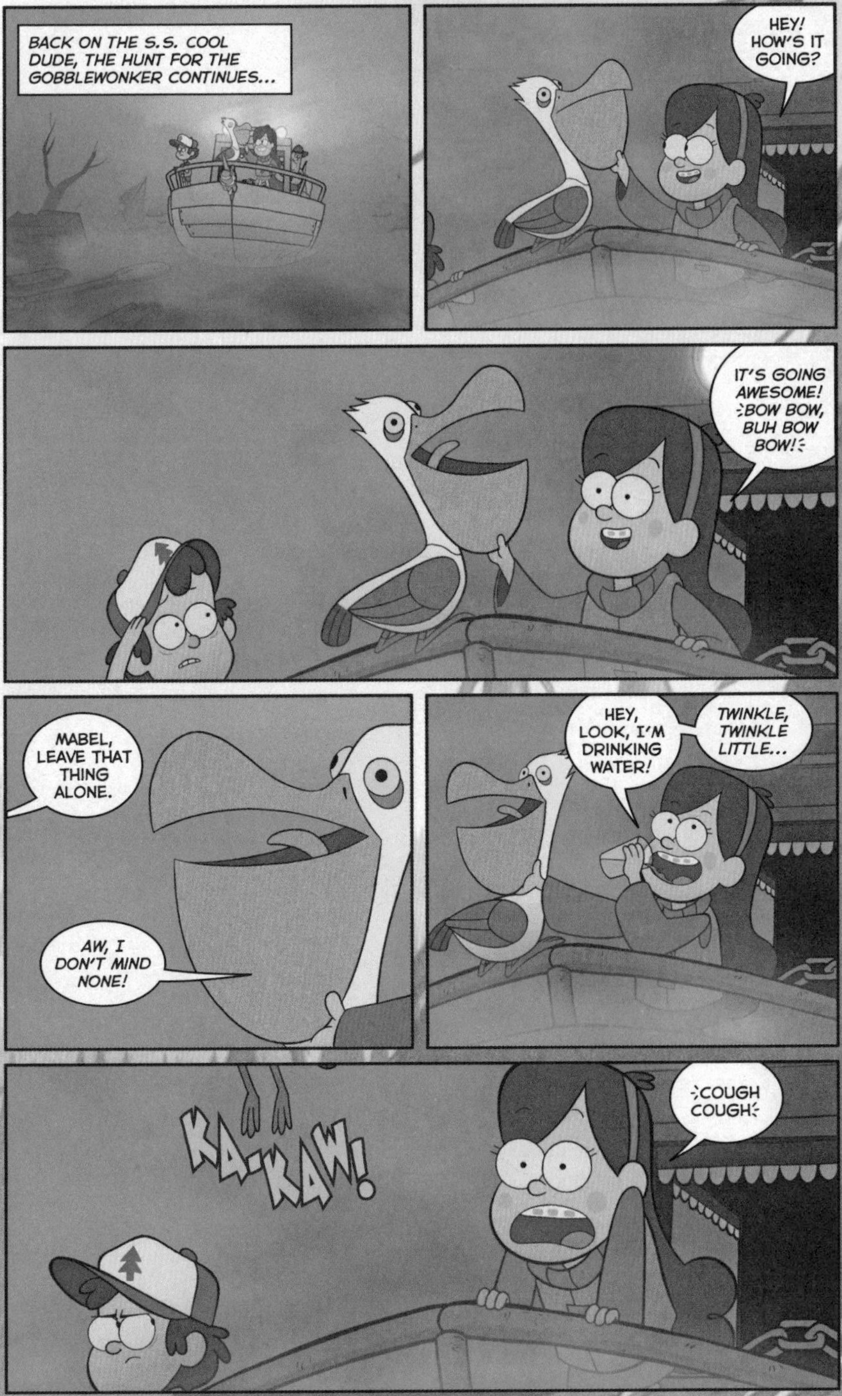
BACK ON THE S.S. COOL DUDE, THE HUNT FOR THE GOBBLEWONKER CONTINUES...
HEY! HOW'S IT GOING?
IT'S GOING AWESOME! BOW BOW, BUH BOW BOW!
MABEL, LEAVE THAT THING ALONE.
AW, I DON'T MIND NONE!
HEY, LOOK, I'M DRINKING WATER!
TWINKLE, TWINKLE LITTLE...
KA-KAW!
COUGH COUGH

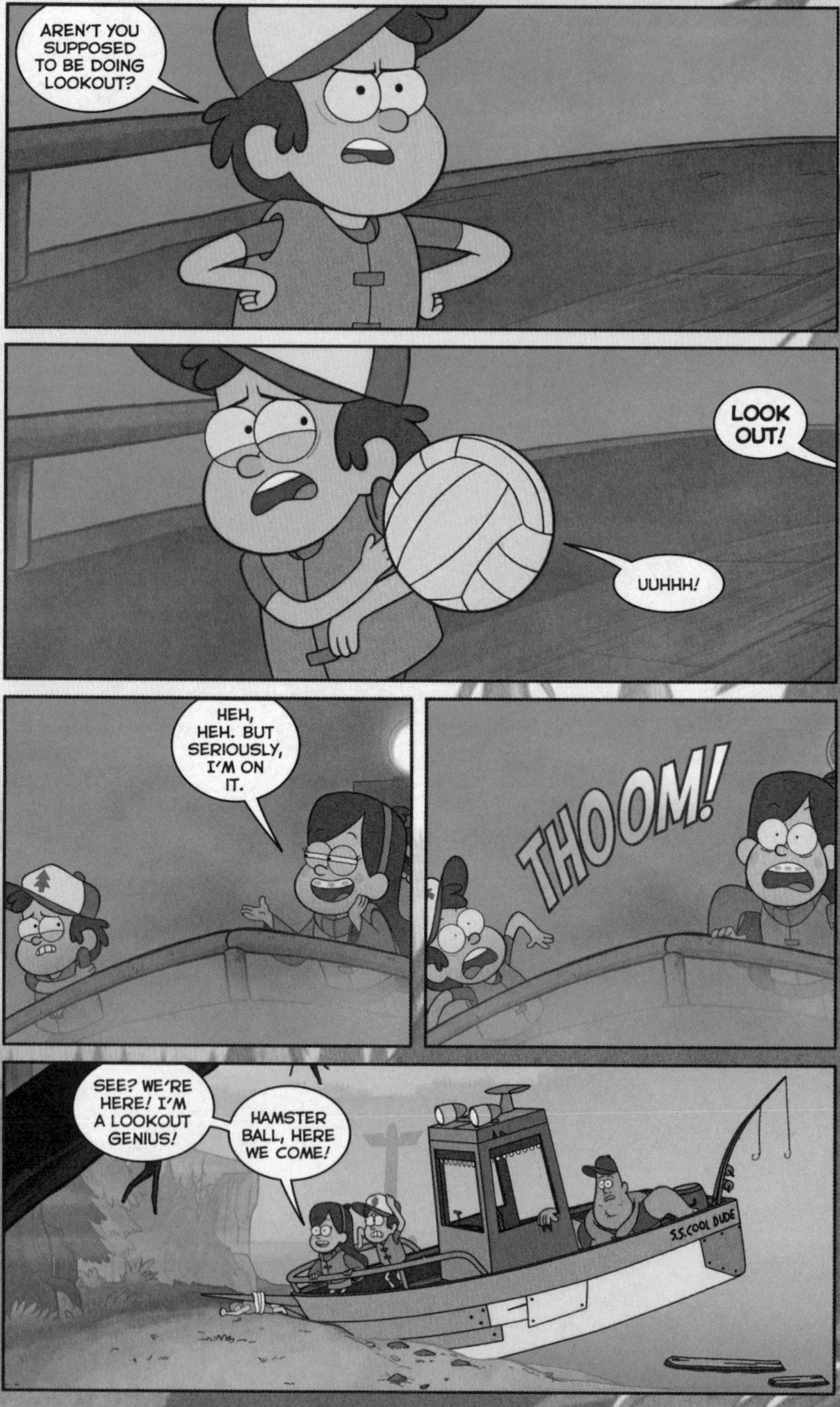
AREN'T YOU SUPPOSED TO BE DOING LOOKOUT?
LOOK OUT!
UUHHH!
HEH, HEH. BUT SERIOUSLY, I'M ON IT.
THOOM!
SEE? WE'RE HERE! I'M A LOOKOUT GENIUS!
HAMSTER BALL, HERE WE COME!
S.S. COOL DUDE

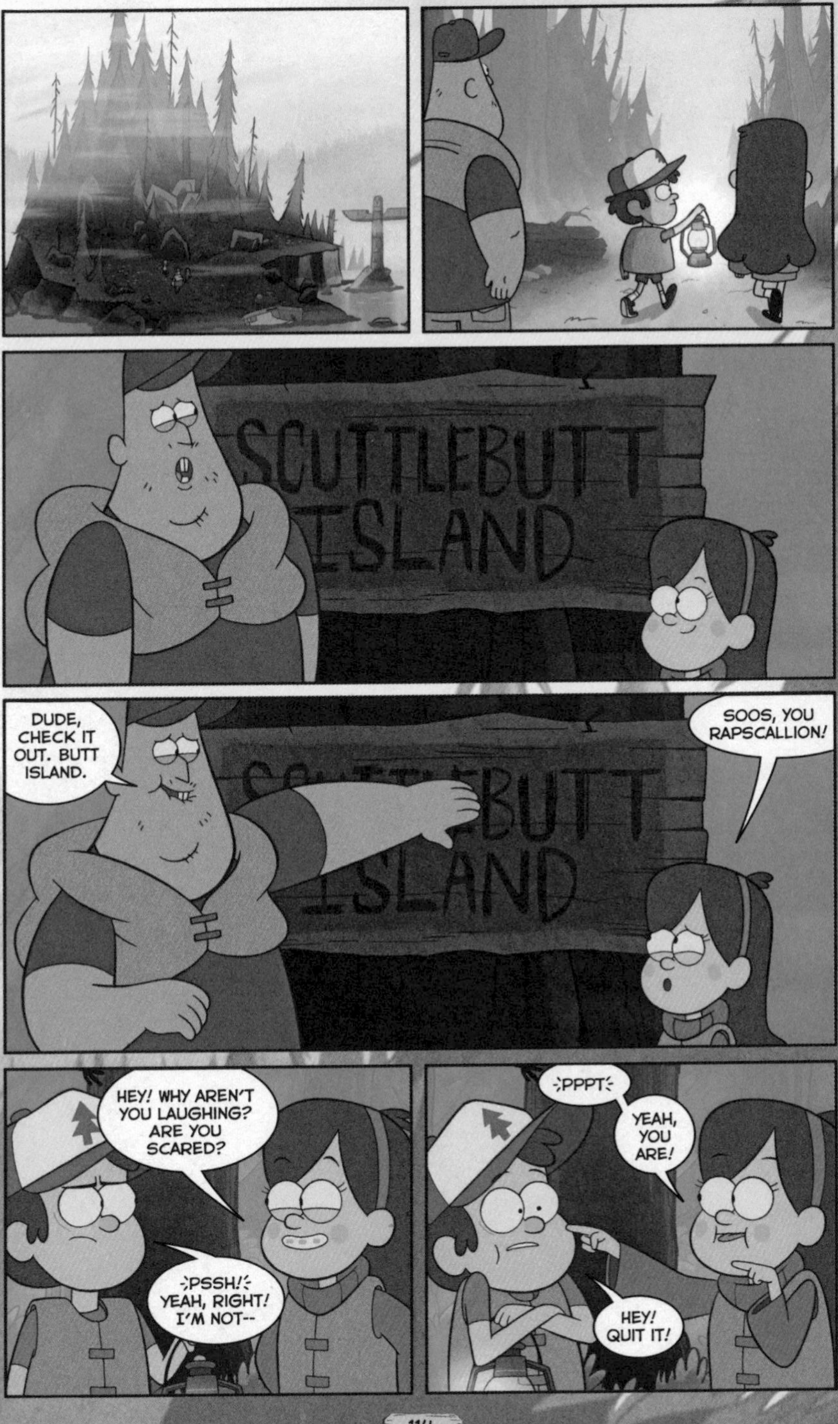
SCUTTLEBUTT ISLAND
DUDE, CHECK IT OUT. BUTT ISLAND.
SOOS, YOU RAPSCALLION!
HEY! WHY AREN'T YOU LAUGHING? ARE YOU SCARED?
PSSH! YEAH, RIGHT! I'M NOT--
PPPT
YEAH, YOU ARE!
HEY! QUIT IT!

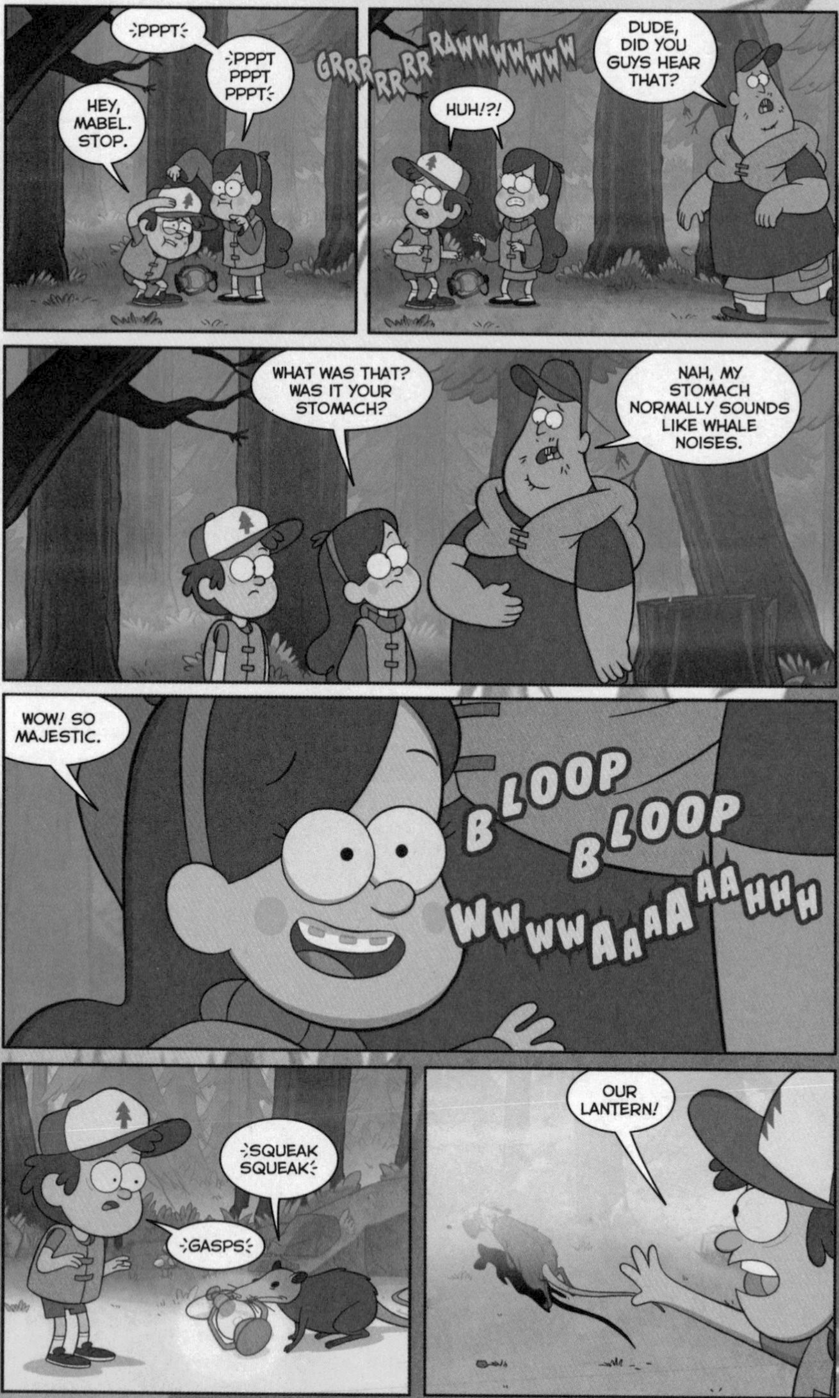
PPPT
PPPT PPPT PPPT
HEY, MABEL. STOP.
GRRRRRRRRAWWWWWWWW
DUDE, DID YOU GUYS HEAR THAT?
HUH!?!
WHAT WAS THAT? WAS IT YOUR STOMACH?
NAH, MY STOMACH NORMALLY SOUNDS LIKE WHALE NOISES.
WOW! SO MAJESTIC.
BLOOP BLOOP
WWWWWAAAAAAHHHH
SQUEAK SQUEAK
GASPS
OUR LANTERN!

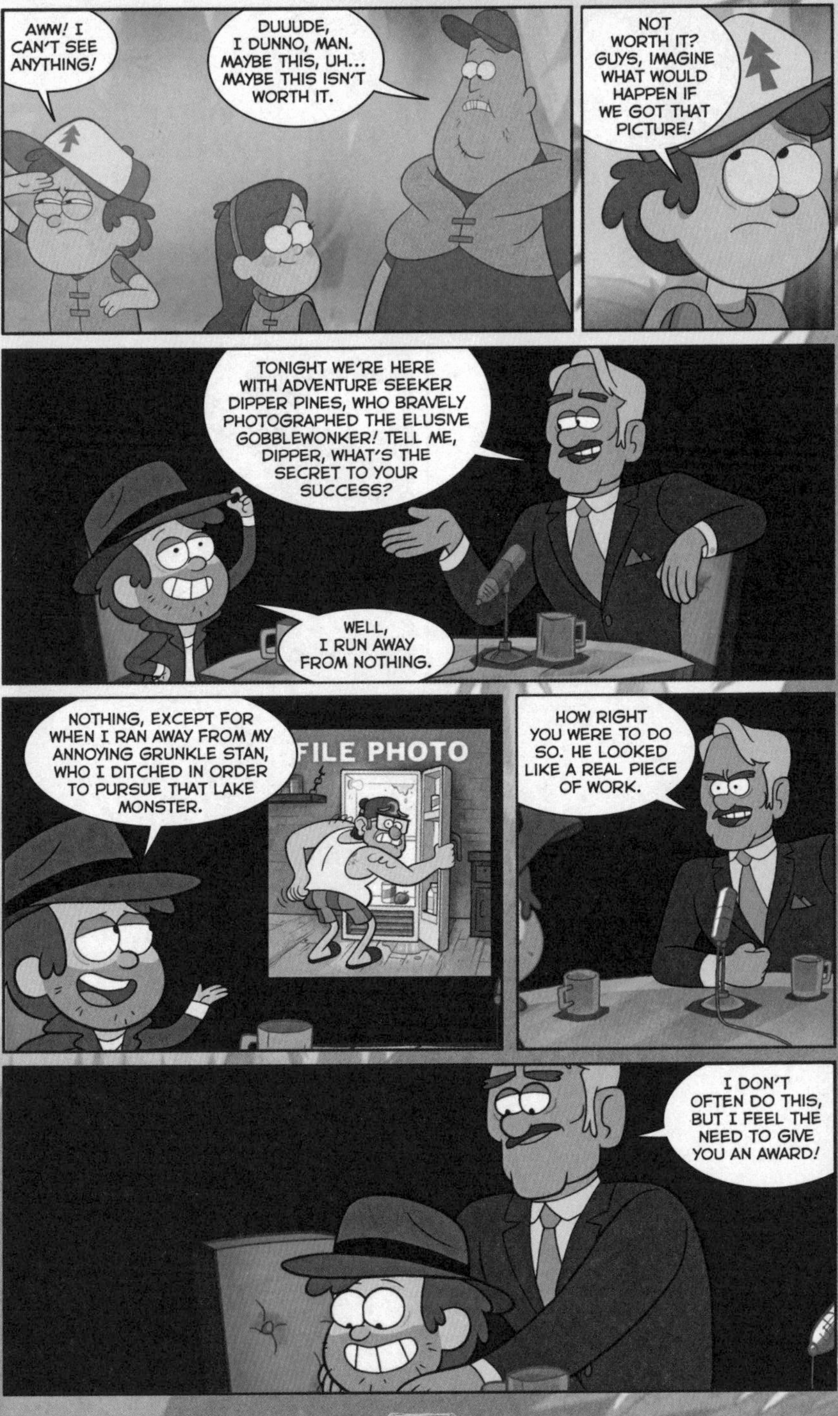
AWW! I CAN'T SEE ANYTHING!
DUUUDE, I DUNNO, MAN. MAYBE THIS, UH... MAYBE THIS ISN'T WORTH IT.
NOT WORTH IT? GUYS, IMAGINE WHAT WOULD HAPPEN IF WE GOT THAT PICTURE!
TONIGHT WE'RE HERE WITH ADVENTURE SEEKER DIPPER PINES, WHO BRAVELY PHOTOGRAPHED THE ELUSIVE GOBBLEWONKER! TELL ME, DIPPER, WHAT'S THE SECRET TO YOUR SUCCESS?
WELL, I RUN AWAY FROM NOTHING.
NOTHING, EXCEPT FOR WHEN I RAN AWAY FROM MY ANNOYING GRUNKLE STAN, WHO I DITCHED IN ORDER TO PURSUE THAT LAKE MONSTER.
FILE PHOTO
HOW RIGHT YOU WERE TO DO SO. HE LOOKED LIKE A REAL PIECE OF WORK.
I DON'T OFTEN DO THIS, BUT I FEEL THE NEED TO GIVE YOU AN AWARD!

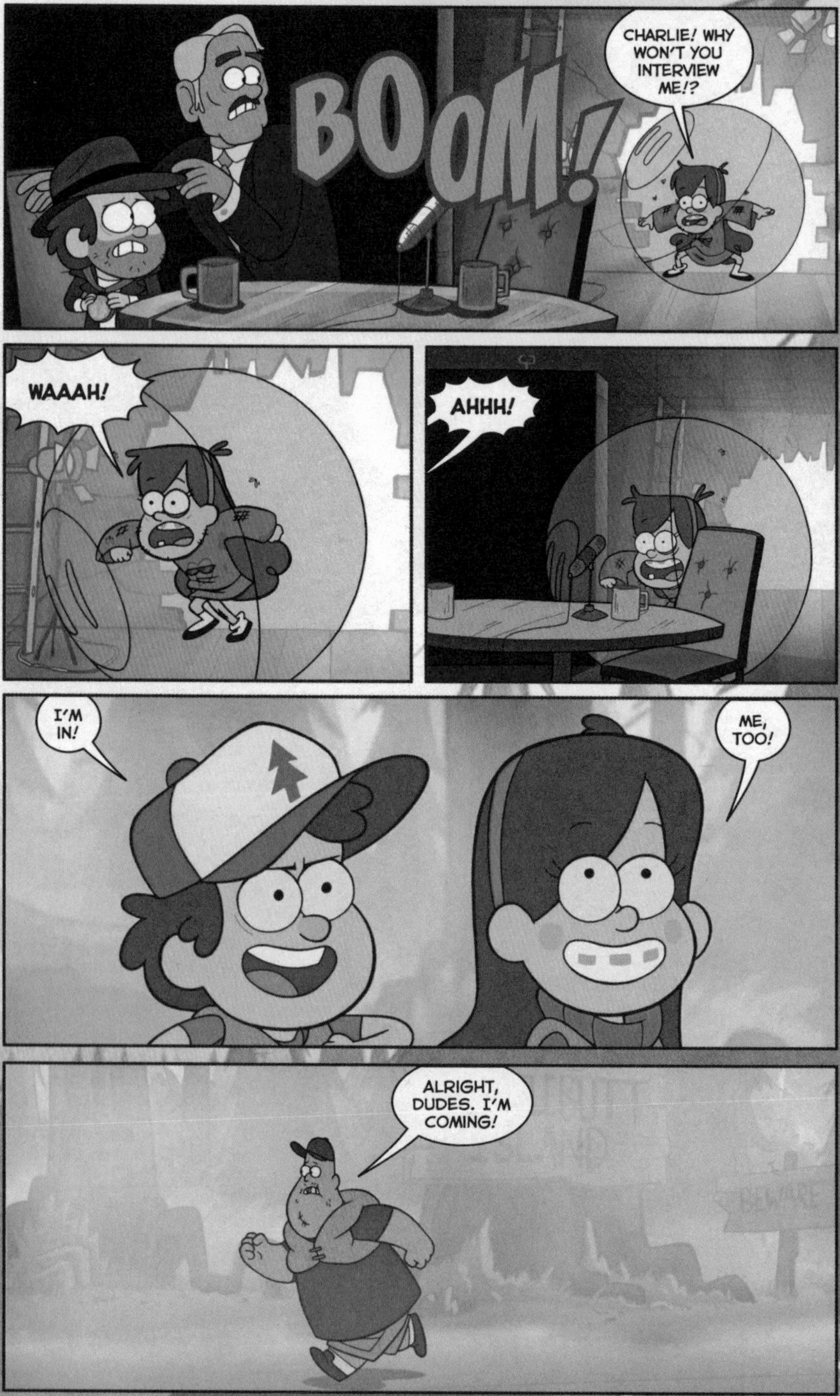
BOOM!
CHARLIE! WHY WON'T YOU INTERVIEW ME!?
WAAAH!
AHHH!
I'M IN!
ME, TOO!
ALRIGHT, DUDES. I'M COMING!

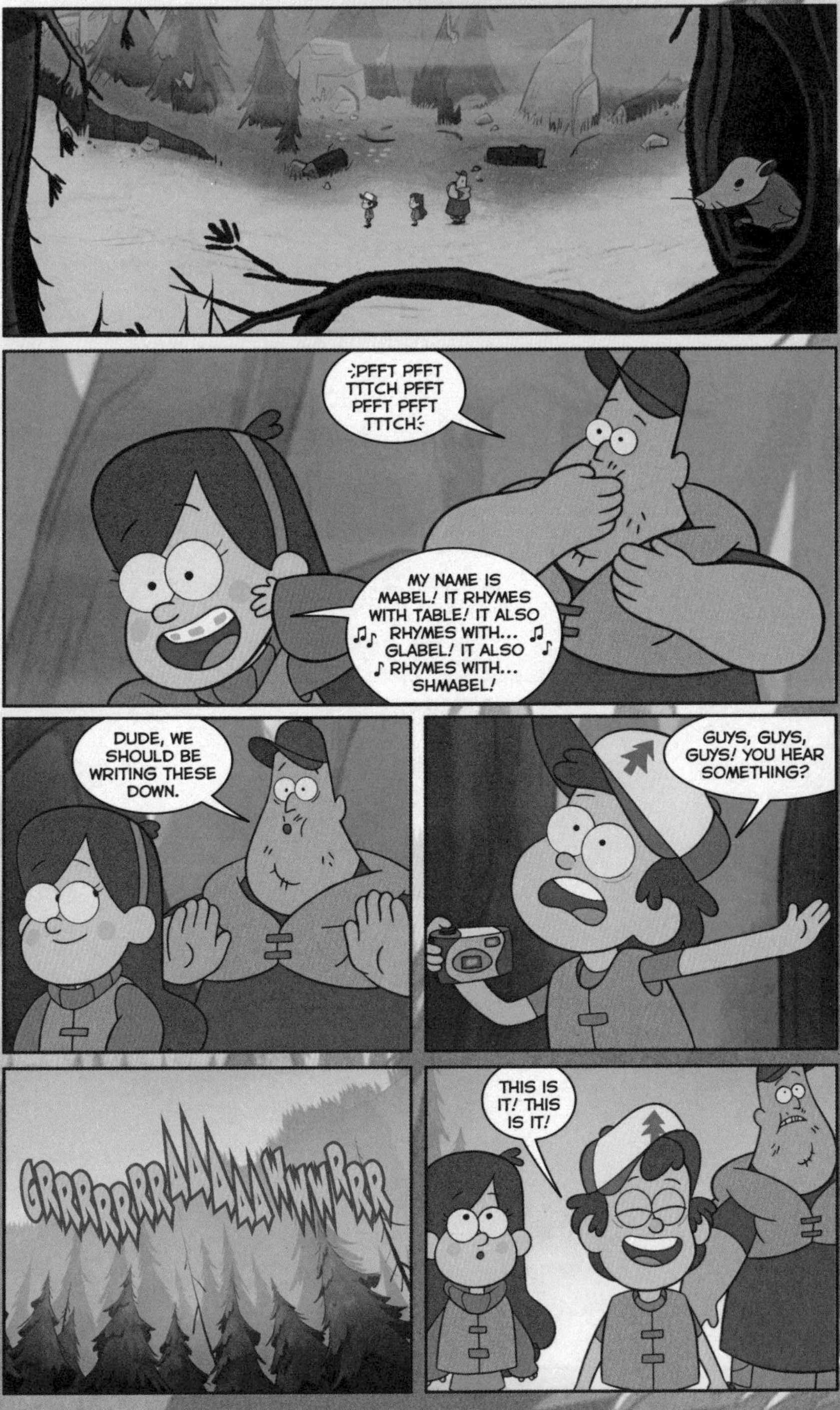
PFFT PFFT TTTCH PFFT PFFT PFFT TTTCH
MY NAME IS MABEL! IT RHYMES WITH TABLE! IT ALSO RHYMES WITH... GLABEL! IT ALSO RHYMES WITH... SHMABEL!
DUDE, WE SHOULD BE WRITING THESE DOWN.
GUYS, GUYS, GUYS! YOU HEAR SOMETHING?
GRRRRRRRAAAAAAHWWWRRR
THIS IS IT! THIS IS IT!

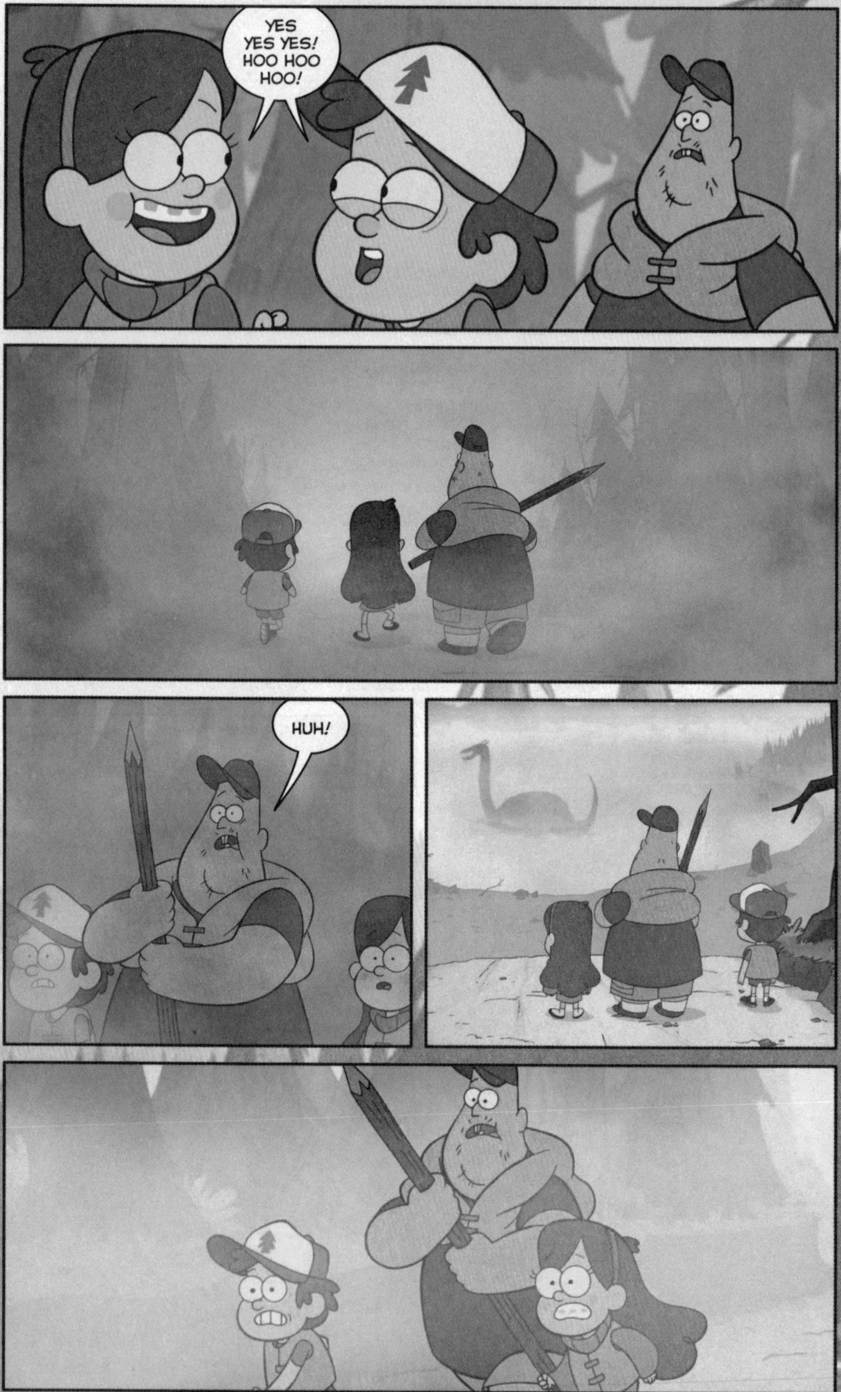
YES YES YES! HOO HOO HOO!
HUH!

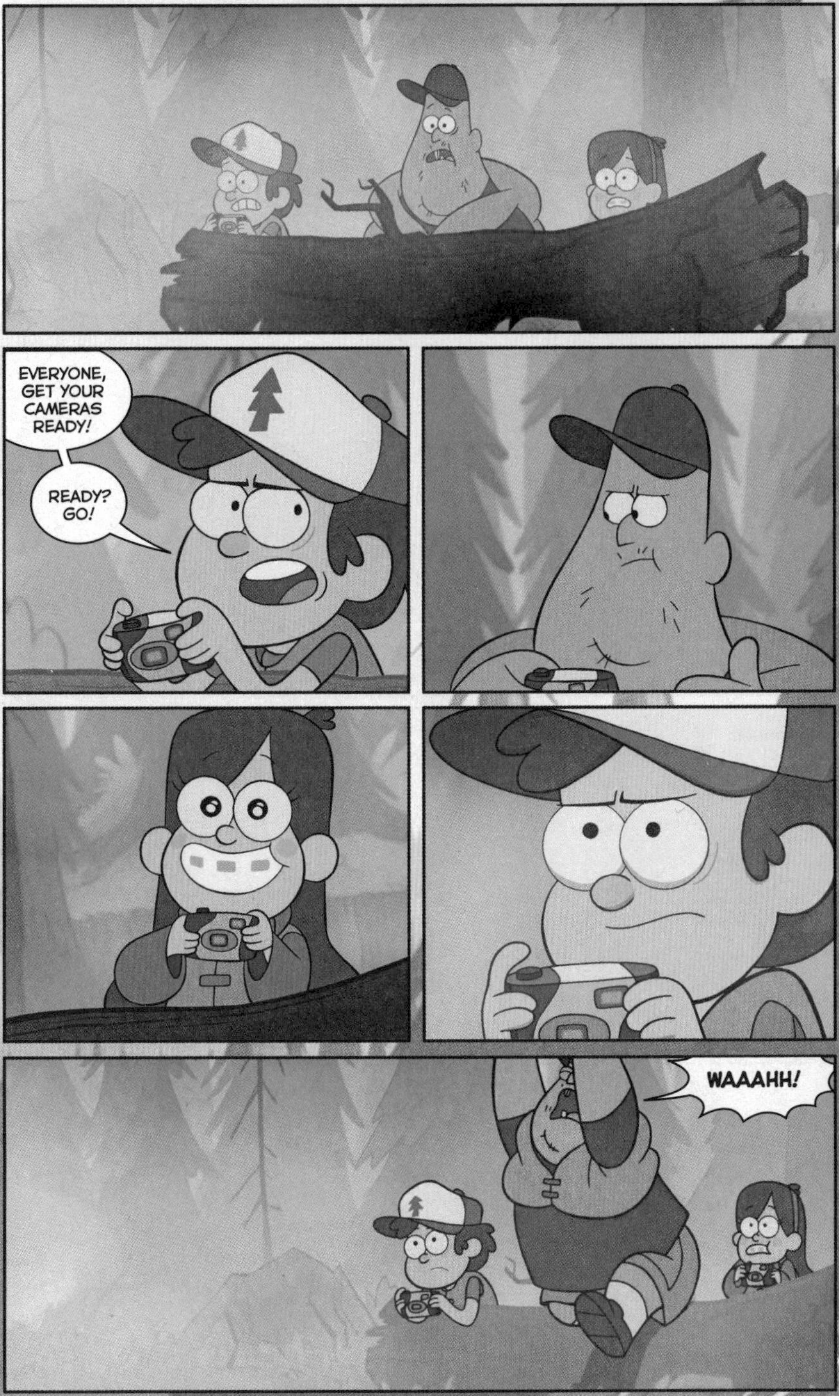
EVERYONE, GET YOUR CAMERAS READY!
READY? GO!
WAAAHH!

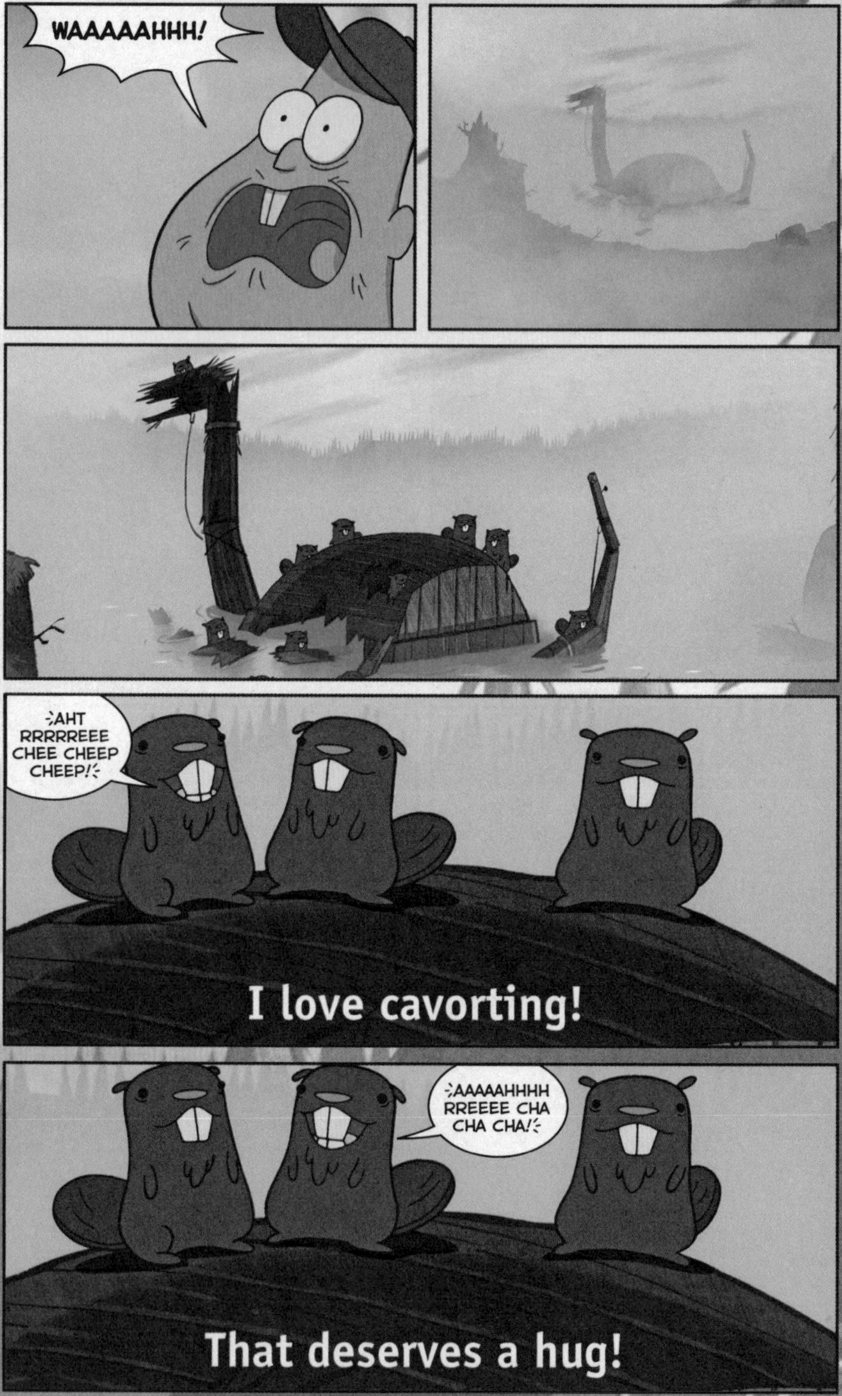
WAAAAAHHH!
-AHT RRRRREEE CHEE CHEEP CHEEP!-
I love cavorting!
-AAAAAHHHH RREEEE CHA CHA CHA!-
That deserves a hug!

BUT... BUT WHAT WAS THAT NOISE, THEN? I HEARD A MONSTER NOISE!

GRRRRR RRRRRR RAAAAAA AWR

GGGRRRRRR RRAAAAAAA AAAWWWR.

SWEET! BEAVER WITH A CHAINSAW.

CLICK!

MAYBE THAT OLD GUY WAS CRAZY AFTER ALL.

-SIGH-

HE **DID** USE THE WORD "SCRABDOODLE."

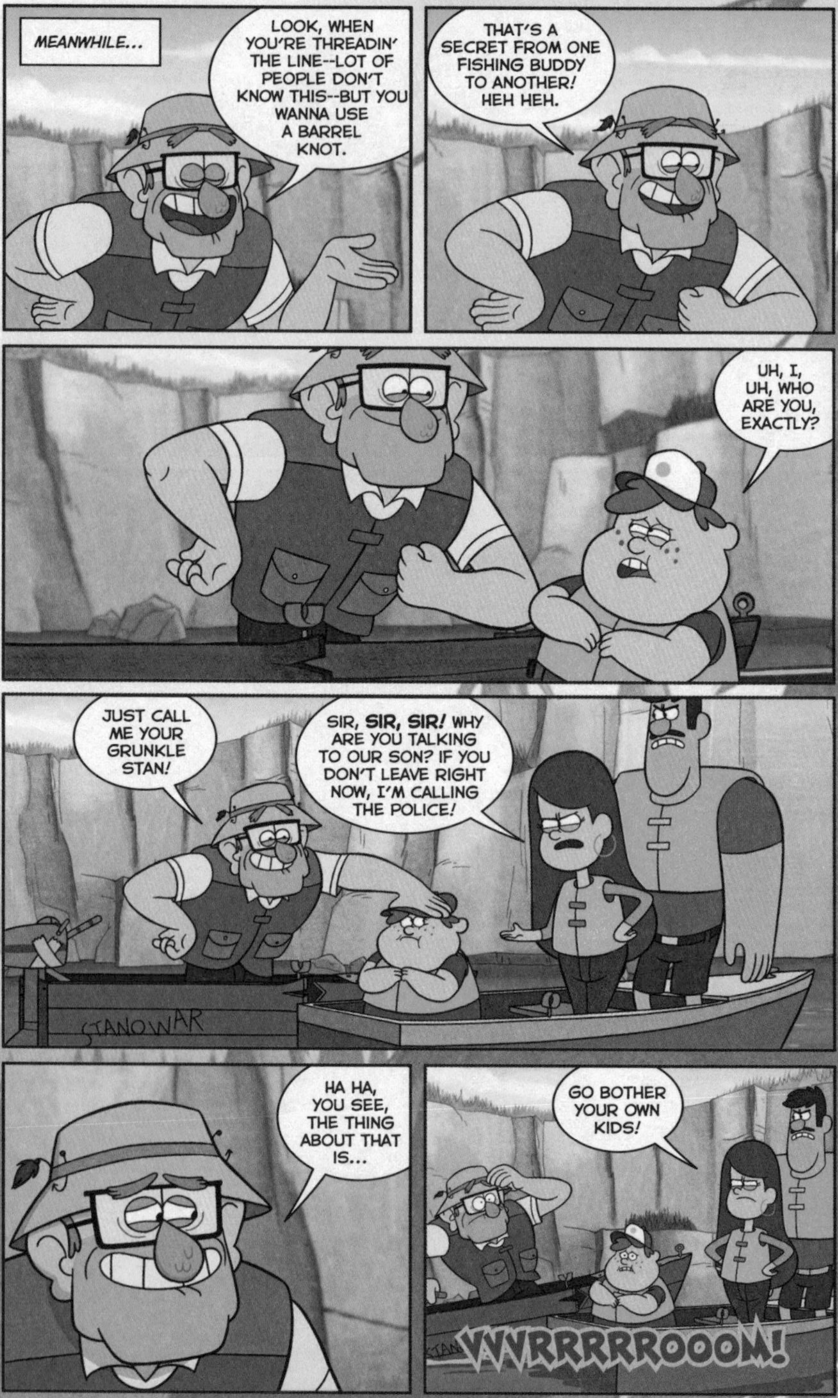
MEANWHILE...
LOOK, WHEN YOU'RE THREADIN' THE LINE--LOT OF PEOPLE DON'T KNOW THIS--BUT YOU WANNA USE A BARREL KNOT.
THAT'S A SECRET FROM ONE FISHING BUDDY TO ANOTHER! HEH HEH.
UH, I, UH, WHO ARE YOU, EXACTLY?
JUST CALL ME YOUR GRUNKLE STAN!
SIR, SIR, SIR! WHY ARE YOU TALKING TO OUR SON? IF YOU DON'T LEAVE RIGHT NOW, I'M CALLING THE POLICE!
STANOWAR
HA HA, YOU SEE, THE THING ABOUT THAT IS...
GO BOTHER YOUR OWN KIDS!
VVVRRRRRROOOM!

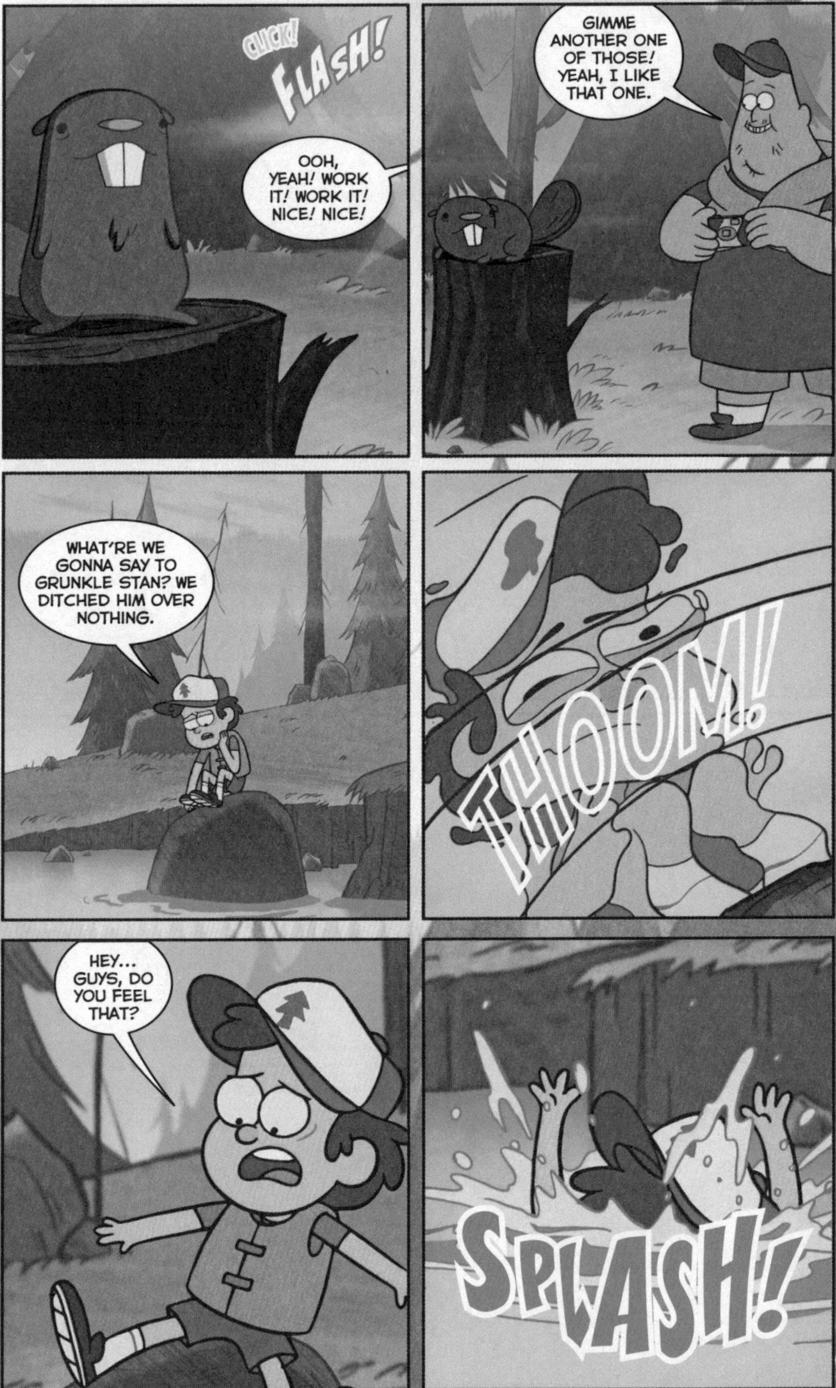
CLICK!
FLASH!
OOH, YEAH! WORK IT! WORK IT! NICE! NICE!
GIMME ANOTHER ONE OF THOSE! YEAH, I LIKE THAT ONE.
WHAT'RE WE GONNA SAY TO GRUNKLE STAN? WE DITCHED HIM OVER NOTHING.
THOOM!
HEY... GUYS, DO YOU FEEL THAT?
SPLASH!

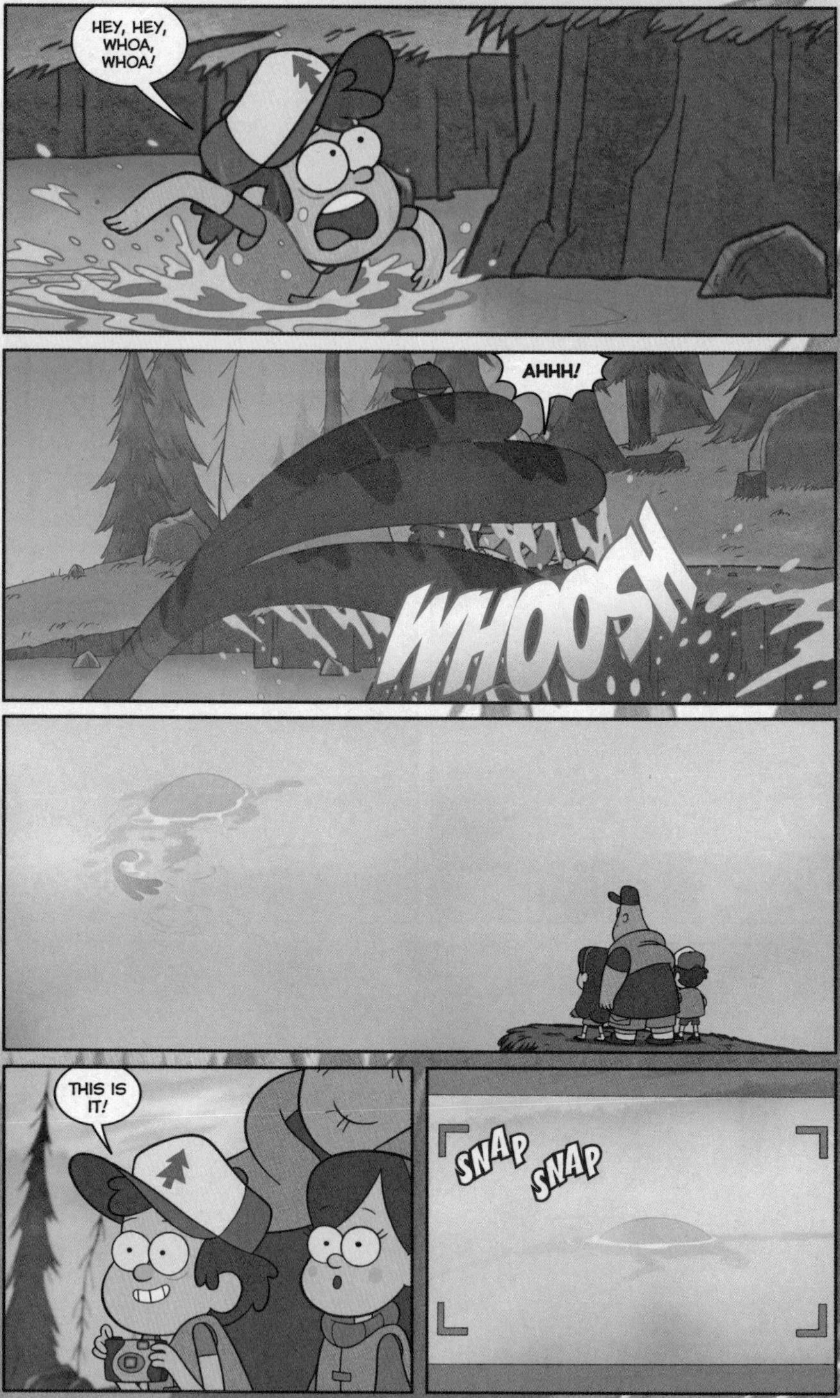
HEY, HEY, WHOA, WHOA!
AHHH!
WHOOSH
THIS IS IT!
SNAP
SNAP

COME ON! THIS IS OUR CHANCE!

WHAT'S WRONG WITH YOU GUYS?

DUDE...?

DIPPER...?

IT'S NOT THAT HARD, ALL RIGHT? ALL YOU GOTTA DO IS POINT, AND SHOOT.

LIKE THIS!

RRRRRRAAAAAAAAAAAWWWR!

RUN!

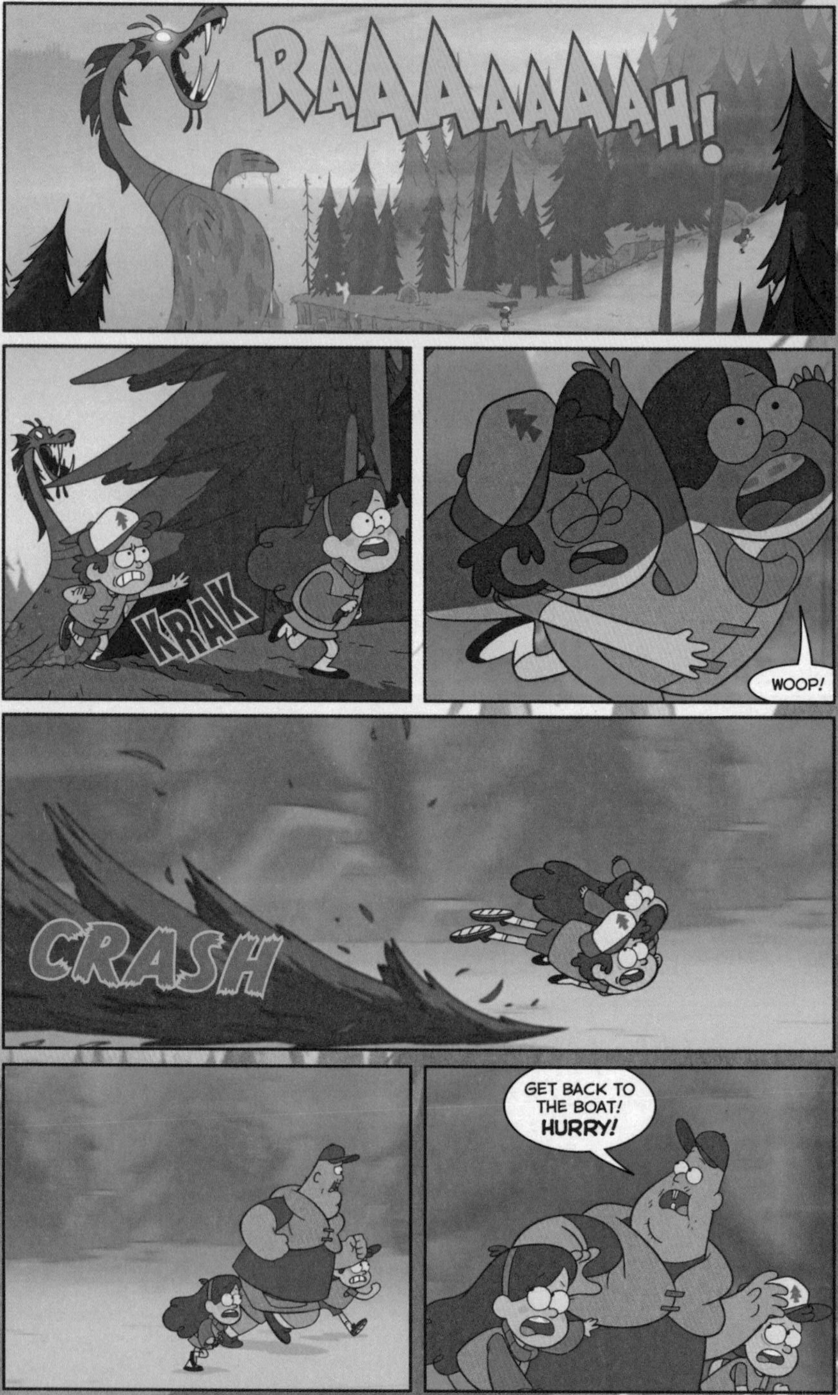
RAAAAAAAAH!
KRAK
WOOP!
CRASH
GET BACK TO THE BOAT! HURRY!

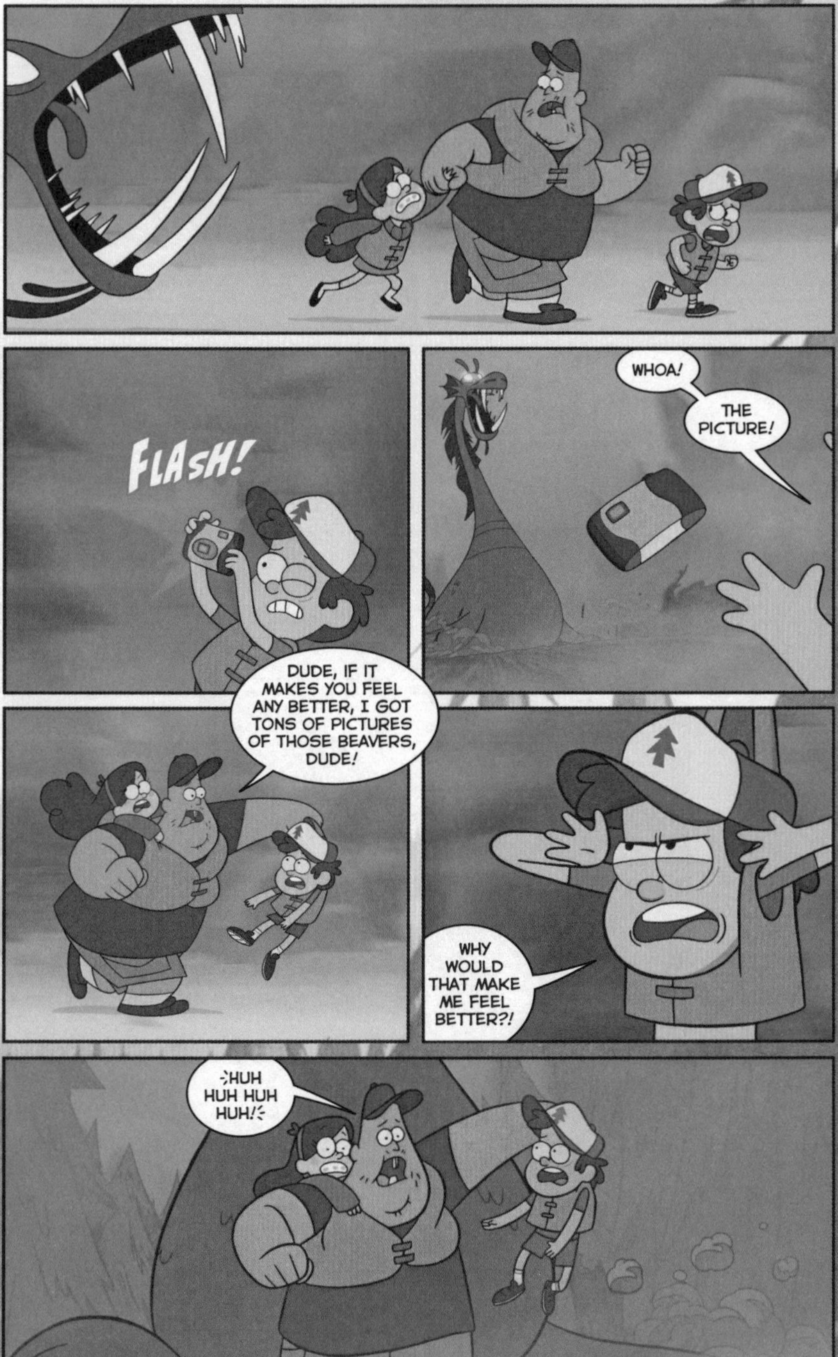
FLASH!
WHOA!
THE PICTURE!
DUDE, IF IT MAKES YOU FEEL ANY BETTER, I GOT TONS OF PICTURES OF THOSE BEAVERS, DUDE!
WHY WOULD THAT MAKE ME FEEL BETTER?!
HUH HUH HUH HUH!

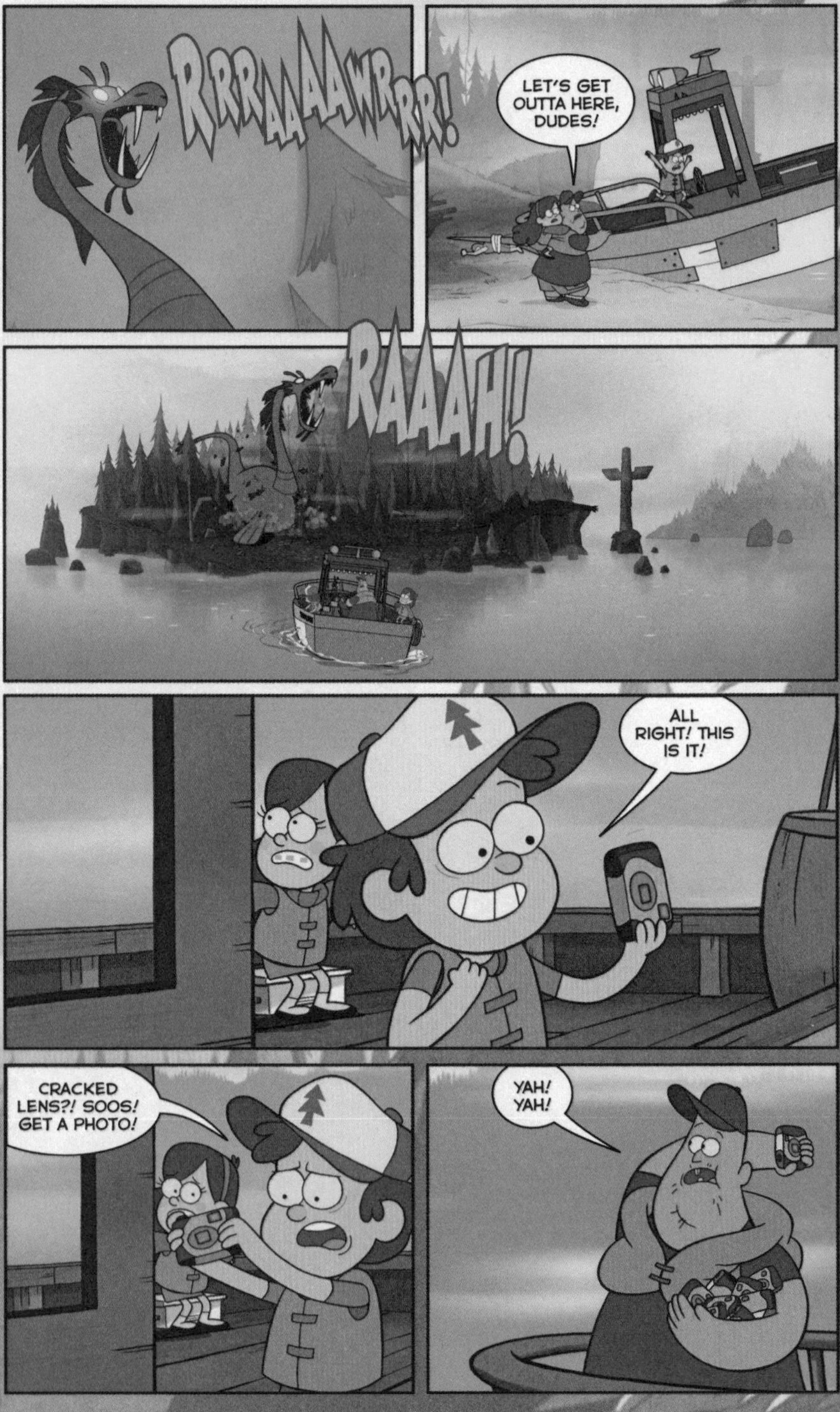
RRRAAAAWRRRR!
LET'S GET OUTTA HERE, DUDES!
RAAAH!
ALL RIGHT! THIS IS IT!
CRACKED LENS?! SOOS! GET A PHOTO!
YAH! YAH!

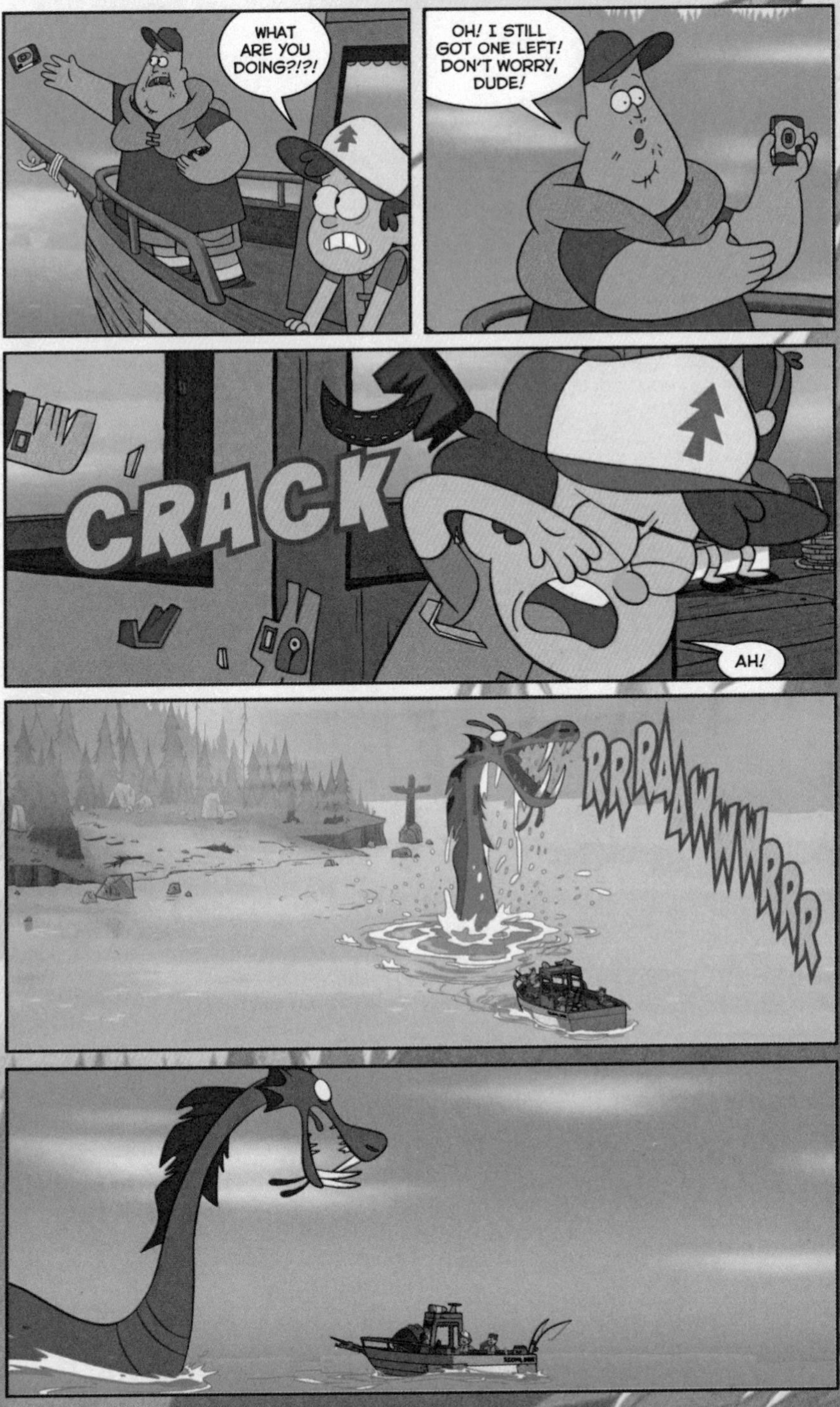
WHAT ARE YOU DOING?!?!
OH! I STILL GOT ONE LEFT! DON'T WORRY, DUDE!
CRACK
AH!
RRRAAWWWRRR

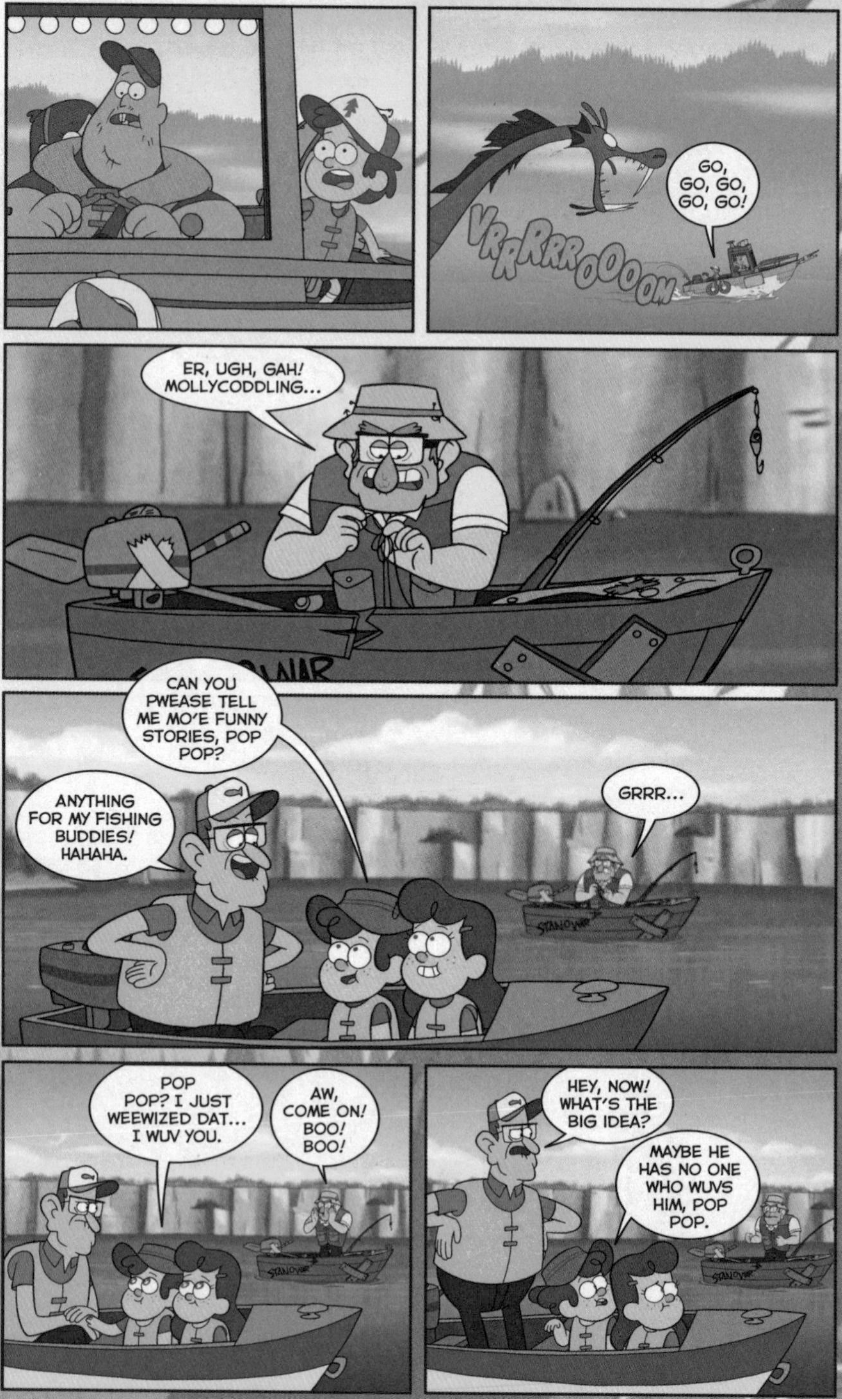
GO, GO, GO, GO, GO!
VRRRRROOOOOM
ER, UGH, GAH! MOLLYCODDLING...
CAN YOU PWEASE TELL ME MO'E FUNNY STORIES, POP POP?
ANYTHING FOR MY FISHING BUDDIES! HAHAHA.
GRRR...
POP POP? I JUST WEEWIZED DAT... I WUV YOU.
AW, COME ON! BOO! BOO!
HEY, NOW! WHAT'S THE BIG IDEA?
MAYBE HE HAS NO ONE WHO WUVS HIM, POP POP.

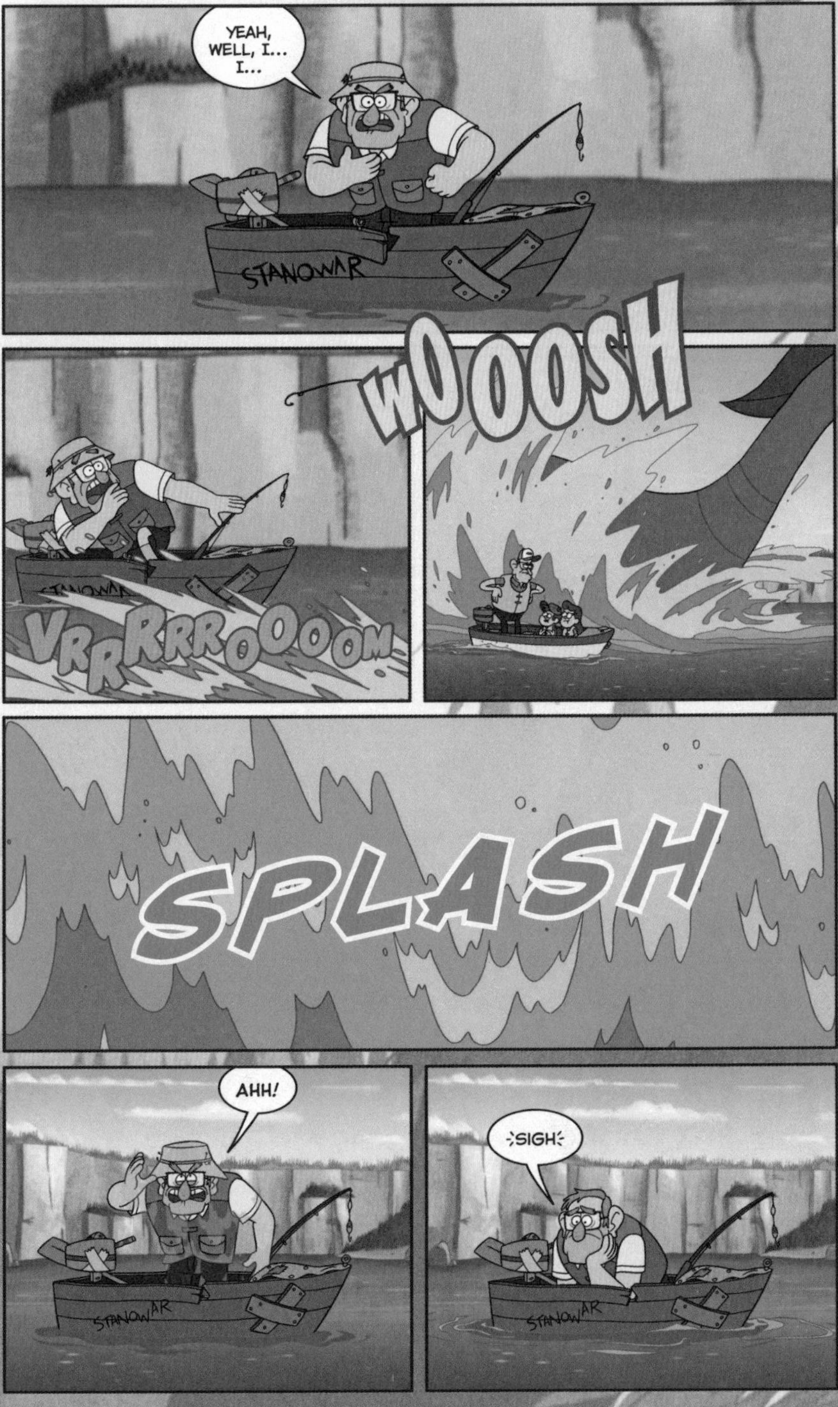
YEAH, WELL, I... I...
STANOWAR
wOOOSH
VRRRRROOOOOM
SPLASH
AHH!
STANOWAR
-SIGH-
STANOWAR

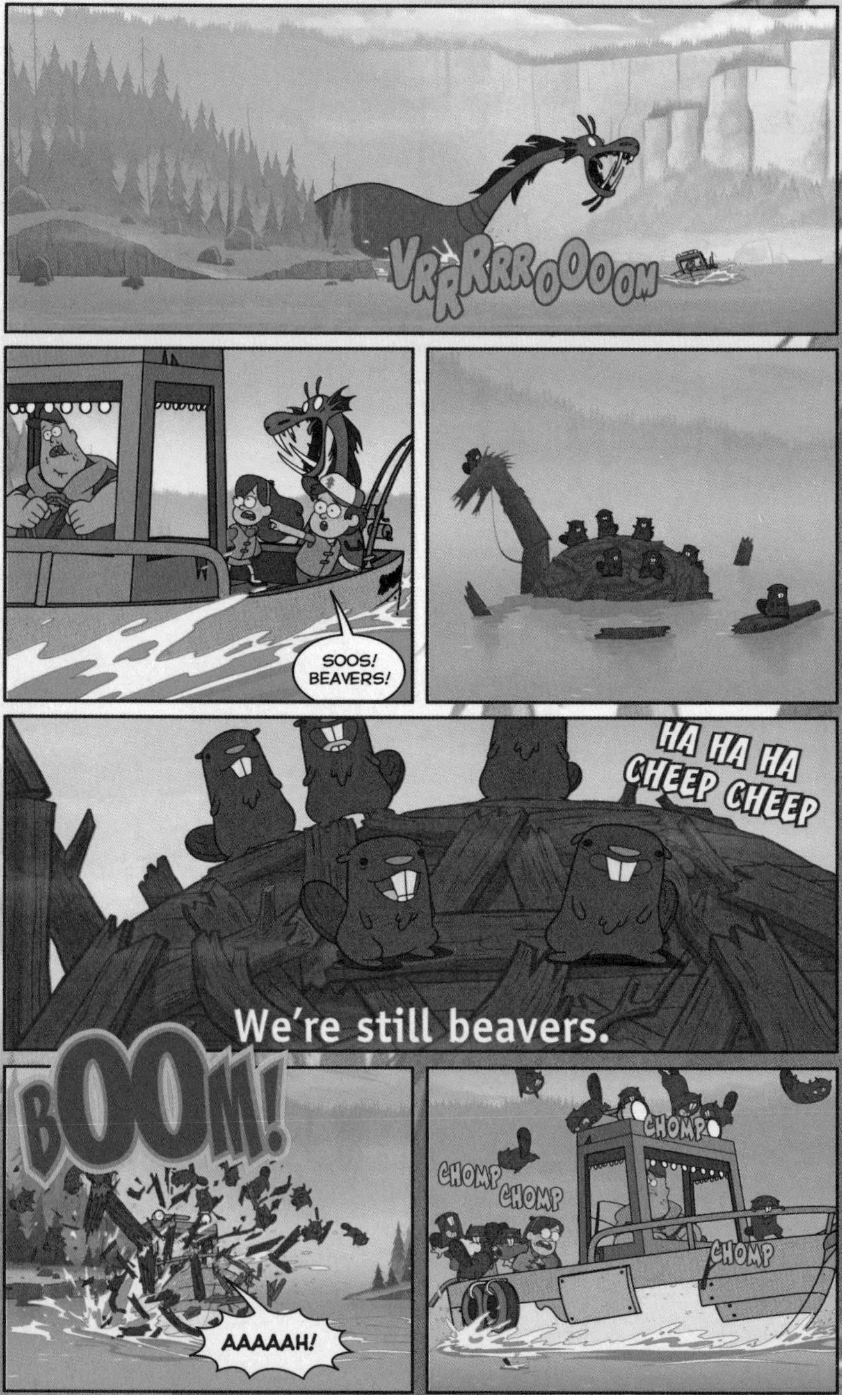
VRRRRROOOOOM
SOOS! BEAVERS!
HA HA HA
CHEEP CHEEP
We're still beavers.
BOOM!
AAAAAH!
CHOMP
CHOMP
CHOMP
CHOMP

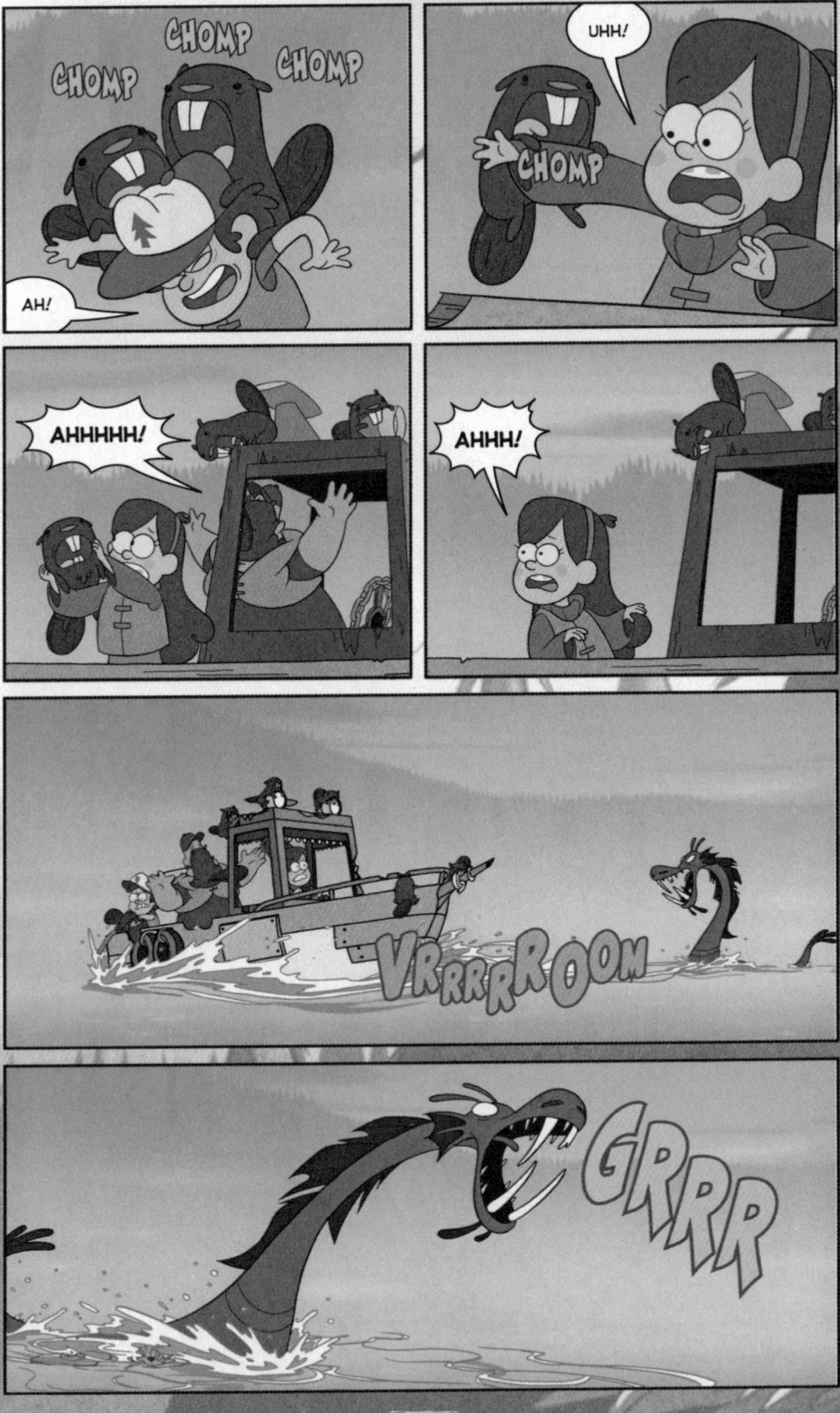
CHOMP
CHOMP
CHOMP
AH!
UHH!
CHOMP
AHHHHH!
AHHH!
VRRRRROOM
GRRRR

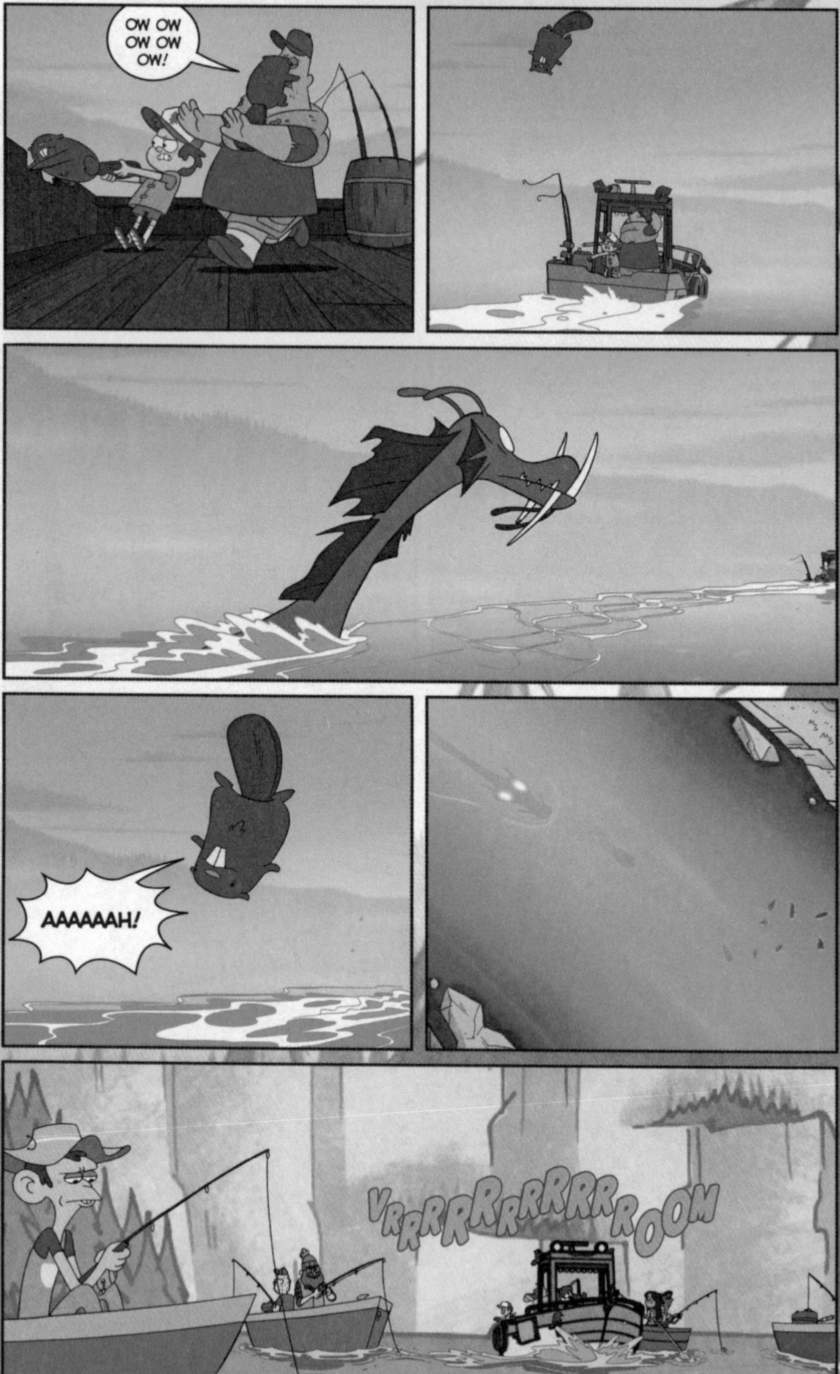
OW OW
OW OW
OW!
AAAAAAH!
VRRRRRRRRRRROOM

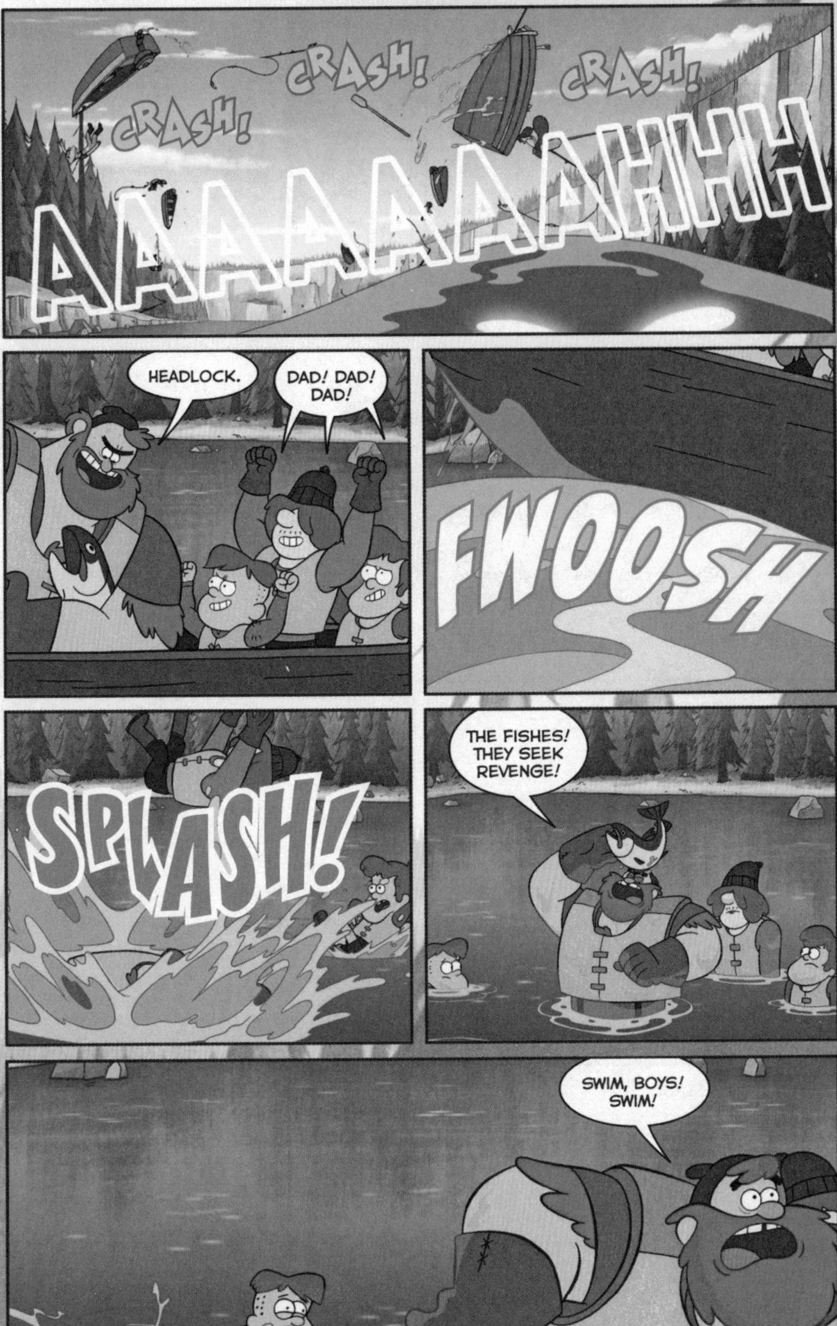
CRASH!
CRASH!
CRASH!
AAAAAAAHHH
HEADLOCK.
DAD! DAD! DAD!
FWOOSH
SPLASH!
THE FISHES! THEY SEEK REVENGE!
SWIM, BOYS! SWIM!

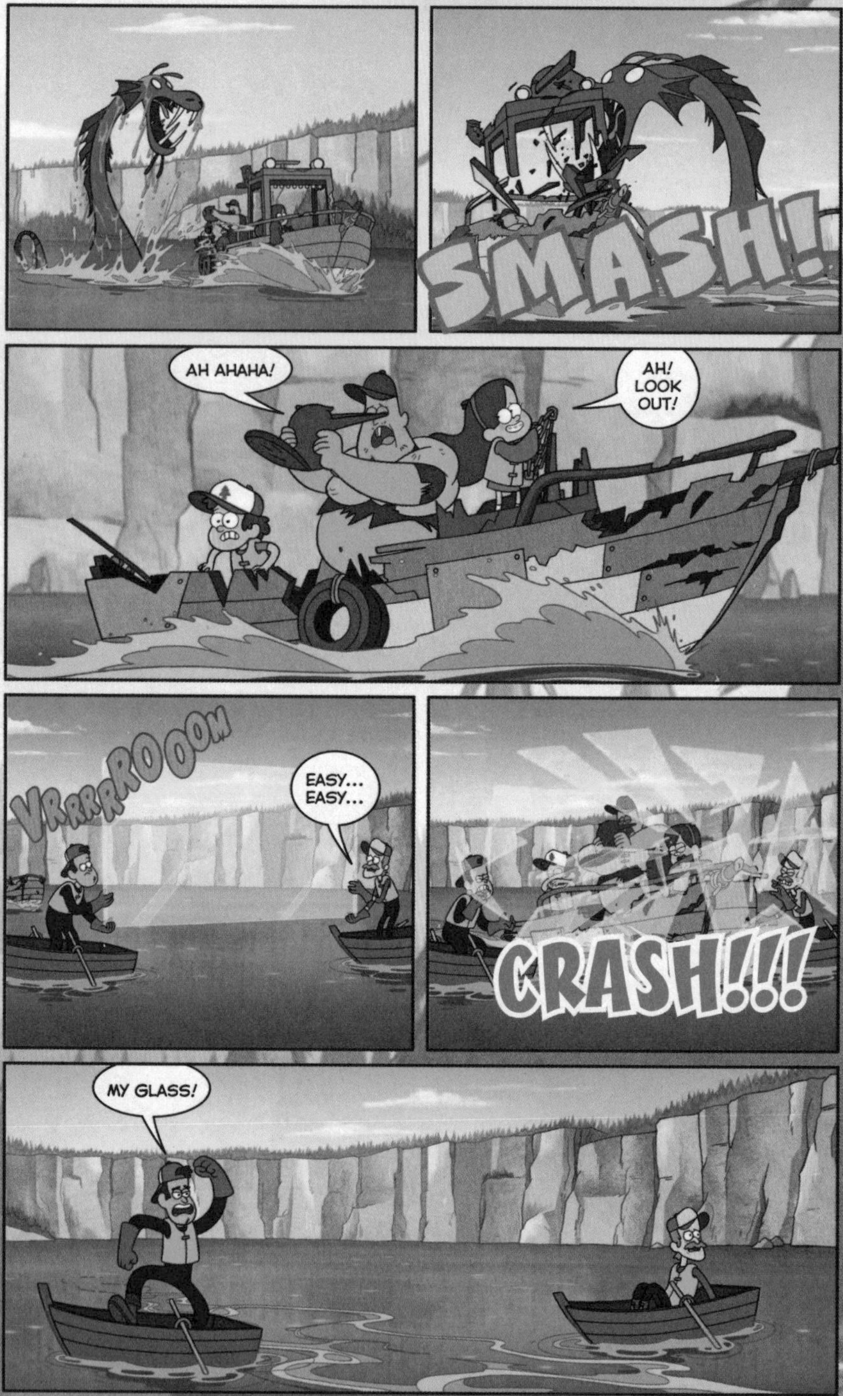
SMASH!!
AH AHAHA!
AH! LOOK OUT!
VRRRRROOOOM
EASY... EASY...
CRASH!!!
MY GLASS!

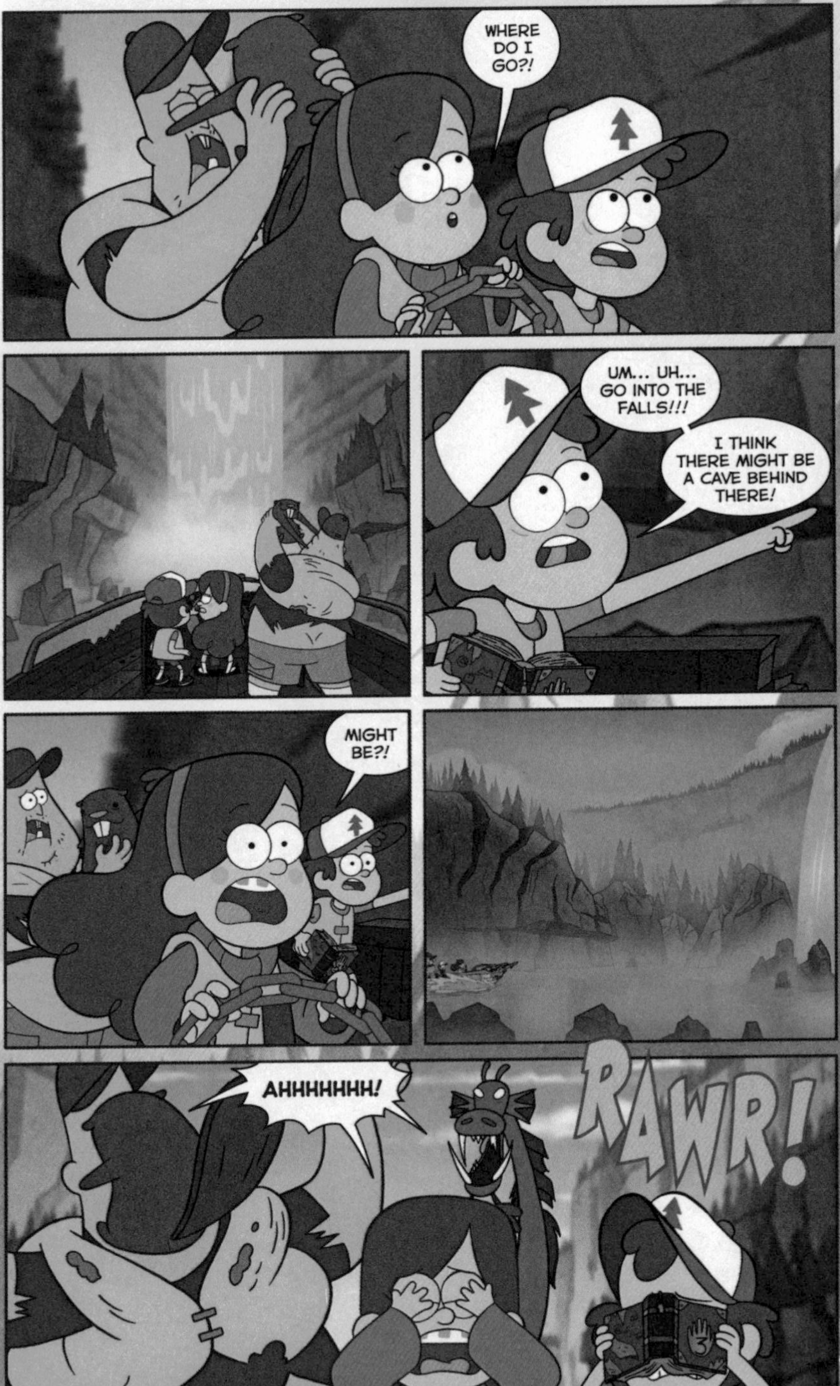
WHERE DO I GO?!
UM... UH... GO INTO THE FALLS!!!
I THINK THERE MIGHT BE A CAVE BEHIND THERE!
MIGHT BE?!
AHHHHHHH!
RAWR!

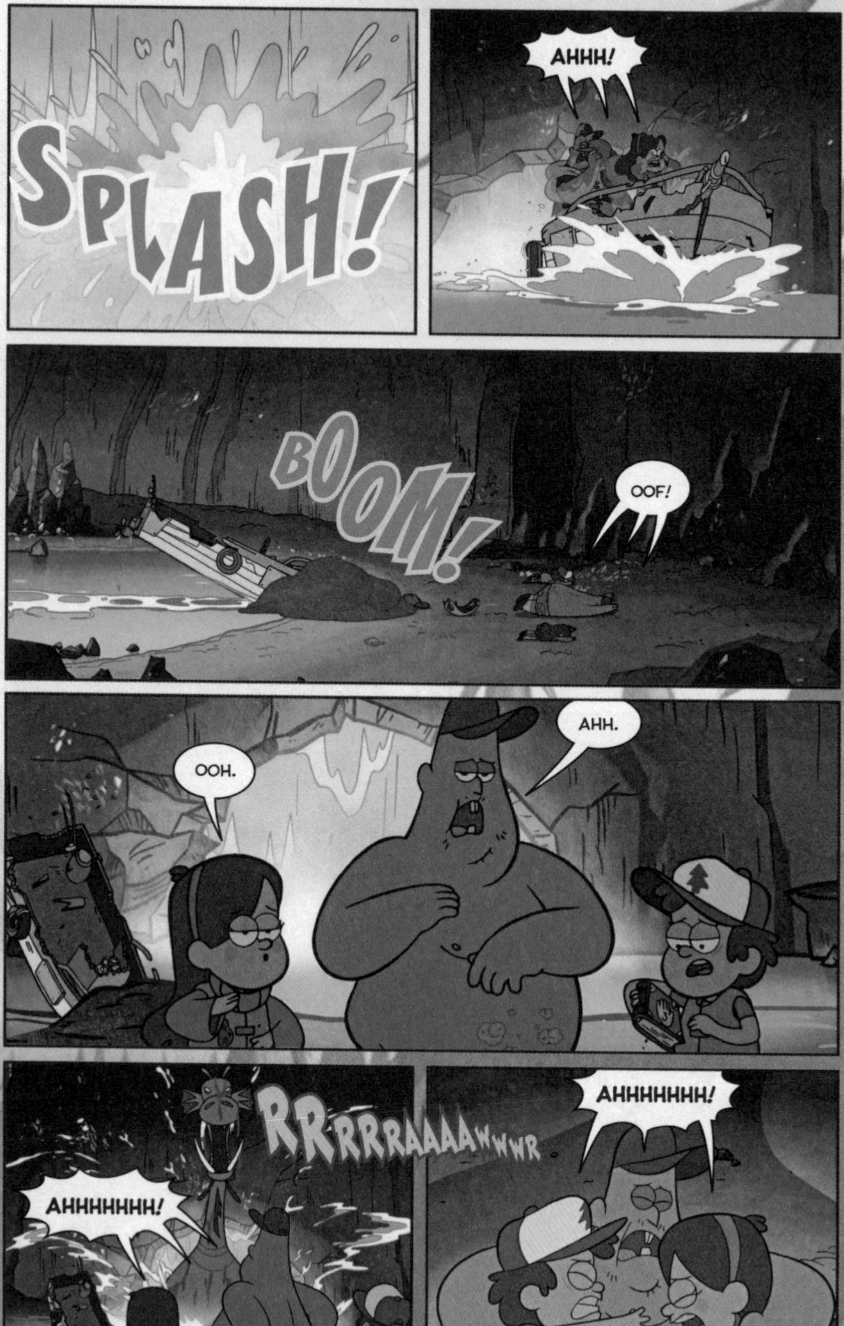
SPLASH!
AHHH!
BOOM!
OOF!
OOH.
AHH.
RRRRRAAAAWWWR
AHHHHHHH!
AHHHHHHH!

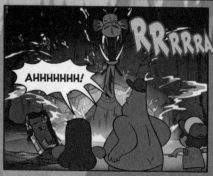

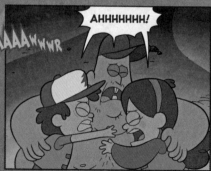

RRRRRRRAWR

SPLASH!

SPLASH!

IT'S STUCK!

HAHA! YEAH!

WAIT. IT'S STUCK?

HUH? HA?!

BOOP.

RRRRR'AAAAAAWWRRR!

FLASH!

CLICK

HAHAHA!

DIDJA GET A GOOD ONE?

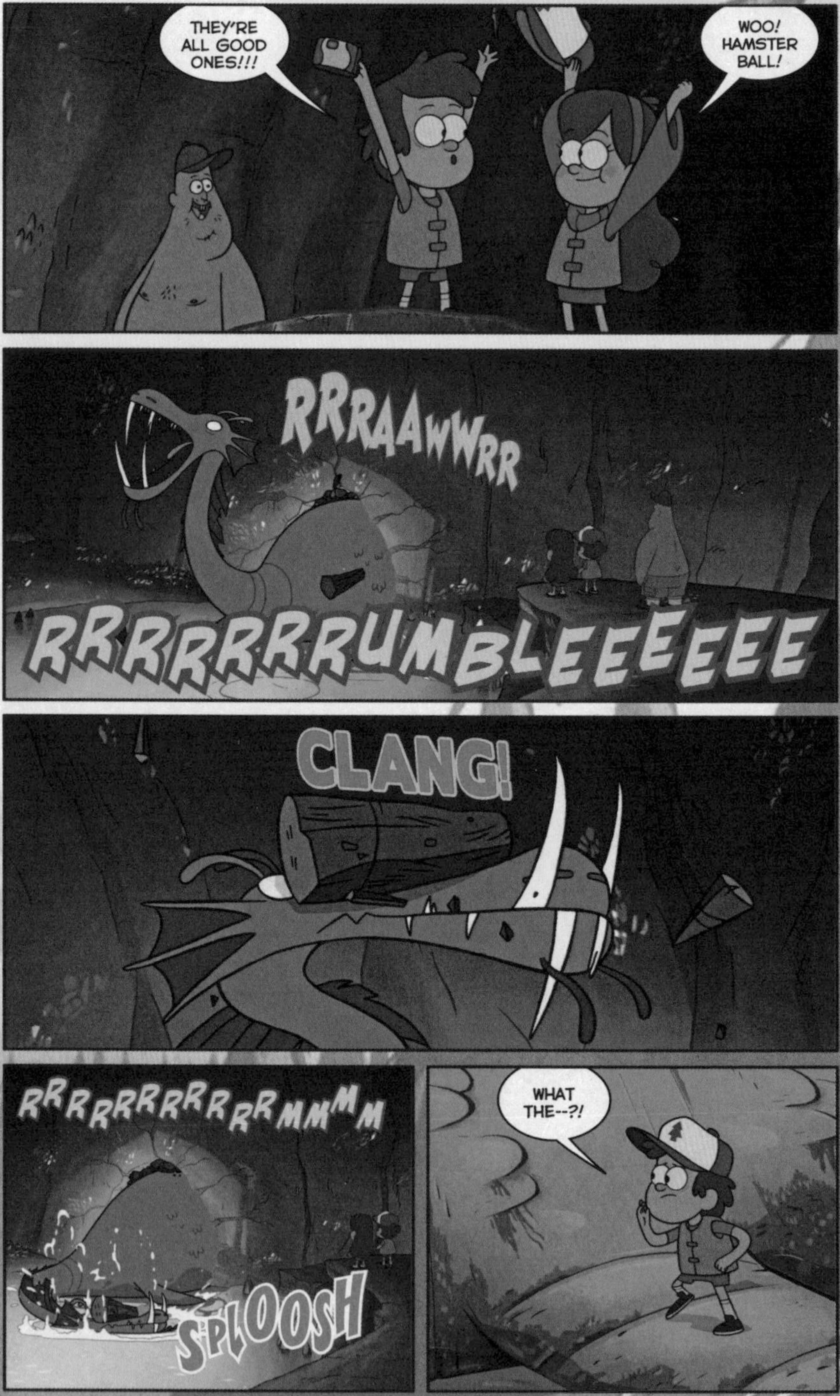
THEY'RE ALL GOOD ONES!!!
WOO! HAMSTER BALL!
RRRAAWWRR
RRRRRRRRUMBLEEEEEE
CLANG!
RRRRRRRRRRRMMMM
SPLOOSH
WHAT THE--?!

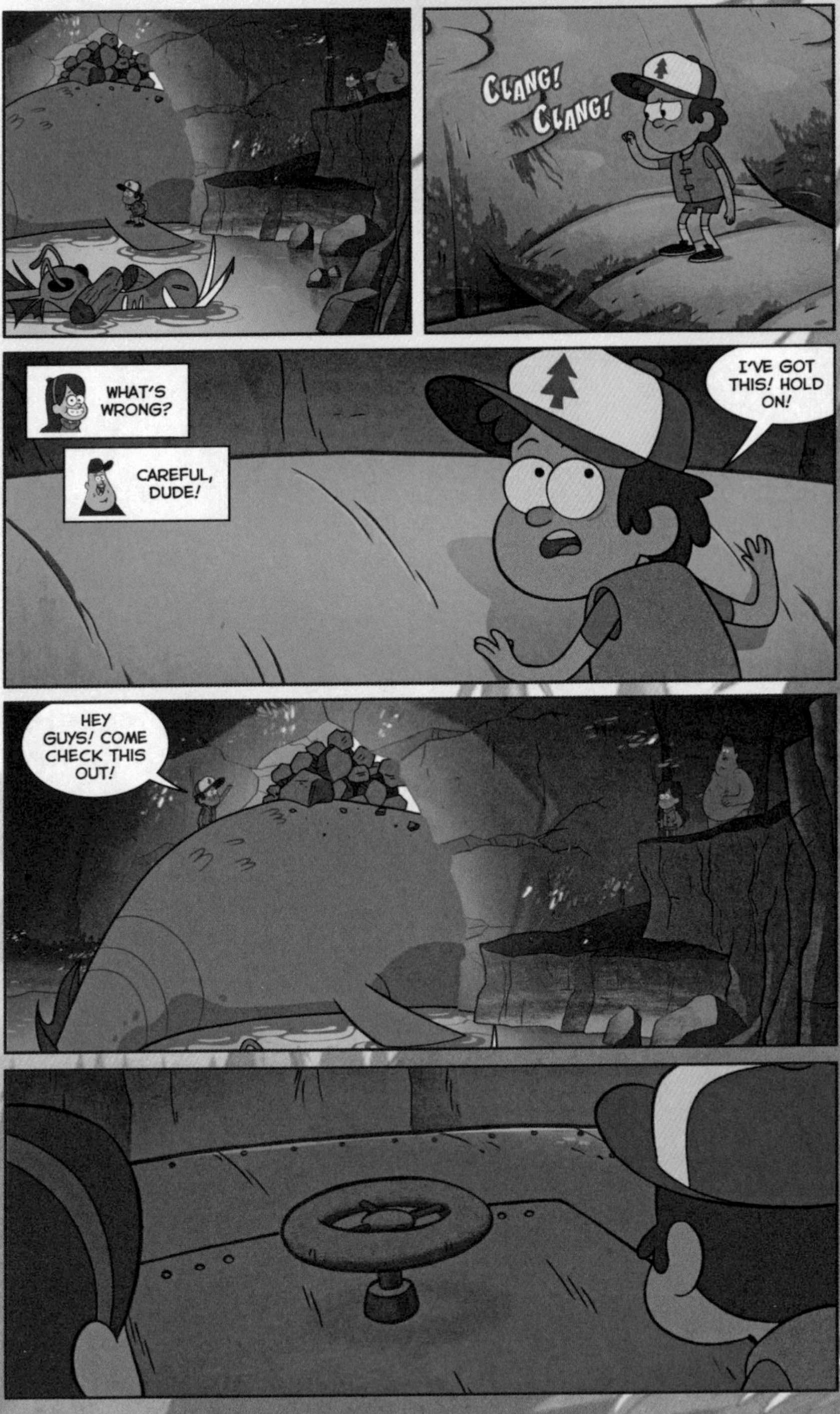
CLANG!
CLANG!
WHAT'S WRONG?
CAREFUL, DUDE!
I'VE GOT THIS! HOLD ON!
HEY GUYS! COME CHECK THIS OUT!

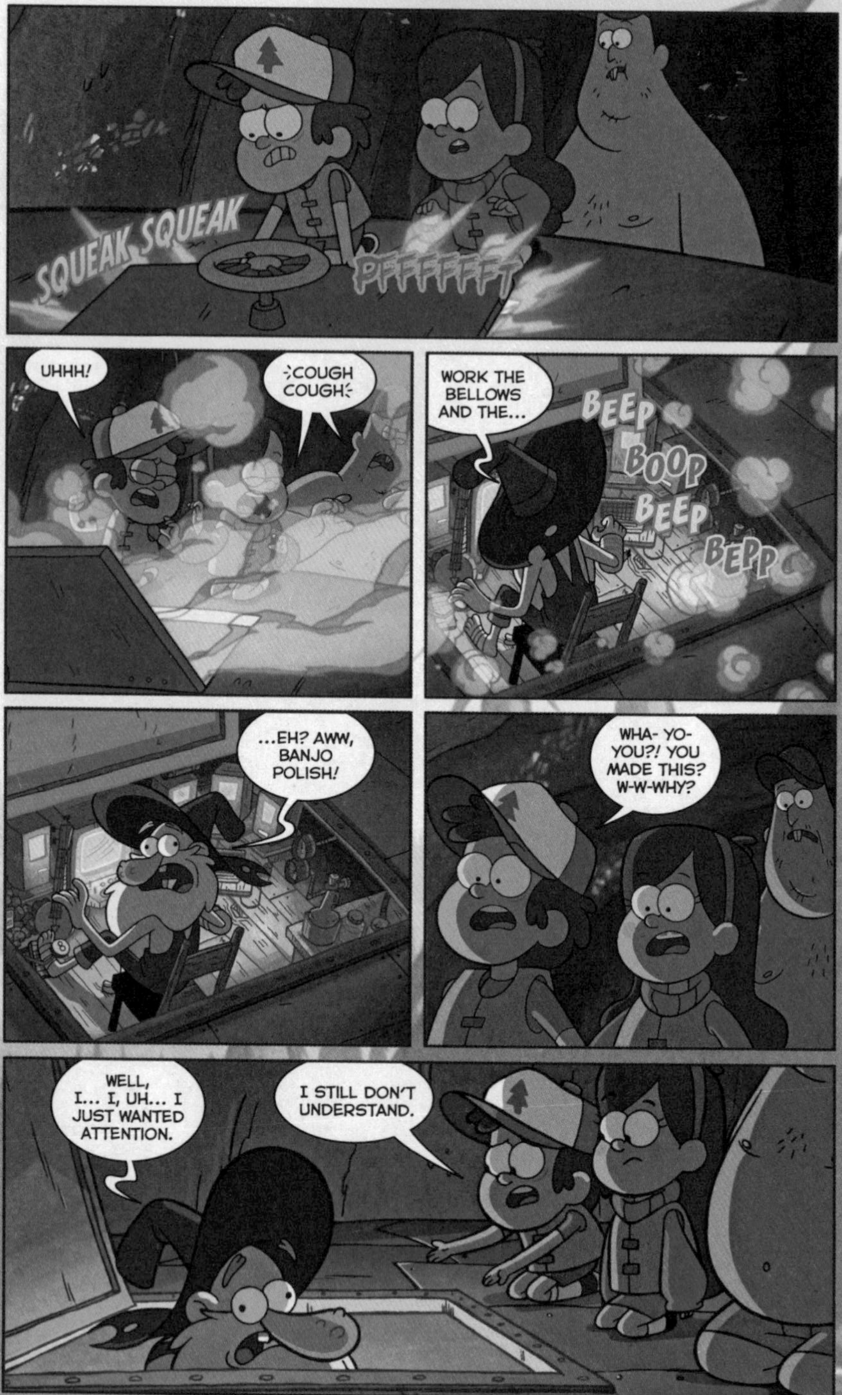
SQUEAK SQUEAK
PFFFFFFFT
UHHH!
COUGH COUGH
WORK THE BELLOWS AND THE...
BEEP BOOP BEEP BEPP
...EH? AWW, BANJO POLISH!
WHA- YO- YOU?! YOU MADE THIS? W-W-WHY?
WELL, I... I, UH... I JUST WANTED ATTENTION.
I STILL DON'T UNDERSTAND.

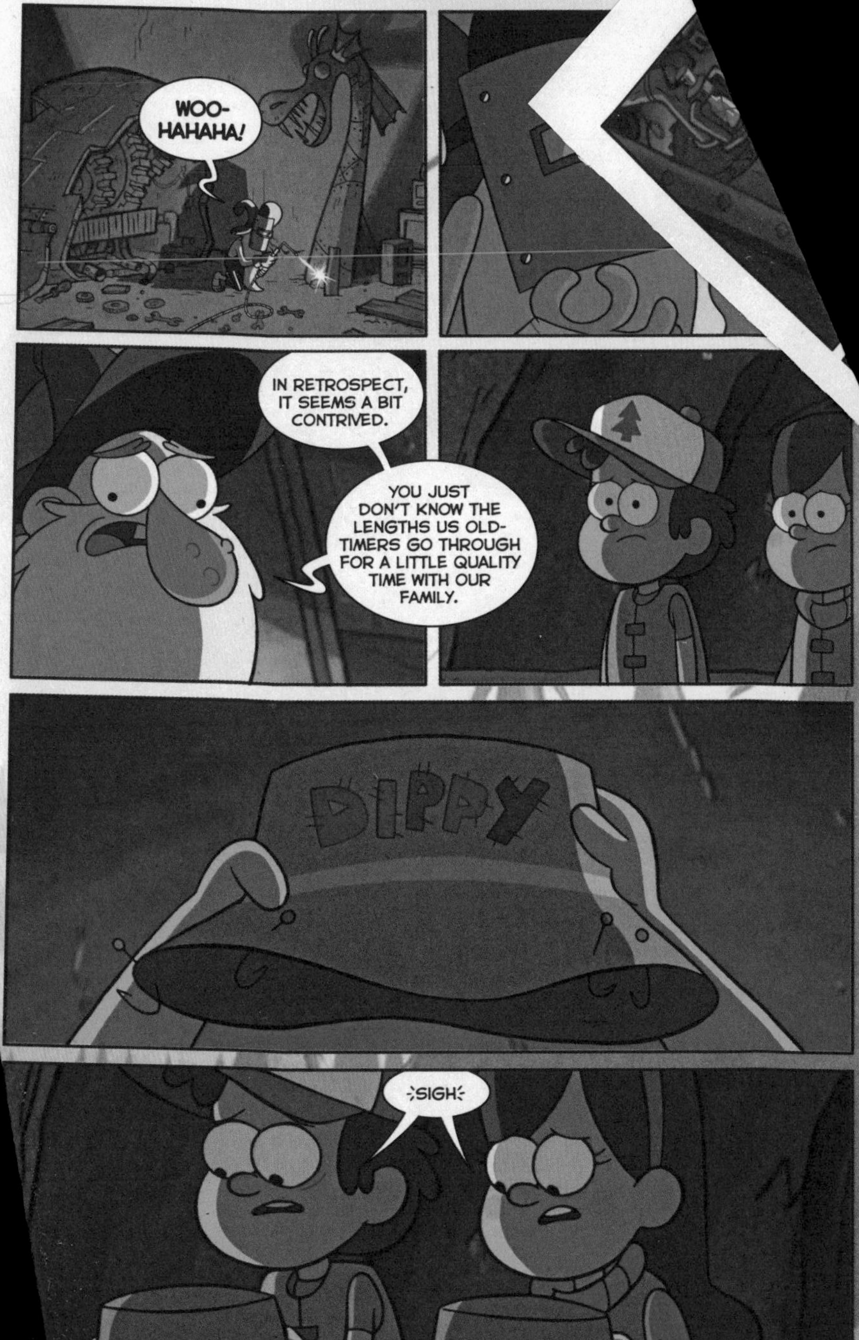

WOO-HAHAHA!
IN RETROSPECT, IT SEEMS A BIT CONTRIVED.
YOU JUST DON'T KNOW THE LENGTHS US OLD-TIMERS GO THROUGH FOR A LITTLE QUALITY TIME WITH OUR FAMILY.
DIPPY
SIGH

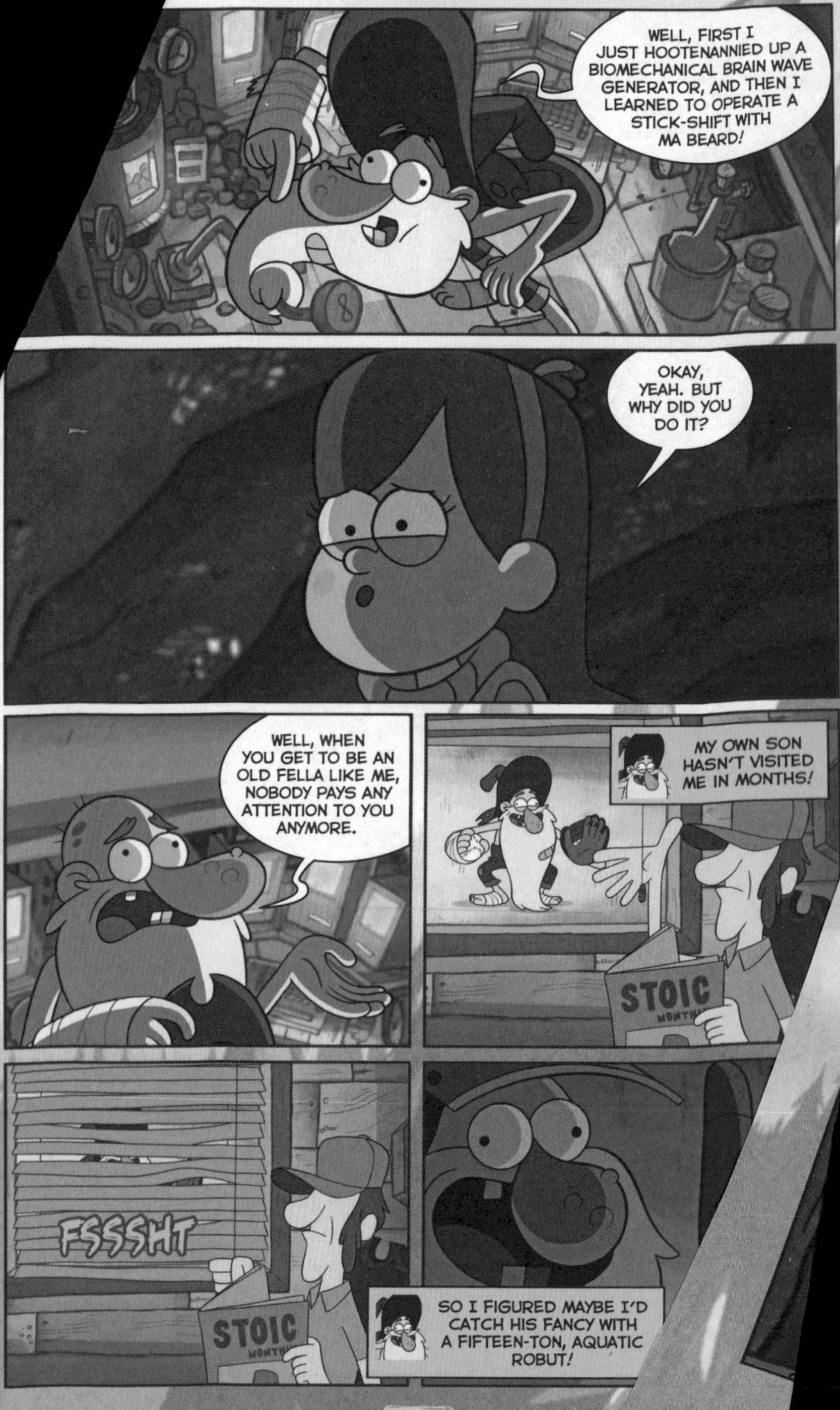
WELL, FIRST I JUST HOOTENANNIED UP A BIOMECHANICAL BRAIN WAVE GENERATOR, AND THEN I LEARNED TO OPERATE A STICK-SHIFT WITH MA BEARD!
OKAY, YEAH. BUT WHY DID YOU DO IT?
WELL, WHEN YOU GET TO BE AN OLD FELLA LIKE ME, NOBODY PAYS ANY ATTENTION TO YOU ANYMORE.
MY OWN SON HASN'T VISITED ME IN MONTHS!
STOIC
FSSSHT
STOIC
SO I FIGURED MAYBE I'D CATCH HIS FANCY WITH A FIFTEEN-TON, AQUATIC ROBUT!

DUDE. I GUESS THE REAL LAKE MONSTER IS YOU TWO. HEH, HEH!

SORRY, THAT JUST LIKE--BOOM--JUST POPPED INTO MY HEAD THERE.

SO, DID YOU EVER TALK TO YOUR SON ABOUT HOW YOU FELT?

NO, SIR, I GOT TO WORK STRAIGHT ON THE ROBUTS!

I MADE LOTS OF ROBUTTS IN MY DAY!

SEA MONSTER

THE GOSSIP

CHAOS!

LIKE WHEN MY WIFE LEFT ME AND I CREATED A HOMICIDAL PTERODACTYL-TRON...

...OR WHEN MY PAL ERNIE DIDN'T COME TO MY RETIREMENT PARTY...

...AND I CONSTRUCTED AN EIGHTY-TON SHAME-BOT THAT EXPLODED THE ENTIRE DOWNTOWN AREA!

HAHAHAHAHA!

DISASTER

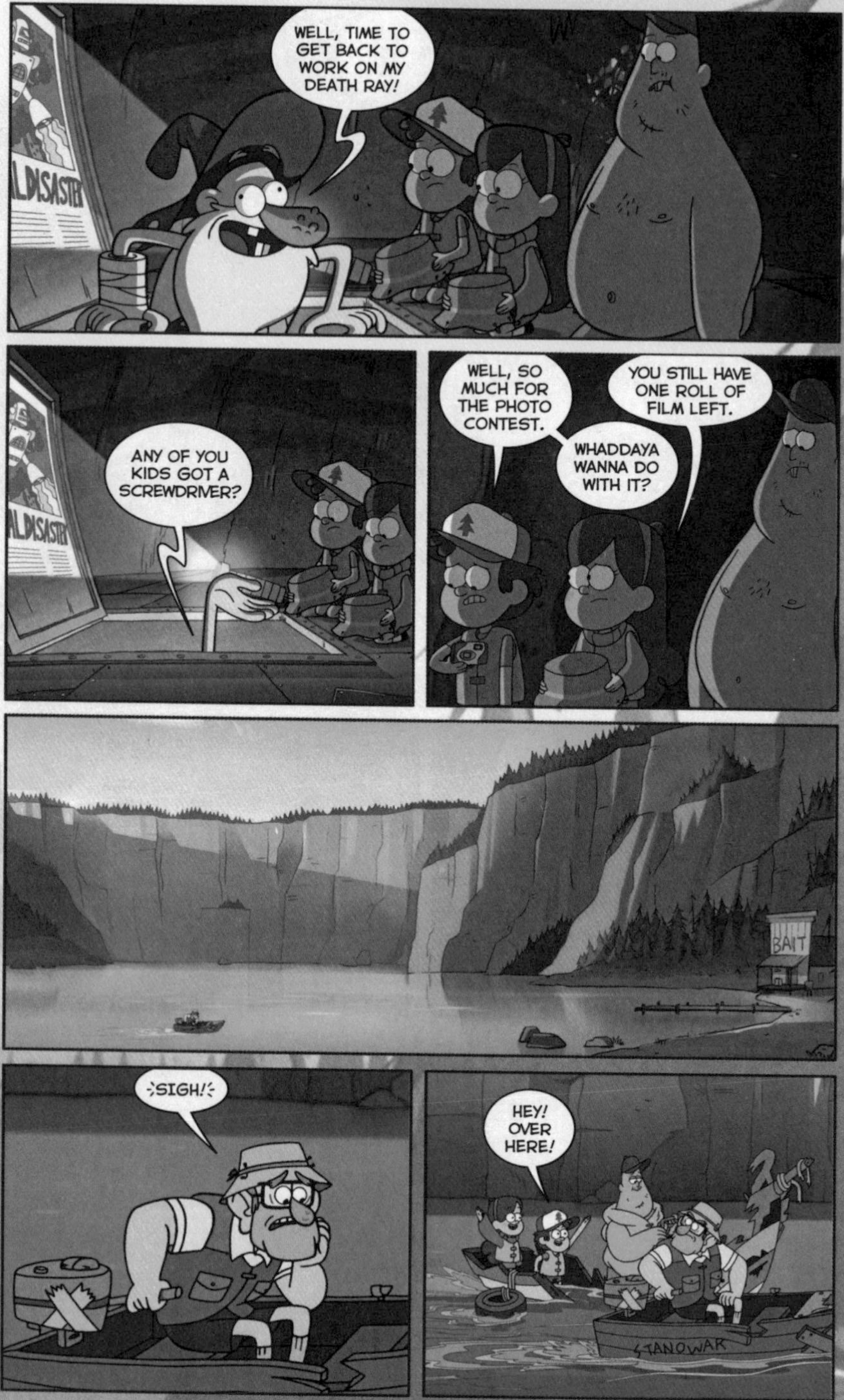
WELL, TIME TO GET BACK TO WORK ON MY DEATH RAY!
ANY OF YOU KIDS GOT A SCREWDRIVER?
WELL, SO MUCH FOR THE PHOTO CONTEST.
YOU STILL HAVE ONE ROLL OF FILM LEFT.
WHADDAYA WANNA DO WITH IT?
BAIT
SIGH!
HEY! OVER HERE!
STANOWAR

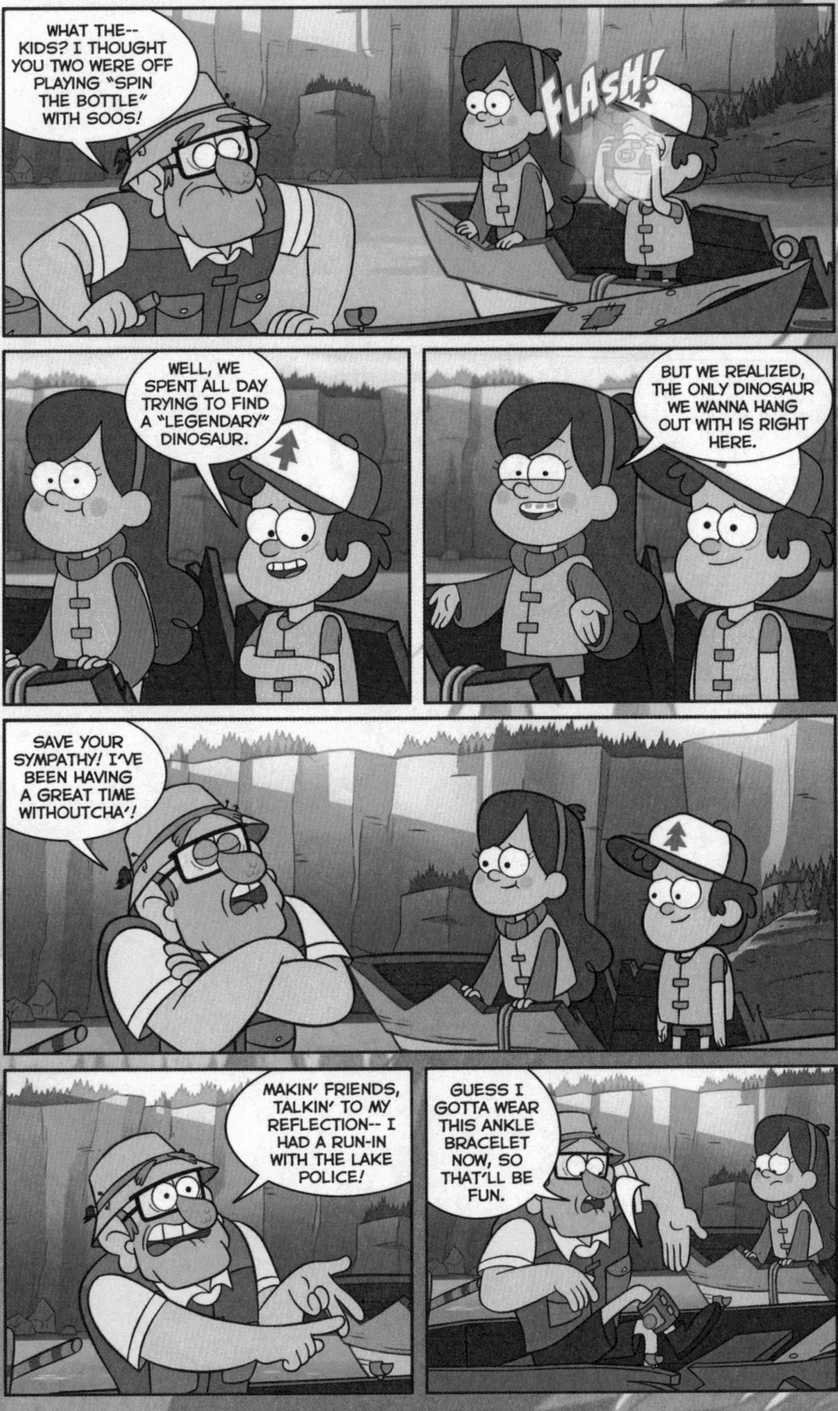
WHAT THE-- KIDS? I THOUGHT YOU TWO WERE OFF PLAYING "SPIN THE BOTTLE" WITH SOOS!
FLASH!
WELL, WE SPENT ALL DAY TRYING TO FIND A "LEGENDARY" DINOSAUR.
BUT WE REALIZED, THE ONLY DINOSAUR WE WANNA HANG OUT WITH IS RIGHT HERE.
SAVE YOUR SYMPATHY! I'VE BEEN HAVING A GREAT TIME WITHOUTCHA'!
MAKIN' FRIENDS, TALKIN' TO MY REFLECTION-- I HAD A RUN-IN WITH THE LAKE POLICE!
GUESS I GOTTA WEAR THIS ANKLE BRACELET NOW, SO THAT'LL BE FUN.

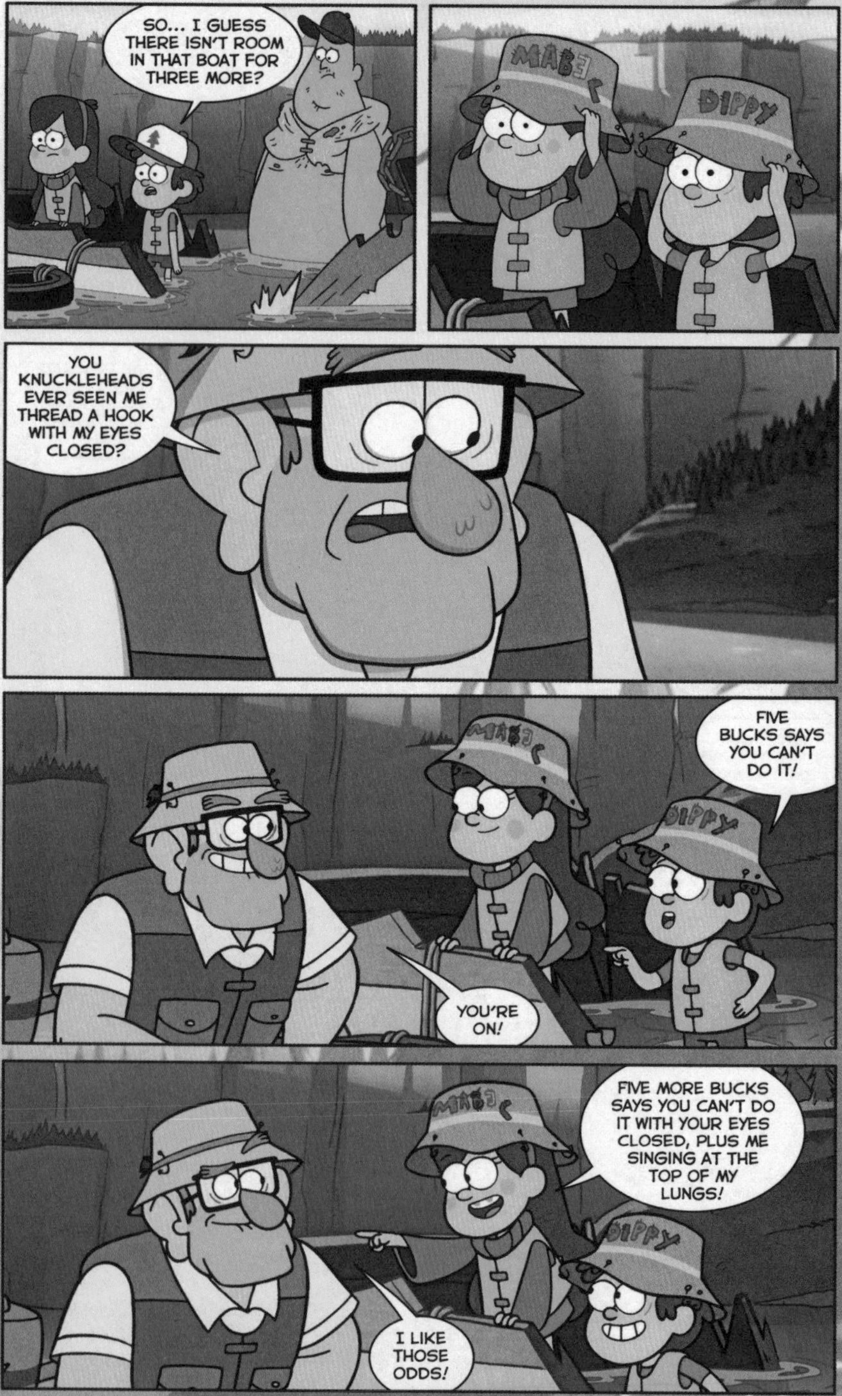
SO... I GUESS THERE ISN'T ROOM IN THAT BOAT FOR THREE MORE?
MABEL
DIPPY
YOU KNUCKLEHEADS EVER SEEN ME THREAD A HOOK WITH MY EYES CLOSED?
FIVE BUCKS SAYS YOU CAN'T DO IT!
YOU'RE ON!
FIVE MORE BUCKS SAYS YOU CAN'T DO IT WITH YOUR EYES CLOSED, PLUS ME SINGING AT THE TOP OF MY LUNGS!
I LIKE THOSE ODDS!

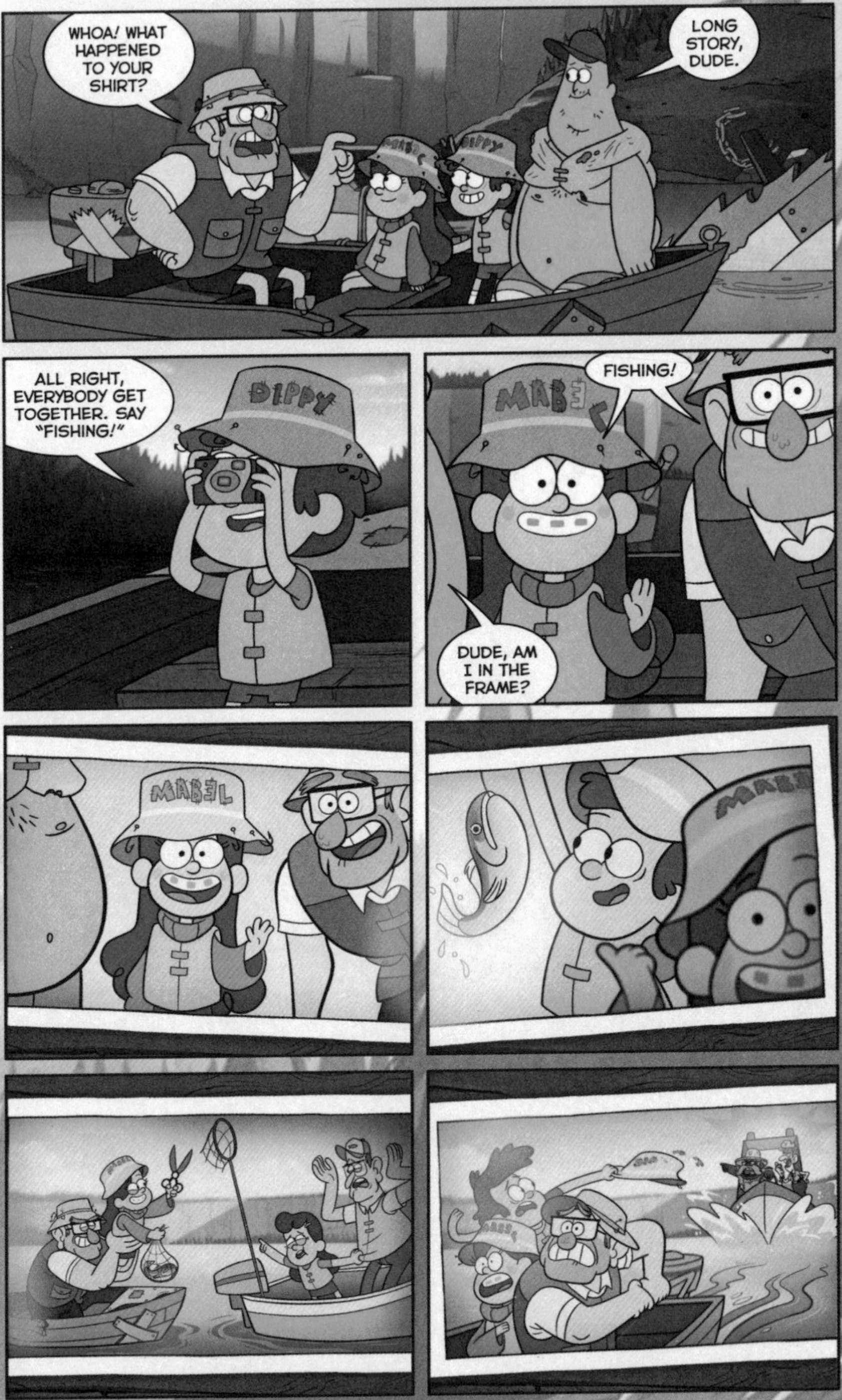
WHOA! WHAT HAPPENED TO YOUR SHIRT?
LONG STORY, DUDE.
ALL RIGHT, EVERYBODY GET TOGETHER. SAY "FISHING!"
FISHING!
DUDE, AM I IN THE FRAME?

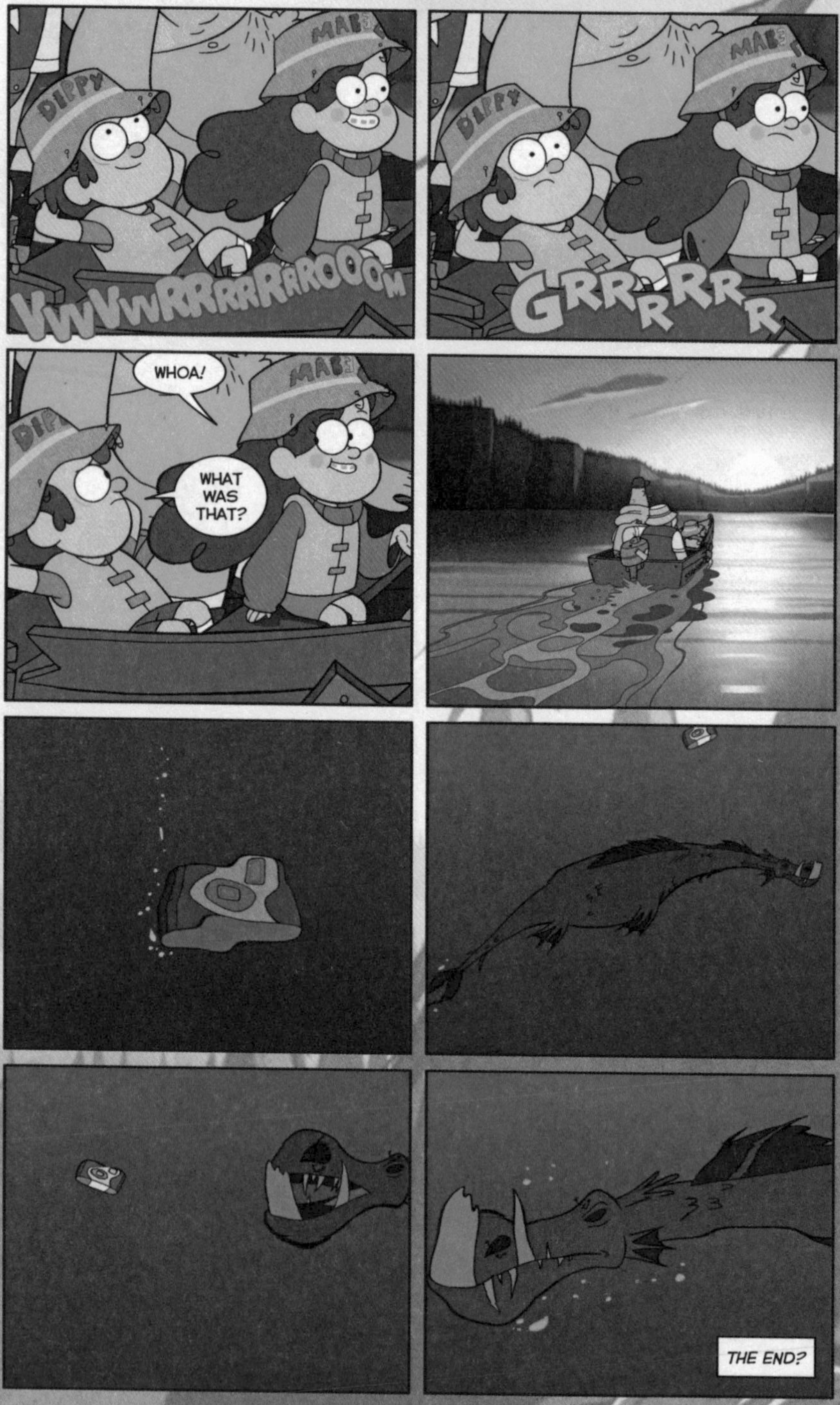
DIPPY
MABEL
VVVVVVRRRRRRRROOOOM
GRRRRRRR
WHOA!
WHAT WAS THAT?
THE END?

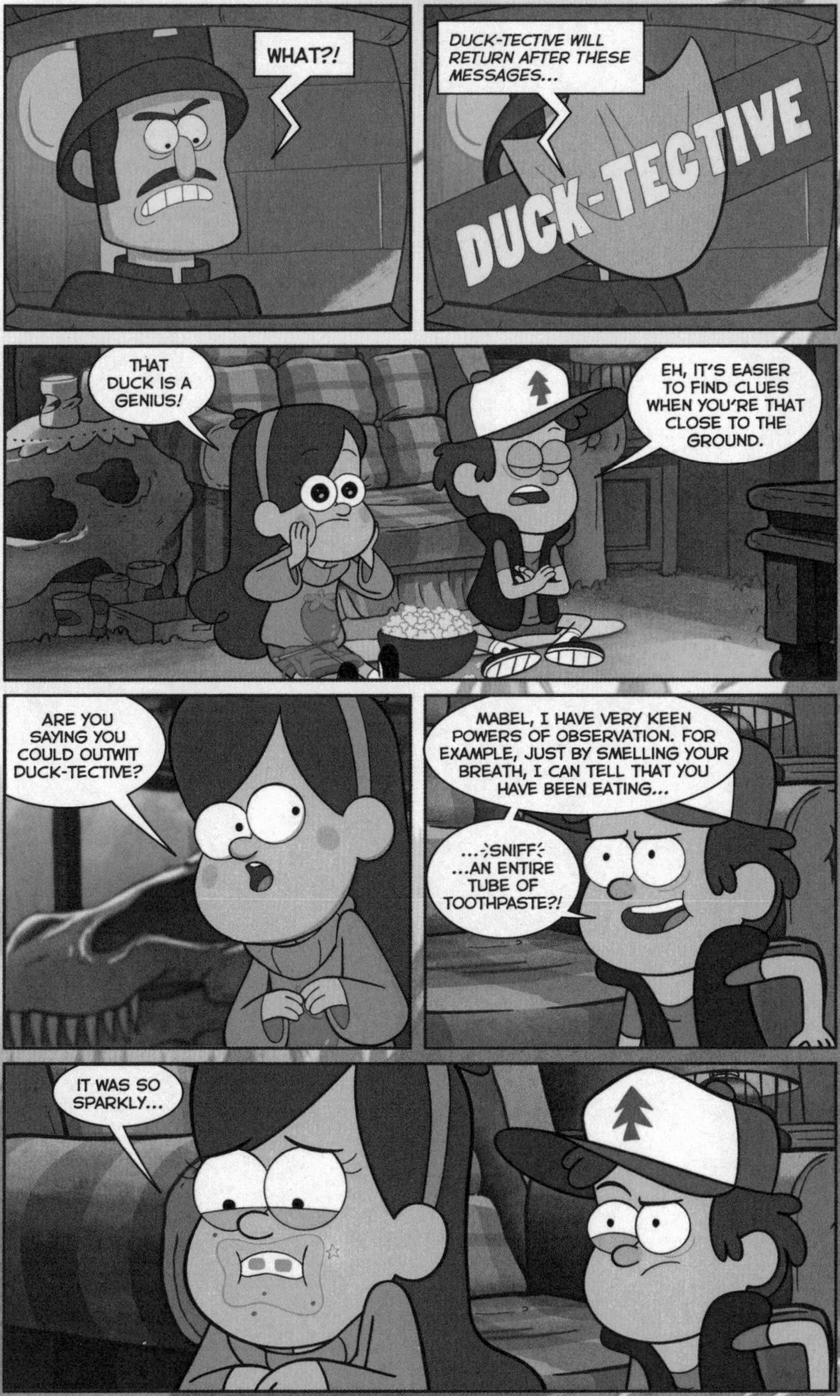
WHAT?!
DUCK-TECTIVE WILL RETURN AFTER THESE MESSAGES...
DUCK-TECTIVE
THAT DUCK IS A GENIUS!
EH, IT'S EASIER TO FIND CLUES WHEN YOU'RE THAT CLOSE TO THE GROUND.
ARE YOU SAYING YOU COULD OUTWIT DUCK-TECTIVE?
MABEL, I HAVE VERY KEEN POWERS OF OBSERVATION. FOR EXAMPLE, JUST BY SMELLING YOUR BREATH, I CAN TELL THAT YOU HAVE BEEN EATING...
...SNIFF ...AN ENTIRE TUBE OF TOOTHPASTE?!
IT WAS SO SPARKLY...

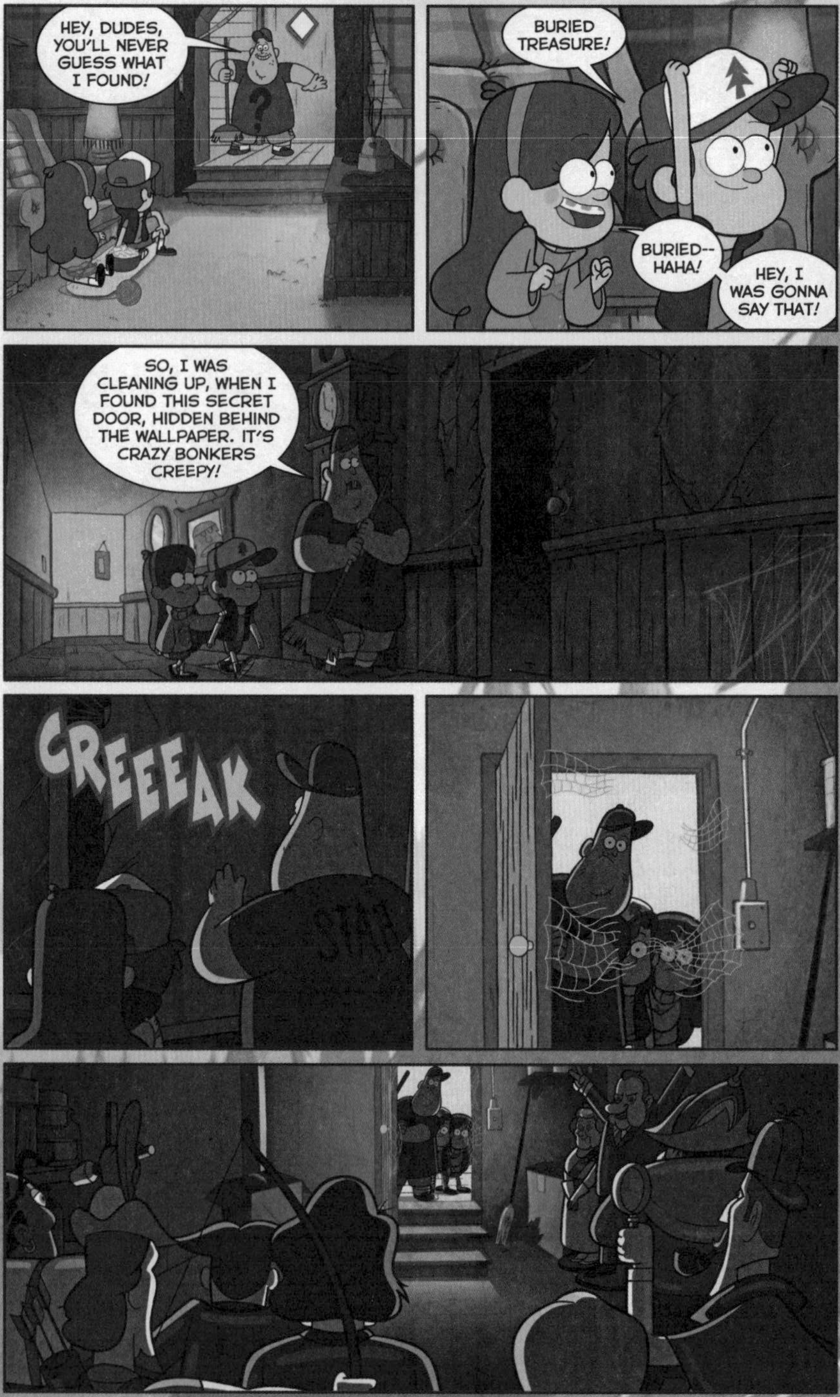
HEY, DUDES, YOU'LL NEVER GUESS WHAT I FOUND!
BURIED TREASURE!
BURIED-- HAHA!
HEY, I WAS GONNA SAY THAT!
SO, I WAS CLEANING UP, WHEN I FOUND THIS SECRET DOOR, HIDDEN BEHIND THE WALLPAPER. IT'S CRAZY BONKERS CREEPY!
CREEEAK

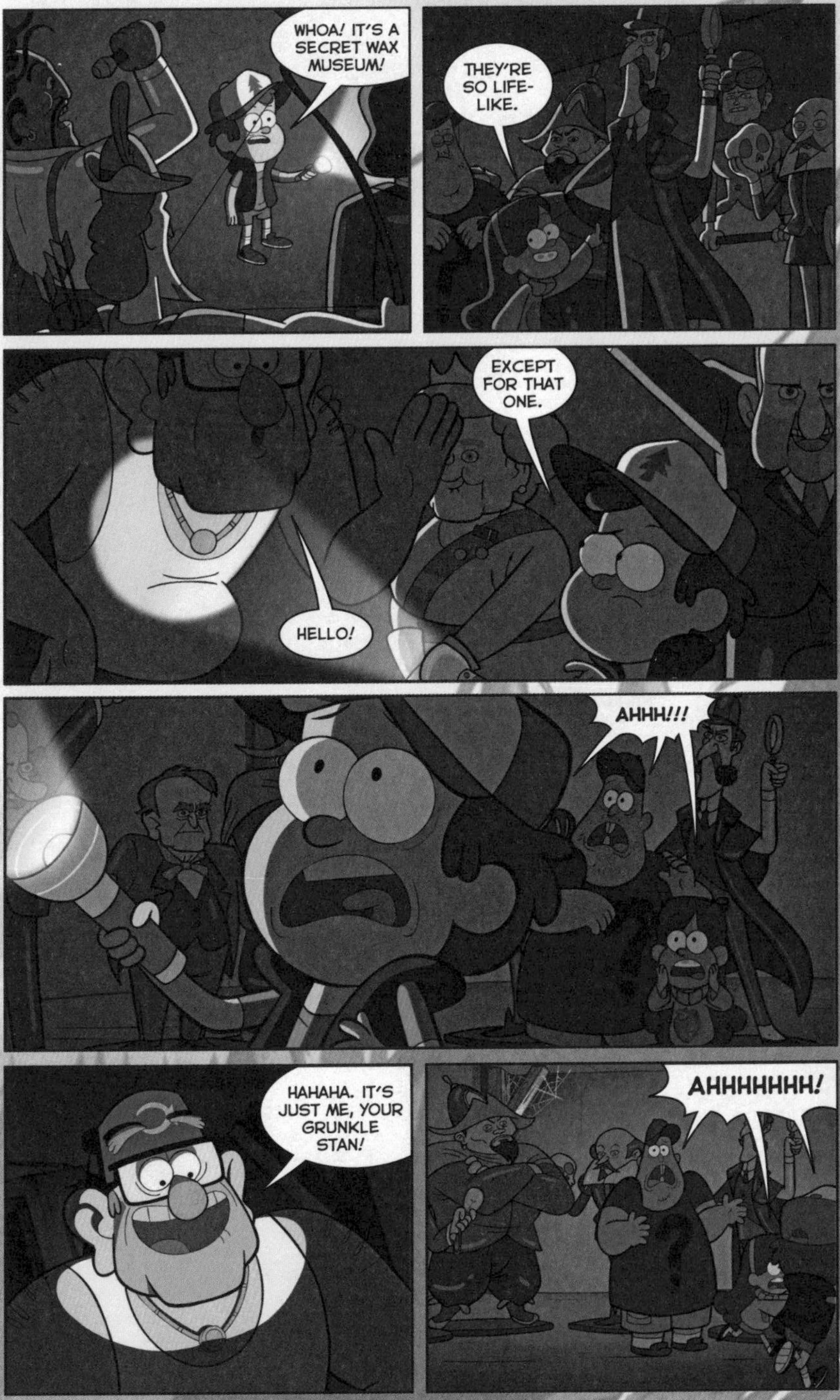
WHOA! IT'S A SECRET WAX MUSEUM!
THEY'RE SO LIFE-LIKE.
EXCEPT FOR THAT ONE.
HELLO!
AHHH!!!
HAHAHA. IT'S JUST ME, YOUR GRUNKLE STAN!
AHHHHHHH!

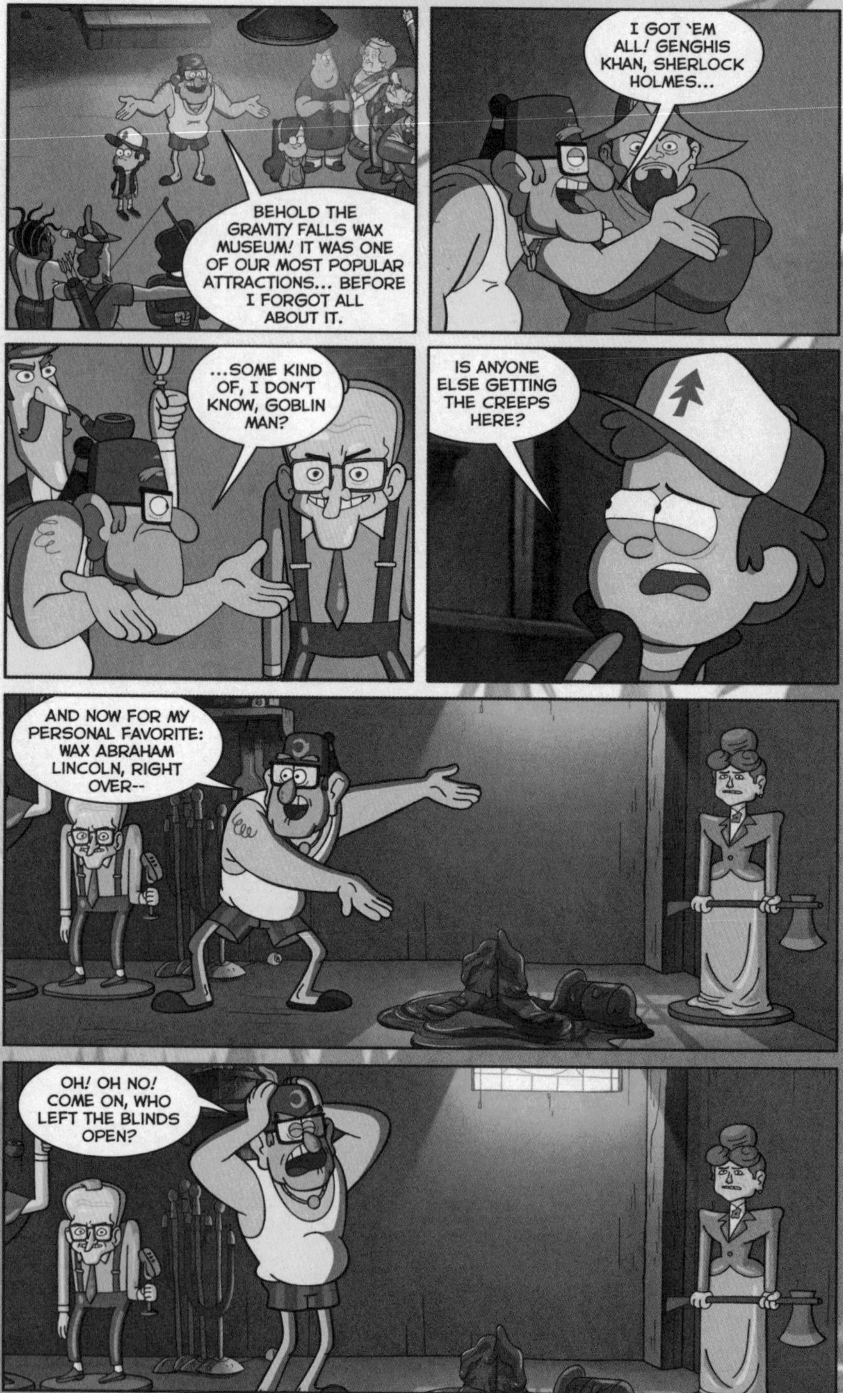
BEHOLD THE GRAVITY FALLS WAX MUSEUM! IT WAS ONE OF OUR MOST POPULAR ATTRACTIONS... BEFORE I FORGOT ALL ABOUT IT.
I GOT 'EM ALL! GENGHIS KHAN, SHERLOCK HOLMES...
...SOME KIND OF, I DON'T KNOW, GOBLIN MAN?
IS ANYONE ELSE GETTING THE CREEPS HERE?
AND NOW FOR MY PERSONAL FAVORITE: WAX ABRAHAM LINCOLN, RIGHT OVER--
OH! OH NO! COME ON, WHO LEFT THE BLINDS OPEN?

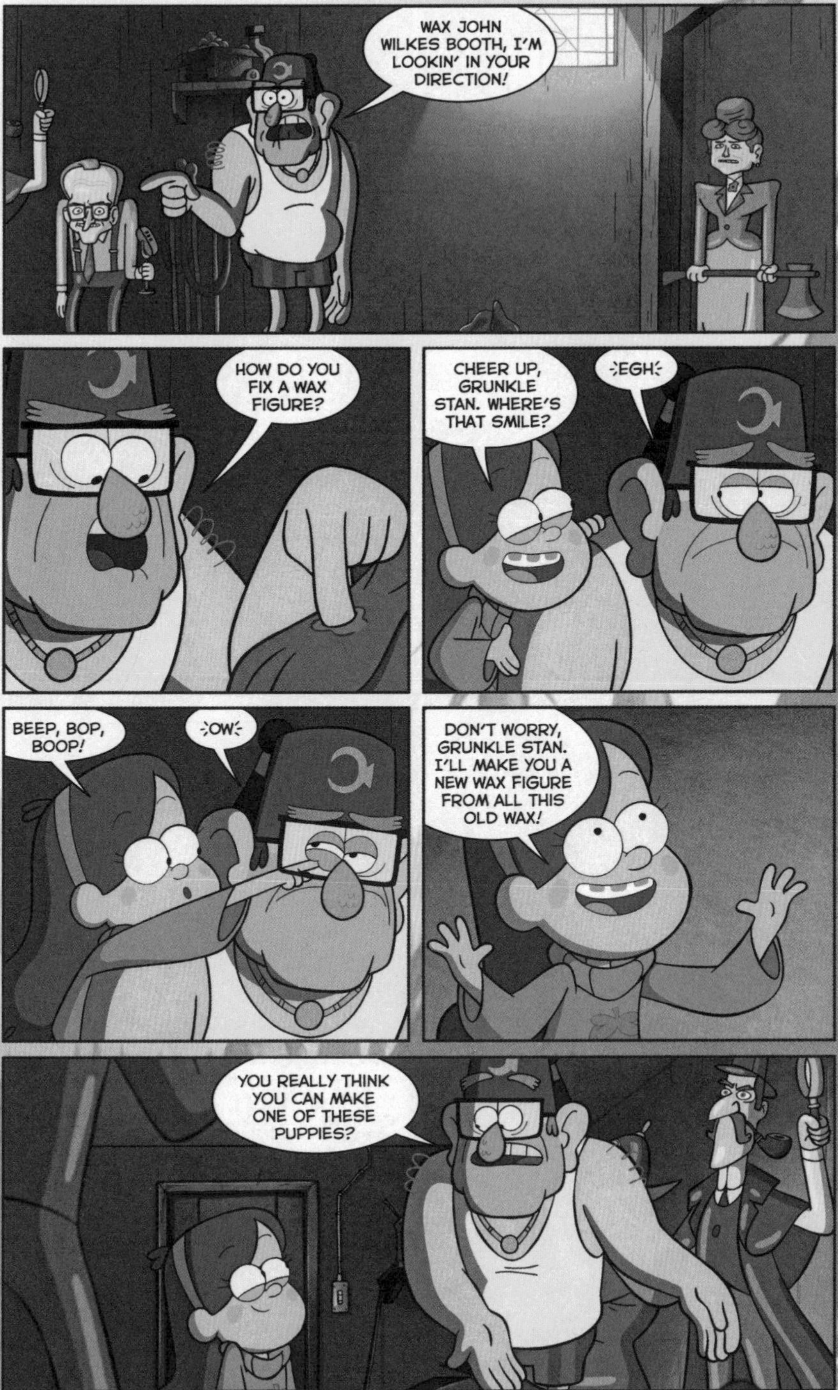
WAX JOHN WILKES BOOTH, I'M LOOKIN' IN YOUR DIRECTION!
HOW DO YOU FIX A WAX FIGURE?
CHEER UP, GRUNKLE STAN. WHERE'S THAT SMILE?
EGH
BEEP, BOP, BOOP!
OW
DON'T WORRY, GRUNKLE STAN. I'LL MAKE YOU A NEW WAX FIGURE FROM ALL THIS OLD WAX!
YOU REALLY THINK YOU CAN MAKE ONE OF THESE PUPPIES?

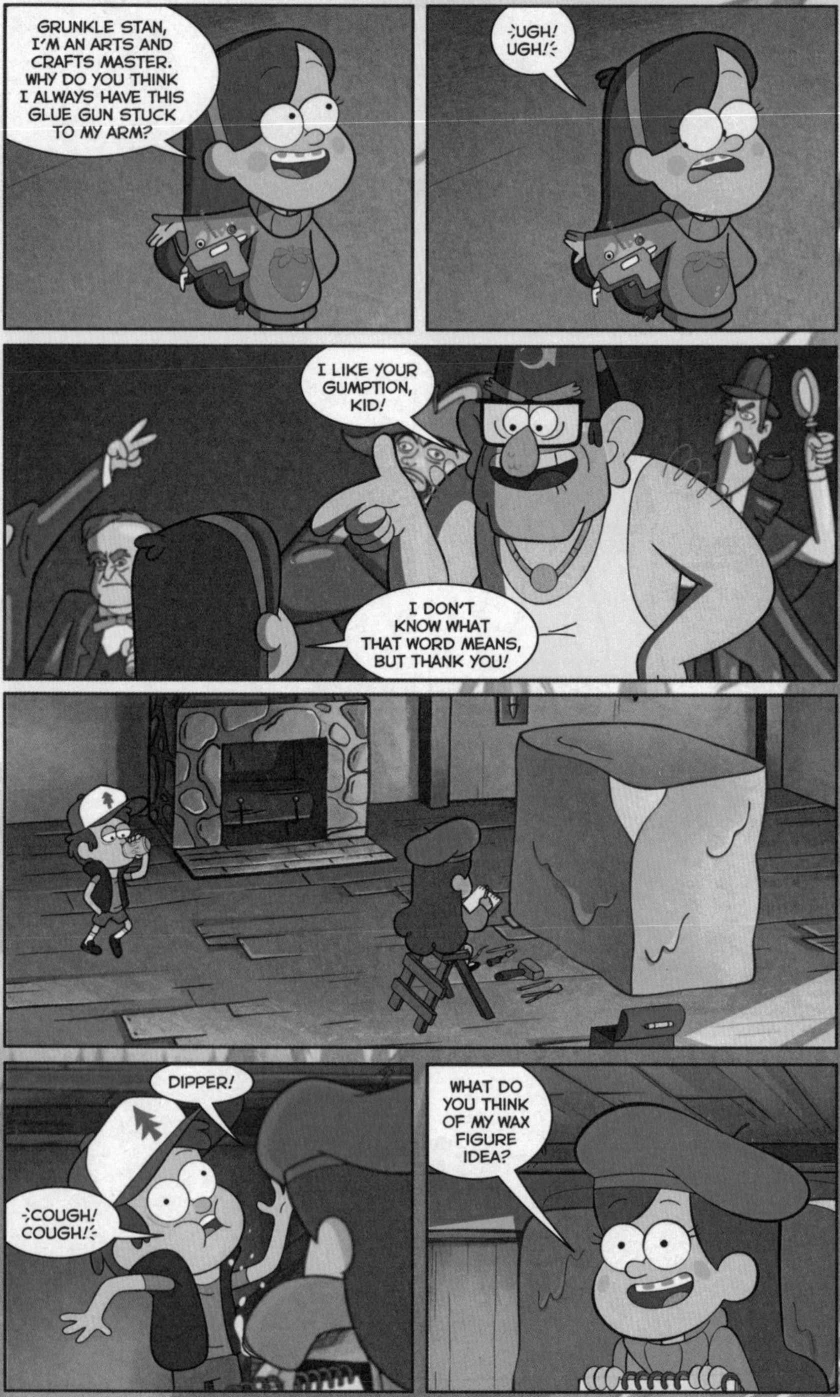
GRUNKLE STAN, I'M AN ARTS AND CRAFTS MASTER. WHY DO YOU THINK I ALWAYS HAVE THIS GLUE GUN STUCK TO MY ARM?
UGH! UGH!
I LIKE YOUR GUMPTION, KID!
I DON'T KNOW WHAT THAT WORD MEANS, BUT THANK YOU!
DIPPER!
COUGH! COUGH!
WHAT DO YOU THINK OF MY WAX FIGURE IDEA?

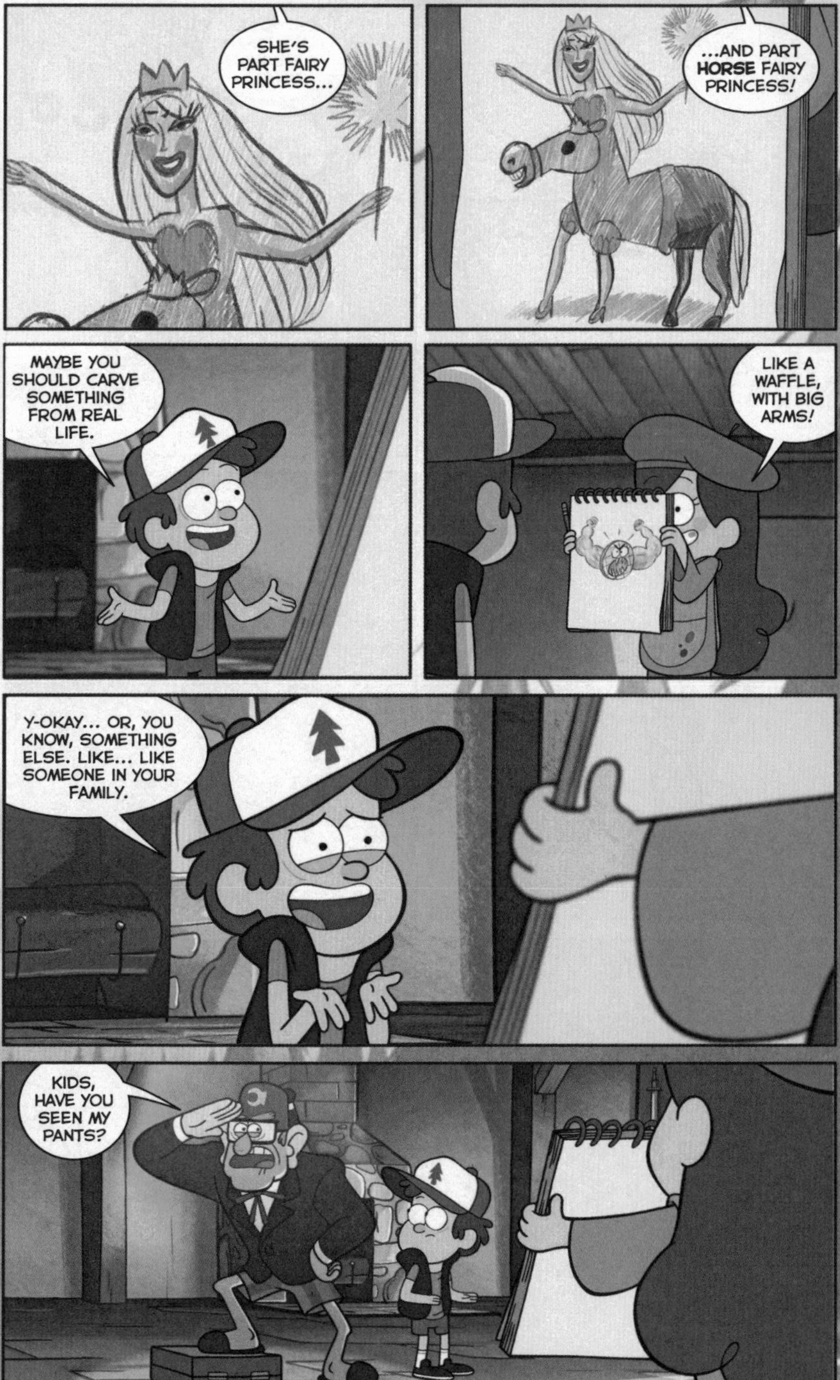
SHE'S PART FAIRY PRINCESS...
...AND PART **HORSE** FAIRY PRINCESS!
MAYBE YOU SHOULD CARVE SOMETHING FROM REAL LIFE.
LIKE A WAFFLE, WITH BIG ARMS!
Y-OKAY... OR, YOU KNOW, SOMETHING ELSE. LIKE... LIKE SOMEONE IN YOUR FAMILY.
KIDS, HAVE YOU SEEN MY PANTS?

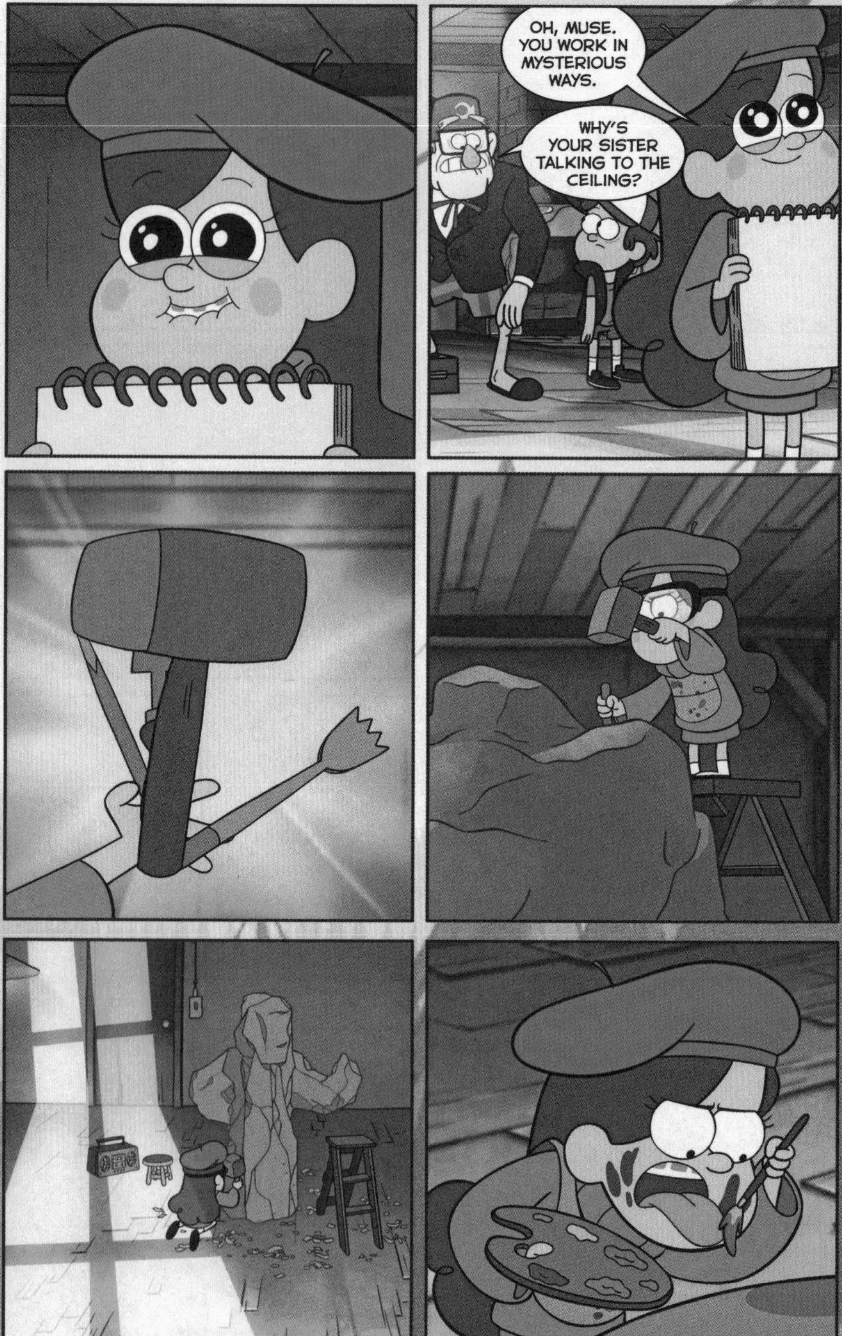
OH, MUSE. YOU WORK IN MYSTERIOUS WAYS.
WHY'S YOUR SISTER TALKING TO THE CEILING?

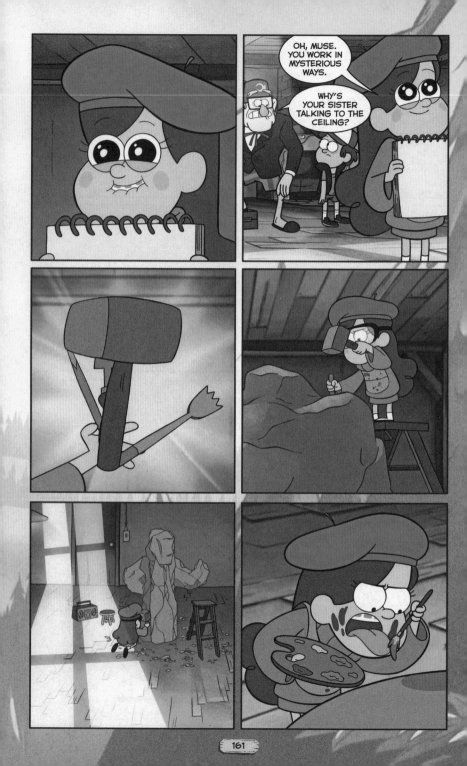

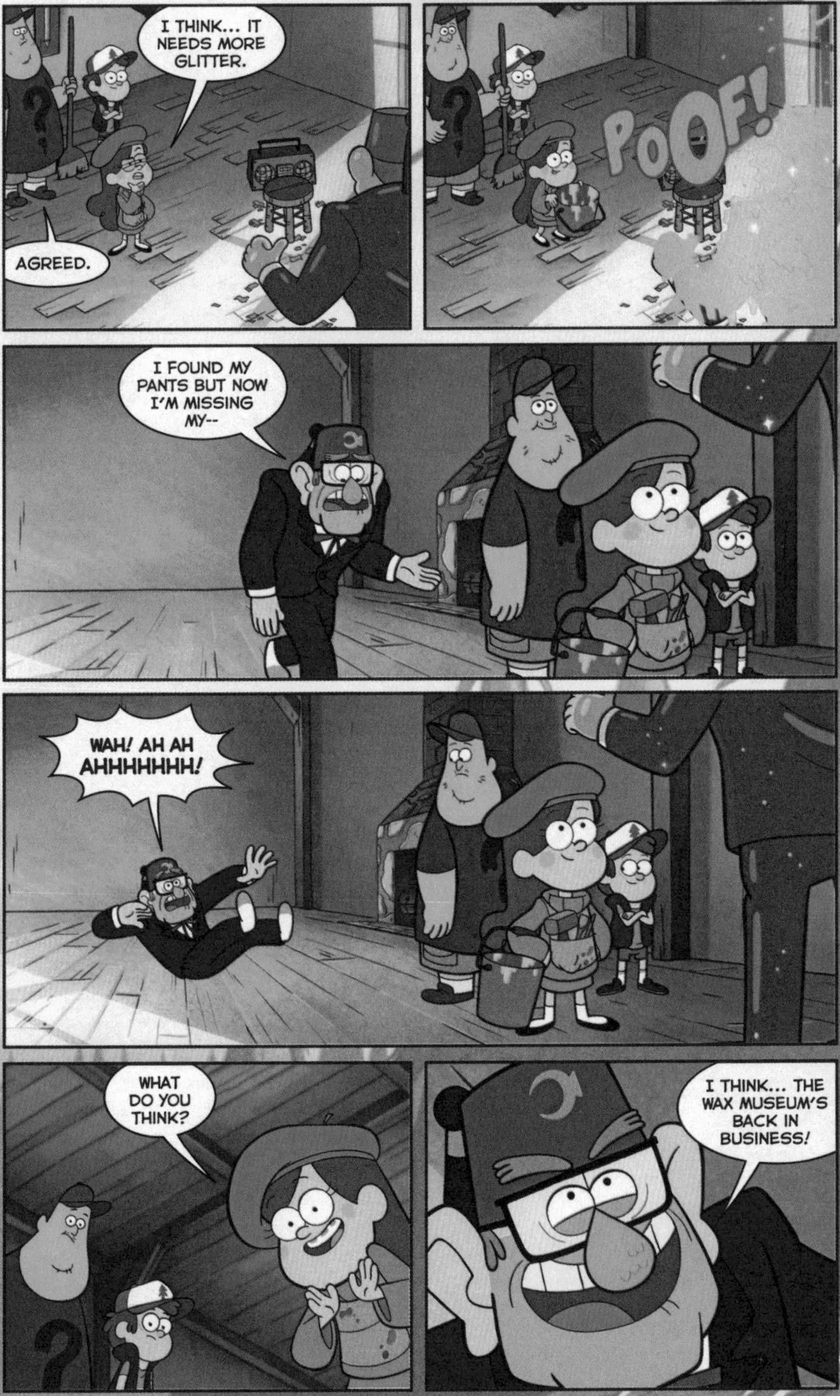
I THINK... IT NEEDS MORE GLITTER.
AGREED.
POOF!
I FOUND MY PANTS BUT NOW I'M MISSING MY--
WAH! AH AH AHHHHHHH!
WHAT DO YOU THINK?
I THINK... THE WAX MUSEUM'S BACK IN BUSINESS!

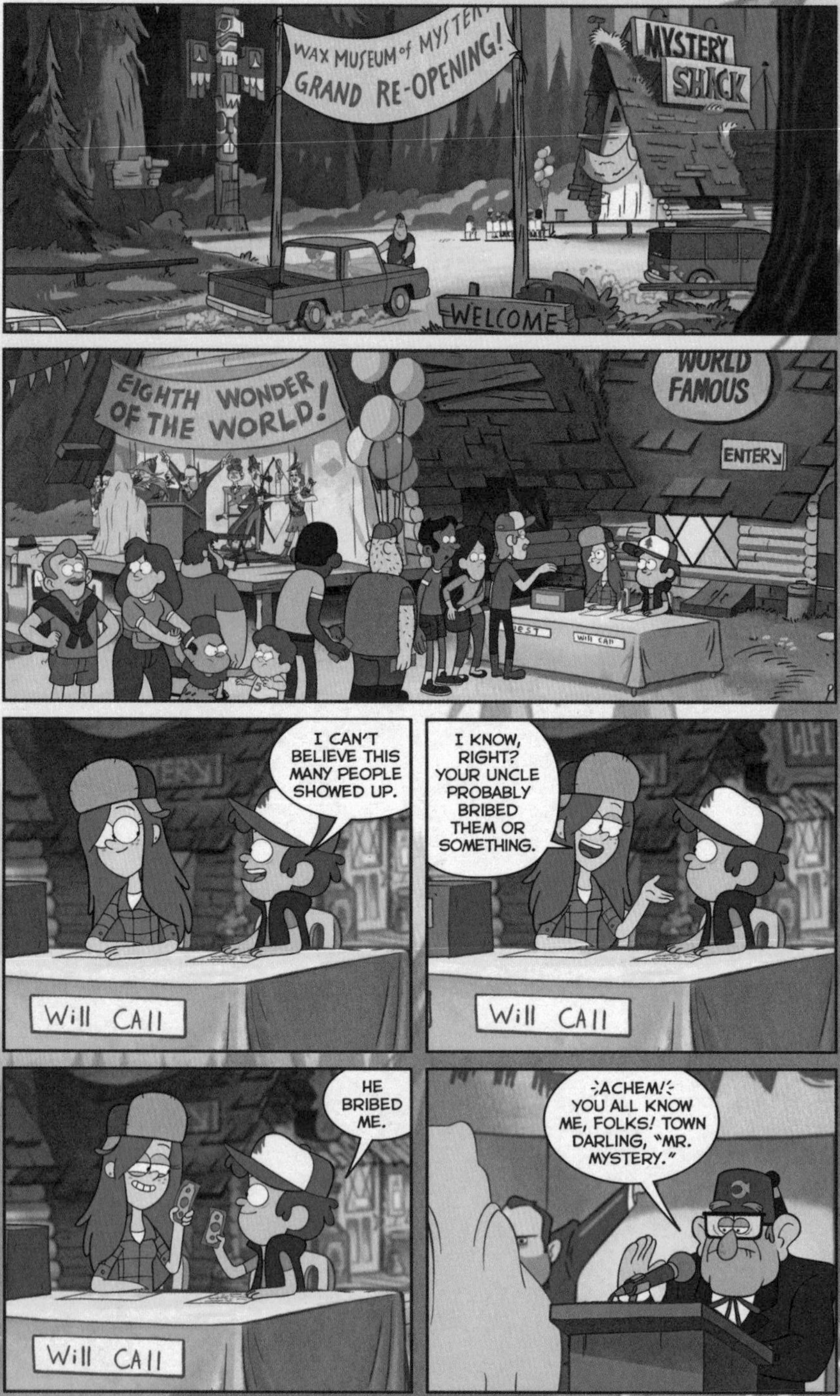
WAX MUSEUM of MYSTERY
GRAND RE-OPENING!
MYSTERY SHACK
WELCOME
EIGHTH WONDER OF THE WORLD!
WORLD FAMOUS
ENTERY
Will CAll
I CAN'T BELIEVE THIS MANY PEOPLE SHOWED UP.
I KNOW, RIGHT? YOUR UNCLE PROBABLY BRIBED THEM OR SOMETHING.
Will CAll
Will CAll
HE BRIBED ME.
Will CAll
ACHEM! YOU ALL KNOW ME, FOLKS! TOWN DARLING, "MR. MYSTERY."

PLEASE, LADIES, CONTROL YOURSELVES!

AS YOU KNOW, I ALWAYS BRING THE PEOPLE OF THIS FAIR TOWN NOVELTIES AND BEFUDDLEMENTS, THE LIKES OF WHICH THE WORLD, HAS NEVER KNOWN.

BUT ENOUGH ABOUT ME. BEHOLD... ME!

EIGHT WONDER OF THE WORLD!

DUN DUUUUN!!

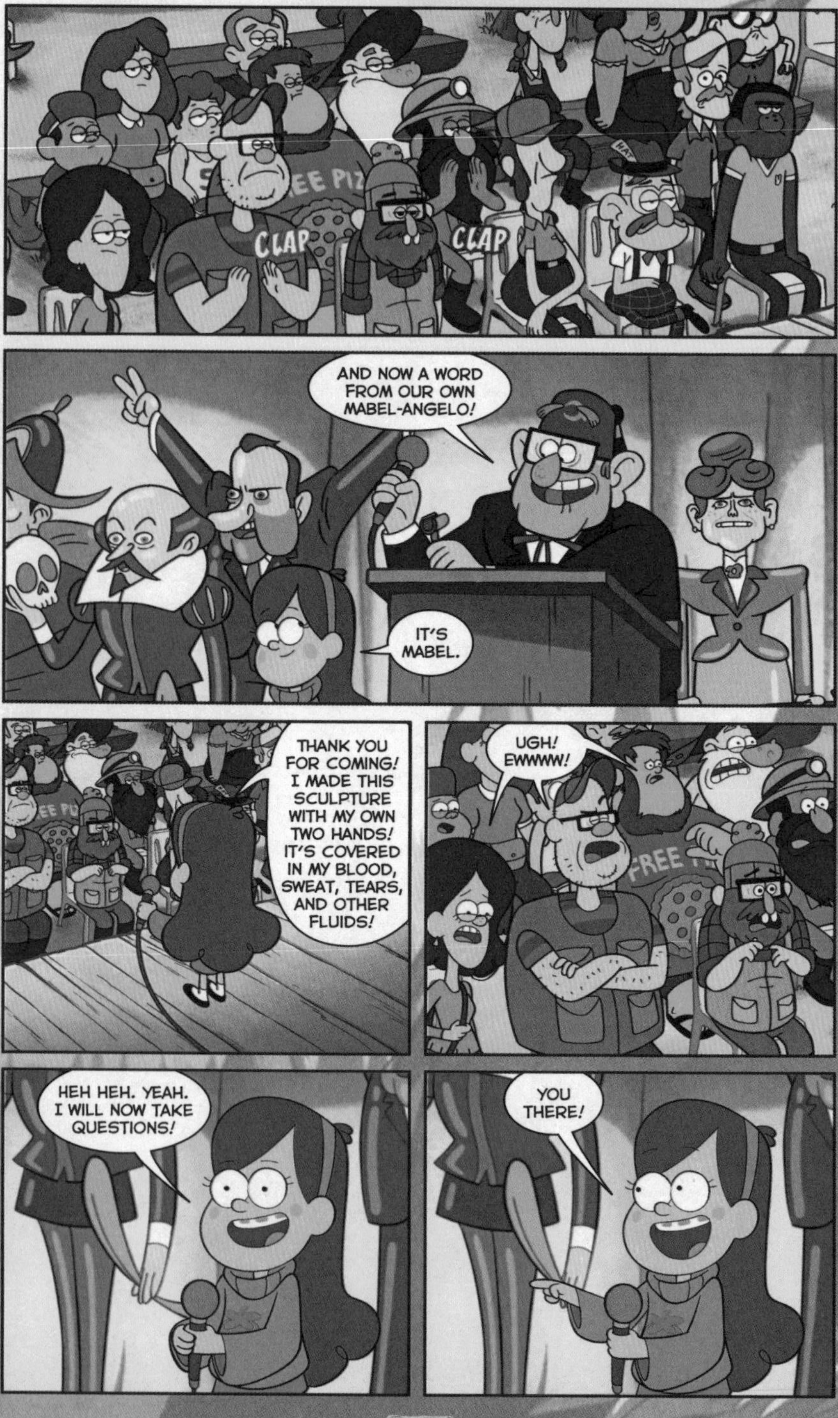
CLAP
CLAP
AND NOW A WORD FROM OUR OWN MABEL-ANGELO!
IT'S MABEL.
THANK YOU FOR COMING! I MADE THIS SCULPTURE WITH MY OWN TWO HANDS! IT'S COVERED IN MY BLOOD, SWEAT, TEARS, AND OTHER FLUIDS!
UGH! EWWWW!
HEH HEH. YEAH. I WILL NOW TAKE QUESTIONS!
YOU THERE!

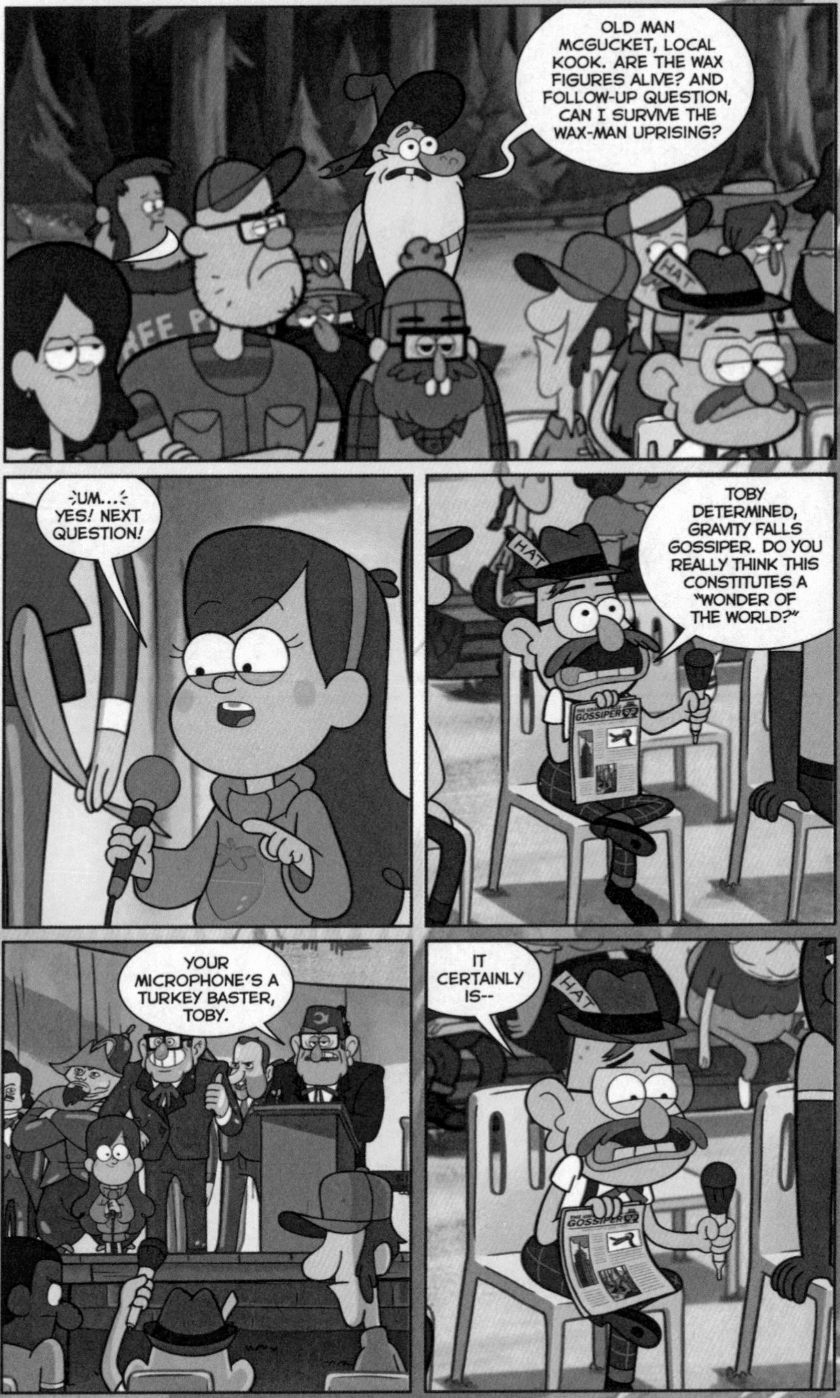
OLD MAN MCGUCKET, LOCAL KOOK. ARE THE WAX FIGURES ALIVE? AND FOLLOW-UP QUESTION, CAN I SURVIVE THE WAX-MAN UPRISING?
HAT
UM... YES! NEXT QUESTION!
TOBY DETERMINED, GRAVITY FALLS GOSSIPER. DO YOU REALLY THINK THIS CONSTITUTES A "WONDER OF THE WORLD?"
HAT
GOSSIPER
YOUR MICROPHONE'S A TURKEY BASTER, TOBY.
IT CERTAINLY IS--
HAT
GOSSIPER

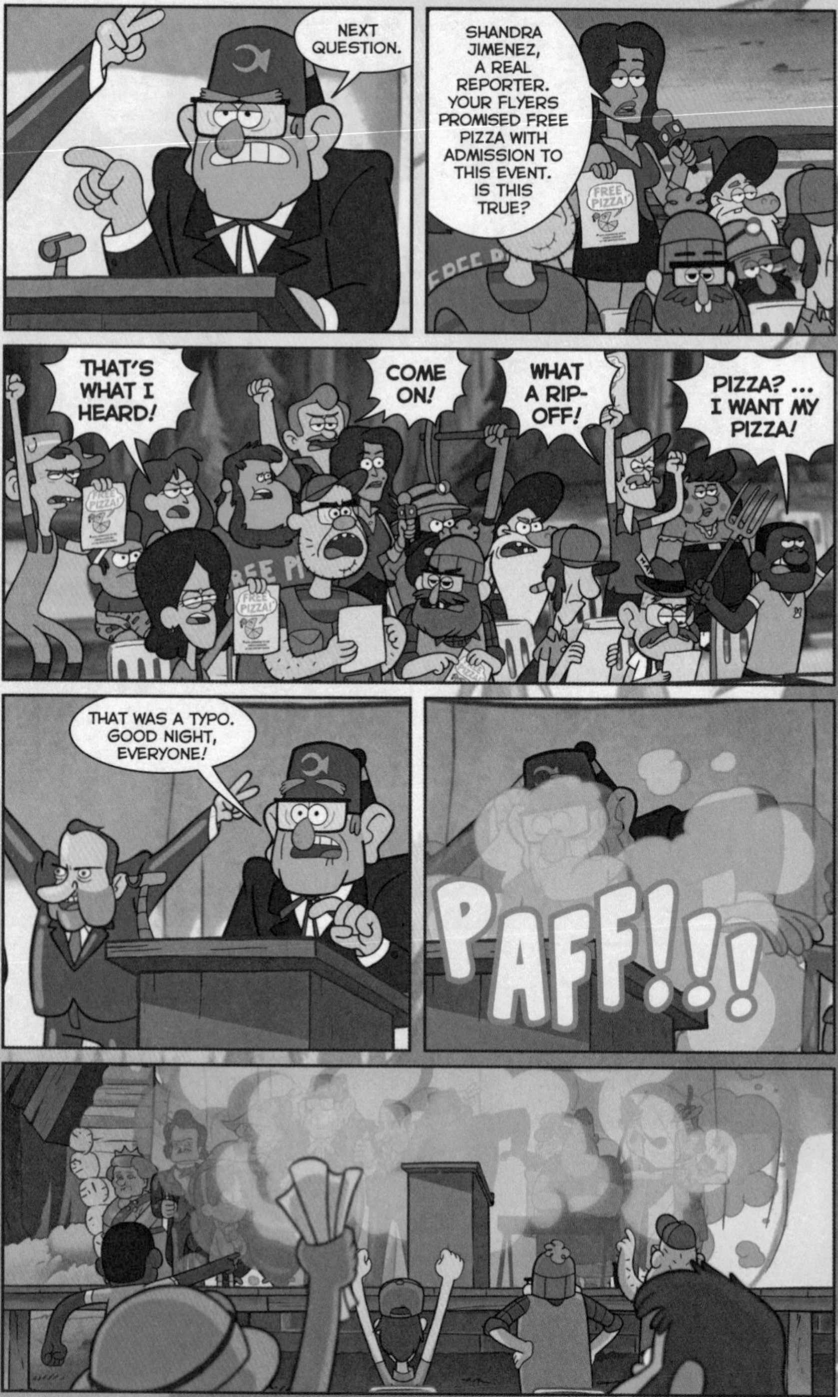
NEXT QUESTION.
SHANDRA JIMENEZ, A REAL REPORTER. YOUR FLYERS PROMISED FREE PIZZA WITH ADMISSION TO THIS EVENT. IS THIS TRUE?
FREE PIZZA!
THAT'S WHAT I HEARD!
COME ON!
WHAT A RIP-OFF!
PIZZA? ... I WANT MY PIZZA!
THAT WAS A TYPO. GOOD NIGHT, EVERYONE!
PAFF!!!

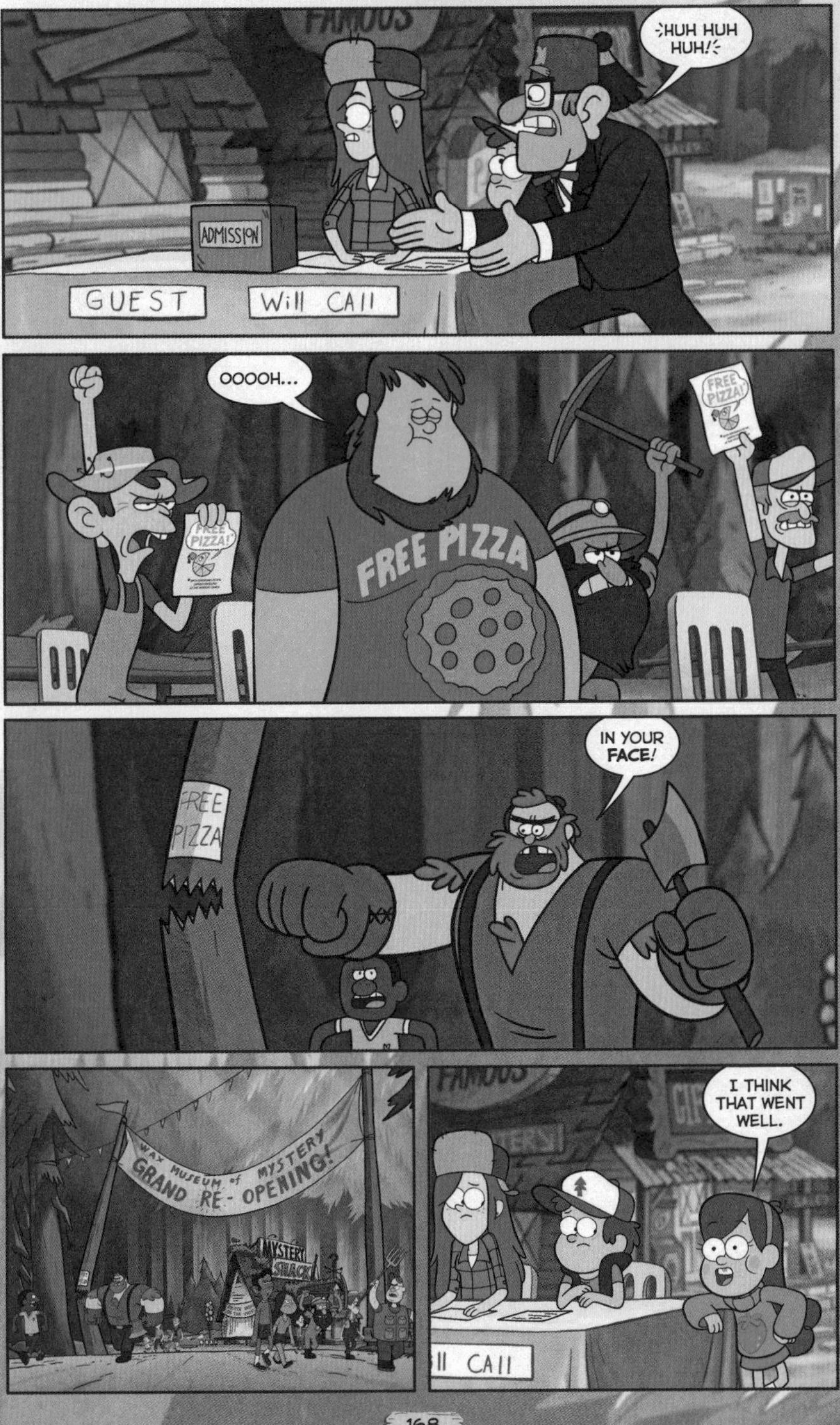
HUH HUH HUH!
ADMISSION
GUEST
Will CAll
OOOOH...
FREE PIZZA!
FREE PIZZA
IN YOUR FACE!
FREE PIZZA
WAX MUSEUM of MYSTERY GRAND RE-OPENING!
MYSTERY SHACK
I THINK THAT WENT WELL.

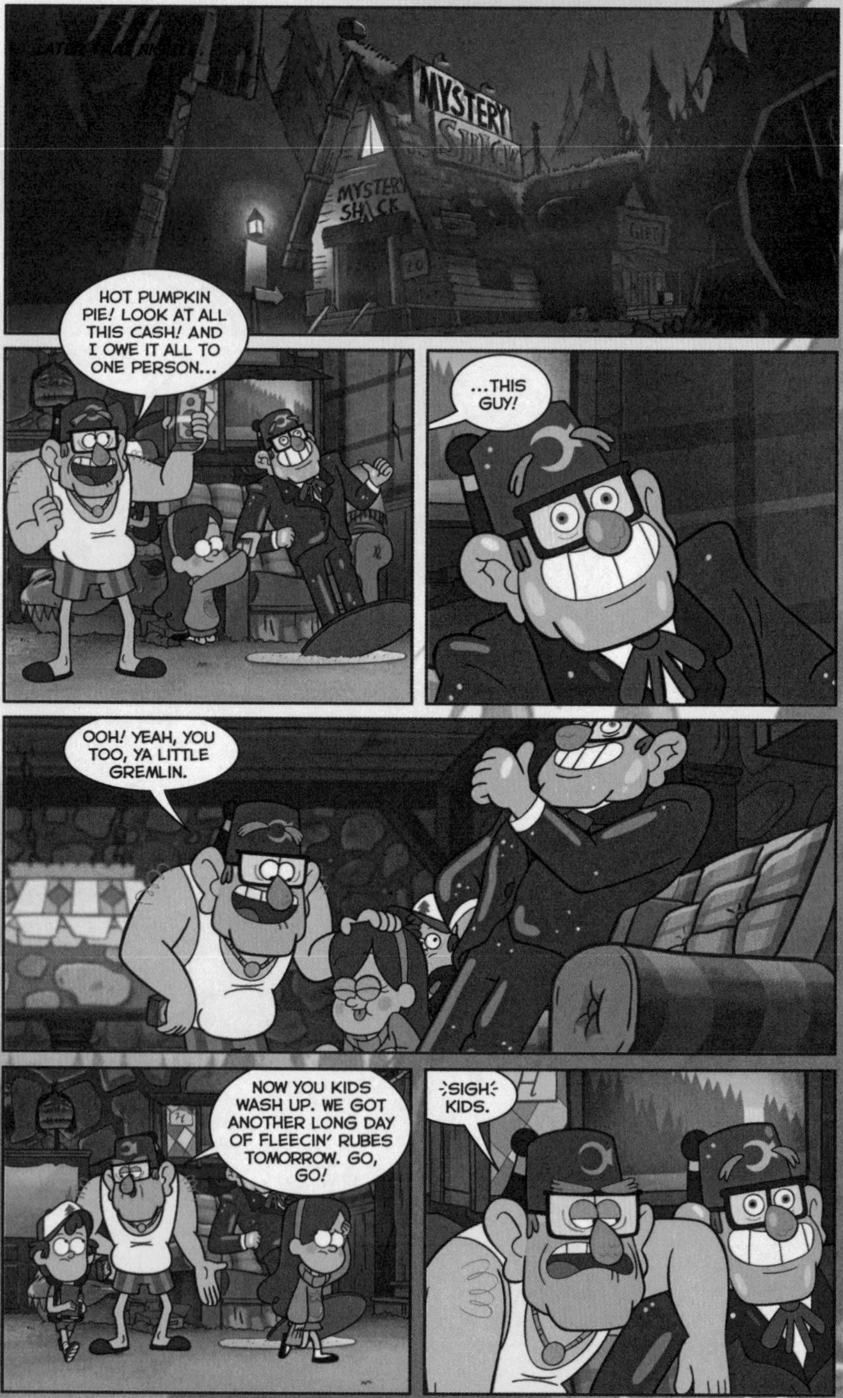
MYSTERY SHACK
MYSTERY SHACK
HOT PUMPKIN PIE! LOOK AT ALL THIS CASH! AND I OWE IT ALL TO ONE PERSON...
...THIS GUY!
OOH! YEAH, YOU TOO, YA LITTLE GREMLIN.
NOW YOU KIDS WASH UP. WE GOT ANOTHER LONG DAY OF FLEECIN' RUBES TOMORROW. GO, GO!
-SIGH- KIDS.

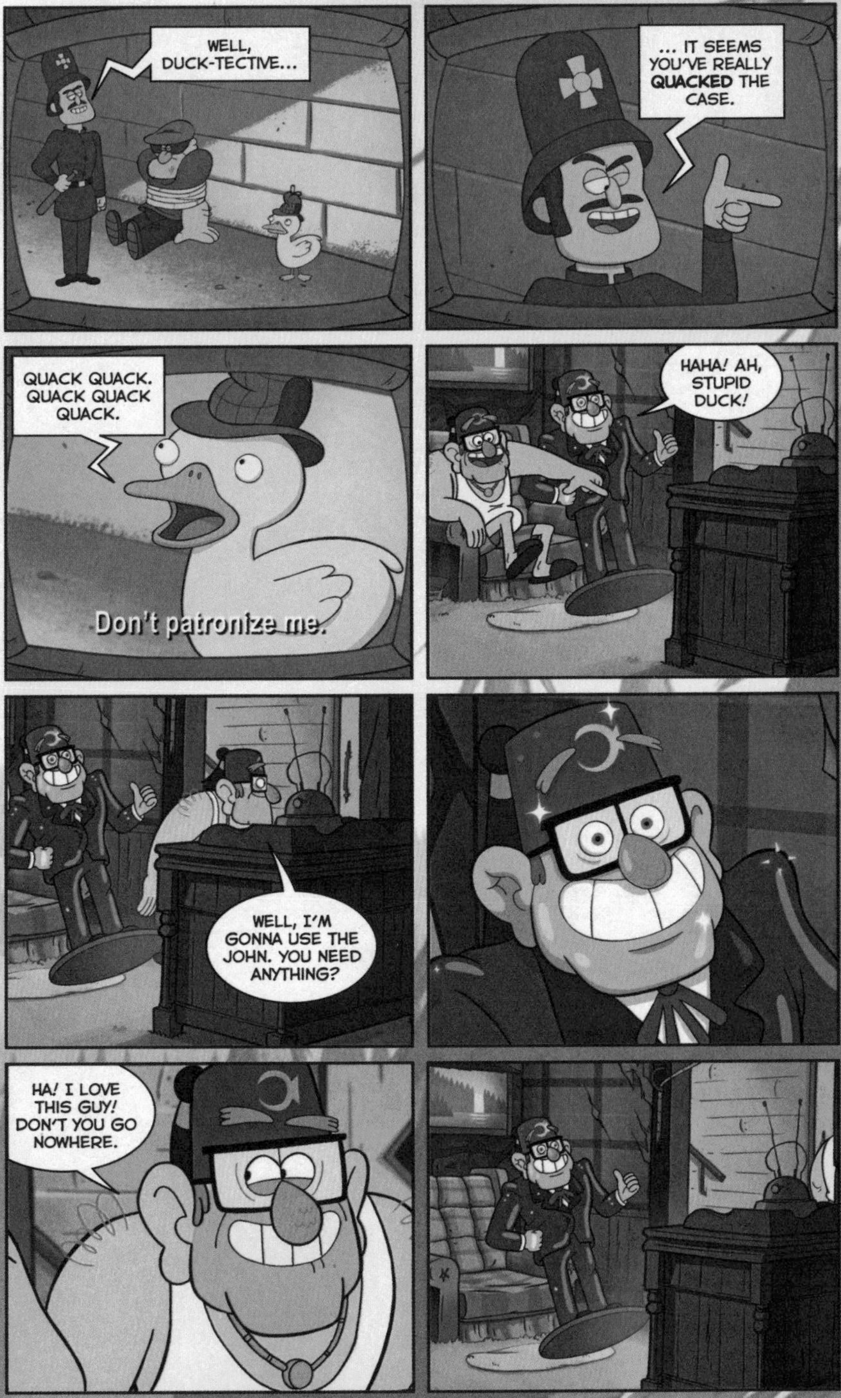
WELL, DUCK-TECTIVE...
... IT SEEMS YOU'VE REALLY QUACKED THE CASE.
QUACK QUACK. QUACK QUACK QUACK.
Don't patronize me.
HAHA! AH, STUPID DUCK!
WELL, I'M GONNA USE THE JOHN. YOU NEED ANYTHING?
HA! I LOVE THIS GUY! DON'T YOU GO NOWHERE.

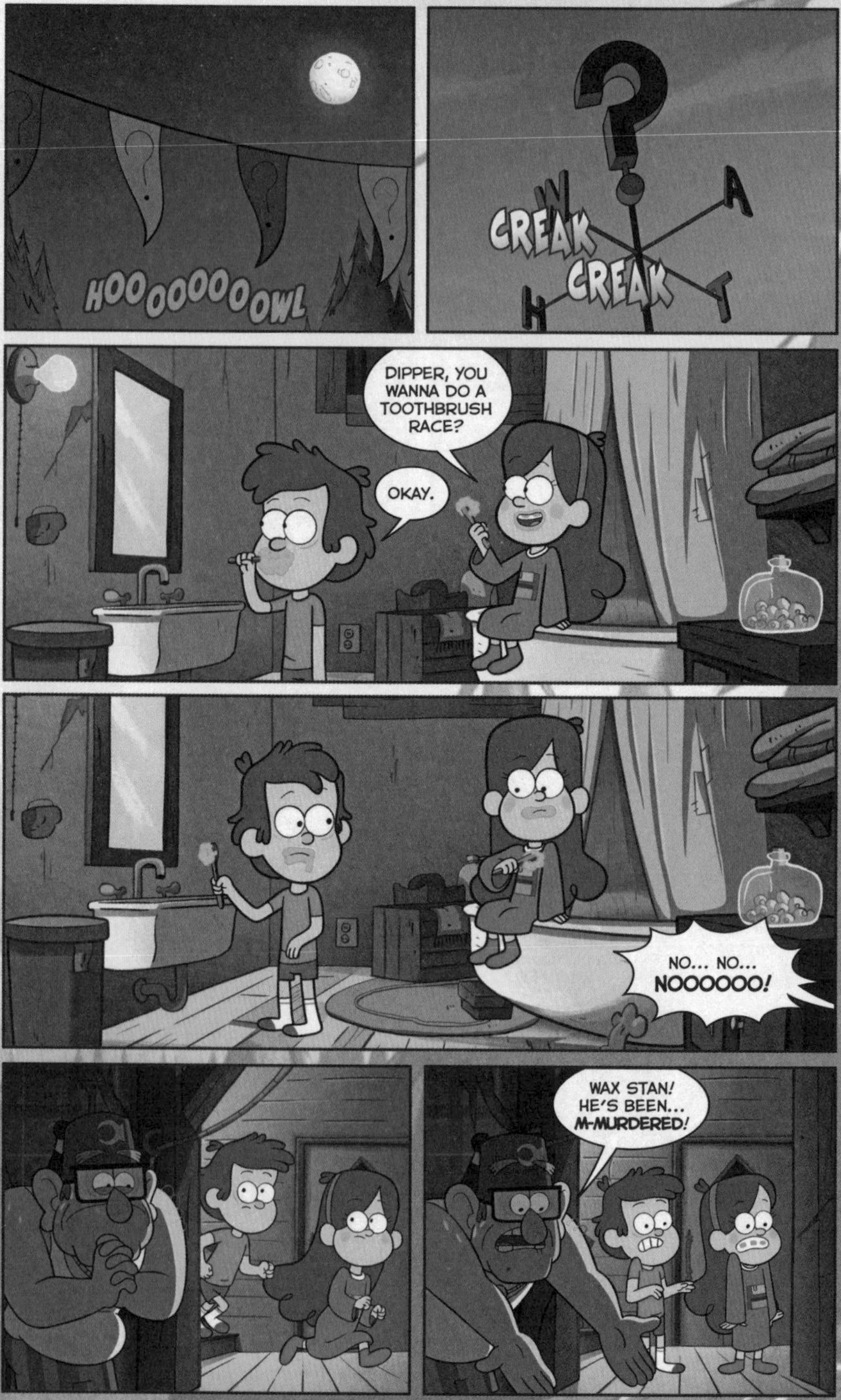
HOOOOOOOOWL
CREAK
CREAK
DIPPER, YOU WANNA DO A TOOTHBRUSH RACE?
OKAY.
NO... NO... NOOOOOO!
WAX STAN! HE'S BEEN... M-MURDERED!

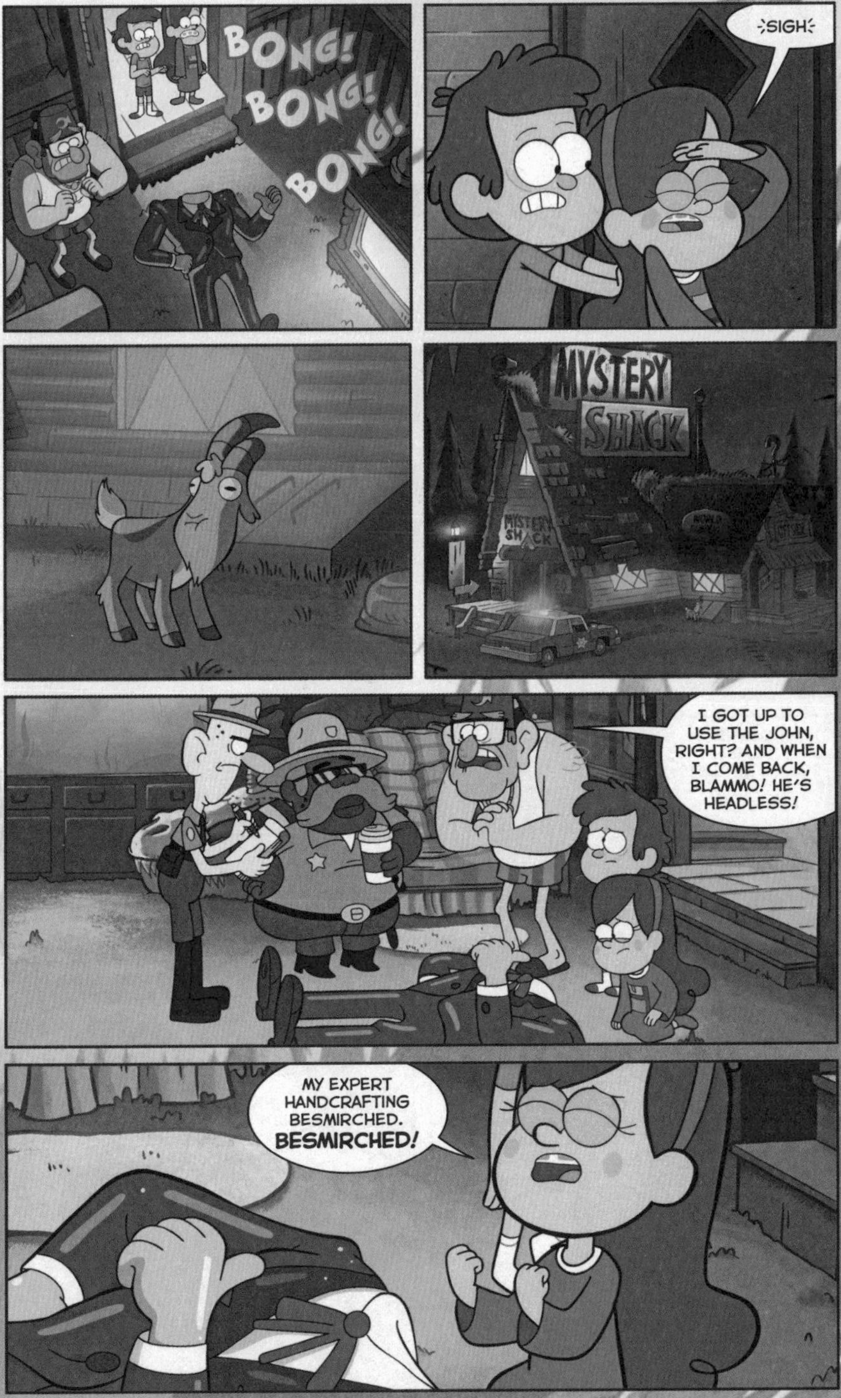
BONG! BONG! BONG!
-SIGH-
MYSTERY SHACK
I GOT UP TO USE THE JOHN, RIGHT? AND WHEN I COME BACK, BLAMMO! HE'S HEADLESS!
MY EXPERT HANDCRAFTING BESMIRCHED. BESMIRCHED!

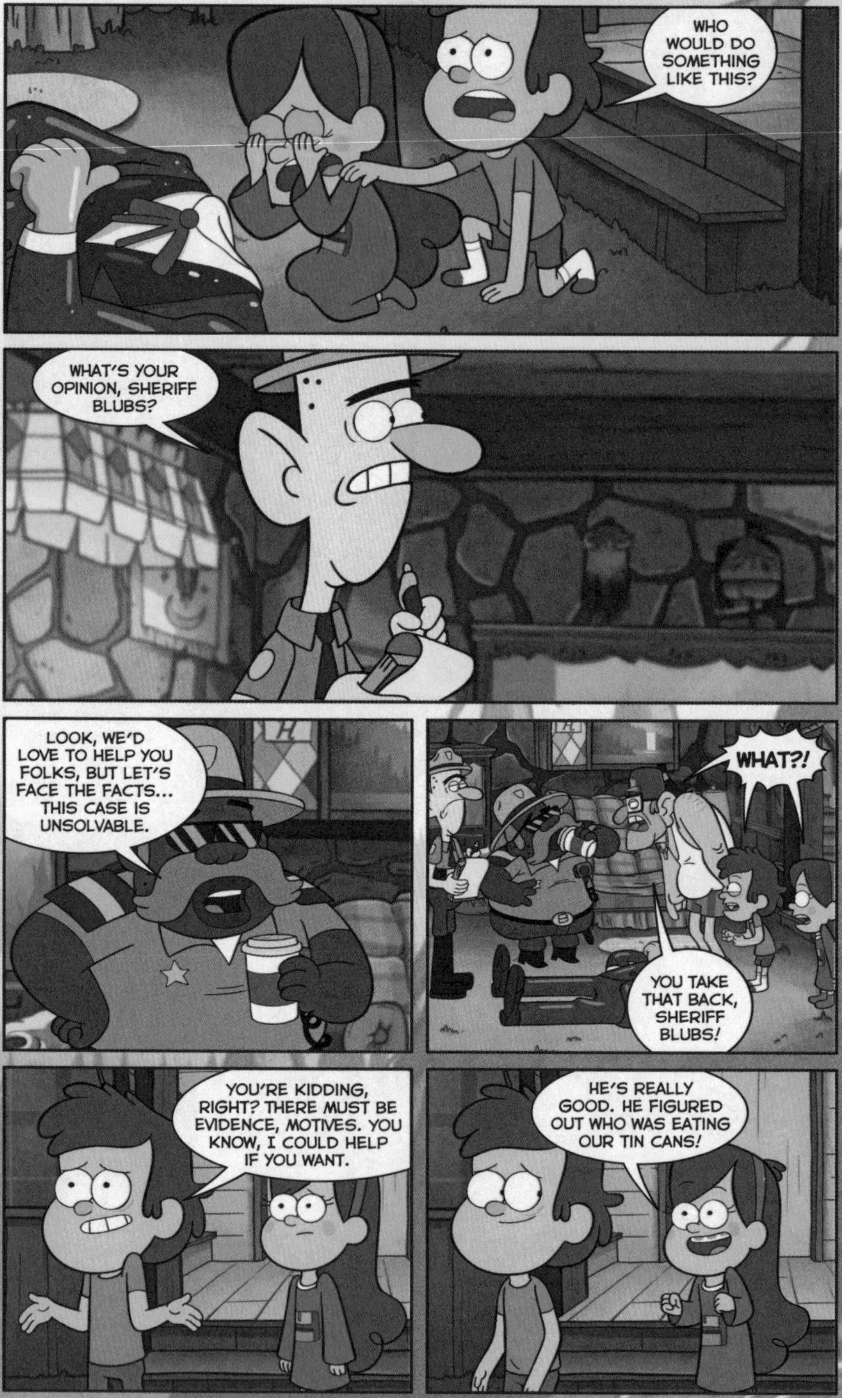
WHO WOULD DO SOMETHING LIKE THIS?
WHAT'S YOUR OPINION, SHERIFF BLUBS?
LOOK, WE'D LOVE TO HELP YOU FOLKS, BUT LET'S FACE THE FACTS... THIS CASE IS UNSOLVABLE.
WHAT?!
YOU TAKE THAT BACK, SHERIFF BLUBS!
YOU'RE KIDDING, RIGHT? THERE MUST BE EVIDENCE, MOTIVES. YOU KNOW, I COULD HELP IF YOU WANT.
HE'S REALLY GOOD. HE FIGURED OUT WHO WAS EATING OUR TIN CANS!

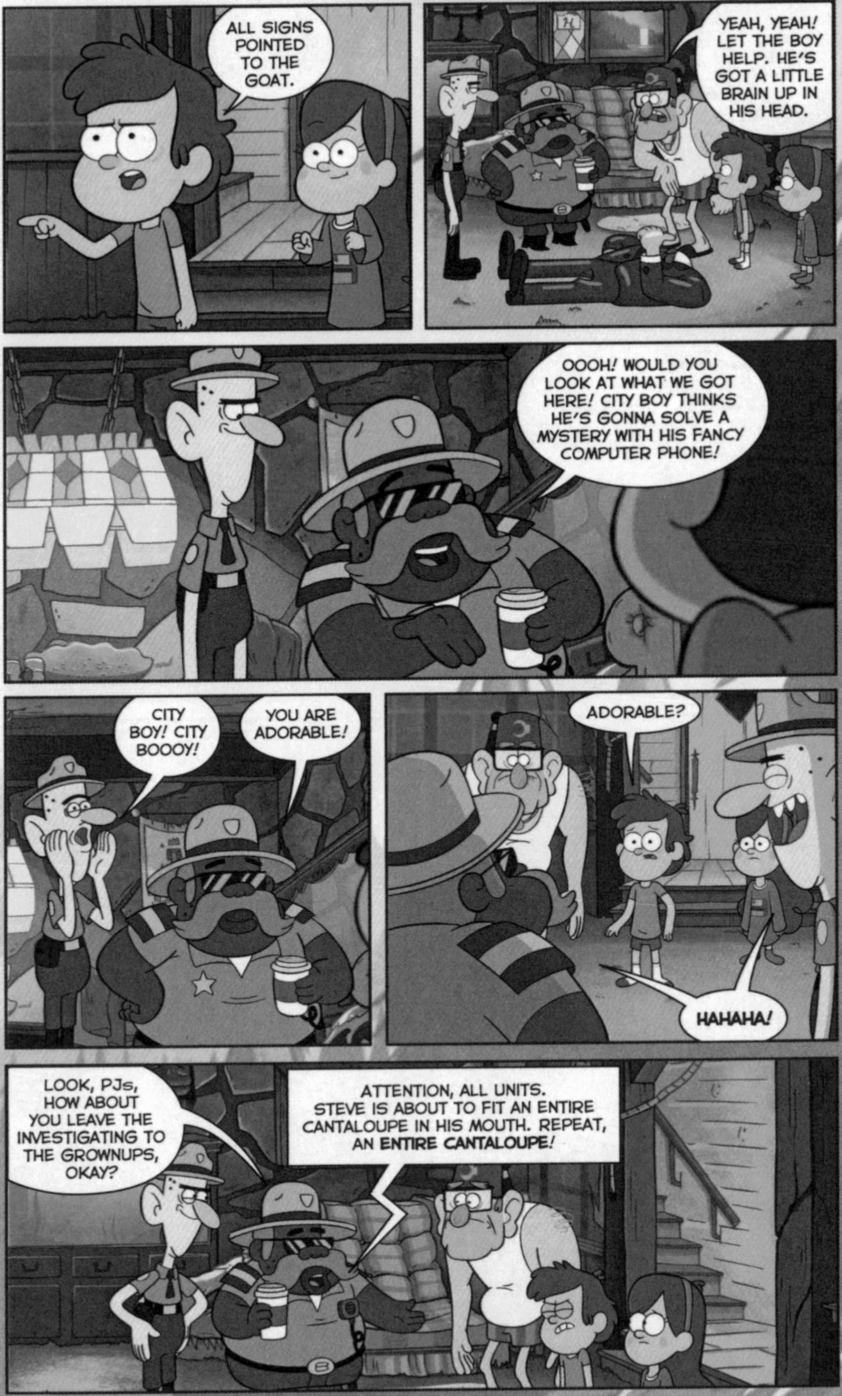
ALL SIGNS POINTED TO THE GOAT.
YEAH, YEAH! LET THE BOY HELP. HE'S GOT A LITTLE BRAIN UP IN HIS HEAD.
OOOH! WOULD YOU LOOK AT WHAT WE GOT HERE! CITY BOY THINKS HE'S GONNA SOLVE A MYSTERY WITH HIS FANCY COMPUTER PHONE!
CITY BOY! CITY BOOOY!
YOU ARE ADORABLE!
ADORABLE?
HAHAHA!
LOOK, PJs, HOW ABOUT YOU LEAVE THE INVESTIGATING TO THE GROWNUPS, OKAY?
ATTENTION, ALL UNITS. STEVE IS ABOUT TO FIT AN ENTIRE CANTALOUPE IN HIS MOUTH. REPEAT, AN ENTIRE CANTALOUPE!

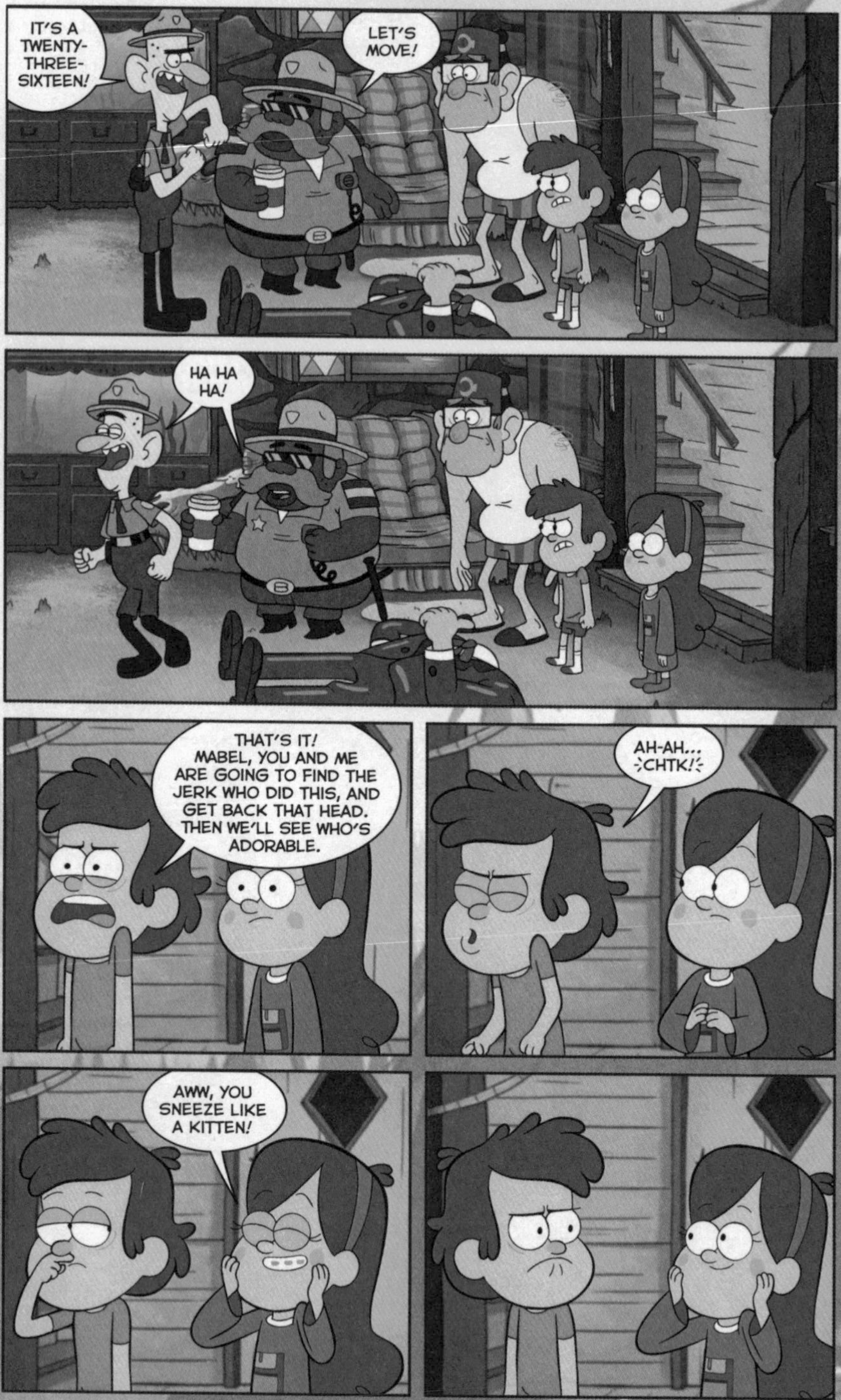
IT'S A TWENTY-THREE-SIXTEEN!
LET'S MOVE!
HA HA HA!
THAT'S IT! MABEL, YOU AND ME ARE GOING TO FIND THE JERK WHO DID THIS, AND GET BACK THAT HEAD. THEN WE'LL SEE WHO'S ADORABLE.
AH-AH... CHTK!
AWW, YOU SNEEZE LIKE A KITTEN!

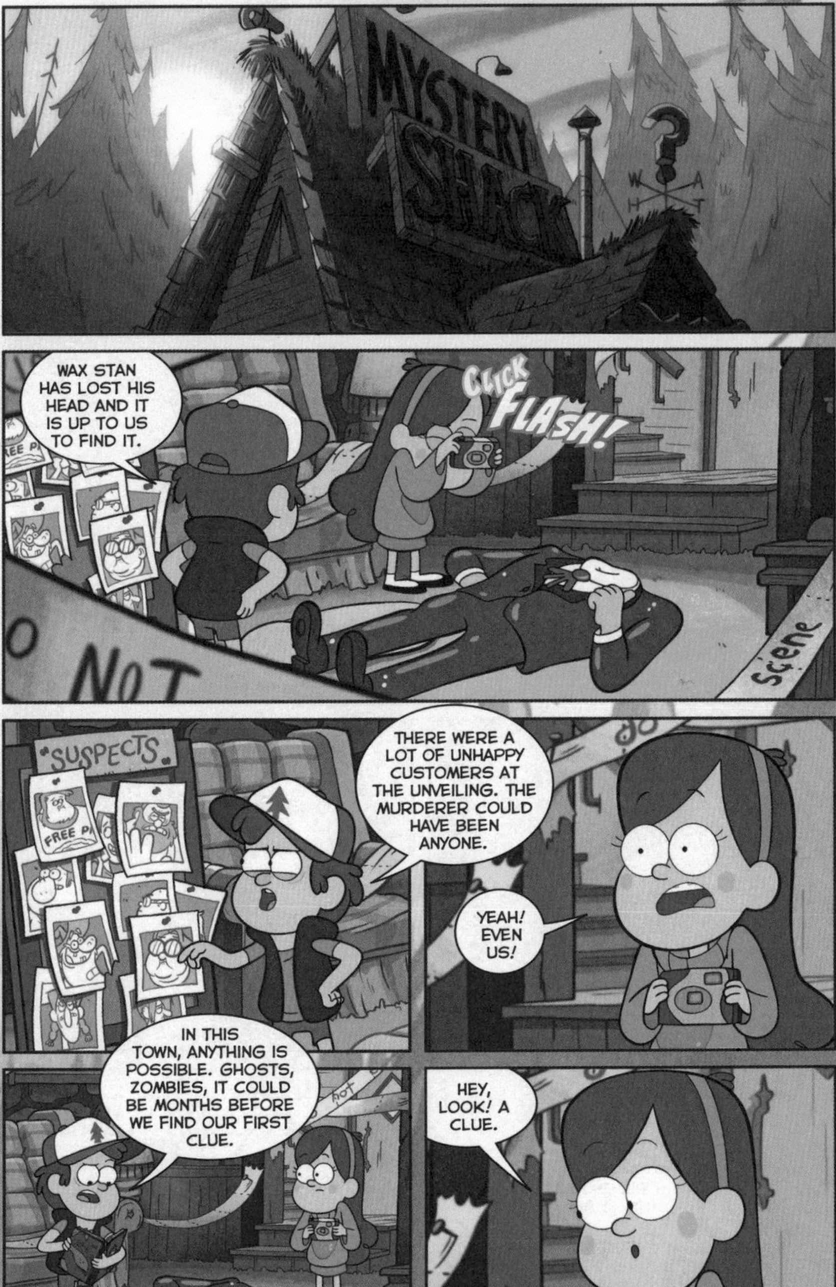
MYSTERY SHACK
WAX STAN HAS LOST HIS HEAD AND IT IS UP TO US TO FIND IT.
CLICK
FLASH!
NOT
scene
SUSPECTS
THERE WERE A LOT OF UNHAPPY CUSTOMERS AT THE UNVEILING. THE MURDERER COULD HAVE BEEN ANYONE.
YEAH! EVEN US!
IN THIS TOWN, ANYTHING IS POSSIBLE. GHOSTS, ZOMBIES, IT COULD BE MONTHS BEFORE WE FIND OUR FIRST CLUE.
HEY, LOOK! A CLUE.

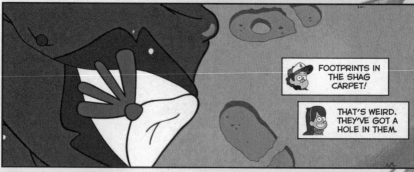

FOOTPRINTS IN THE SHAG CARPET!

THAT'S WEIRD. THEY'VE GOT A HOLE IN THEM.

AND THEY'RE LEADING TO...

:GASP!:

SO, WHAT DO YOU THINK?

IN MY OPINION... THIS IS AN AX.

WAIT A MINUTE. THE LUMBERJACK!

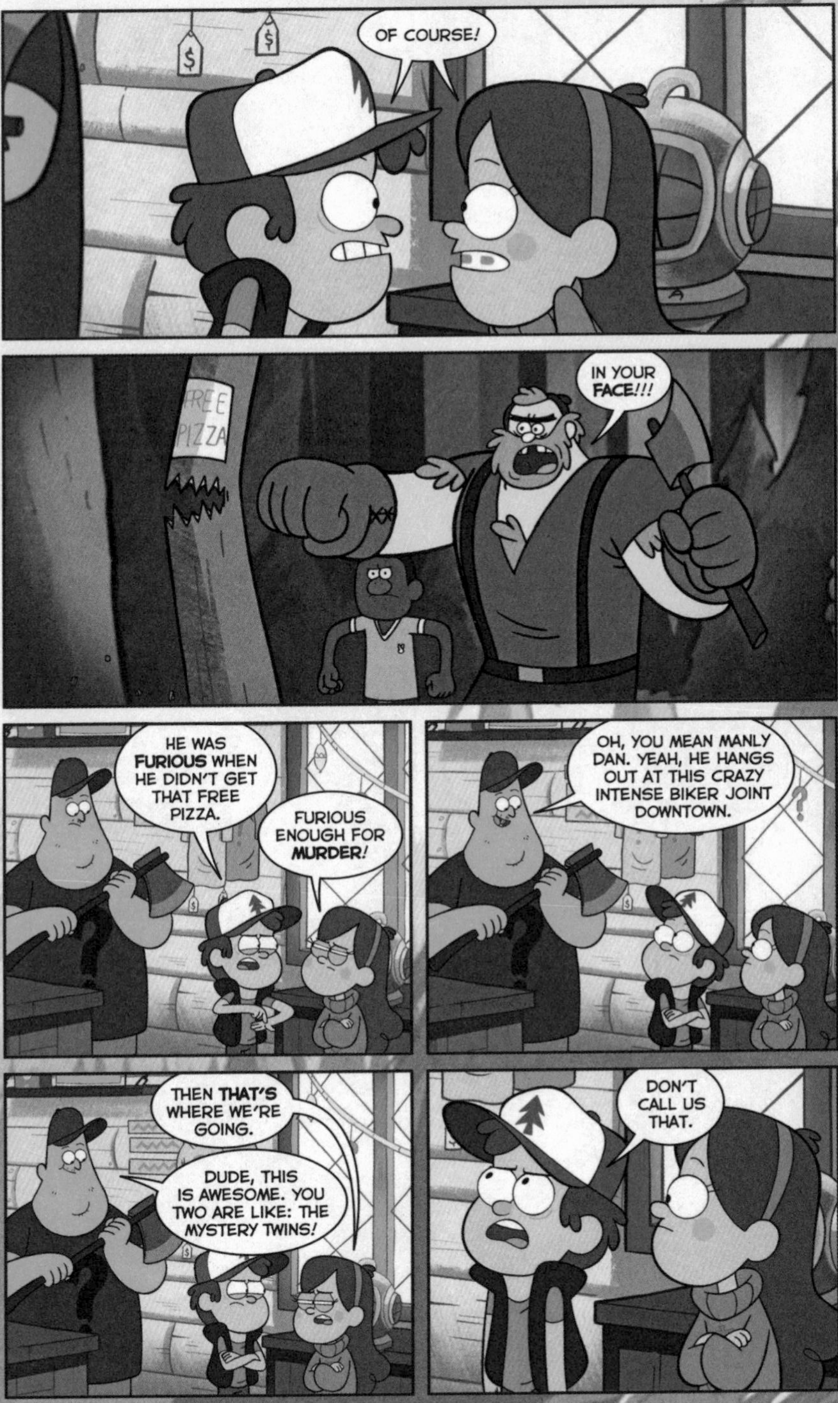
OF COURSE!
FREE PIZZA
IN YOUR FACE!!!
HE WAS FURIOUS WHEN HE DIDN'T GET THAT FREE PIZZA.
FURIOUS ENOUGH FOR MURDER!
OH, YOU MEAN MANLY DAN. YEAH, HE HANGS OUT AT THIS CRAZY INTENSE BIKER JOINT DOWNTOWN.
THEN THAT'S WHERE WE'RE GOING.
DUDE, THIS IS AWESOME. YOU TWO ARE LIKE: THE MYSTERY TWINS!
DON'T CALL US THAT.

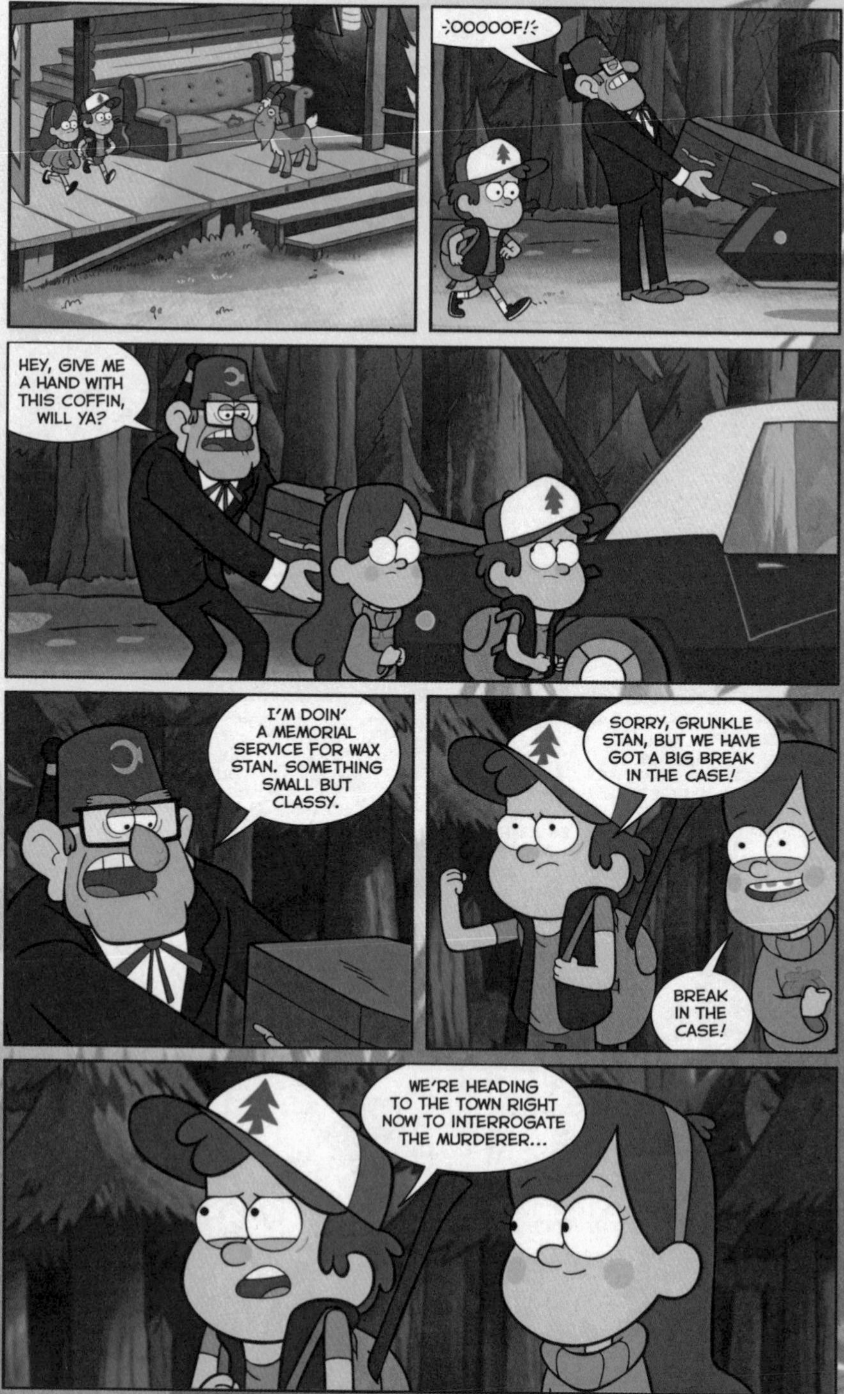
OOOOOF!
HEY, GIVE ME A HAND WITH THIS COFFIN, WILL YA?
I'M DOIN' A MEMORIAL SERVICE FOR WAX STAN. SOMETHING SMALL BUT CLASSY.
SORRY, GRUNKLE STAN, BUT WE HAVE GOT A BIG BREAK IN THE CASE!
BREAK IN THE CASE!
WE'RE HEADING TO THE TOWN RIGHT NOW TO INTERROGATE THE MURDERER...

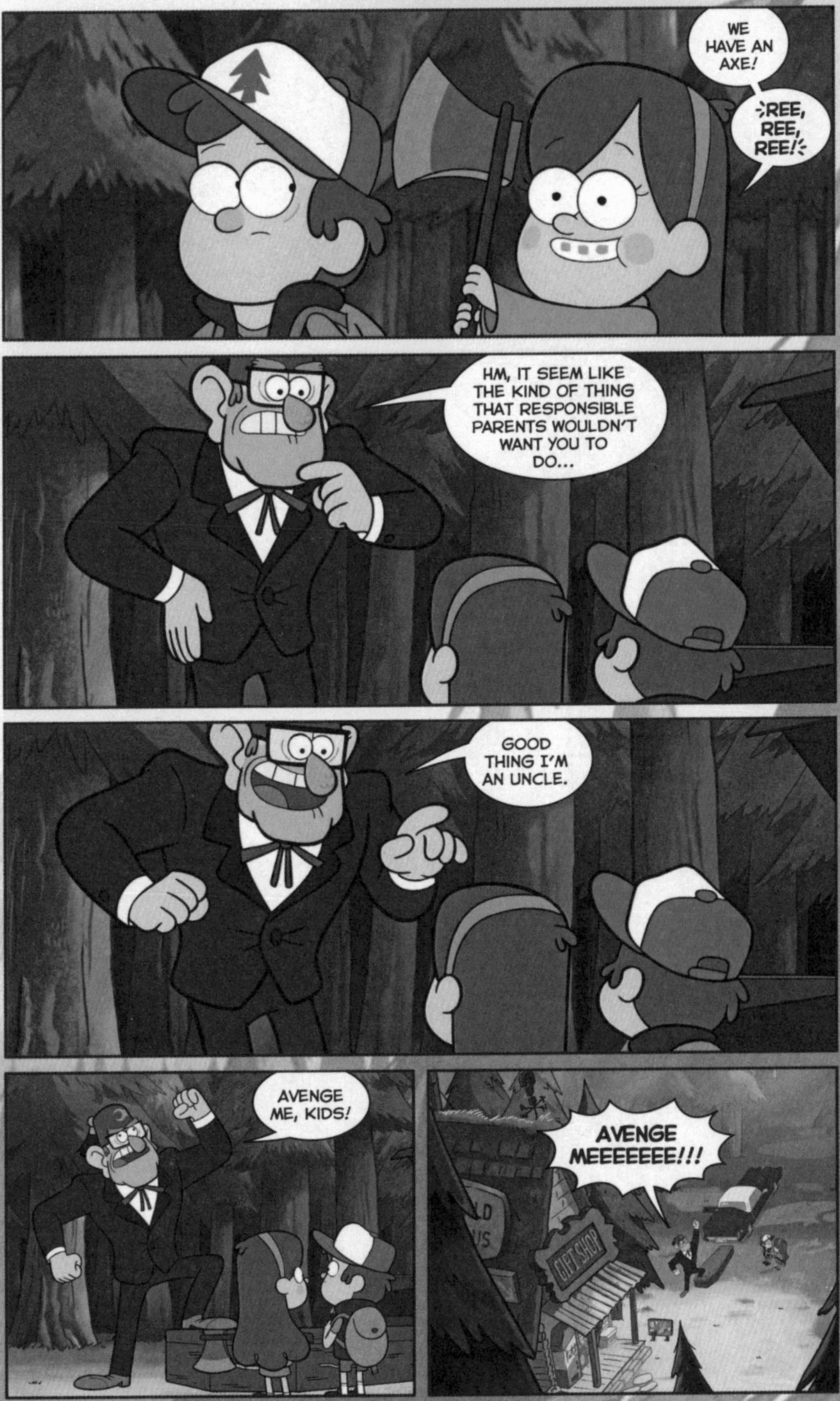
WE HAVE AN AXE!
REE, REE, REE!
HM, IT SEEM LIKE THE KIND OF THING THAT RESPONSIBLE PARENTS WOULDN'T WANT YOU TO DO...
GOOD THING I'M AN UNCLE.
AVENGE ME, KIDS!
AVENGE MEEEEEEE!!!
GIFT SHOP

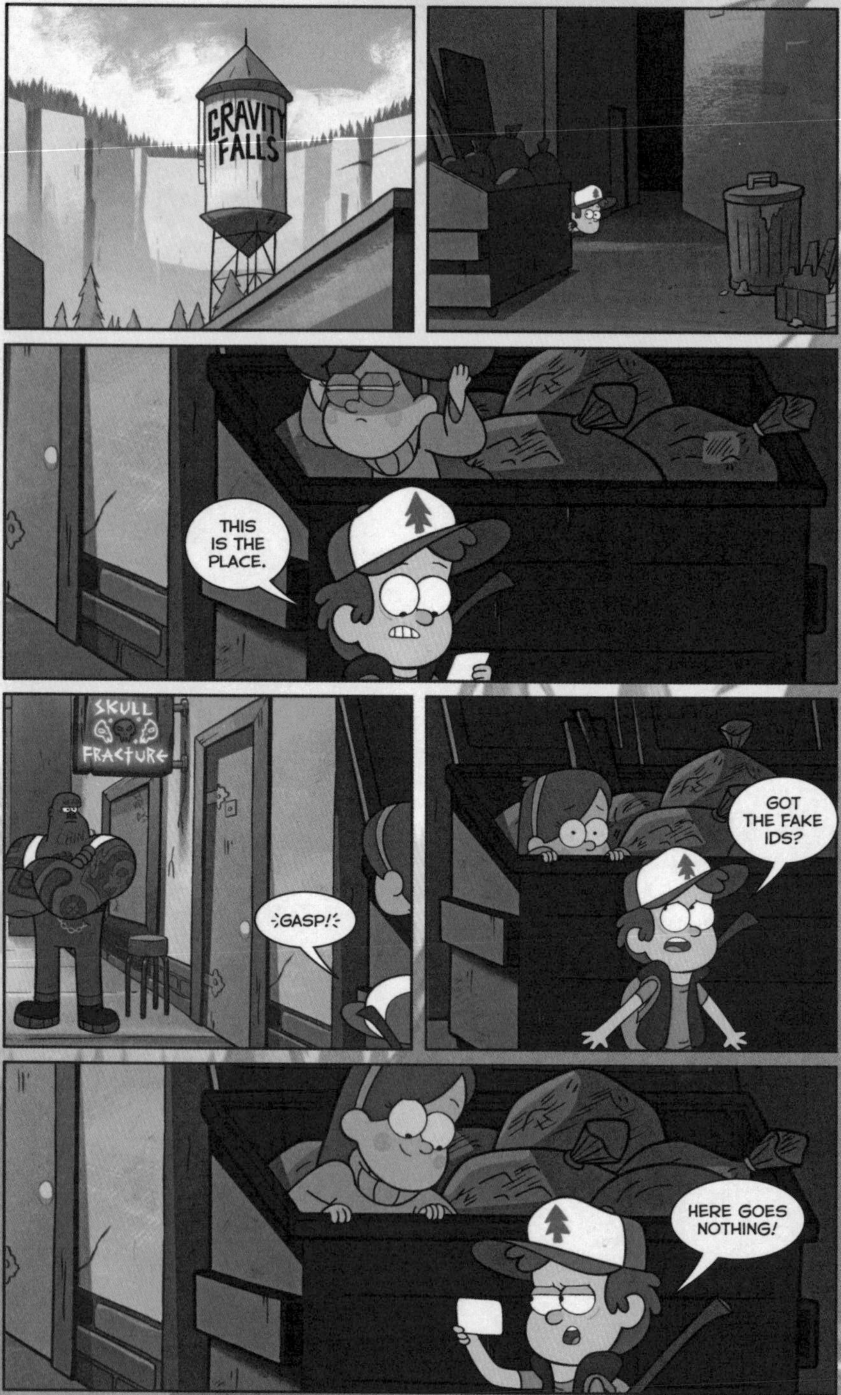
GRAVITY FALLS
THIS IS THE PLACE.
SKULL FRACTURE
GASP!
GOT THE FAKE IDS?
HERE GOES NOTHING!

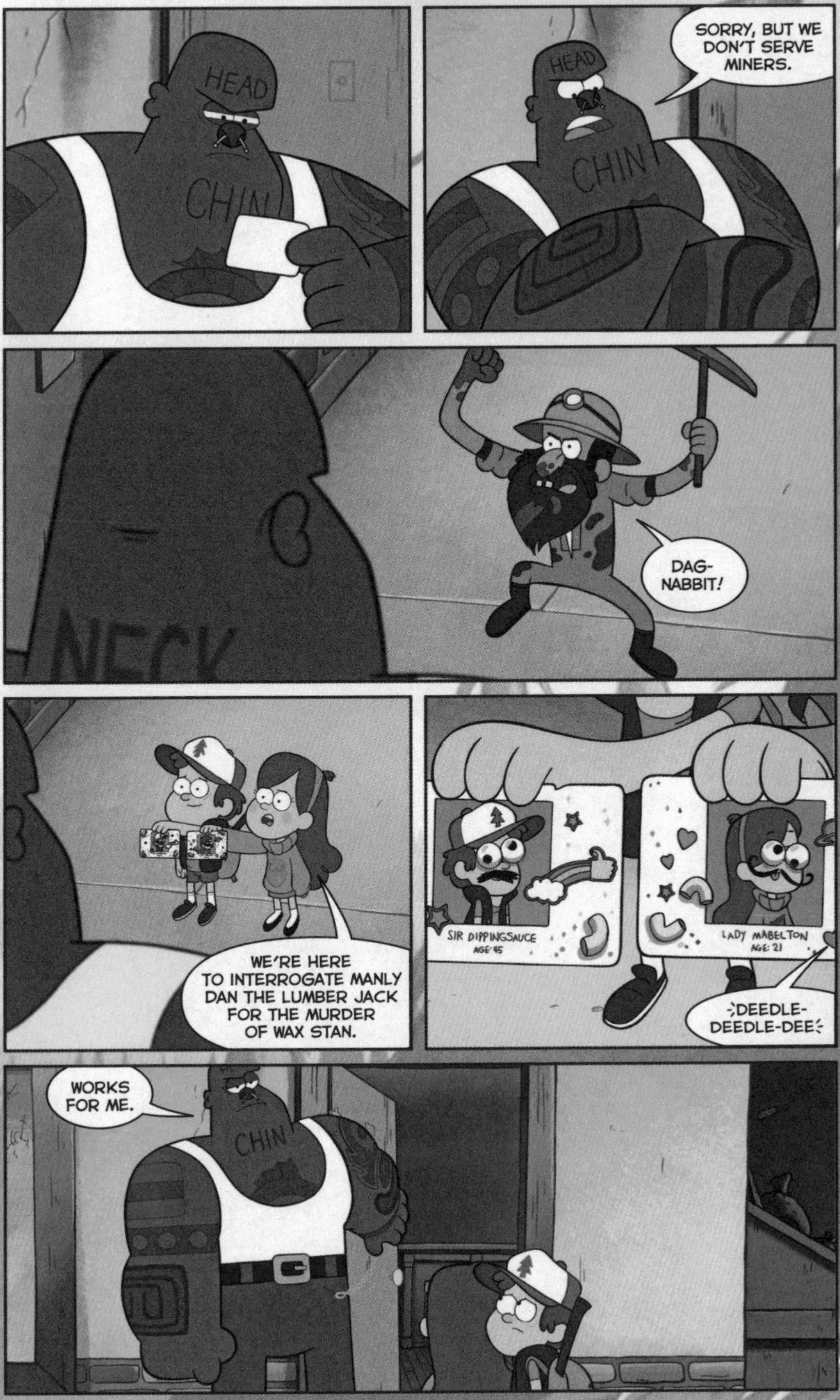
HEAD
CHIN
HEAD
CHIN
SORRY, BUT WE DON'T SERVE MINERS.
NECK
DAG-NABBIT!
WE'RE HERE TO INTERROGATE MANLY DAN THE LUMBER JACK FOR THE MURDER OF WAX STAN.
SIR DIPPINGSAUCE
AGE: 45
LADY MABELTON
AGE: 21
DEEDLE-DEEDLE-DEE
WORKS FOR ME.
CHIN

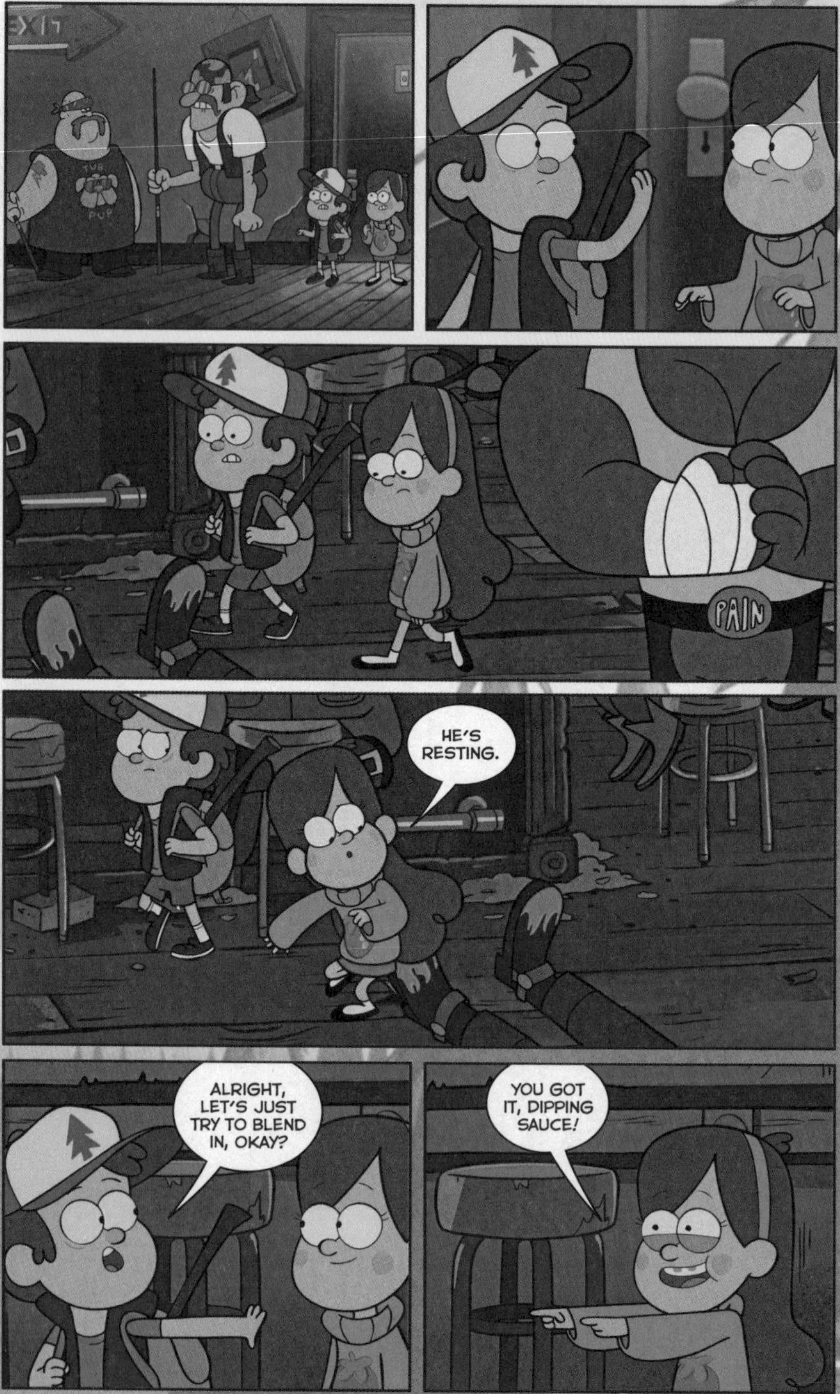
EXIT
TUB PUP
PAIN
HE'S RESTING.
ALRIGHT, LET'S JUST TRY TO BLEND IN, OKAY?
YOU GOT IT, DIPPING SAUCE!

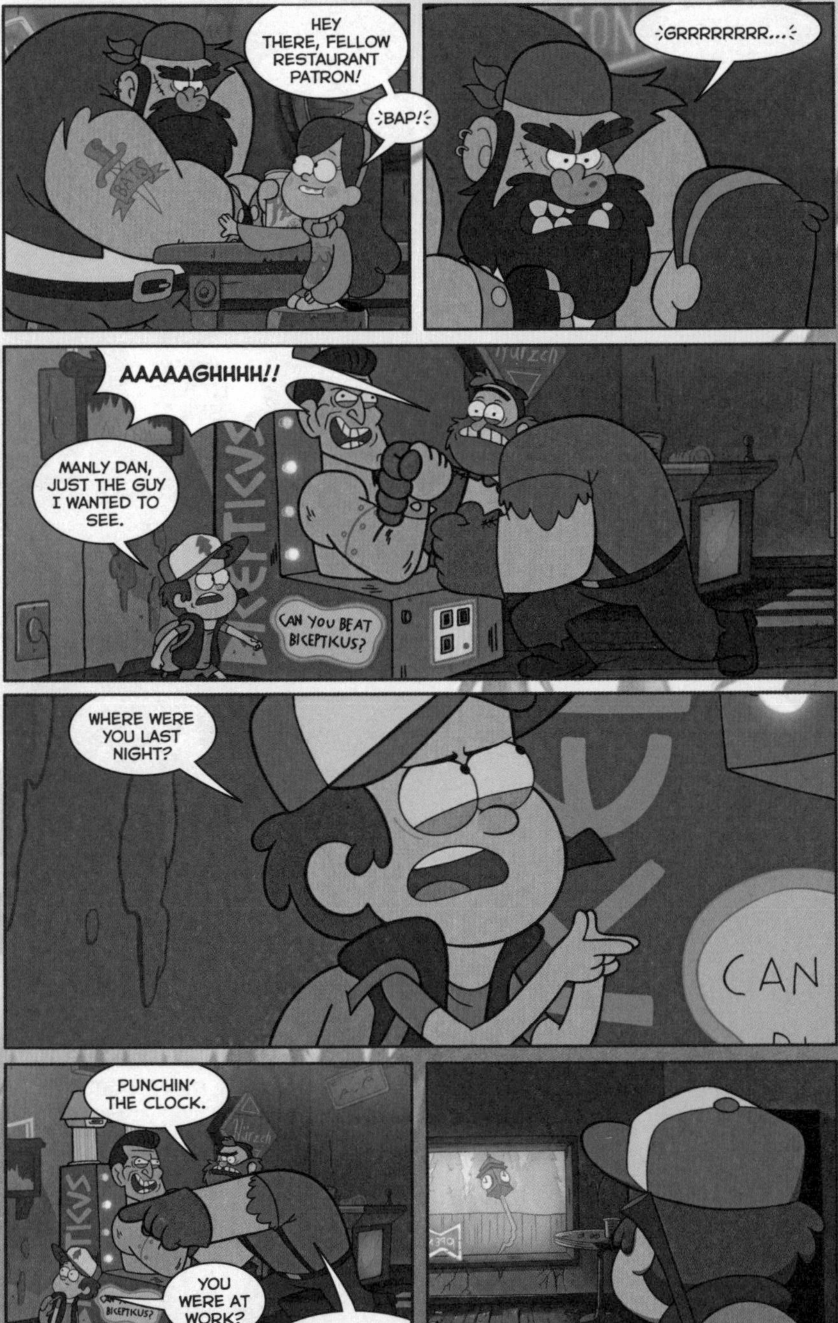
HEY THERE, FELLOW RESTAURANT PATRON!
BAP!
BATS
GRRRRRRRR...
AAAAAGHHHH!!
MANLY DAN, JUST THE GUY I WANTED TO SEE.
CAN YOU BEAT BICEPTIKUS?
WHERE WERE YOU LAST NIGHT?
CAN
PUNCHIN' THE CLOCK.
YOU WERE AT WORK?
NO, I WAS PUNCHIN' THAT CLOCK!

10 O'CLOCK, THE TIME OF THE MURDER.

SO, I GUESS YOU'VE NEVER SEEN THIS BEFORE?

CAN YOU BEAT BICEPTIKUS?

LISTEN LITTLE GIRL!

HEY, ACTUALLY I'M A--

--I WOULDN'T PICK MY TEETH WITH THAT AX. IT'S LEFT HANDED! I ONLY USE MY RIGHT HAND, THE **MANLY HAND!!!**

CAN YOU BEAT BICEPTIKUS?

RRRRRAWRRR!

GIT IM'! GIT IM'! HEHEHE!

CAN YOU BEAT BICEPTIKUS?

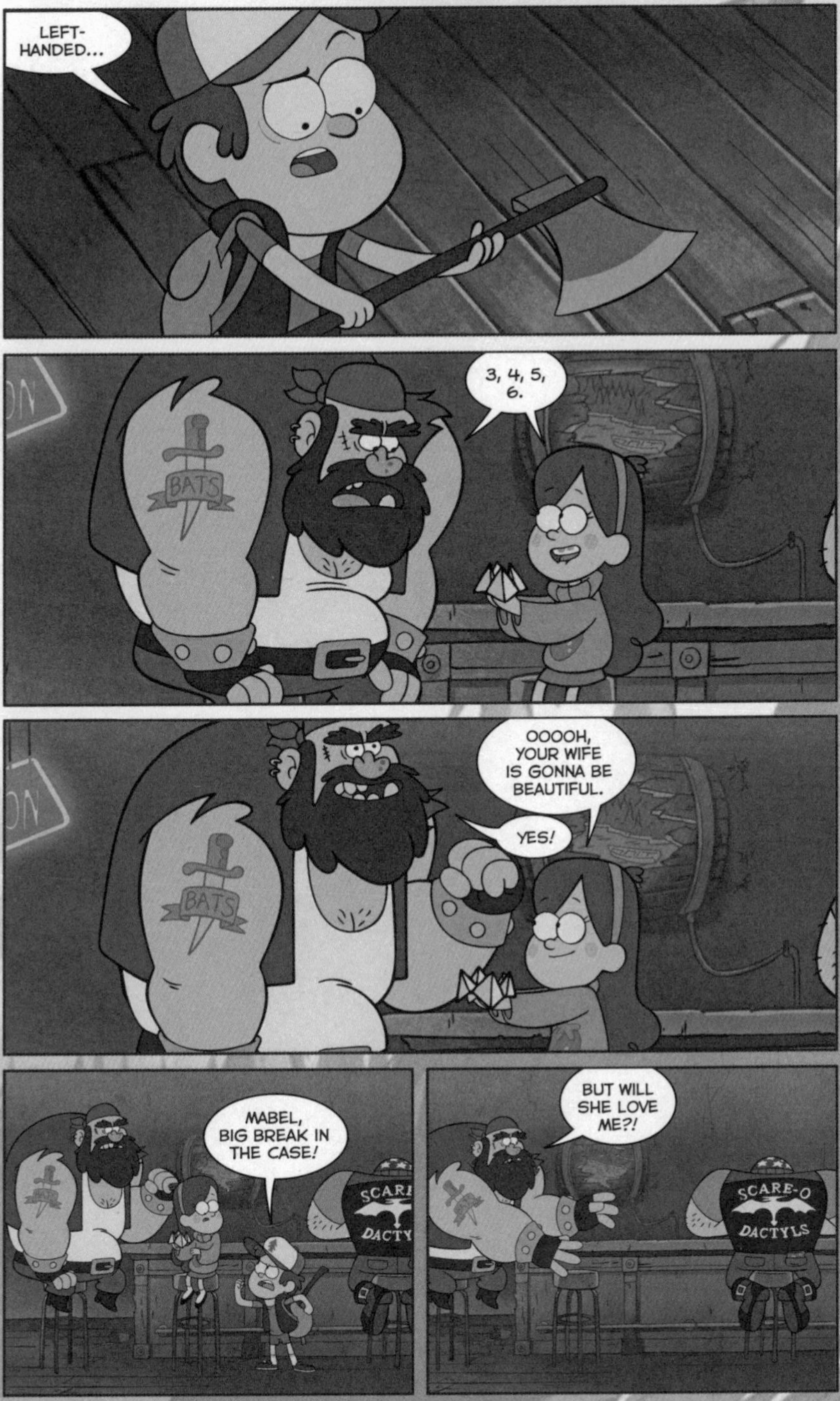
LEFT-HANDED...
3, 4, 5, 6.
OOOOH, YOUR WIFE IS GONNA BE BEAUTIFUL.
YES!
BATS
MABEL, BIG BREAK IN THE CASE!
BUT WILL SHE LOVE ME?!
SCARE-O DACTYLS

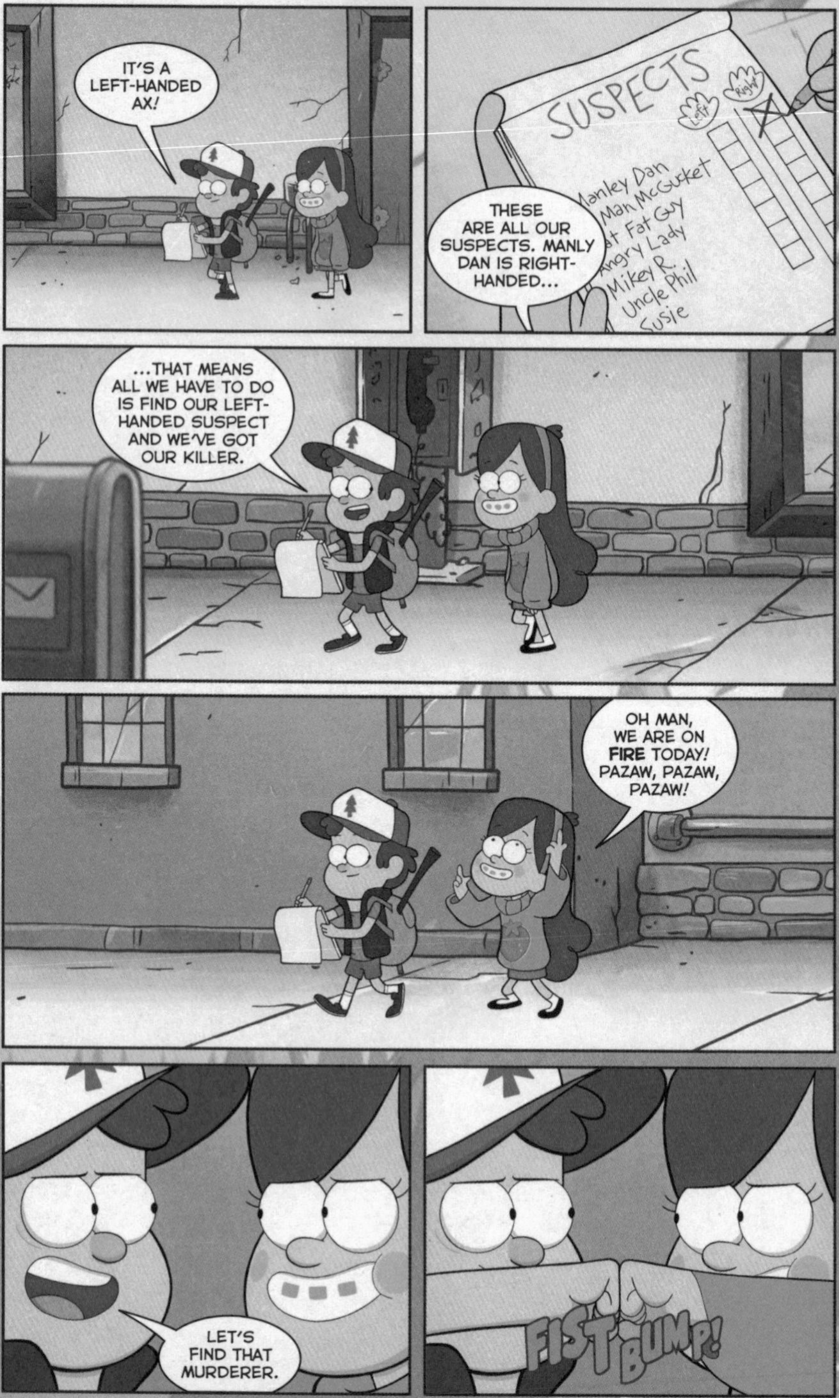
IT'S A LEFT-HANDED AX!
SUSPECTS
Left
Right
Manley Dan
Man McGucket
Fat Fat Guy
Angry Lady
Mikey R.
Uncle Phil
Susie
THESE ARE ALL OUR SUSPECTS. MANLY DAN IS RIGHT-HANDED...
...THAT MEANS ALL WE HAVE TO DO IS FIND OUR LEFT-HANDED SUSPECT AND WE'VE GOT OUR KILLER.
OH MAN, WE ARE ON **FIRE** TODAY! PAZAW, PAZAW, PAZAW!
LET'S FIND THAT MURDERER.
FIST BUMP!

Manley Dan
Old Man McGucket
That Fat Guy
Angry Lady
Mikey R.
Uncle Phil
Susie

Manley Dan
Old Man McGucket
That Fat Guy
Angry Lady
Mikey R.
Uncle Phil
Susie

Left | Right

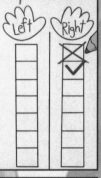

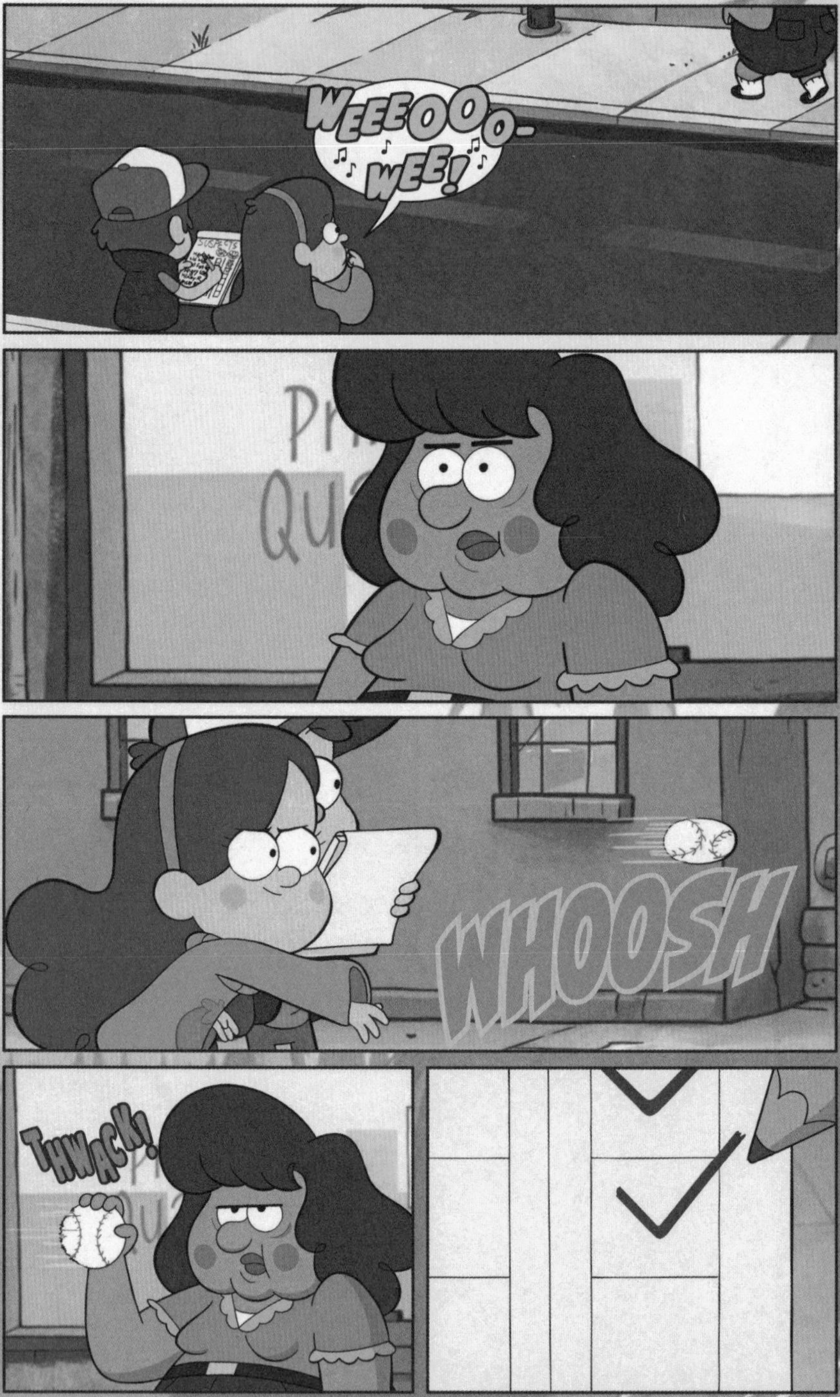
WEEEOOO-WEE!
WHOOSH
THWACK!

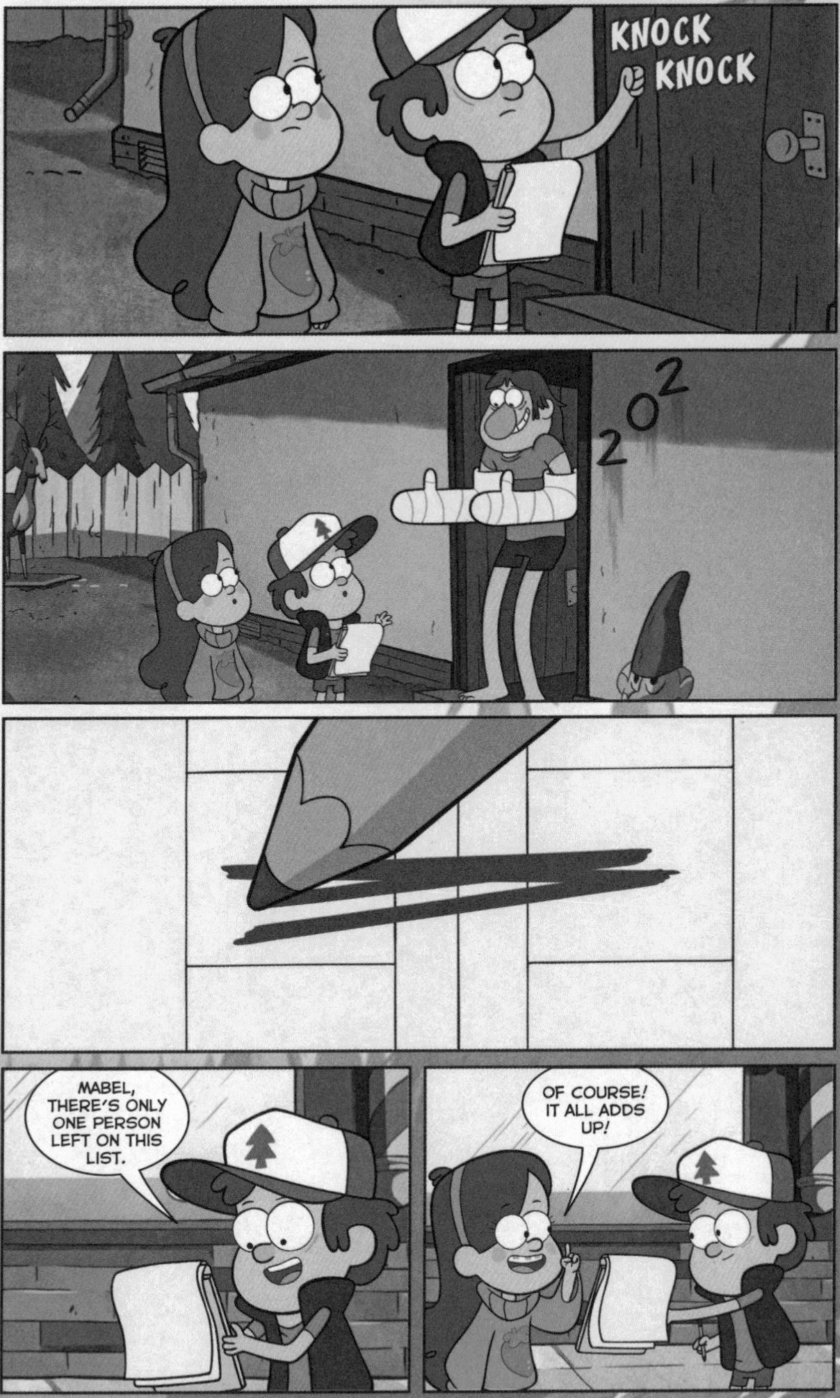
KNOCK
KNOCK
ZOZ
MABEL, THERE'S ONLY ONE PERSON LEFT ON THIS LIST.
OF COURSE! IT ALL ADDS UP!

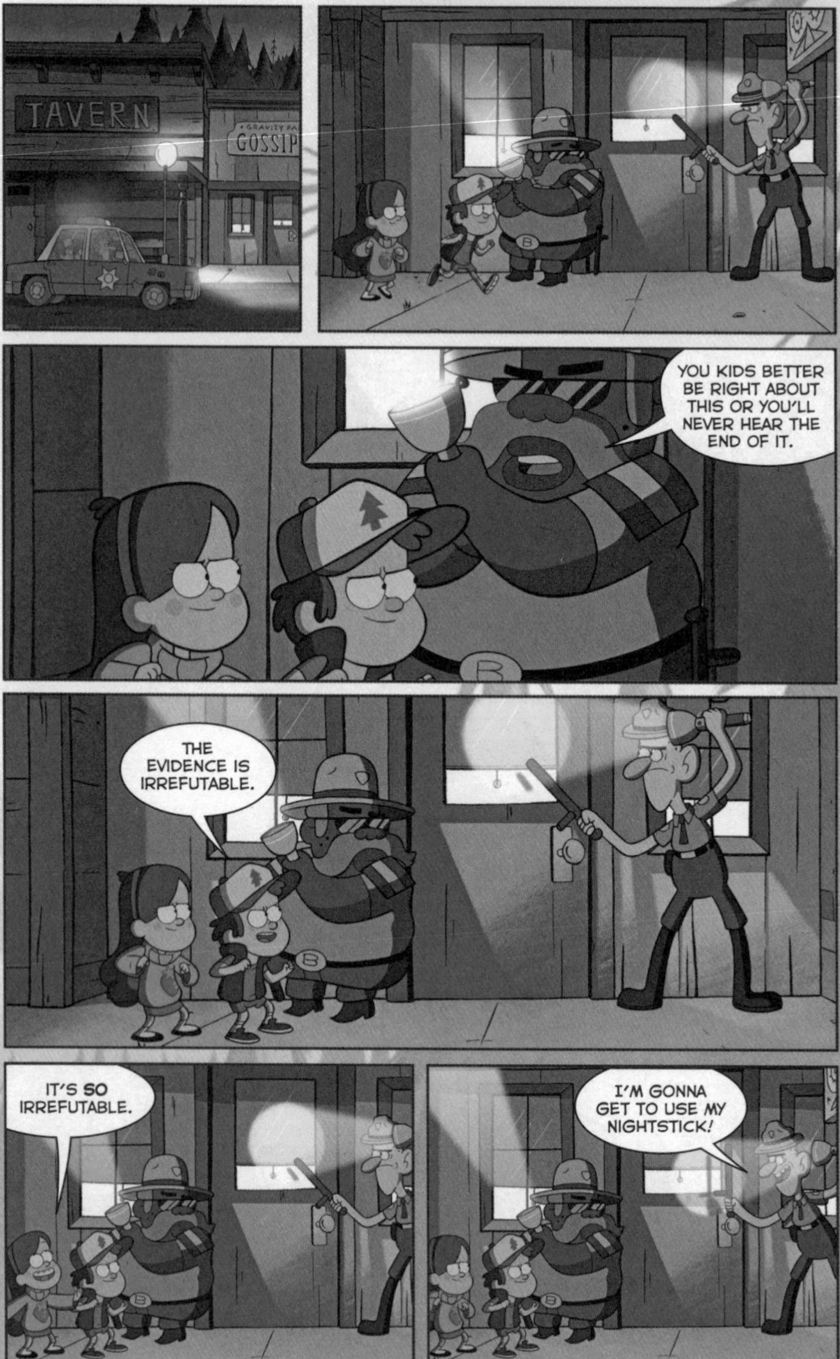
TAVERN
GRAVITY FALLS GOSSIP
YOU KIDS BETTER BE RIGHT ABOUT THIS OR YOU'LL NEVER HEAR THE END OF IT.
THE EVIDENCE IS IRREFUTABLE.
IT'S SO IRREFUTABLE.
I'M GONNA GET TO USE MY NIGHTSTICK!

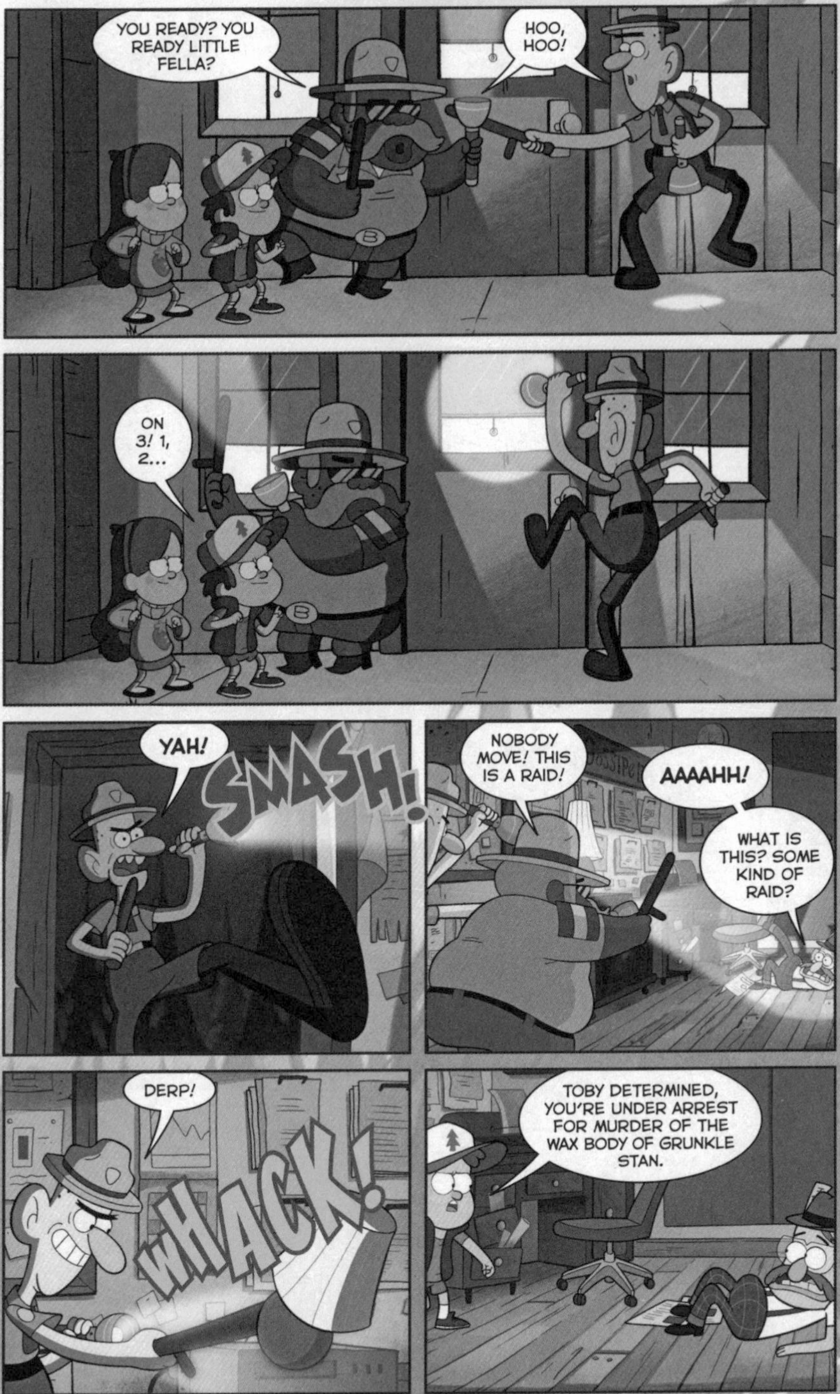
YOU READY? YOU READY LITTLE FELLA?
HOO, HOO!
ON 3! 1, 2...
YAH!
SMASH!
NOBODY MOVE! THIS IS A RAID!
AAAAHH!
WHAT IS THIS? SOME KIND OF RAID?
DERP!
WHACK!
TOBY DETERMINED, YOU'RE UNDER ARREST FOR MURDER OF THE WAX BODY OF GRUNKLE STAN.

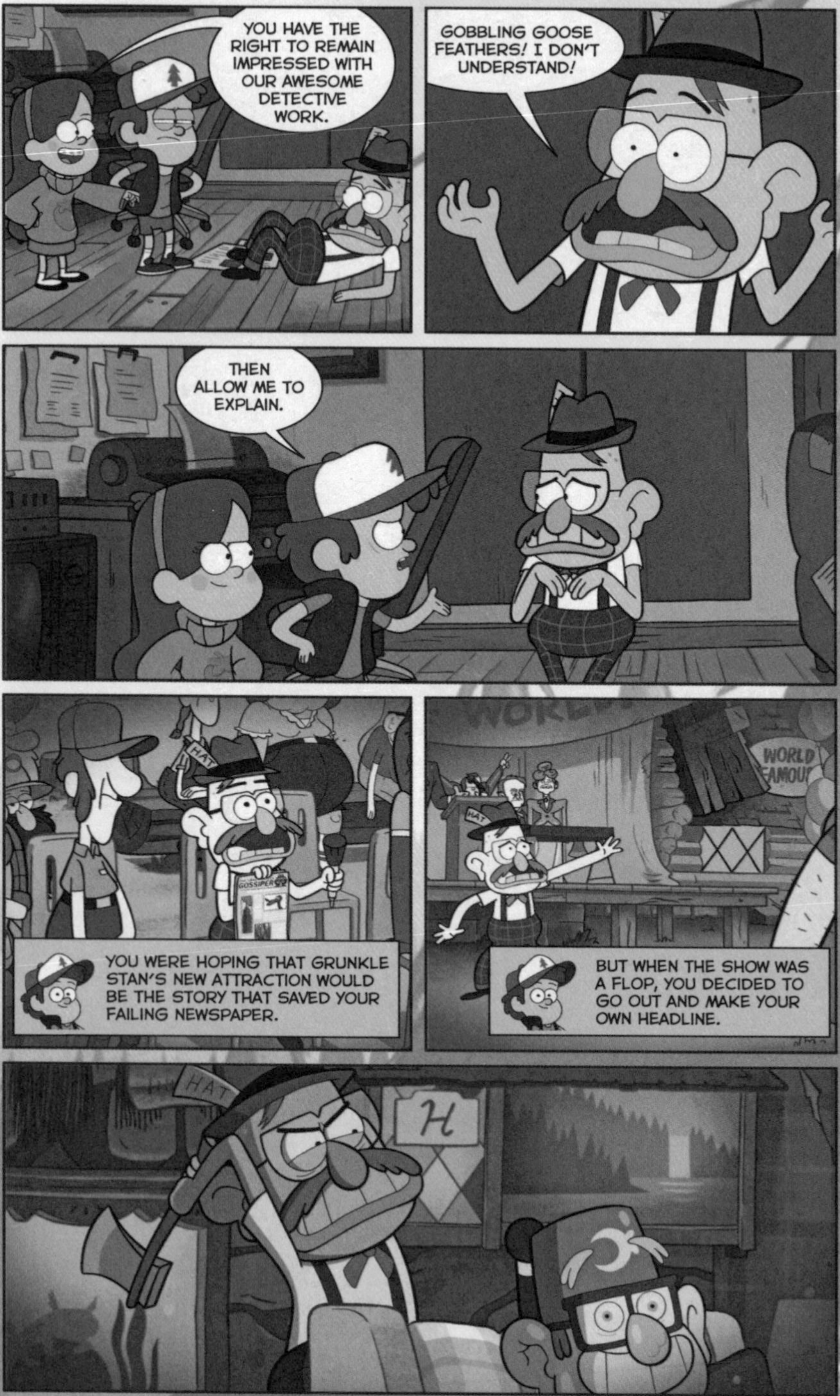
YOU HAVE THE RIGHT TO REMAIN IMPRESSED WITH OUR AWESOME DETECTIVE WORK.
GOBBLING GOOSE FEATHERS! I DON'T UNDERSTAND!
THEN ALLOW ME TO EXPLAIN.
HAT
GOSSIPER
YOU WERE HOPING THAT GRUNKLE STAN'S NEW ATTRACTION WOULD BE THE STORY THAT SAVED YOUR FAILING NEWSPAPER.
WORLD FAMOU
HAT
BUT WHEN THE SHOW WAS A FLOP, YOU DECIDED TO GO OUT AND MAKE YOUR OWN HEADLINE.
HAT
H

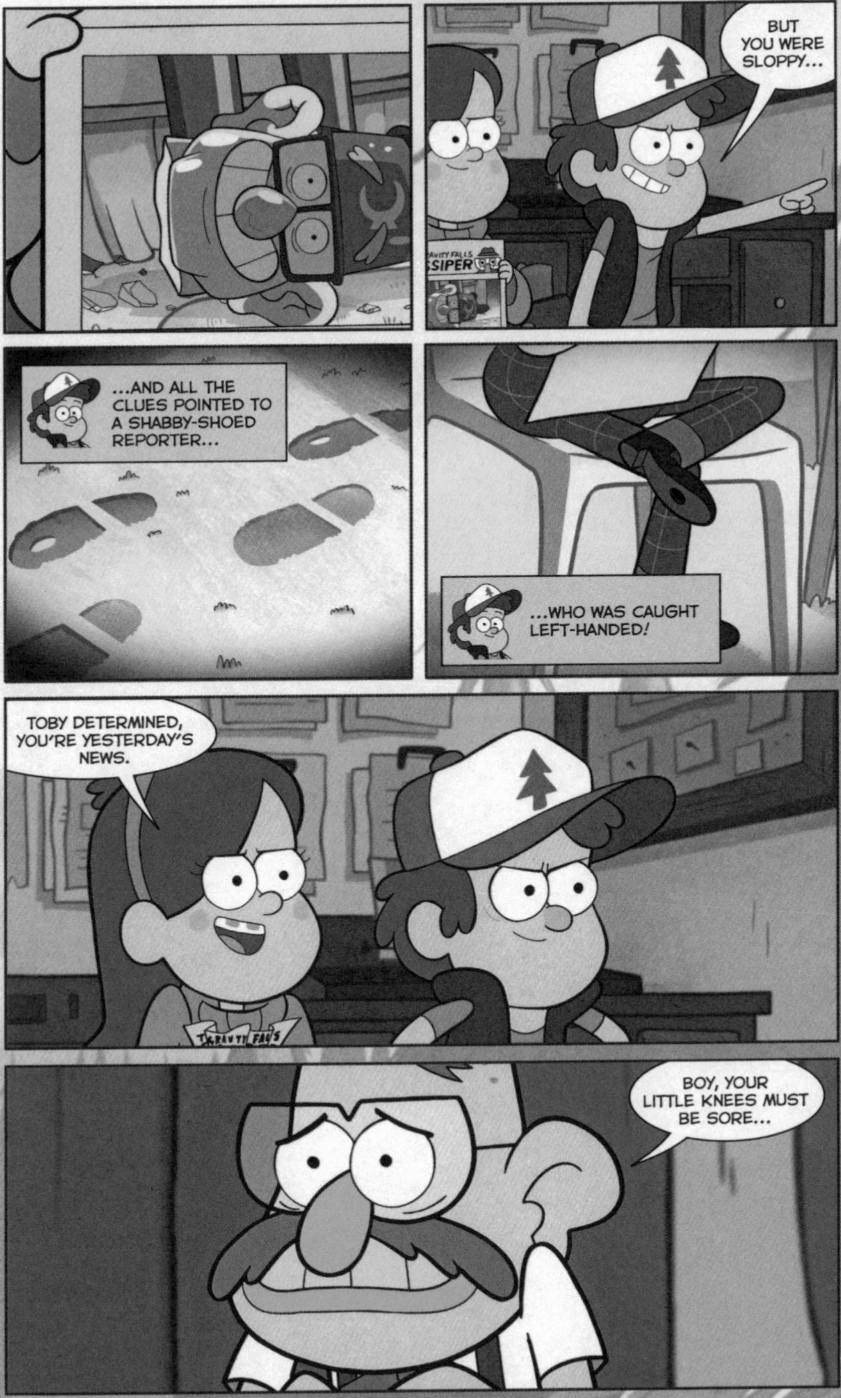
BUT YOU WERE SLOPPY...
RAVITY FALLS
SSIPER
...AND ALL THE CLUES POINTED TO A SHABBY-SHOED REPORTER...
...WHO WAS CAUGHT LEFT-HANDED!
TOBY DETERMINED, YOU'RE YESTERDAY'S NEWS.
BOY, YOUR LITTLE KNEES MUST BE SORE...

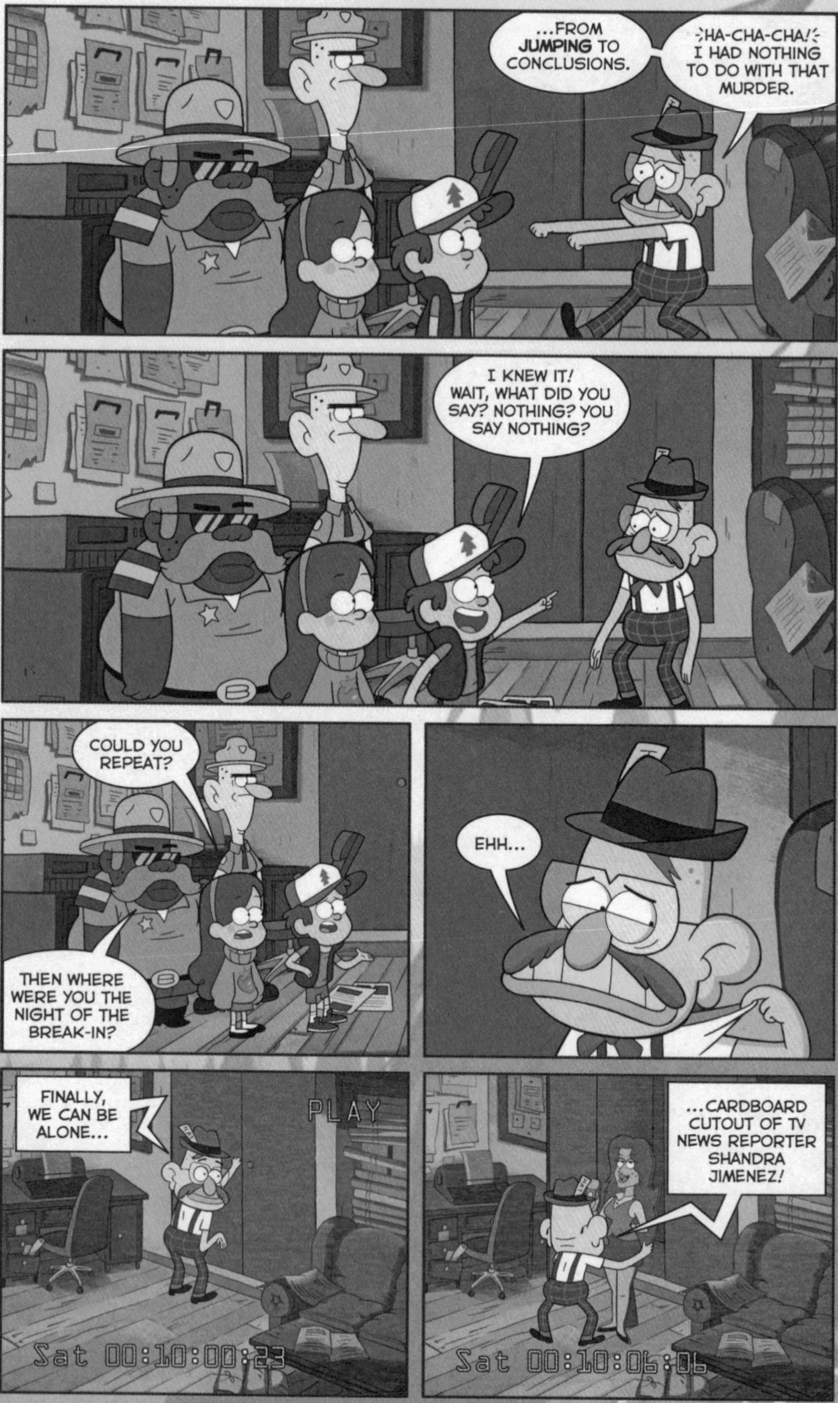
...FROM JUMPING TO CONCLUSIONS.
HA-CHA-CHA! I HAD NOTHING TO DO WITH THAT MURDER.
I KNEW IT! WAIT, WHAT DID YOU SAY? NOTHING? YOU SAY NOTHING?
COULD YOU REPEAT?
THEN WHERE WERE YOU THE NIGHT OF THE BREAK-IN?
EHH...
FINALLY, WE CAN BE ALONE...
PLAY
Sat 00:10:00:23
...CARDBOARD CUTOUT OF TV NEWS REPORTER SHANDRA JIMENEZ!
Sat 00:10:06:06

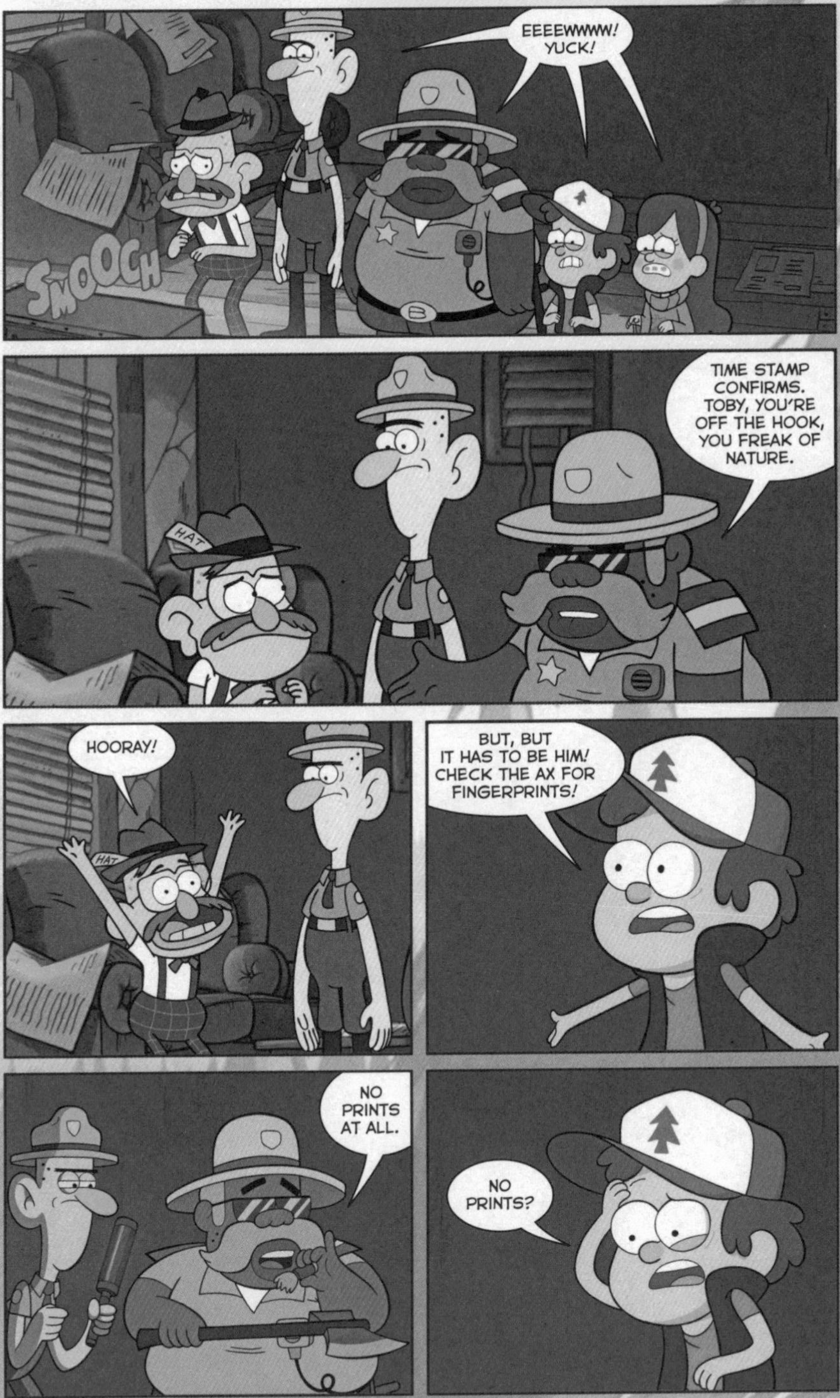
EEEEWWWW! YUCK!
SMOOCH
TIME STAMP CONFIRMS. TOBY, YOU'RE OFF THE HOOK, YOU FREAK OF NATURE.
HAT
HOORAY!
HAT
BUT, BUT IT HAS TO BE HIM! CHECK THE AX FOR FINGERPRINTS!
NO PRINTS AT ALL.
NO PRINTS?

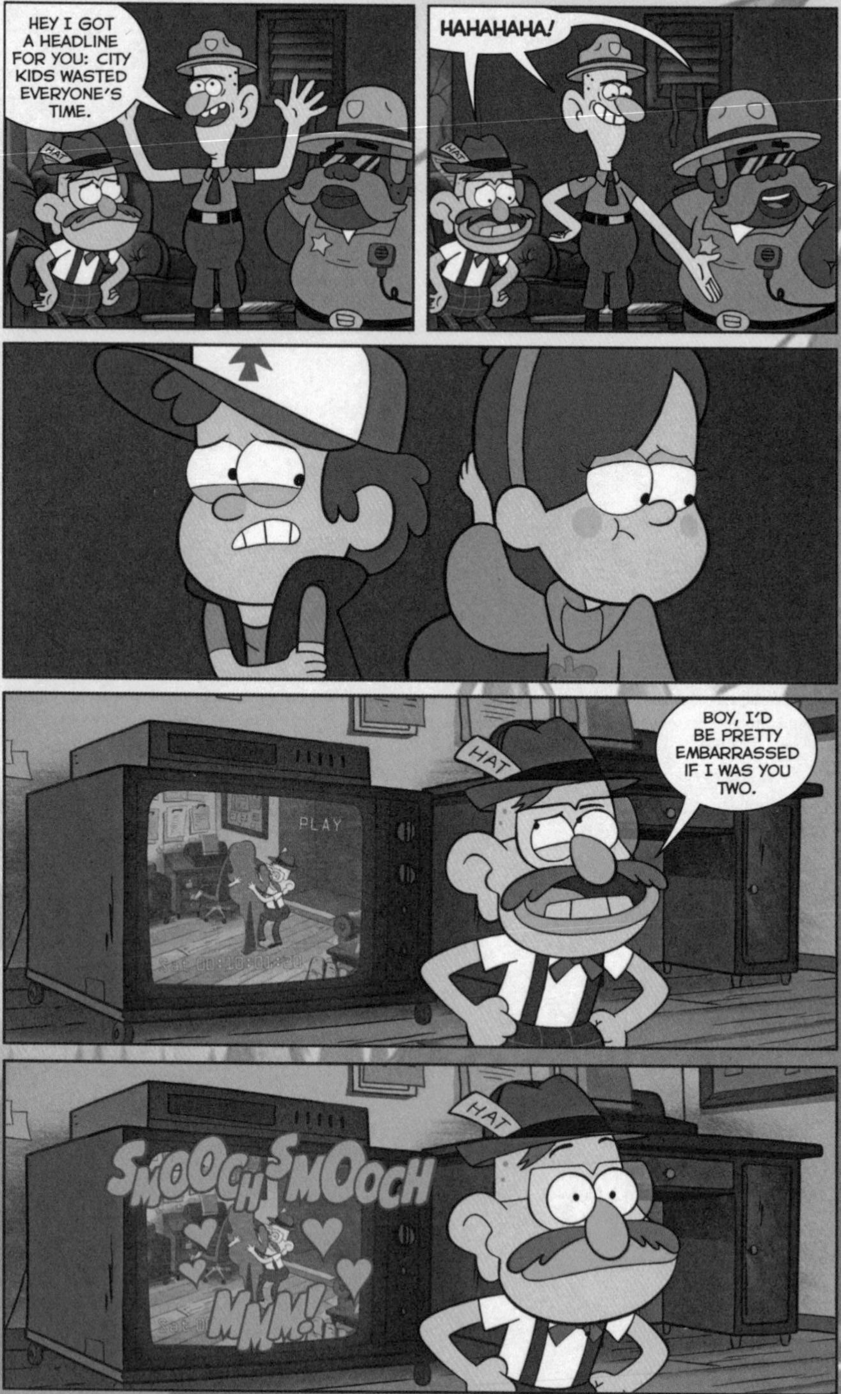
HEY I GOT A HEADLINE FOR YOU: CITY KIDS WASTED EVERYONE'S TIME.
HAT
HAHAHAHA!
HAT
HAT
BOY, I'D BE PRETTY EMBARRASSED IF I WAS YOU TWO.
PLAY
HAT
SMOOCH SMOOCH
MMM!

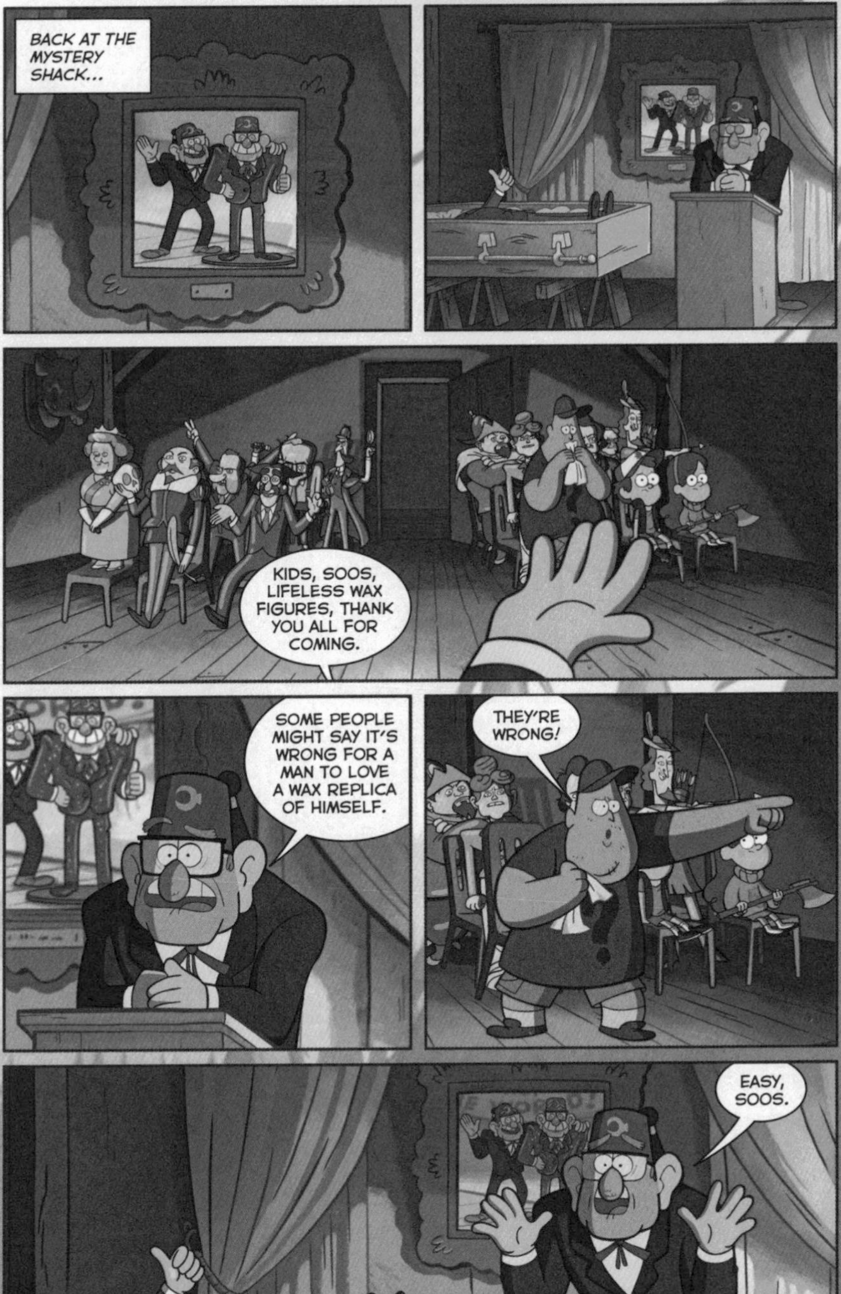
BACK AT THE MYSTERY SHACK...
KIDS, SOOS, LIFELESS WAX FIGURES, THANK YOU ALL FOR COMING.
SOME PEOPLE MIGHT SAY IT'S WRONG FOR A MAN TO LOVE A WAX REPLICA OF HIMSELF.
THEY'RE WRONG!
EASY, SOOS.

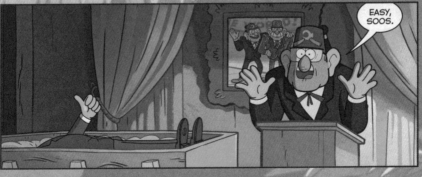

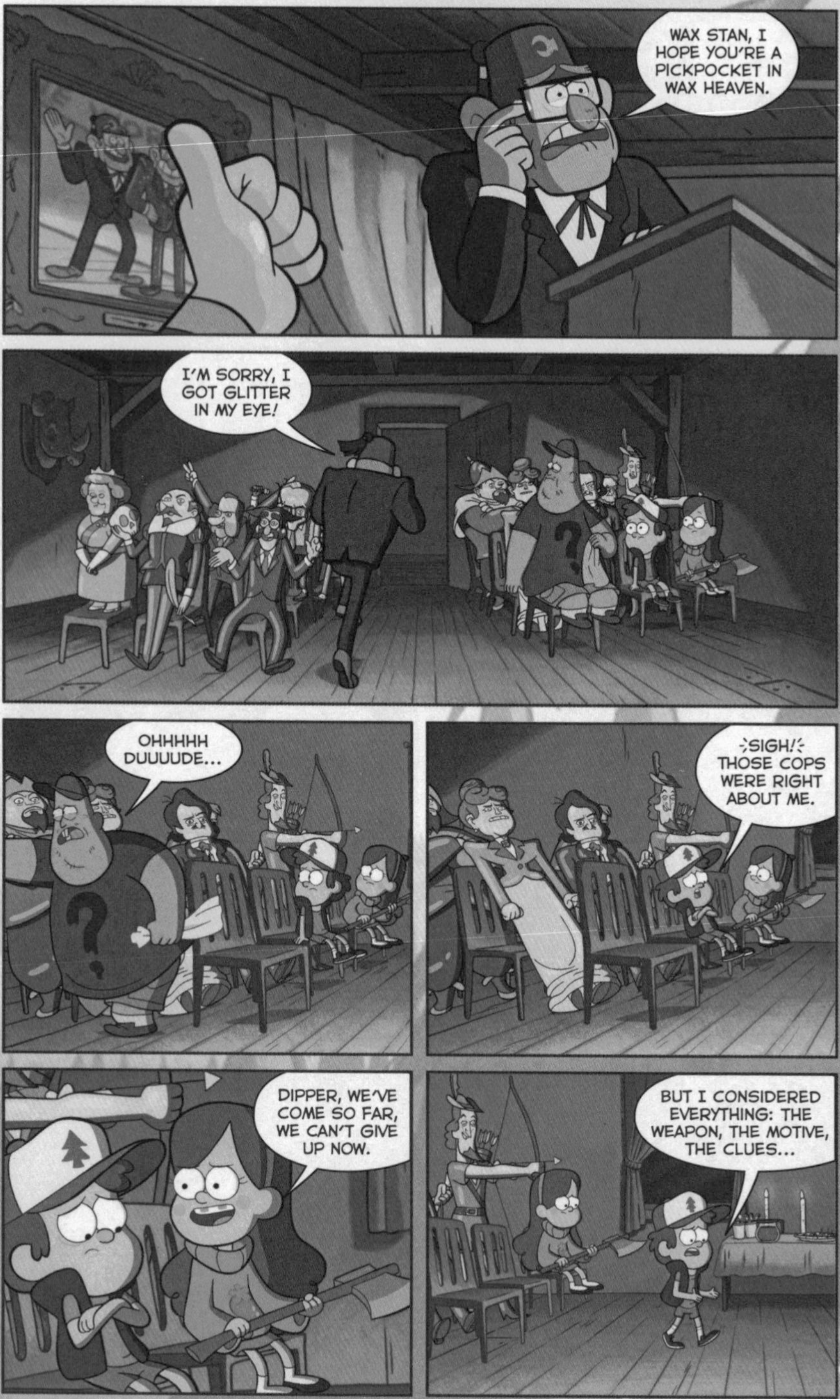
WAX STAN, I HOPE YOU'RE A PICKPOCKET IN WAX HEAVEN.
I'M SORRY, I GOT GLITTER IN MY EYE!
OHHHHH DUUUUDE...
SIGH! THOSE COPS WERE RIGHT ABOUT ME.
DIPPER, WE'VE COME SO FAR, WE CAN'T GIVE UP NOW.
BUT I CONSIDERED EVERYTHING: THE WEAPON, THE MOTIVE, THE CLUES...

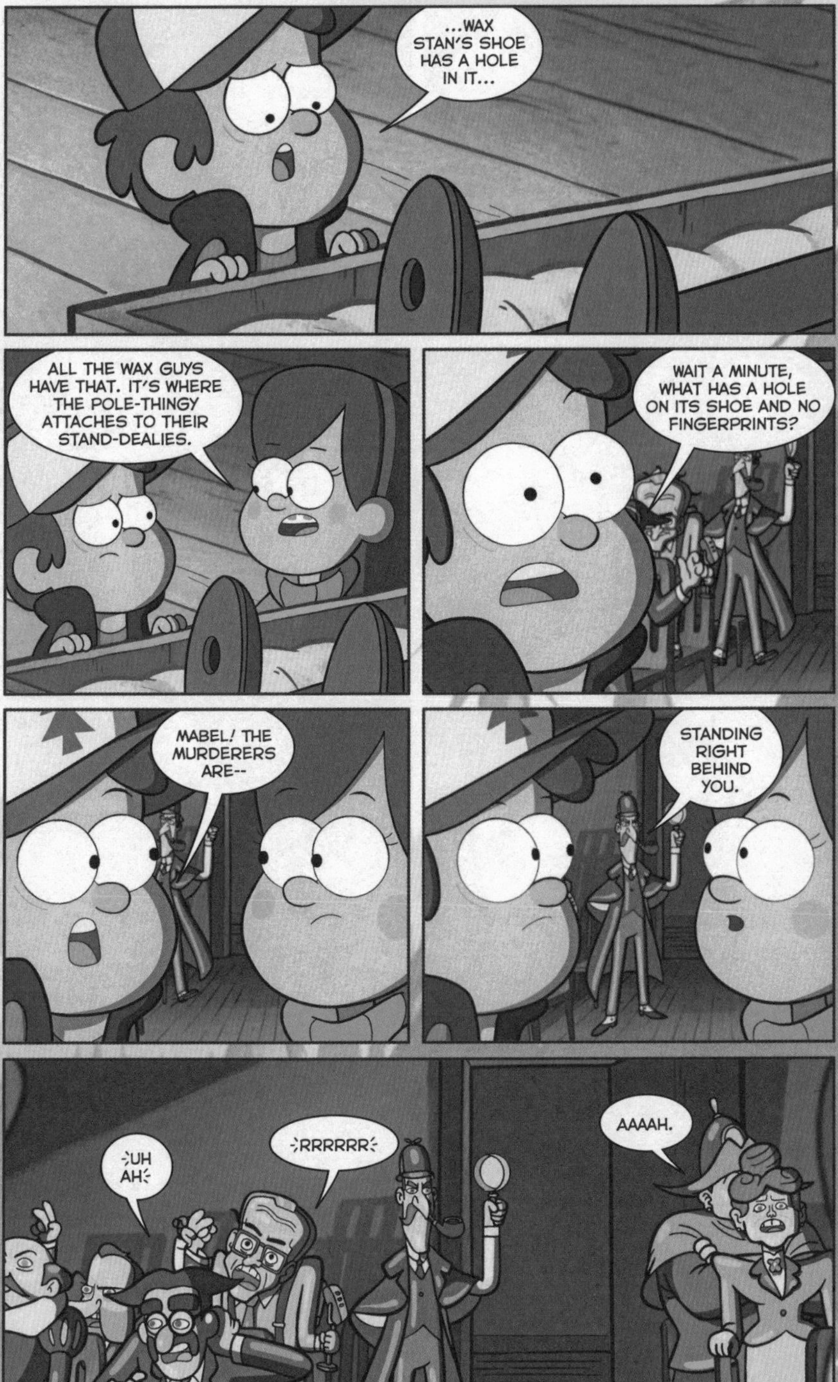
...WAX STAN'S SHOE HAS A HOLE IN IT...
ALL THE WAX GUYS HAVE THAT. IT'S WHERE THE POLE-THINGY ATTACHES TO THEIR STAND-DEALIES.
WAIT A MINUTE, WHAT HAS A HOLE ON ITS SHOE AND NO FINGERPRINTS?
MABEL! THE MURDERERS ARE--
STANDING RIGHT BEHIND YOU.
UH AH
RRRRRR
AAAAH.

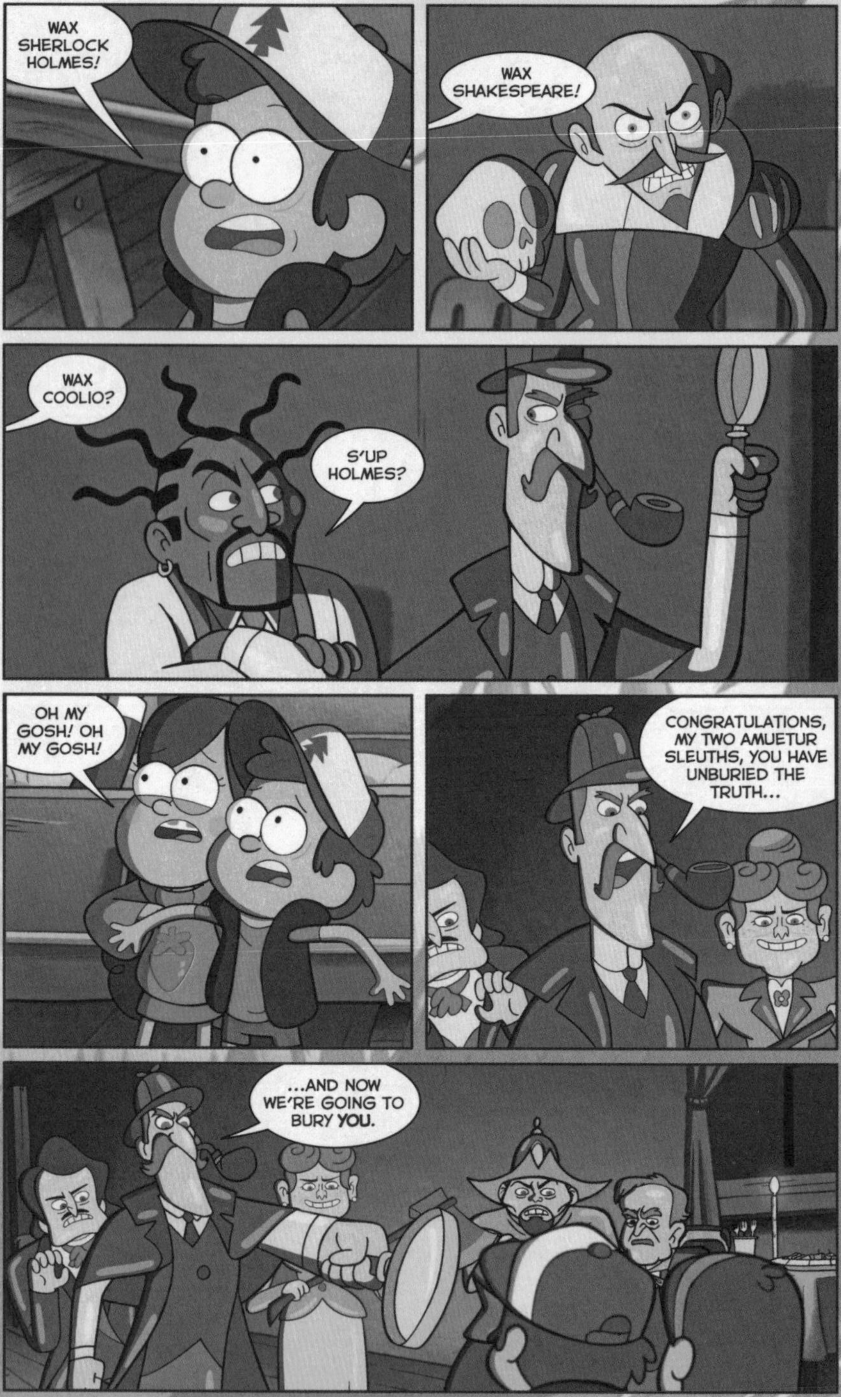
WAX SHERLOCK HOLMES!
WAX SHAKESPEARE!
WAX COOLIO?
S'UP HOLMES?
OH MY GOSH! OH MY GOSH!
CONGRATULATIONS, MY TWO AMUETUR SLEUTHS, YOU HAVE UNBURIED THE TRUTH...
...AND NOW WE'RE GOING TO BURY **YOU**.

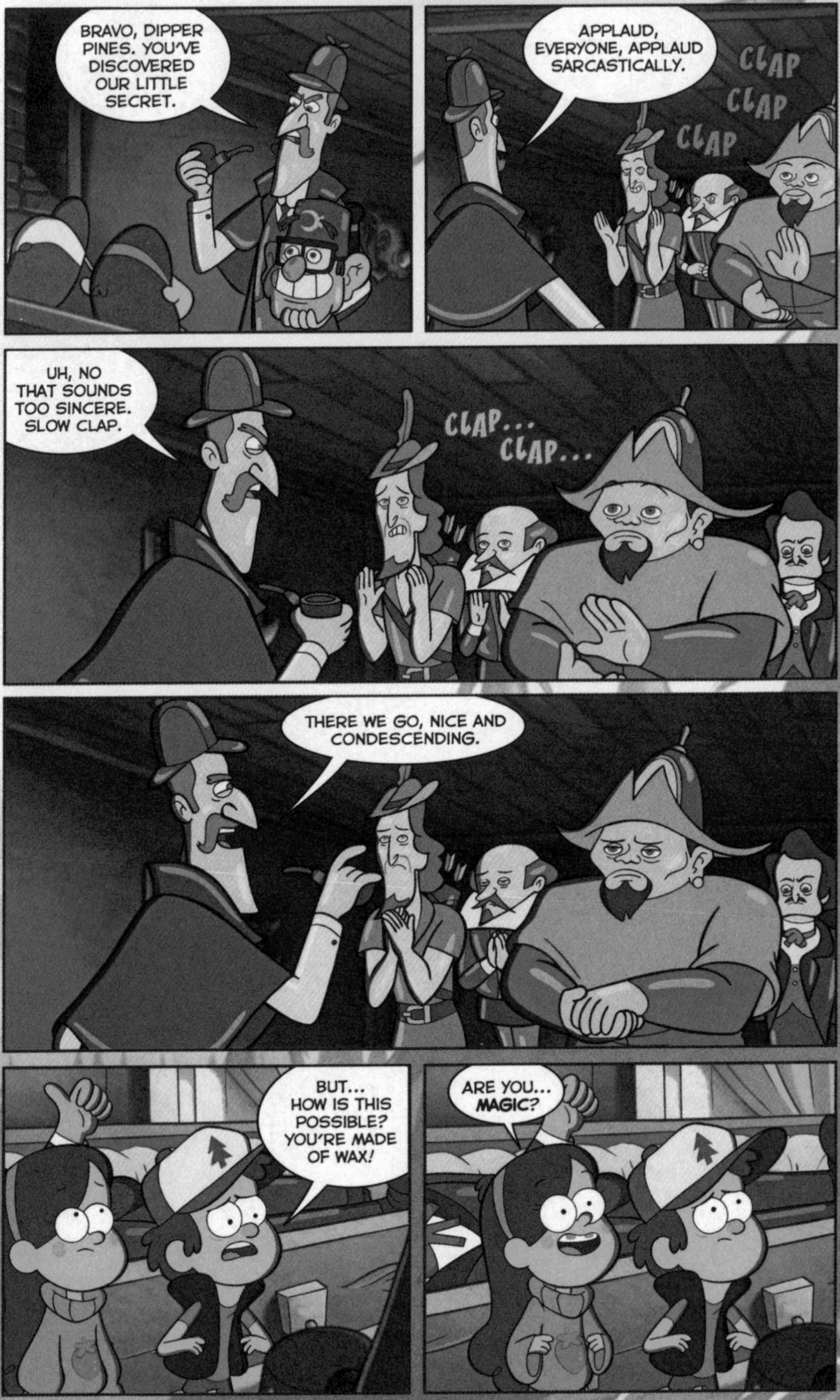

BRAVO, DIPPER PINES. YOU'VE DISCOVERED OUR LITTLE SECRET.
APPLAUD, EVERYONE, APPLAUD SARCASTICALLY.
CLAP CLAP CLAP
UH, NO THAT SOUNDS TOO SINCERE. SLOW CLAP.
CLAP... CLAP...
THERE WE GO, NICE AND CONDESCENDING.
BUT... HOW IS THIS POSSIBLE? YOU'RE MADE OF WAX!
ARE YOU... MAGIC?

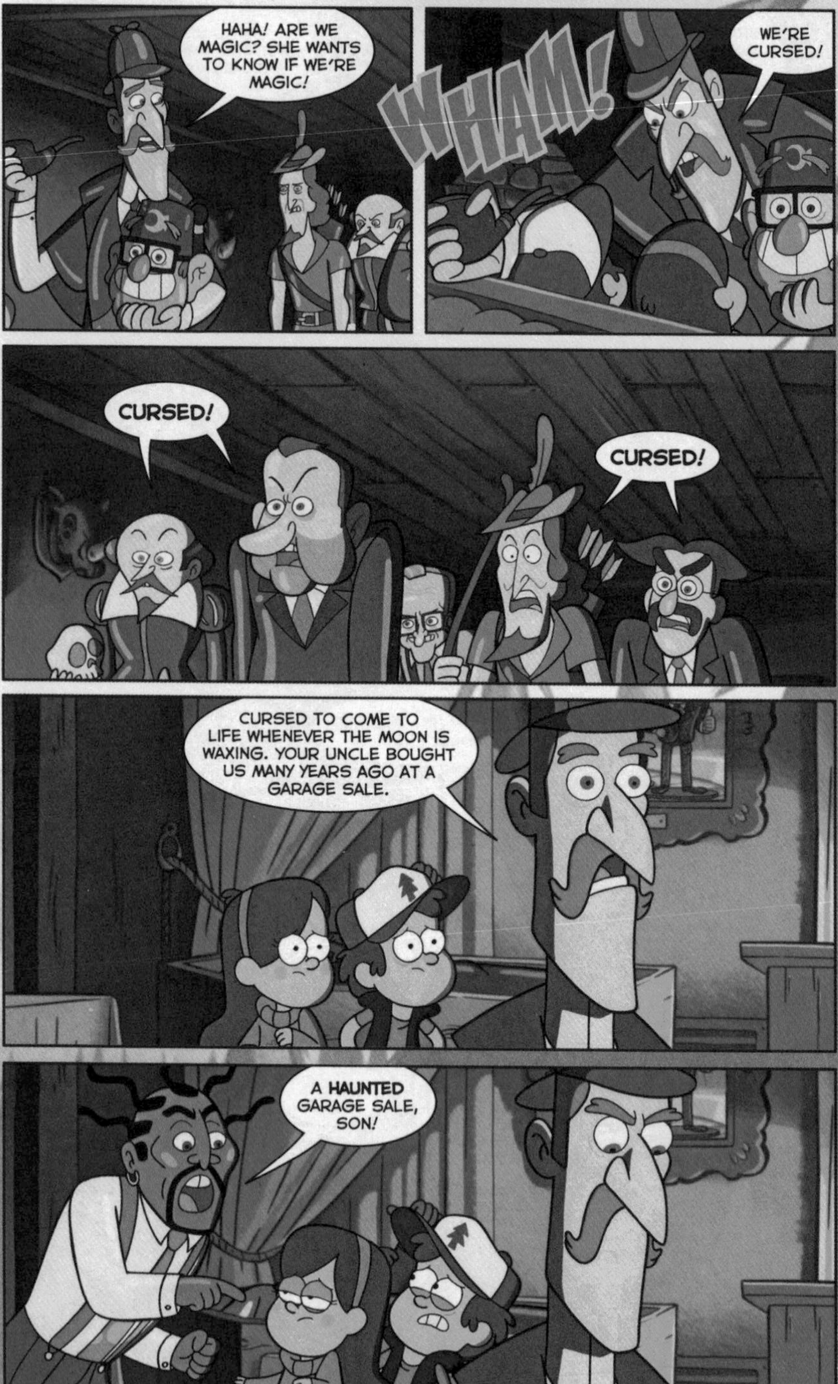
HAHA! ARE WE MAGIC? SHE WANTS TO KNOW IF WE'RE MAGIC!
WHAM!
WE'RE CURSED!
CURSED!
CURSED!
CURSED TO COME TO LIFE WHENEVER THE MOON IS WAXING. YOUR UNCLE BOUGHT US MANY YEARS AGO AT A GARAGE SALE.
A **HAUNTED** GARAGE SALE, SON!

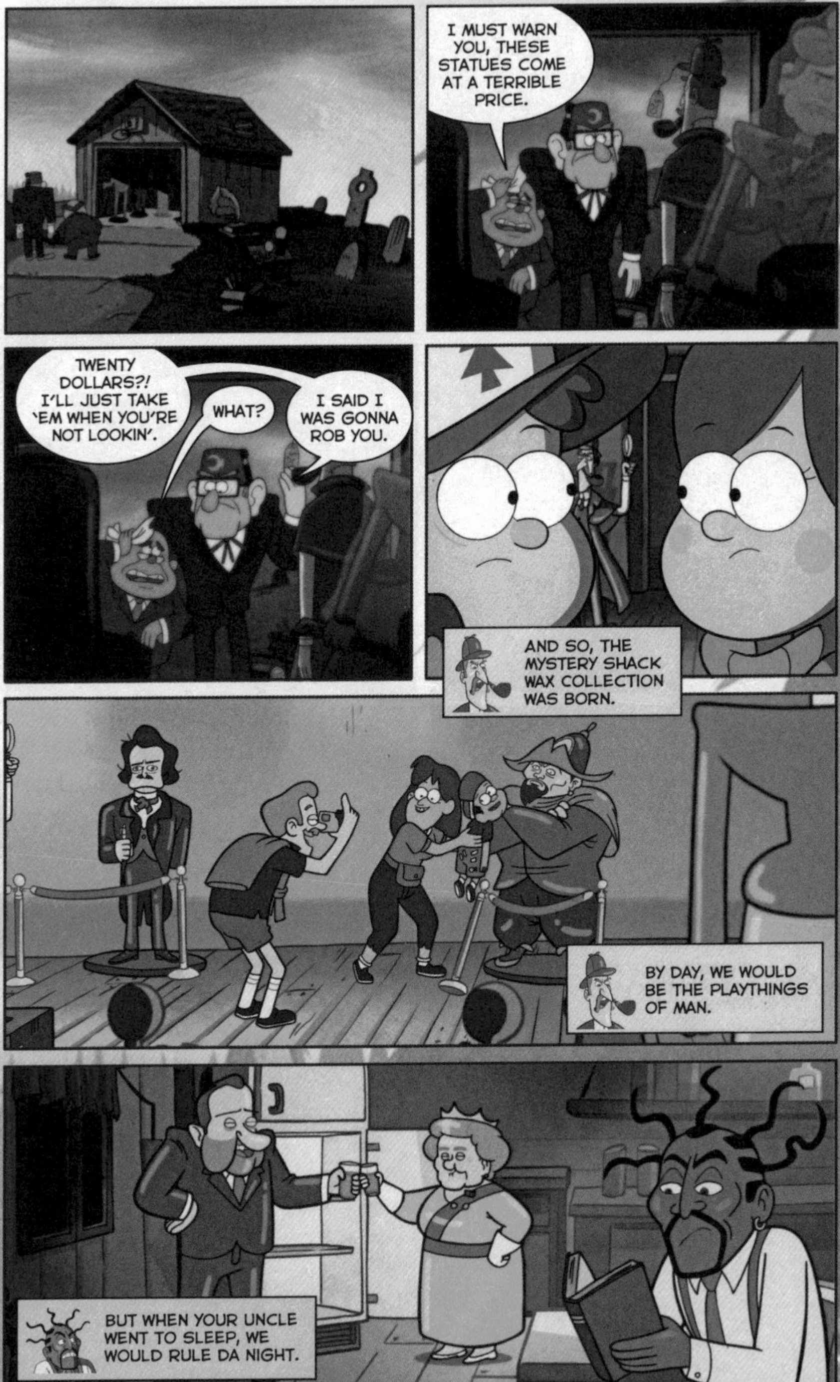
I MUST WARN YOU, THESE STATUES COME AT A TERRIBLE PRICE.
TWENTY DOLLARS?! I'LL JUST TAKE 'EM WHEN YOU'RE NOT LOOKIN'.
WHAT?
I SAID I WAS GONNA ROB YOU.
AND SO, THE MYSTERY SHACK WAX COLLECTION WAS BORN.
BY DAY, WE WOULD BE THE PLAYTHINGS OF MAN.
BUT WHEN YOUR UNCLE WENT TO SLEEP, WE WOULD RULE DA NIGHT.

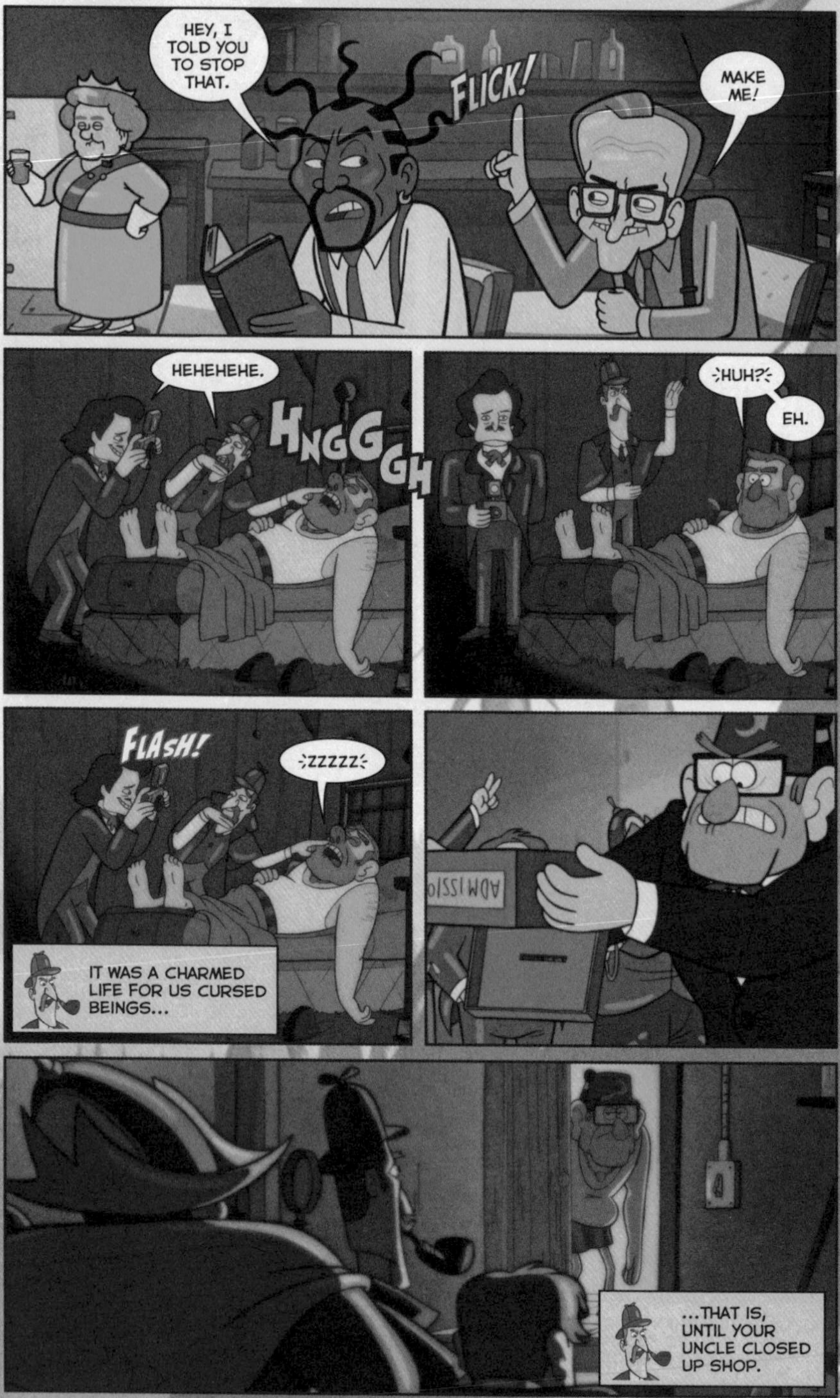
HEY, I TOLD YOU TO STOP THAT.
FLICK!
MAKE ME!
HEHEHEHE.
HNGGGH
HUH?
EH.
FLASH!
ZZZZZ
ADMISSIO
IT WAS A CHARMED LIFE FOR US CURSED BEINGS...
...THAT IS, UNTIL YOUR UNCLE CLOSED UP SHOP.

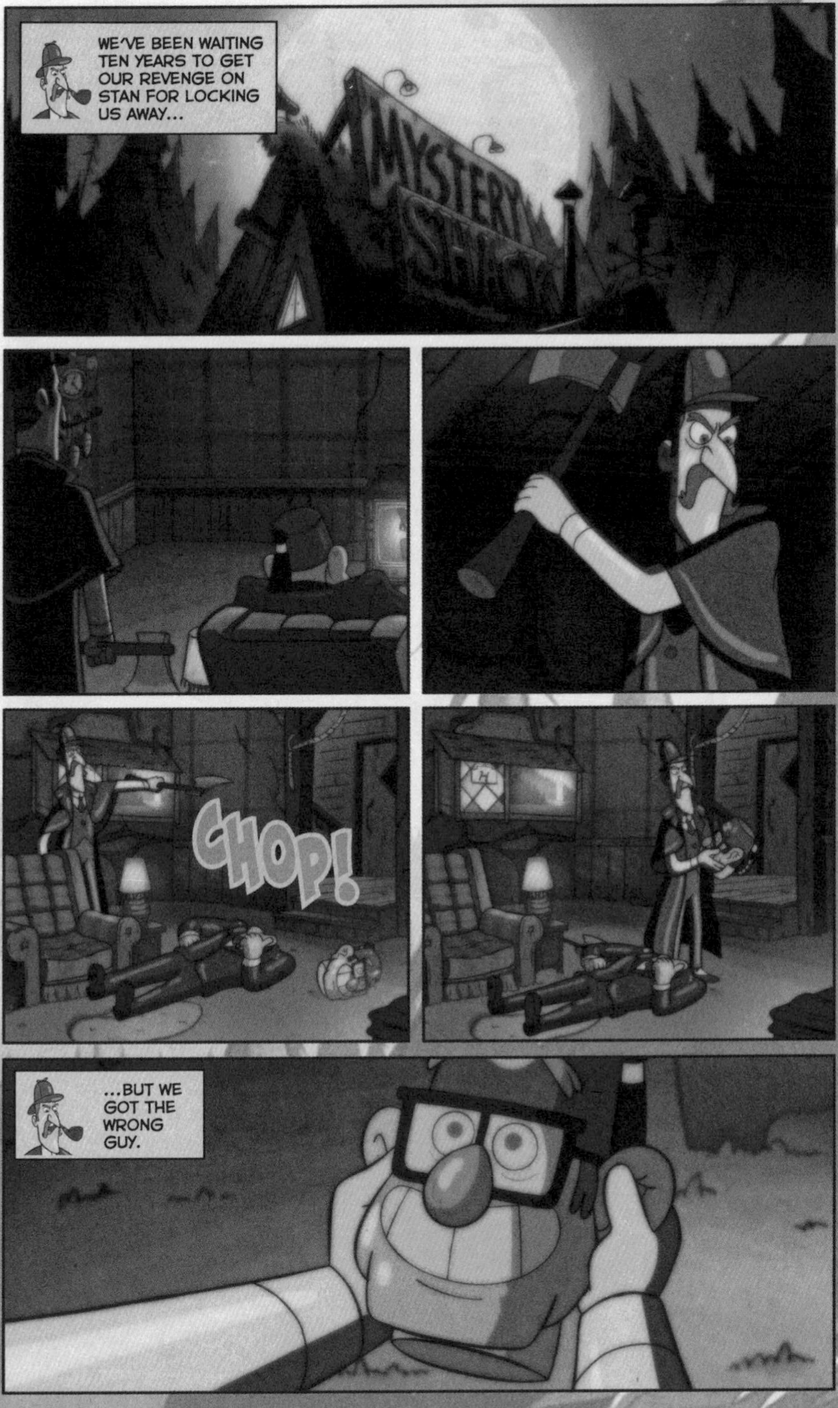
WE'VE BEEN WAITING TEN YEARS TO GET OUR REVENGE ON STAN FOR LOCKING US AWAY...
MYSTERY SHACK
CHOP!
...BUT WE GOT THE WRONG GUY.

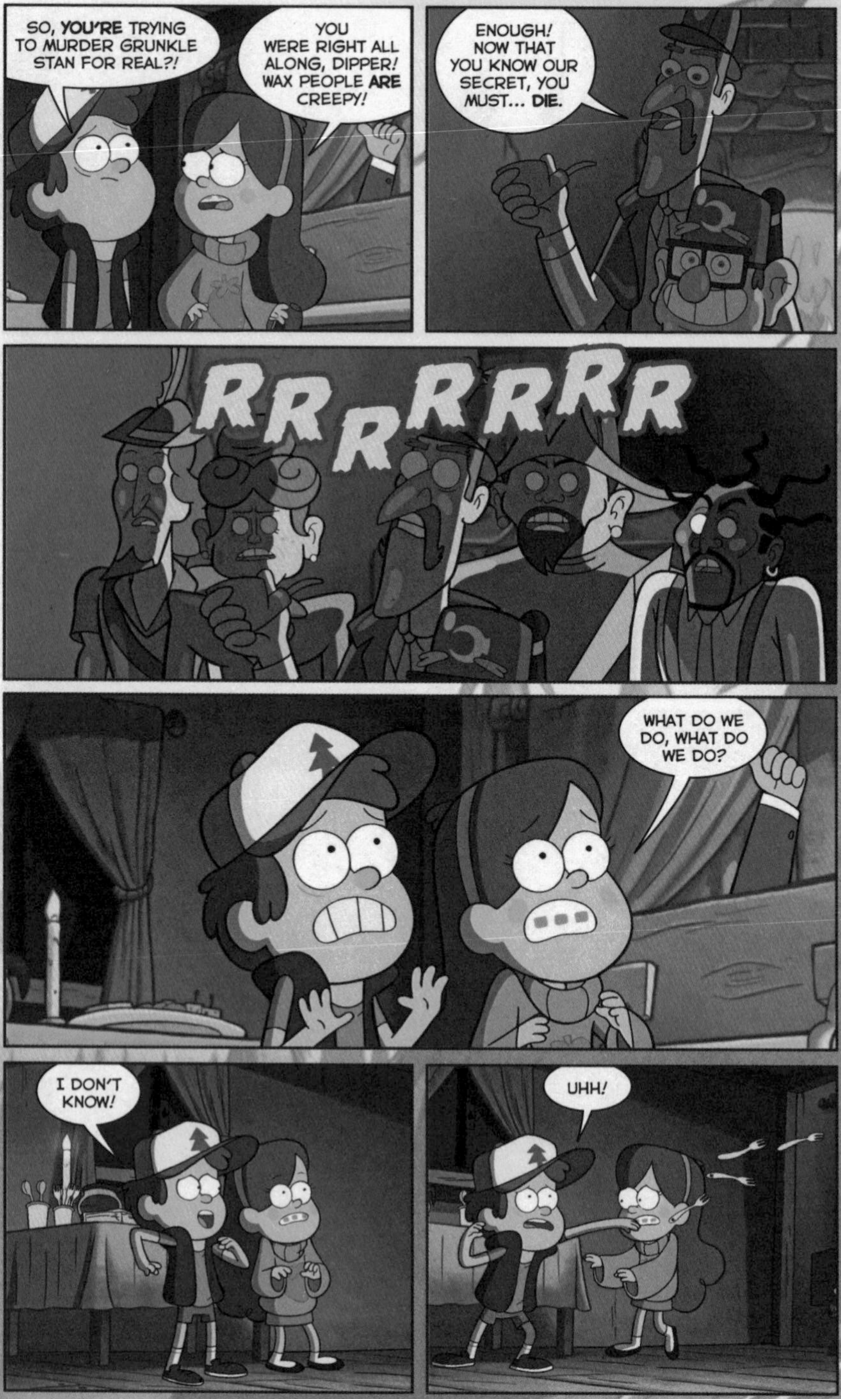
SO, YOU'RE TRYING TO MURDER GRUNKLE STAN FOR REAL?!
YOU WERE RIGHT ALL ALONG, DIPPER! WAX PEOPLE ARE CREEPY!
ENOUGH! NOW THAT YOU KNOW OUR SECRET, YOU MUST... DIE.
RRRRRRRR
WHAT DO WE DO, WHAT DO WE DO?
I DON'T KNOW!
UHH!

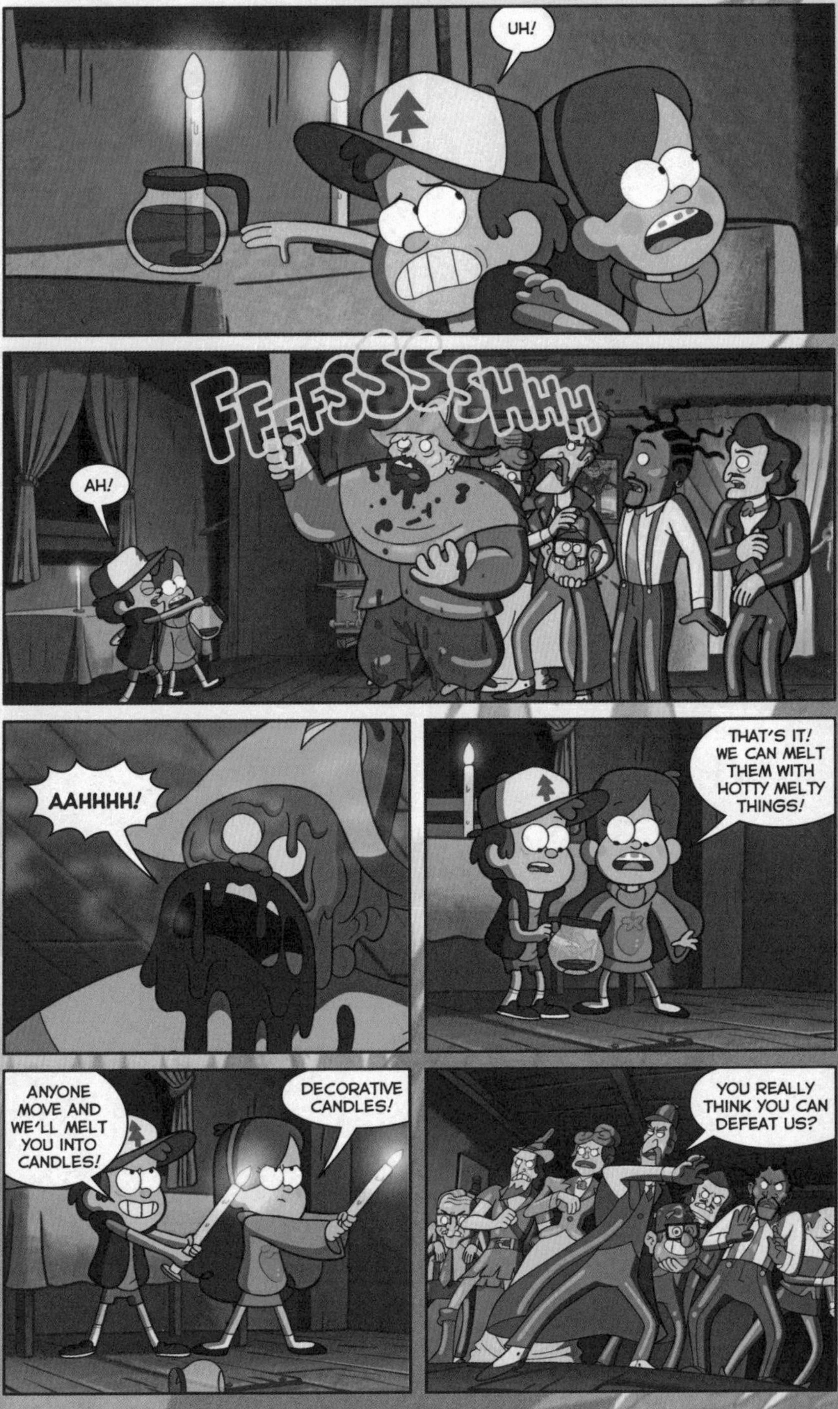
UH!
FF-FSSSSHHH
AH!
AAHHHH!
THAT'S IT! WE CAN MELT THEM WITH HOTTY MELTY THINGS!
ANYONE MOVE AND WE'LL MELT YOU INTO CANDLES!
DECORATIVE CANDLES!
YOU REALLY THINK YOU CAN DEFEAT US?

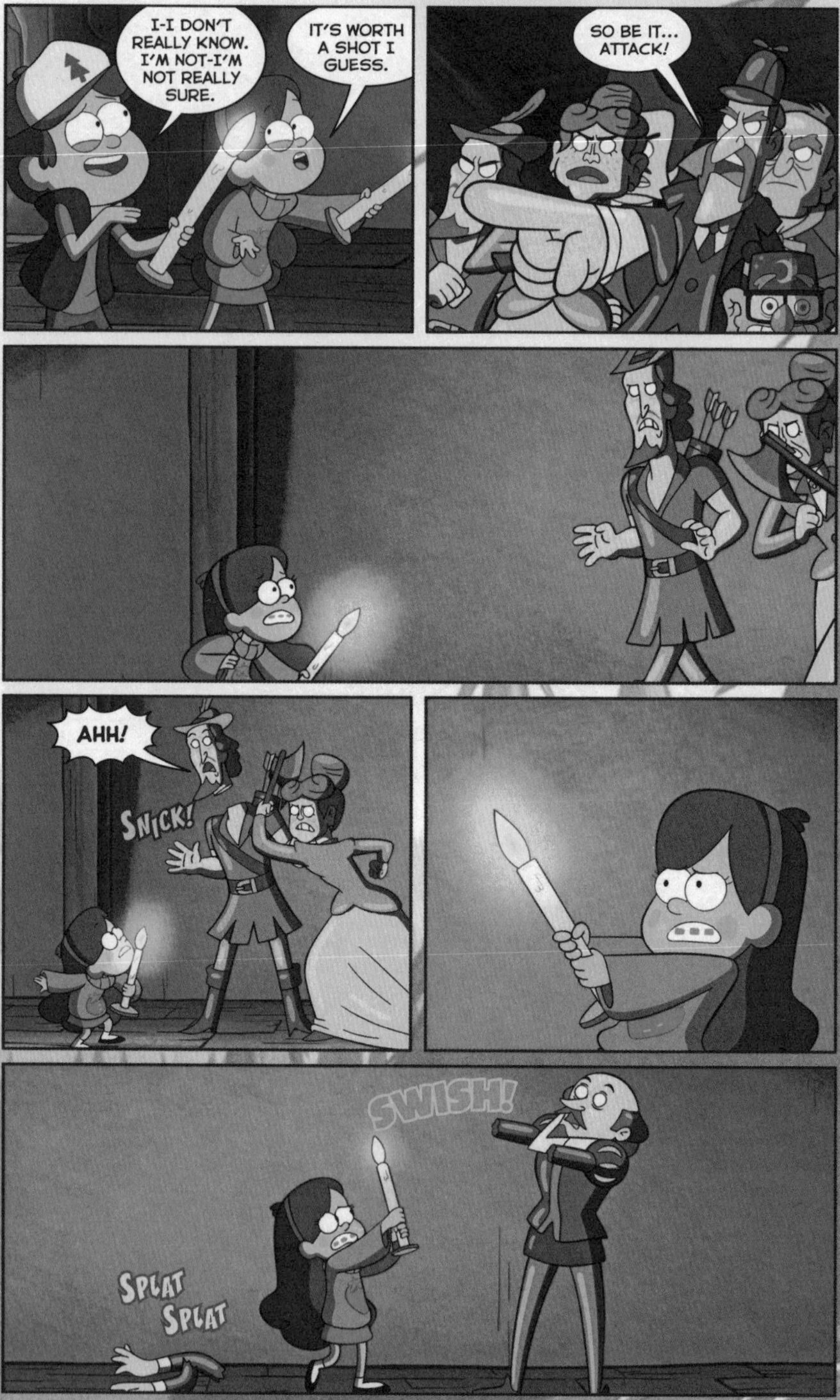
I-I DON'T REALLY KNOW. I'M NOT-I'M NOT REALLY SURE.
IT'S WORTH A SHOT I GUESS.
SO BE IT... ATTACK!
AHH!
SNICK!
SWISH!
SPLAT
SPLAT

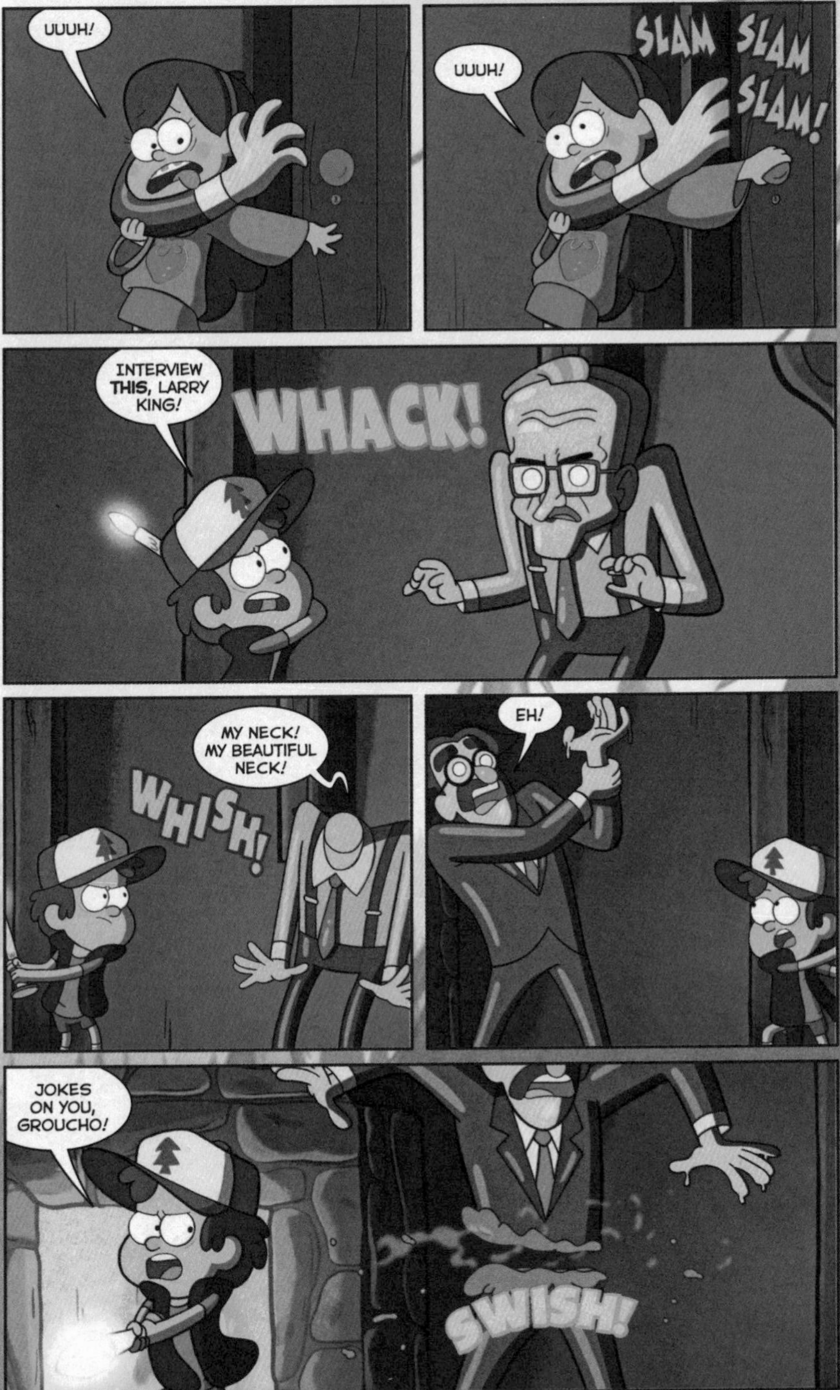
UUUH!
UUUH!
SLAM SLAM SLAM!
INTERVIEW THIS, LARRY KING!
WHACK!
MY NECK! MY BEAUTIFUL NECK!
WHISH!
EH!
JOKES ON YOU, GROUCHO!
SWISH!

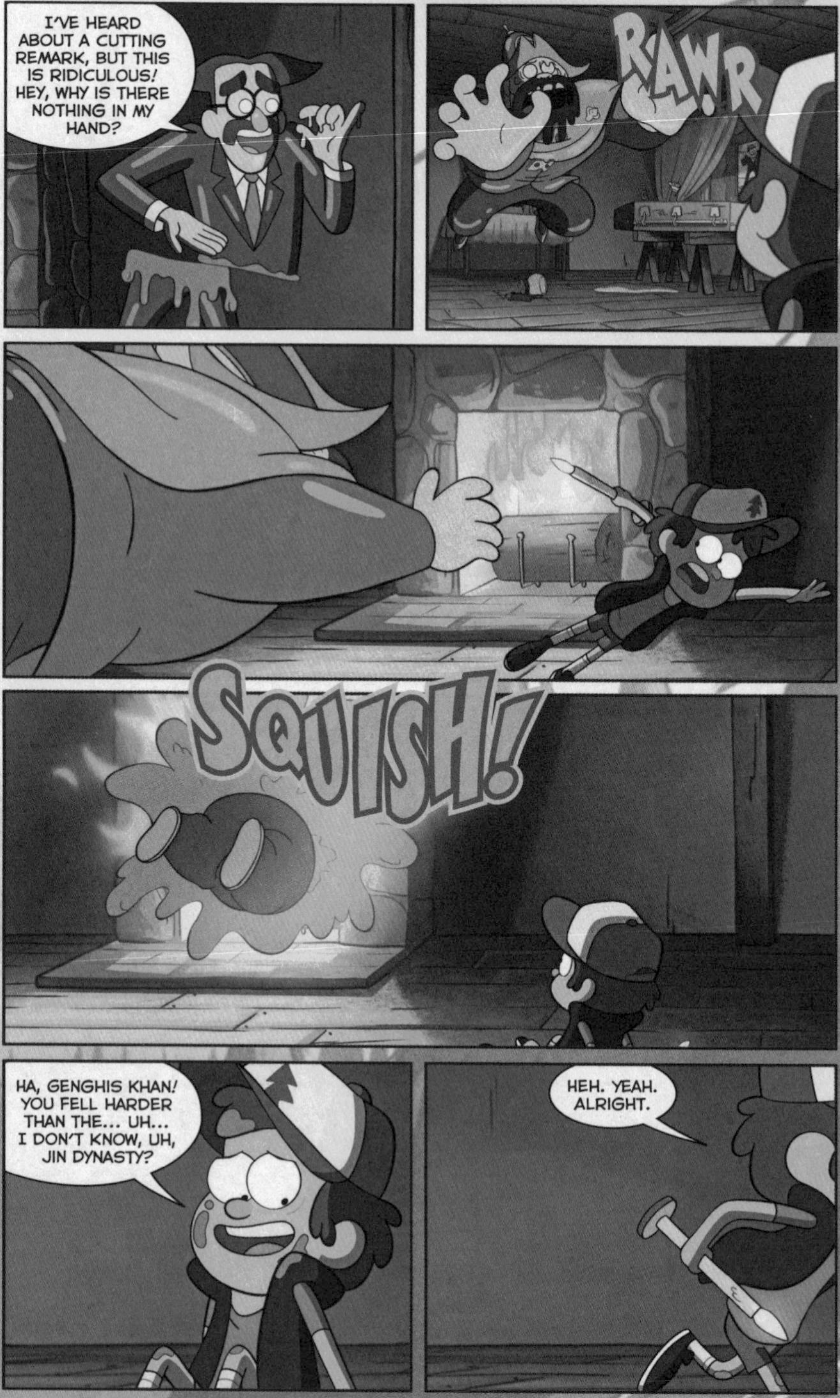
I'VE HEARD ABOUT A CUTTING REMARK, BUT THIS IS RIDICULOUS! HEY, WHY IS THERE NOTHING IN MY HAND?
RAWR
SQUISH!
HA, GENGHIS KHAN! YOU FELL HARDER THAN THE... UH... I DON'T KNOW, UH, JIN DYNASTY?
HEH. YEAH. ALRIGHT.

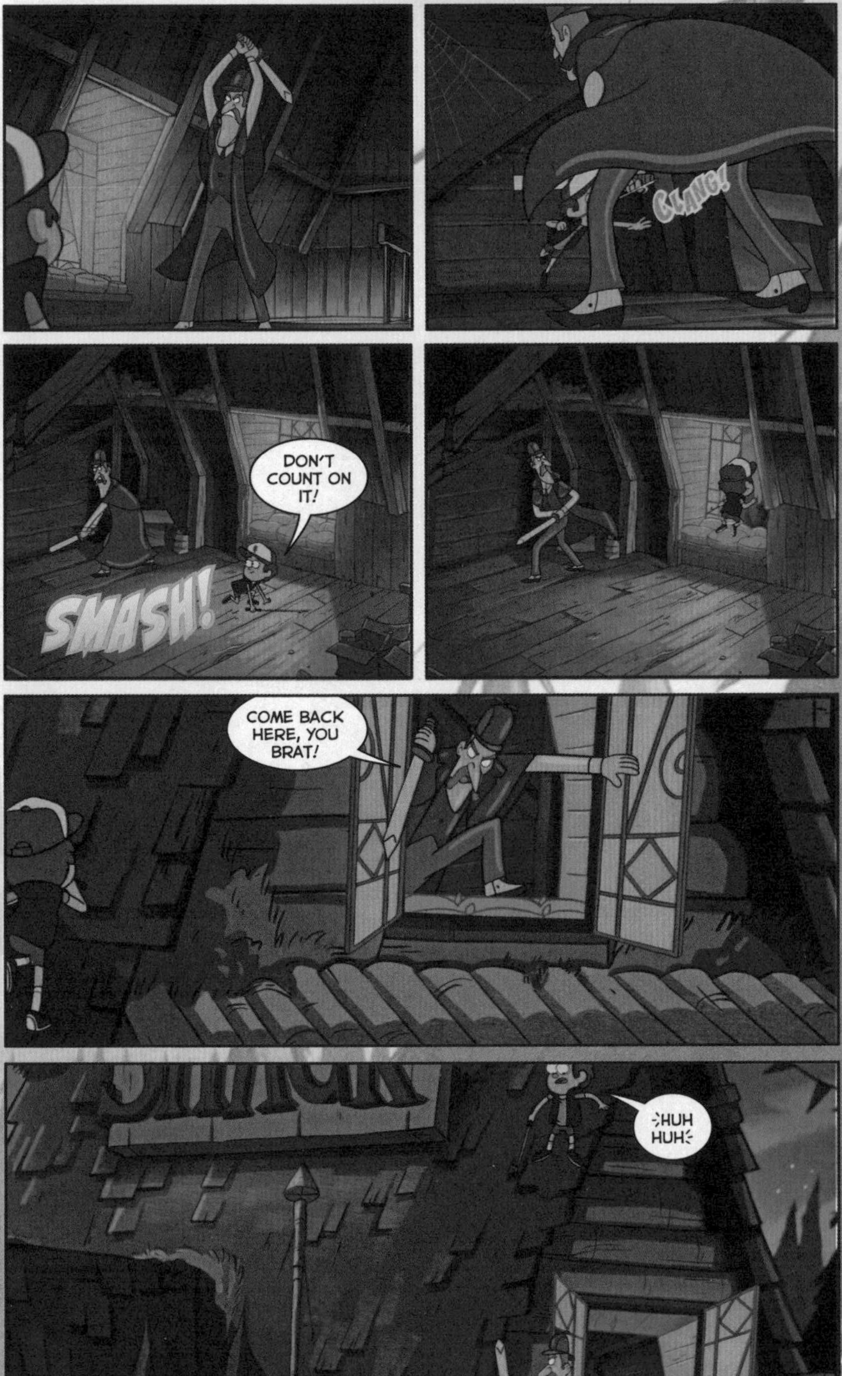
CLANG!
DON'T COUNT ON IT!
SMASH!
COME BACK HERE, YOU BRAT!
HUH HUH

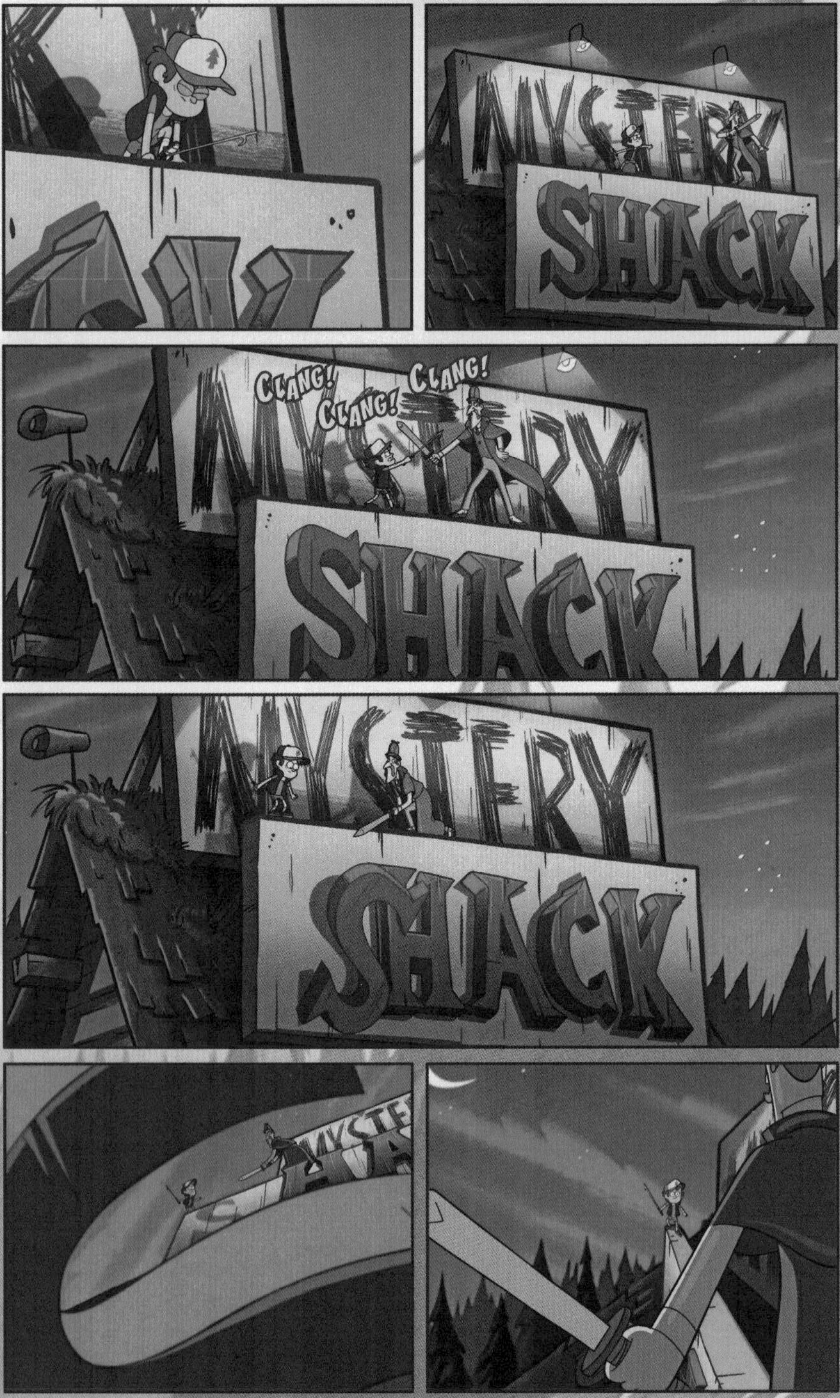
MYSTERY
SHACK
CLANG!
CLANG!
CLANG!

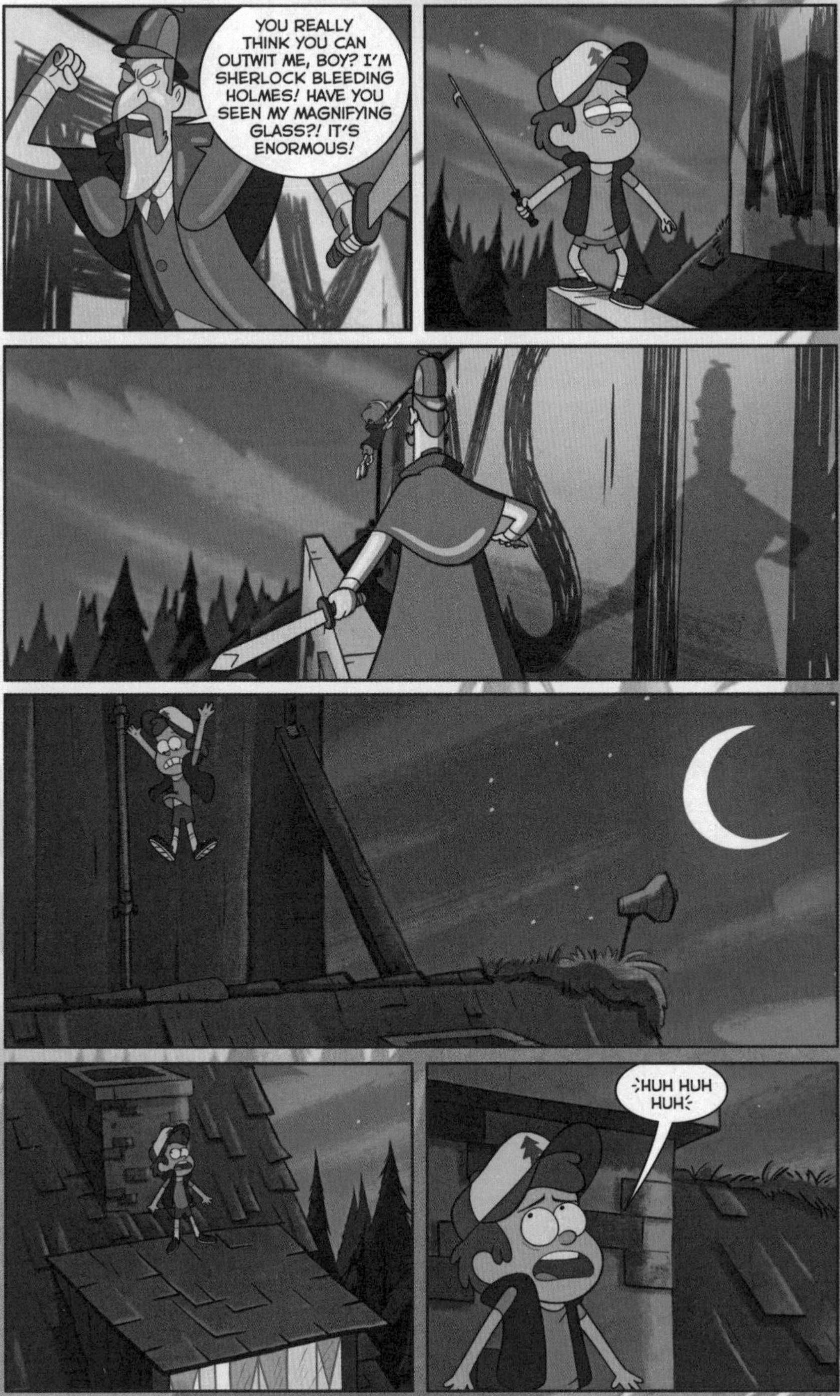
YOU REALLY THINK YOU CAN OUTWIT ME, BOY? I'M SHERLOCK BLEEDING HOLMES! HAVE YOU SEEN MY MAGNIFYING GLASS?! IT'S ENORMOUS!
HUH HUH HUH

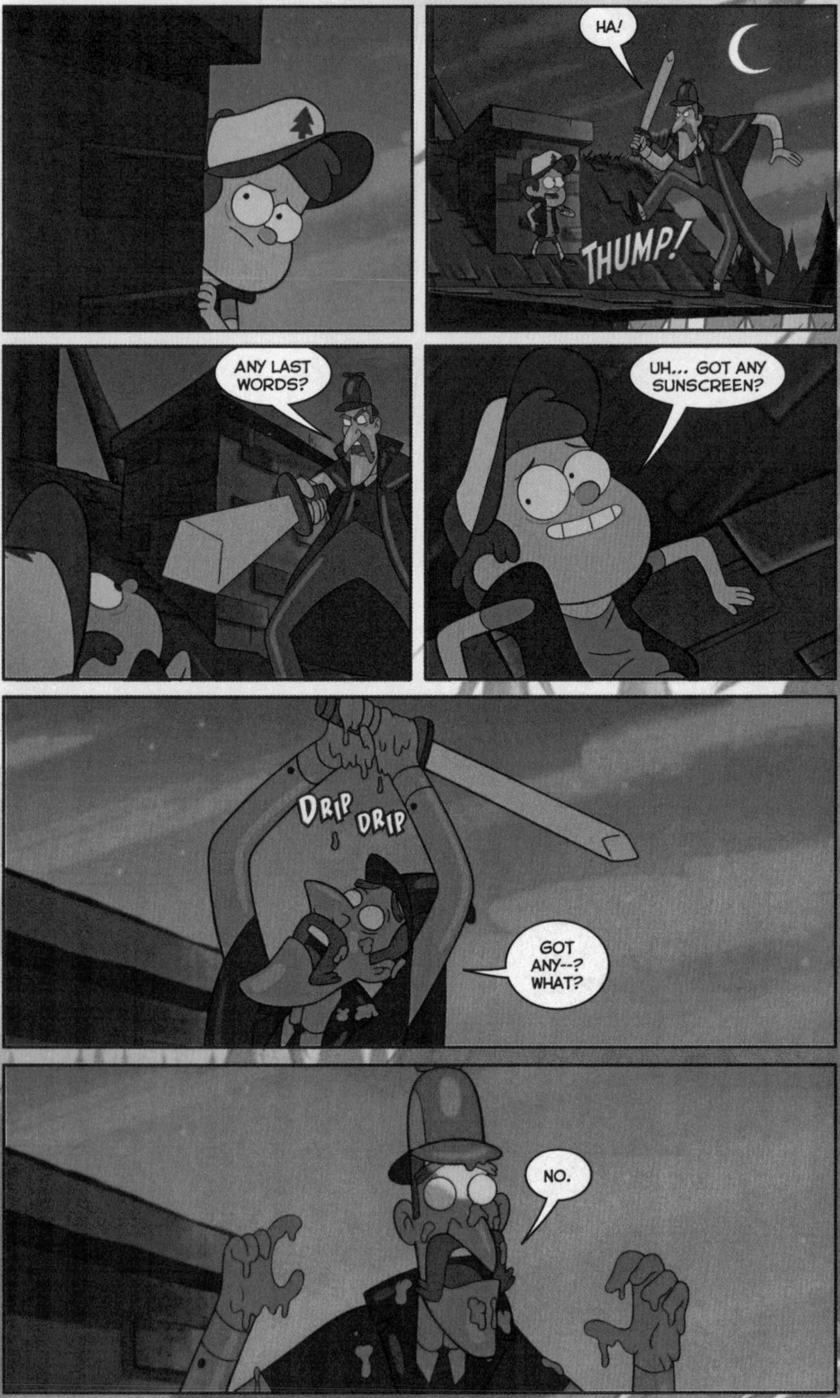
HA!
THUMP!
ANY LAST WORDS?
UH... GOT ANY SUNSCREEN?
DRIP DRIP
GOT ANY--? WHAT?
NO.

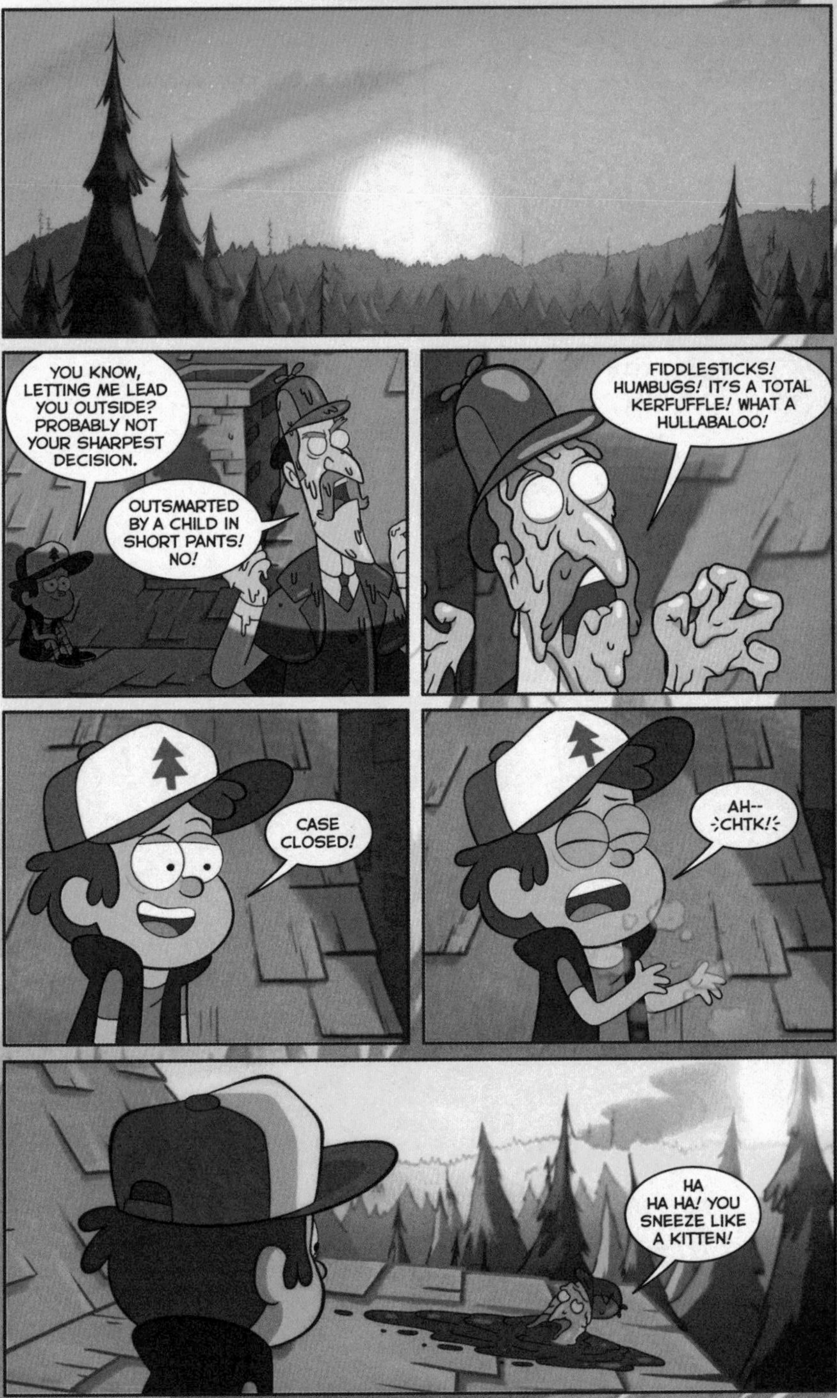
YOU KNOW, LETTING ME LEAD YOU OUTSIDE? PROBABLY NOT YOUR SHARPEST DECISION.
OUTSMARTED BY A CHILD IN SHORT PANTS! NO!
FIDDLESTICKS! HUMBUGS! IT'S A TOTAL KERFUFFLE! WHAT A HULLABALOO!
CASE CLOSED!
AH-- CHTK!
HA HA HA! YOU SNEEZE LIKE A KITTEN!

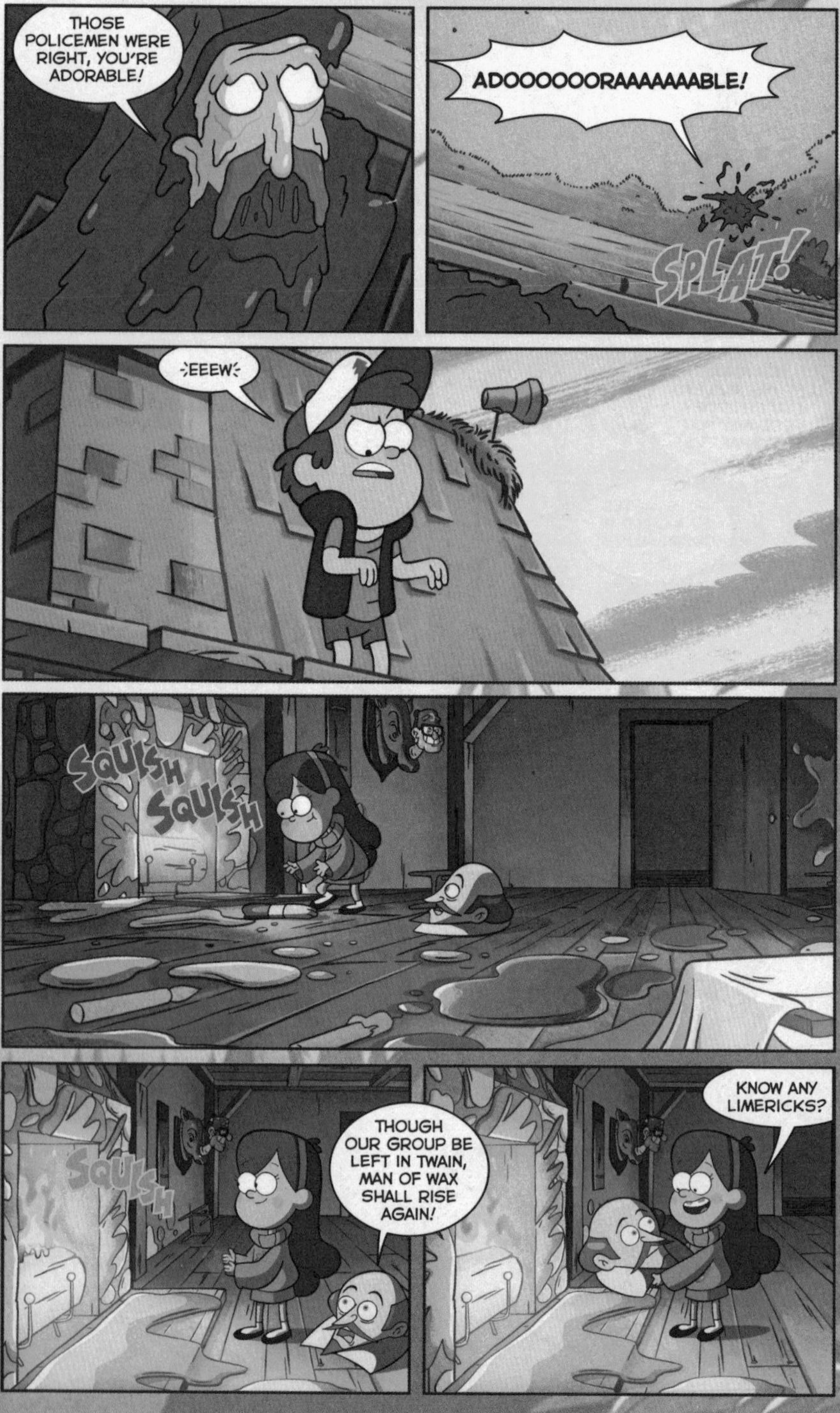
THOSE POLICEMEN WERE RIGHT, YOU'RE ADORABLE!
ADOOOOOORAAAAAAABLE!
SPLAT!
EEEW
SQUISH
SQUISH
SQUISH
THOUGH OUR GROUP BE LEFT IN TWAIN, MAN OF WAX SHALL RISE AGAIN!
KNOW ANY LIMERICKS?

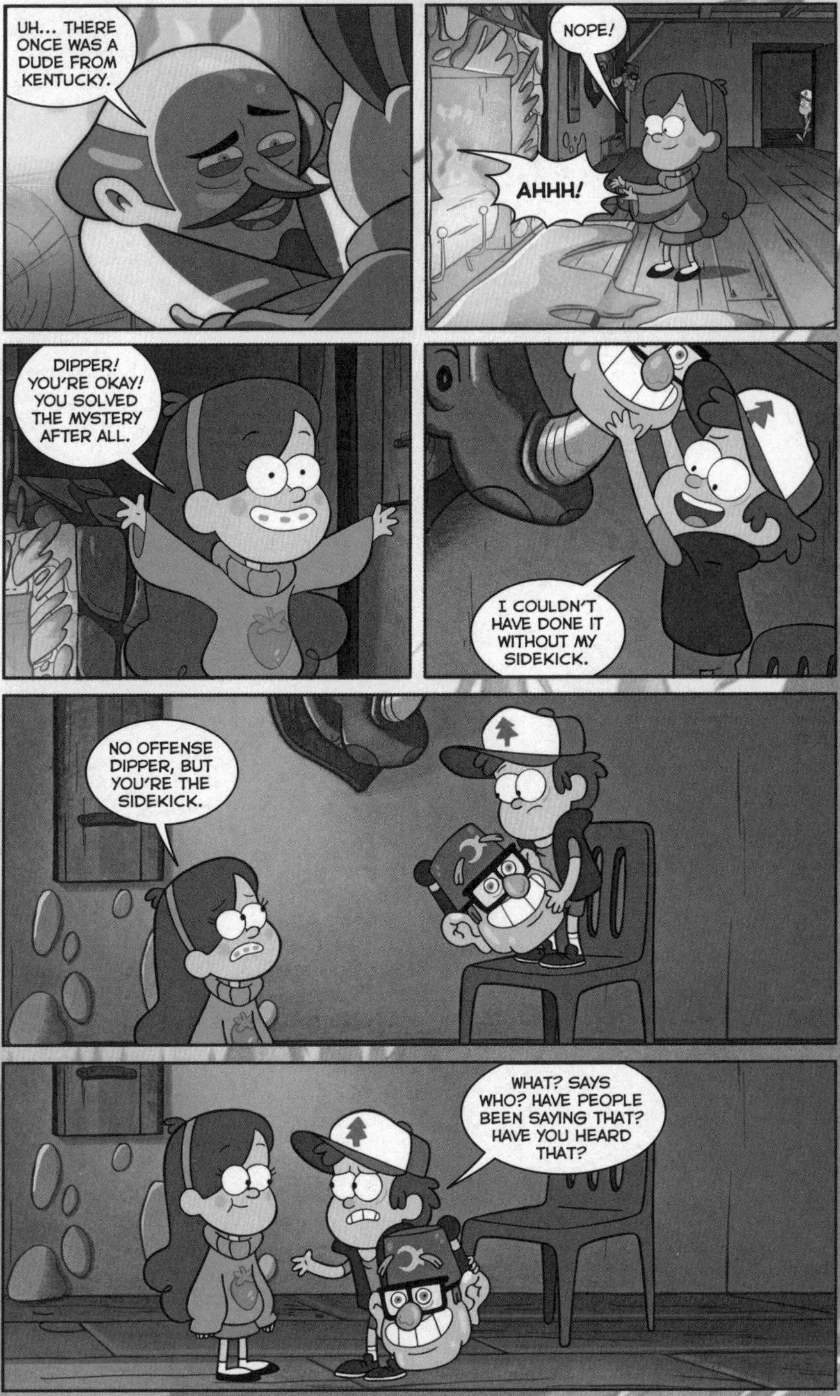
UH... THERE ONCE WAS A DUDE FROM KENTUCKY.
NOPE!
AHHH!
DIPPER! YOU'RE OKAY! YOU SOLVED THE MYSTERY AFTER ALL.
I COULDN'T HAVE DONE IT WITHOUT MY SIDEKICK.
NO OFFENSE DIPPER, BUT YOU'RE THE SIDEKICK.
WHAT? SAYS WHO? HAVE PEOPLE BEEN SAYING THAT? HAVE YOU HEARD THAT?

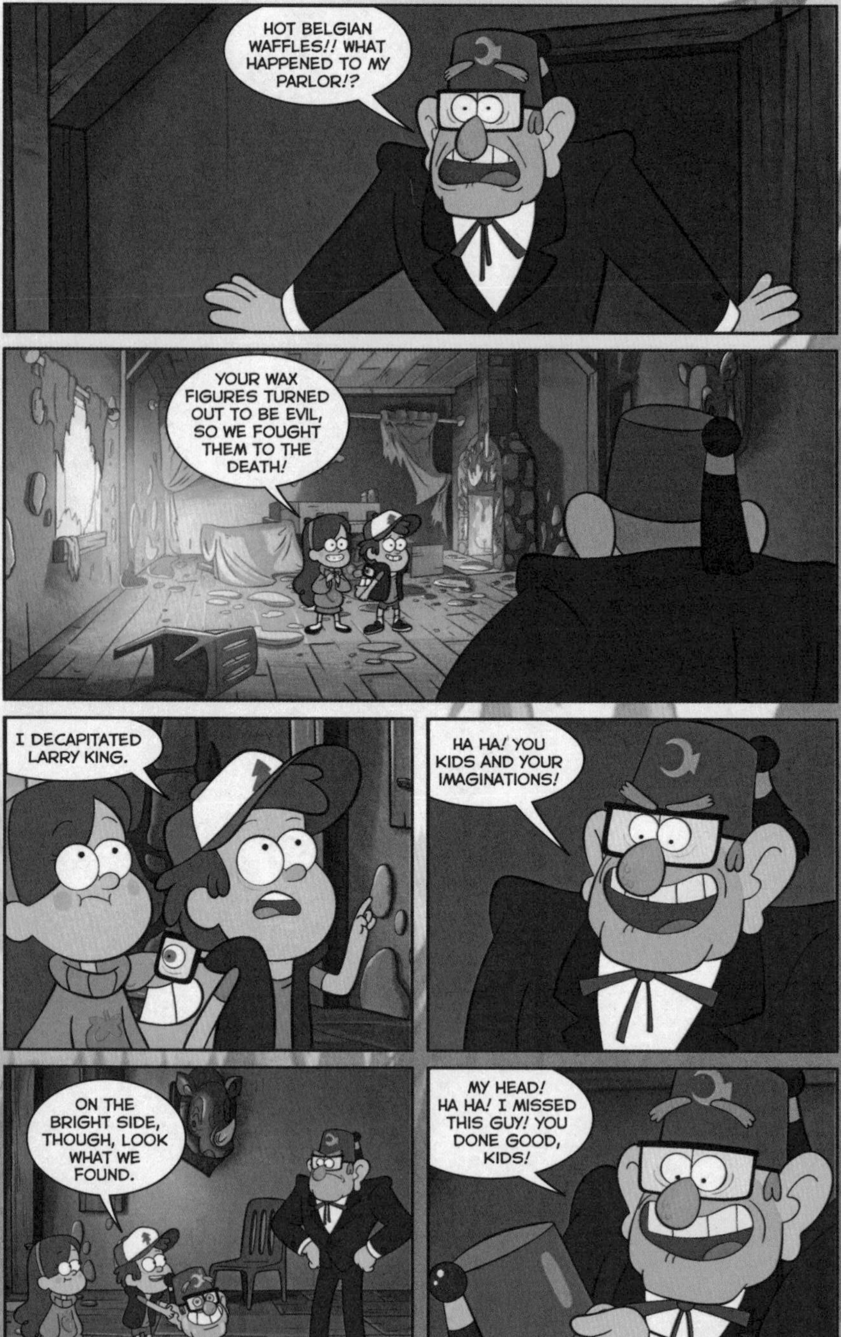
HOT BELGIAN WAFFLES!! WHAT HAPPENED TO MY PARLOR!?
YOUR WAX FIGURES TURNED OUT TO BE EVIL, SO WE FOUGHT THEM TO THE DEATH!
I DECAPITATED LARRY KING.
HA HA! YOU KIDS AND YOUR IMAGINATIONS!
ON THE BRIGHT SIDE, THOUGH, LOOK WHAT WE FOUND.
MY HEAD! HA HA! I MISSED THIS GUY! YOU DONE GOOD, KIDS!

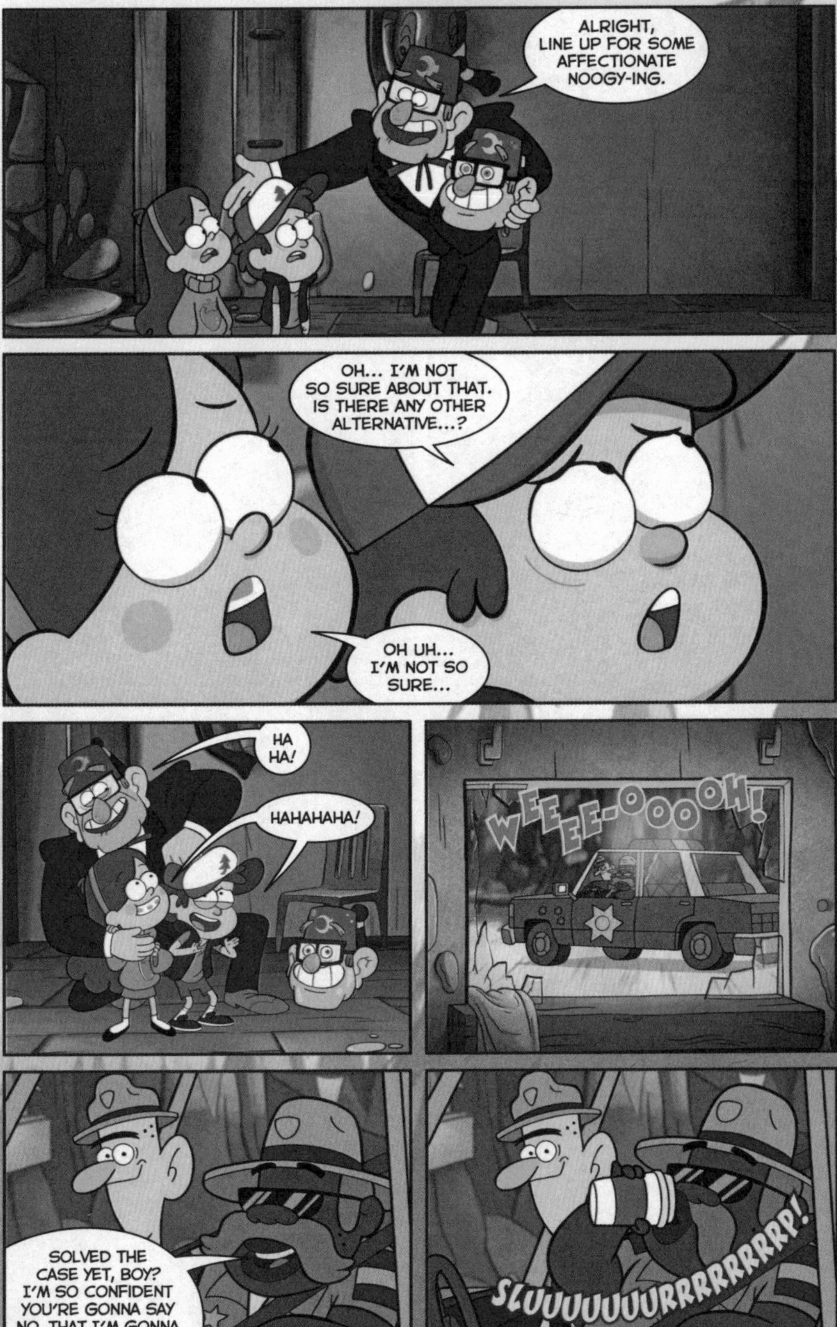
ALRIGHT, LINE UP FOR SOME AFFECTIONATE NOOGY-ING.
OH... I'M NOT SO SURE ABOUT THAT. IS THERE ANY OTHER ALTERNATIVE...?
OH UH... I'M NOT SO SURE...
HA HA!
HAHAHAHA!
WEEEE-OOOOOH!
SOLVED THE CASE YET, BOY? I'M SO CONFIDENT YOU'RE GONNA SAY NO, THAT I'M GONNA TAKE A LONG, SLOW SIP FROM MY CUP OF COFFEE.
SLUUUUUUURRRRRRRP!

ACTUALLY, THE ANSWER IS YES.

⸎BLU BLU BLU--⸎

SPPPPPPPPBBBBBT!

AHHHH!

SPPPPPPPPBBBBBT!

IT BURNS! IT BURNS!

MY EYES!

VRRROOOM

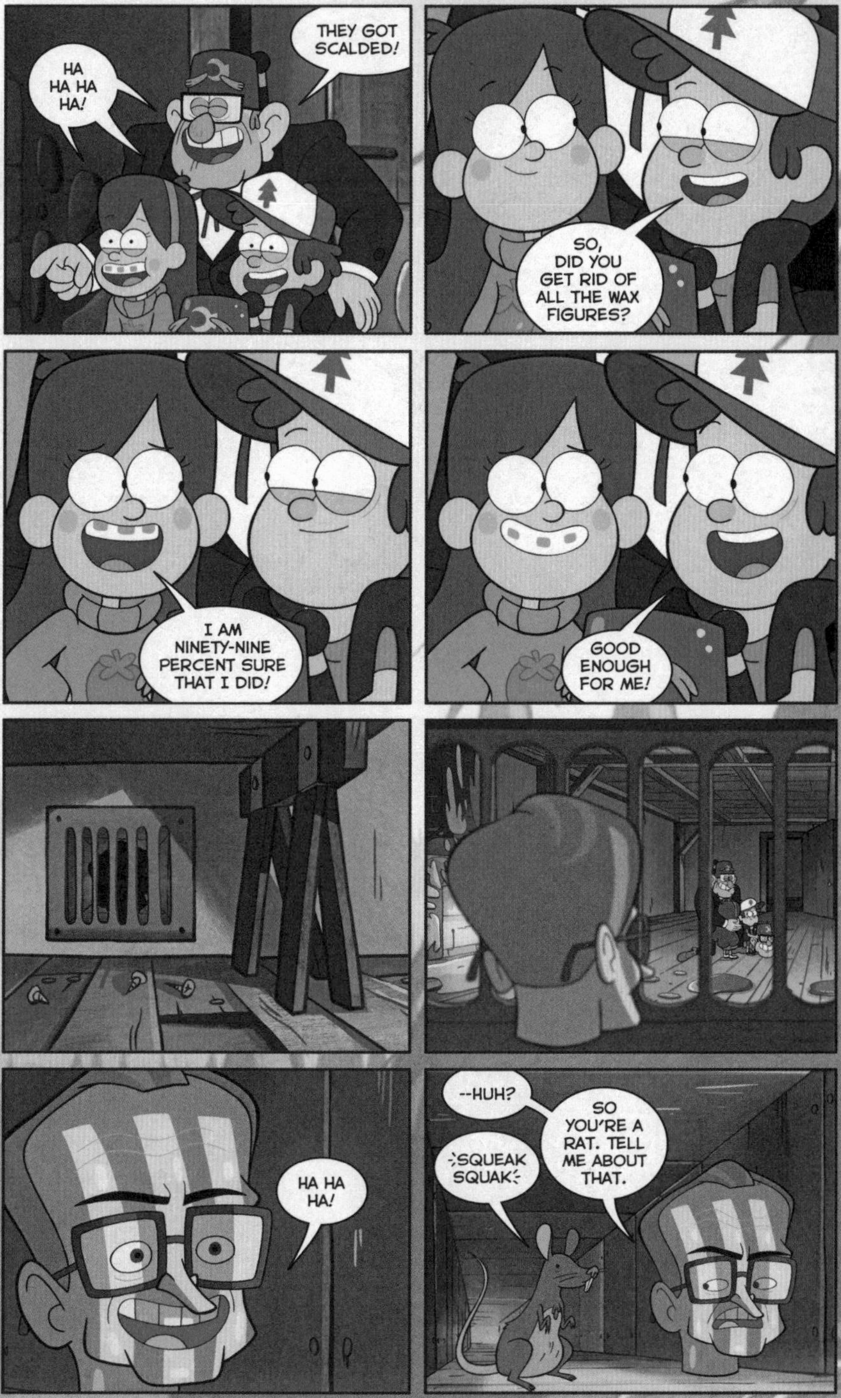
HA HA HA HA!
THEY GOT SCALDED!
SO, DID YOU GET RID OF ALL THE WAX FIGURES?
I AM NINETY-NINE PERCENT SURE THAT I DID!
GOOD ENOUGH FOR ME!
HA HA HA!
--HUH?
SO YOU'RE A RAT. TELL ME ABOUT THAT.
SQUEAK SQUAK

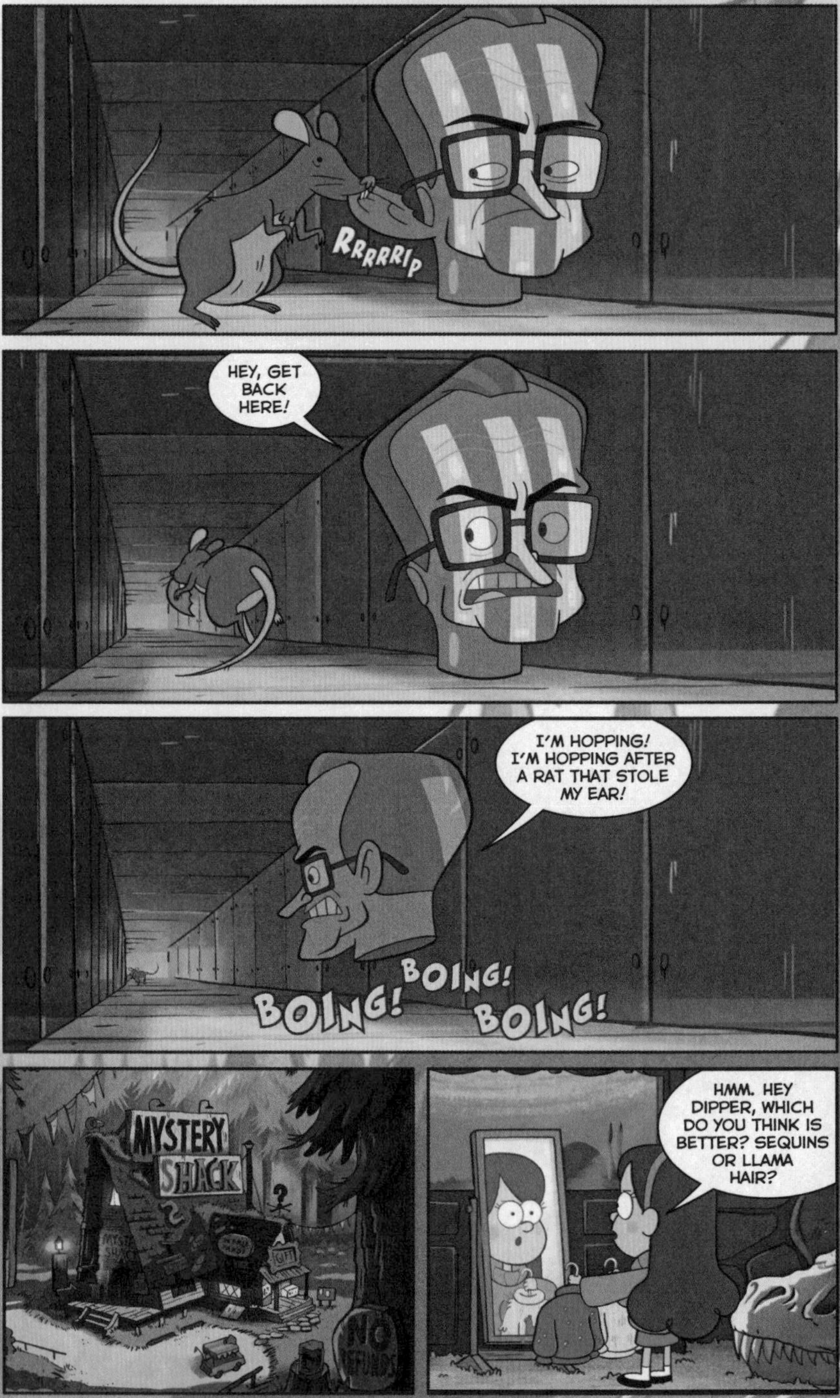
RRRRRIP
HEY, GET BACK HERE!
I'M HOPPING! I'M HOPPING AFTER A RAT THAT STOLE MY EAR!
BOING! BOING! BOING!
MYSTERY SHACK
NO REFUNDS
HMM. HEY DIPPER, WHICH DO YOU THINK IS BETTER? SEQUINS OR LLAMA HAIR?

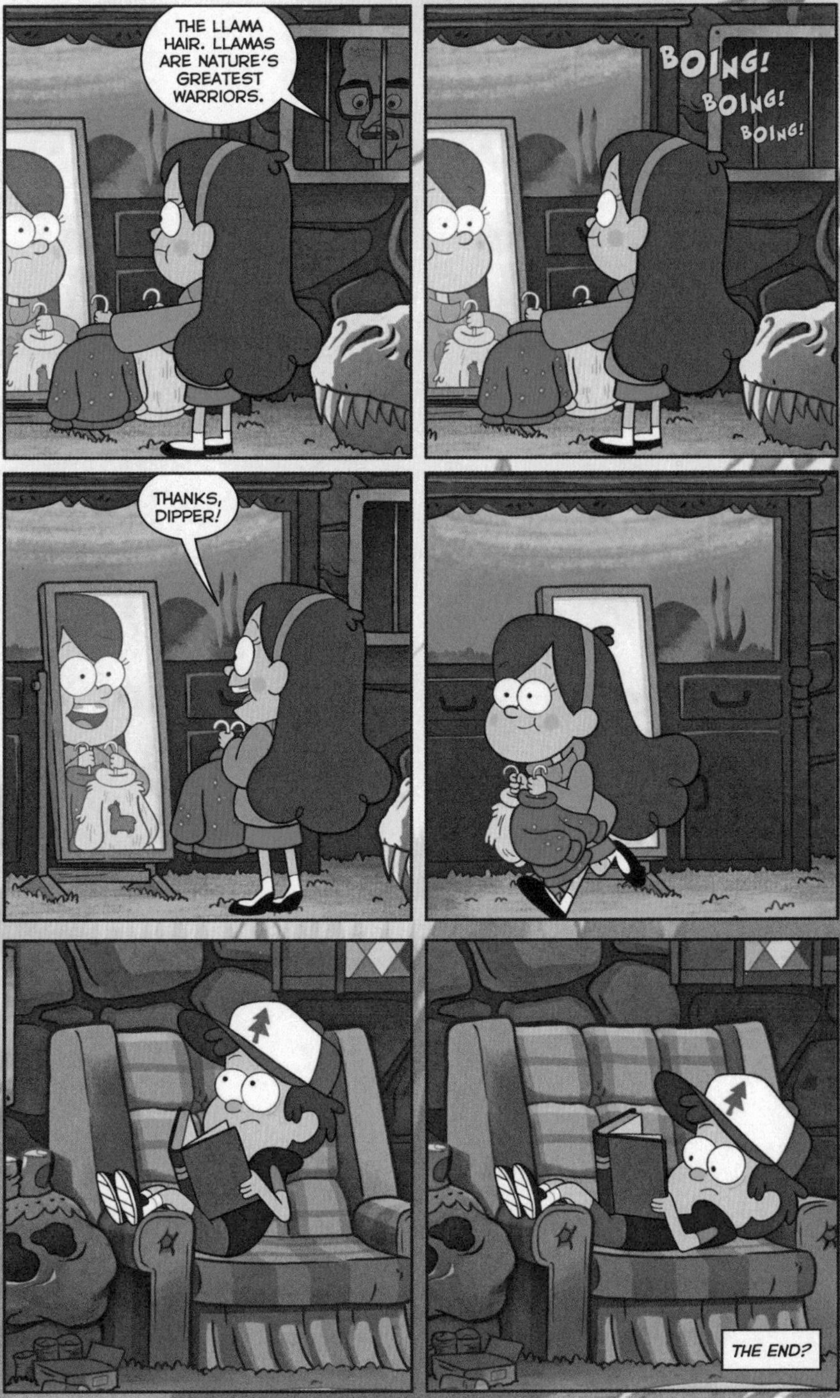
THE LLAMA HAIR. LLAMAS ARE NATURE'S GREATEST WARRIORS.
BOING!
BOING!
BOING!
THANKS, DIPPER!
THE END?